Judge's Girls

Books by Sharina Harris

Judge's Girls

(Im)Perfectly Happy

Judge's Girls

sharina harris

KENSINGTON BOOKS
www.kensingtonbooks.com

KENSINGTON BOOKS are published by

Kensington Publishing Corp.
119 West 40th Street
New York, NY 10018

All Kensington titles, imprints, and distributed lines are available at special quantity discounts for bulk purchases for sales promotion, premiums, fund-raising, educational, or institutional use.

Special book excerpts or customized printings can also be created to fit specific needs. For details, write or phone the office of the Kensington Sales Manager: Kensington Publishing Corp., 119 West 40th Street, New York, NY 10018. Attn. Sales Department. Phone: 1-800-221-2647.

Kensington and the K logo Reg. U.S. Pat. & TM Off.

ISBN-13: 978-1-4967-2566-0 (ebook)
ISBN-10: 1-4967-2566-2 (ebook)

ISBN-13: 978-1-4967-2565-3
ISBN-10: 1-4967-2565-4
First Kensington Trade Paperback Printing: November 2020

10 9 8 7 6 5 4 3 2 1

Printed in the United States of America

Acknowledgments

Thanks so much to my critique partners: Constance Gillam, Pamela Varnado, Mary Marvella, and Ison Hill! This book is so much better because of you. Thank you for fun Saturday mornings and passionate debates about our characters.

Thanks to my agent, Amanda Leuck—I was at one of the lowest points in my life when I got the "call" and you were the light in my dark. I so appreciate you!

To my mother, Pamela. Thank you for answering all my lawyer questions!

To my husband and son—thanks for creating the space to allow me to write. To my dad, stepmom, and stepsisters—thanks for being loving and supportive. I love our blended families.

Special thanks to Brian M. for providing research on substance abuse impact and counseling centers. Denise, thanks for making the connection happen!

And finally, thank you, readers!

PROLOGUE

MAYA

Saturday morning, March 14ᵗʰ
6 days since Daddy died

Pastor Davies strode toward the solid oak lectern, a thick, maroon-colored Bible in hand. Sunshine streaming through the stained glass cast red and green lights against his weathered face. "Let the church say amen."

"Amen," the congregation responded.

I couldn't. My throat felt like grains of sand in an hourglass. A hundred pairs of eyes were aimed at me, watching my every move even though they couldn't see me through the black lace veil covering my face. I stroked a coin, Daddy's lucky penny, between my forefinger and thumb. The cool from the copper soothed me.

"Oh, Lawd." Aunt Lisa waved a black lace handkerchief in the air, her arms jiggling with the motion. "Not my baby, sweet Jesus. Not. My. Baby!" Aunt Lisa jumped from the seat and walk-hopped to the front of the church. She threw herself on the black and silver casket, moaning and groaning and body shaking.

That's right, Aunt Lisa. Give them a show. Move the attention away from me.

"Take me instead, Lord!" Aunt Lisa patted her chest and looked toward Black Jesus in the mural above the baptism pool.

My daddy's other sister, Aunt Eloisa, wailed from the pew. She didn't dare run up like Aunt Lisa. Aunt Eloisa had bad knees, bad ankles, bad joints—bad everything if you let her tell it.

Daddy would hate this. He hated spectacles and pomp and circumstance.

If he were here, he'd tell Aunt Lisa to sit down and tell Pastor Davies to get on with it.

But if he were here, he'd be alive. And I wouldn't be at his funeral.

Exhausted from crying myself to sleep. Exhausted from heaving the two crackers I'd just managed to swallow before my stomach churned. Exhausted from taking care of my stepsister.

Exhausted from making sure my stepmother hadn't burned the house down.

Pastor Davies looked over his shoulder and nodded to the minister seated to the right of the pulpit. I couldn't remember his name, but he'd always been nice the few times I'd attended service. He sighed and hefted his portly physique up. The chair squeaked and shifted, as the red velvet cushion on top of the chair rose like dough.

"All right, Sister Lisa." The minister's soothing and patient voice could barely be heard over the wails. "Go on back to the pew, now. Sit down with your family."

Aunt Clara Bell, my great-aunt who'd raised Daddy and his sisters after my grandmother died, waved Aunt Lisa back. "Come sit down, so we can pay our respects to Joe. It's a funeral, not *The Price Is Right.*"

Aunt Lisa wailed louder. Minister Simpson, who'd been

seated toward the left side of the pulpit, gently grabbed her elbow and guided her away from the casket. She slumped from his grip like a toddler in the throes of a tantrum. Her black, mad-hatter hat fell to the ground, as she flopped onto the floor and howled.

"Hush now," the minister's voice grew agitated. "Judge Joe's in a better place."

In a better place. What better place could there be than here with me? The tsunami was building, churning my insides, flooding my lungs. I couldn't breathe. I was angry—so damn angry and hurt. I couldn't move past the vow he'd made twenty-two years ago.

He should be here. He promised.

The penny heated between my fingers, but I couldn't stop rubbing it. I couldn't stop the memories from bowling me over.

"Swear it, Daddy. Swear on your lucky penny that you'll never leave me."

Daddy, so big and so strong, was like the oak tree in our backyard that I'd loved to climb—solid and steadfast. But the day Mama died he'd fallen, and he'd crumbled. And at five years old I didn't know what was scarier—Mama's lifeless body or Daddy's lifeless eyes.

I don't know if it was my small fists banging on his legs, or the tears that soaked his pants, but he suddenly dropped to his knees. His brown eyes glistened with a wetness that left me cold even though the sun warmed my skin. He looked at me, and he *saw* me. He choked on a breath as if he were coming back to life.

He took the penny from my fingers and vowed, *"I promise, Maya. I'm here to stay."*

I believed him. But I'm not five years old anymore. Twenty-seven years old, mad at the world, mad at God. Mad at Daddy for saddling me with his second wife, Jeanie, who couldn't bear to see his casket. So instead of sitting in the pew with his family, she'd run out of the sanctuary and locked herself in the bathroom. After everything Daddy endured for that woman: my family giving him crap for marrying a white woman fifteen years his junior, his so-called friends freezing him out because they didn't think it was *right*. And how had she repaid him? With cowardice.

Sniffles cut through my fog of anger. *Ryder.* My shadow. The only good thing Jeanie had done with her life had been birthing a beautiful and brilliant daughter.

The squeeze from Ryder's hand gave me a sliver of comfort. Though, from the red that inflamed her baby blues, and from the puffy bags under her eyes, she needed comforting, too. I tilted my head on her shoulder and pulled her into a side hug. "We'll be okay," I managed to whisper.

Her arm squeezed my waist. "Promise?" Her voice shaky and desperate, much like my own when I'd asked Daddy the same request. I wanted to give her the world, but I couldn't utter the lie.

But I did stop rubbing the penny. It wasn't lucky after all.

CHAPTER 1

MAYA
ALL BLACK EVERYTHING

Monday morning, March 23rd
15 days since Daddy died

*D*amn.

I pushed the heavy glass door, lunch bag and empty mug in hand, ready to start back after a brief hiatus from Dickerson, Hill, and Sanders Law Firm.

I wasn't cursing about my return to work, or the fact that I felt just as lost as I had two weeks ago when Daddy died. No, I cursed because I wasn't ready for well-wishes.

Or fake wishes.

Marc Sanders, one of the owners and a partner, would be authentic. David Nero, a fellow staff attorney and my nemesis, would give me fake sympathy. But I was an adult and a Donaldson. We didn't run away from difficulty, we conquered it. So, I marched into the breakroom, my pink, four-point-seven-two-inch Louboutins clicking against the tile announcing my arrival. Marc stopped mid-conversation with David, giving him the universal "hold up" finger. David pressed his lips together, likely very annoyed at my noisy entrance that took time away from his precious mentor.

My pace brisk, I strode over and opened the door to the fridge and then placed my lunch inside. "Gentlemen." I nodded and moved a few steps over to the coffee machine.

"Heeyyy, Maya." Marc's firm grip grasped my shoulder as I waited for the coffee to drip. "How're you holding up?"

I fixed my lips into a not-too-happy yet not-too-sad smile and then turned around. "I'm okay."

"Your father will be missed." His brown eyes drooped a bit at the corners. "Did I ever tell you he helped me get my first client?"

I shook my head, though he'd told me a few times already. It made people happy to share memories of Daddy.

I let Marc ramble on while I tried to anchor myself to his words, attempting to hold back the tidal wave of grief that threatened to consume and carry me away.

Breathe. Focus. Smile. Nod.

"Here I was, thinking I'm a hotshot with my brand-spanking-new law degree, and just like that"—Marc snapped his fingers—"I thought I could take over this small town. I strutted around, giving out my cards, wearing a full suit and sporting a heavy Jersey accent. No one, I mean, NO ONE"—he waved a hand—"would touch me with a ten-foot pole. Then I get *really* desperate and start hanging out at the courthouse. Judge Joe takes me to the side, tells me that instead of walking around like my shit don't stink, I needed to look people in the eye when I talked to them. After that, well . . ." He waved his hand again. "Proof's in the pudding. Judge Joe . . ." Marc sighed. "He was a hell of a guy."

Everyone loved Dad. The brilliant attorney turned judge had a heart of gold. Instead of sending screw-up kids to jail, he'd allowed the offenders to invest in the community. Although he'd had a soft spot and granted second chances, Daddy wasn't a pushover. The repeat offenders found that out with the loud clack of his gavel and a prison sentence.

Marc stuffed his hands into his pockets and bobbed his head. He did this every time he was winding up or ramping down a closing argument or a conversation.

Say something before it gets sad and awkward.

The last of my coffee dripped into my favorite mug that stated: I LIKE MY COFFEE BLACK, LIKE MY SOUL. I grabbed my cup and then leaned against the counter. "I'm truly grateful for the meal vouchers. I hadn't had a chance to mail out thank-you cards, and I—"

"Of course, you haven't."

"But I—"

Marc waved away my fake protest. "I'm sure you have a million and one things to do. When my mother, God rest her soul, passed on, I barely had time to come up for air. I know you have a lot of people cooking for you right now. When things settle, and you need a break, use the vouchers."

David cleared his throat as if I needed a reminder of his slimy presence. He stood right beside Marc, nodding at everything Marc had said to me about Daddy.

David, an all-star pro at the art of bullshitting, attended every networking event. If the owners went golfing, he'd worm his way into an invite. And it worked for him. He got awarded the big cases that would earn big dollars, and the ones that were so slam dunk you'd have to be fresh out of law school to lose.

"If you're too busy for work, I'm happy to chip in. I've made great strides with Mrs. Stevenson, and I'm happy to take it to trial while you . . . grieve." David's tone left a Sweet'N Low aftertaste in my mouth.

Hell no, you cannot steal my case.

"Thank you for the offer, David, but that won't be necessary." I puppeteered a smile.

Another partner, Roland Hill, strode into the kitchen. My

pulse raced at NASCAR speeds. I cleared my throat and returned my attention to David.

"Are you sure, Maya?" David's unibrow lifted in solidarity.

"Very. I've been looking at your notes, tightening up a few things. I'll take the interviews from here. Thanks for the research, but Mrs. Stevenson seemed excited to have me back onboard."

Marc nodded. "Tell me about it. She kept asking for you and wanted your address to send flowers and food. You've got the magic touch with her, for sure."

"Thanks, Marc."

The case had initially been assigned to David. Six months ago, the widow had been a wreck when she first came to the firm and could barely get out a word without breaking down.

Back then, David stomped out of the meeting room into the cafeteria where many of us had been eating lunch. "I can't understand a damn thing she's saying, other than 'Dan's dead.' Anyway, I've got the Billings case that's going to trial next week. Can someone else take her?"

Katy, our paralegal, smiled and said, "Maya, your case just wrapped up today, didn't it?"

I already had three or four more cases than all other junior attorneys, but since I was put on the spot by Thing 1 and Katy, Thing 2, I said yes. Besides, I hated it when clients were dismissed because they were emotional.

After our consultation, I'd discovered that her case had the potential to bring in major money, seeing as her husband was killed in a tractor trailer accident.

I worked with Mrs. Stevenson and nursed her back to emotional health. After a few meetings she laughed and smiled again.

All that to say, hell, fuck no, David wouldn't be taking over my case. Not to mention, a successful win for this case would damn near solidify my spot as a partner.

I mustered up another smile. *Mouth open, check. Teeth on display. Double check.* "Thank you again for your research. You really shine in that area."

David narrowed his eyes, knowing I'd relegated him to a research assistant, not a trial attorney.

"Glad to see you both working together." Marc patted David's back. "And Maya, it's good to have you back. The team meetings have been boring without your spirited debates."

I gave him a smile, a real one this time, and saluted him with my coffee. "I'm a Donaldson. We always have something colorful to add."

After I stepped into my office, I did my usual routine: boot laptop, sip coffee, and kick off shoes. I put my cell on silent and pushed it to the edge of my desk.

Now what?

My take-on-the-world attitude disappeared.

I plopped my mug on the desk and pushed my feet against the floor, swiveling my chair around. Every time it stopped moving, I pushed myself off, again and again, twirling around like I had all the time in the world.

A sliver of silver caught my attention. I didn't need to look at the picture in the frame, my mind's eye clearly recalled the image: me and Daddy at my law school graduation.

Me with a big smile, all teeth and a little gum and my eyes so squinty they looked closed. Daddy's long arms wrapped around my shoulders while he kissed my cheek. His attention was focused on me. I don't think he was aware of the camera.

Daddy had been wistful that day with broad smiles and bear hugs.

"I'm so proud of you, Baby Girl. Your mama would've been proud of you, too, graduating at the top of your class." Dad stepped back, pride etched on his chestnut-brown face. *"Mark my words, you're going to change the world."*

On our way home from the ceremony, I'd asked Daddy to

stop by Mama's grave. On special milestones, Daddy and I left her flowers. I always thanked her for giving me life. But, when Jeanie's mouth began to tremble and her face turned tomato red, he brushed me off.

"It's been a long day, Baby Girl. Let's go later. Just the two of us."

We never went to share my news. *We never will.* A mass of pain sat over my left eye where it made camp over the past two weeks. Anytime I thought of Daddy it thumped like a bass drum. Thoughts of Daddy were convoluted: grief, then anger, chased by guilt. "Not here." I pressed my fingers against my eyelids. "Not now."

Both my parents were gone. Mama had been reduced to mental snapshots of braiding my hair, bedtime stories and singing in the choir. Memories of Mama were fond but fading.

Memories of Daddy were torture.

Nausea slammed into my stomach, threatening to propel two ounces of coffee and two tons of agony. My mind whirred, never focusing on one thing but skipping like a scratched record.

His easy smile falling off when he realized he'd burned our toast.

Daddy casting a fishing rod in the lake while he stumbled through the birds-and-the-bees talk, attempting to keep it scientific until he got frustrated and said, *"Boys only want one thing."*

I hooked the creepy crawler and slid it down the hook. I smiled a little. I didn't shriek or cry like I did last time. Daddy said I needed to be tough because the world was hard. "What's the thing boys want, Daddy?"

"To feel you up and let you down."

I shook my head. "Can you really say all boys, because you said to never generalize a group—"

"Yes. All of them." He nodded once and told me to be quiet and bait my line.

"Bored already?"

I dropped my feet to the ground to stop the spinning and focused on the familiar voice.

I swallowed and licked my lips. "Mr. Hill."

"Miss Donaldson." His brown, almond-shaped eyes roved over me, sending electric zings down my body.

Mr. Tall, Dark and Handsome, as one of the paralegals called him, shot me a killer smile, biting down on one corner of his lips. He was usually clean-shaven but in the past few months he'd grown a beard. I wasn't a fan of beards, but the look worked for him. His impressive gray suit covered even more impressive muscles. His shoulders were so broad I wondered if he lifted boulders instead of hundred-pound weights.

I squirmed in my seat, and his eyes ignited. He knew damn well what he was doing.

Refraining from rolling my eyes, I crossed my arms and cleared my throat.

"Can I help you, Mr. Hill?" *And knock on the damn door next time.*

He was a partner at the firm and technically my boss, but I didn't report to him. Regardless, he knew I preferred he knock before entering.

"No, I don't need anything. I'm checking in on you. It's your first day back, you have some major cases underway, and I figured—"

"You figured I couldn't handle it, Mr. Hill."

"Maya." His tone compassionate yet reproving. He knew I knew better.

I dropped my head and averted my gaze.

"You can talk to me, you know."

"I know." I swallowed, my throat drier than sandpaper.

"B-but if I do . . ." I swallowed again, but this time I looked up, taking in a deep breath—an attempt to remove the quiver from my voice. "I need to work," I whispered. "I need to be around people." I sniffed before the tears crawled up my throat.

He nodded. "I figured the first day back would be rough for you. And I know how you love caramel macchiatos." He brought around the hand he'd been keeping behind his back and revealed a cup from the only Starbucks that was clear across town.

I leaned forward, hand outstretched. "Skim milk?"

"And no whip. I'm not some amateur." He gave me the hot beverage.

I took a deep breath and accepted the offering. "Thank you, Roland."

"You're always welcome, Maya." His eyes lit and dancing with a secret he was dying to tell.

I grabbed a file from the corner of my desk. "I really am ready to work now." I smiled. "Thanks."

He nodded, shooting me another hot look. Just before he turned to leave, he paused at the door. "I'll be seeing you, Maya."

"Yes." I gave him a wobbly smile. "I suspect you will."

His mouth quirked at the corners. He turned and left my office.

I sipped the hot beverage. My spirts had lifted, but I still couldn't focus.

Thrumming my fingers, my eyes drifted back to the very thing I tried to avoid, my phone.

"Don't do it," I chided myself.

But I needed to hear Daddy's voice. The last voicemail he left before he died.

"Screw it." Leaning over, I grabbed my phone and punched in the code for voicemail.

"Hey, Baby Girl. I know you're working late. I saw the oil light blinking so I'm going to pick up your car and swing it by Tony's shop." A deep sigh rattled my receiver. "Okay, that's not the real reason I called you. I've been thinking about our talk on the lake. I was wrong for what I said. I think you'll make a great partner. I was just mad because I always thought you'd want to start a firm with your old man. But Marc's a good guy—not as good as me—but he knows what he's doing. So, go for partner. Just know that you'll have to work twice as hard to get it. Keep a cool head at all times and don't let 'em see you sweat. Okay, we'll talk more this Sunday. Bye, Baby Girl. Oh, wait, one more thing. Do me a favor and swing by Aunt Clara Bell's before you come over on Sunday. She's making banana pudding." He lowered his voice. "Don't want Jeanie to get all worked up about it."

I put my phone down and squeezed my eyes shut. I could recite the message by now, but the jab of pain never lessened. After hearing Daddy's voice, pure joy filled my center. Warm and soothing, like hot tea and honey.

Just as quickly as joy arrived, pain took over, hitting me like a one-two punch. I didn't want to get up. I wanted to sit there and bleed. Maybe catch my breath after the gut punch.

But Daddy wouldn't want that.

Tears rushed to the surface. I squeezed my eyelids tight, my breath coming out in pants. My eyes flew open and it felt as if a wet, hazy filter blurred my vision. With the side of my fingers, I dashed tears away and reinforced the dam that threatened to break free and flood me.

"I won't let you down, Daddy. I'll make partner."

Monday evening, March 23rd
15 days

The day had passed, and the sun had begun its descent. I pushed away from my desk, massaging my eyes. Thankfully, I was nearly caught up on Mrs. Stevenson's case. Although David had done an excellent job the few weeks I was away, his notes hadn't been easy to decipher.

The man wanted me to come to him and ask a bunch of questions. And with his office located squarely between two partners at the firm, they would witness my multiple walks of shame had I not been determined to figure out things on my own. If I called him, he would've put me on speaker and if I emailed, he would've copied our bosses in his reply. I knew this because he'd done it before—make me look inept while he got all the glory.

I didn't let it slide. I took my complaints to Roland, the youngest and most approachable partner, not to mention David's boss. Roland thanked me and told me he'd resolve it. I don't know what Roland said to David, but ever since, David was more careful in how he spoke to me in front of the partners.

Still, I'd been burned. And now I'd take my evenings to catch up rather than ask that snake for help. Besides, I had no plans and work kept depression at bay.

After packing up my briefcase, I set off for home. Tonight, I'd catch up on my other two cases while binge-watching bad reality TV. Most people would assume that I only watched *Law & Order* and *How to Get Away with Murder,* but after hours of scouring legalese, my mind needed a break. *Big Brother* had been my latest guilty pleasure and I'd mastered the art of listening while working.

After my short trip home to my apartment, I showered and ordered Chinese food.

"Cookies. I need cookies." Decision made, I pulled ingredients from my pantry: flour, old-fashioned oats, brown sugar, and raisins.

The doorbell rang. I glanced at my watch. "That was quick." I'd just ordered the food fifteen minutes ago. The bell rang again. "Coming, coming." I grabbed my wallet, rushed to the entrance and yanked open the door.

Instead of my usual pimply-faced, teenage guy, Roland leaned against the doorframe. The three-piece suit he'd worn earlier had been replaced by a denim shirt. A liberal number of buttons were undone to reveal his hard chest.

"Rola—" Before I could finish his name, he rushed me, cupped my jaw, pressed me into the wall, and kissed me senseless. The door slammed behind us. He lifted me in the air, and I wrapped my legs around his waist, kissing him with equal intensity. Somehow, he walked us to the couch. I pushed myself up and arched my back while he stared down at me as if I were a dream. His dream.

My breath stalled in my lungs. I was equally pleased and dismayed. I needed to focus on making partner, not being his dream girl.

This thing, this attraction we had for each other, wasn't a relationship. It was a long-standing booty call. Yes, a little over a year ago we mutually decided to make our booty calls exclusive with occasional trips out of town. But one of us would stop it when the time was right. Most likely, me.

I cleared my throat, my chest now heaving under his intense gaze. "What are you doing here?"

"I needed to see you."

"But it's Monday."

He shrugged. "I needed to see you. I think our seeing each other only on Tuesdays and Saturdays is a stupid rule, anyway." He lowered himself beside me, reached for the remote and muted the television. "How're you holding up?" His thumb grazed my lips. I shivered from his warm touch.

"Some days are better than others." I pushed him off and scooted away. "The caramel macchiato helped."

He hooked his leg around mine and pulled me closer to face

him, all the while giving me the infamous Roland Hill look. The one he used to cross-examine witnesses, eyes narrowed, lips pinched, and head tilted. The subtle, yet stern look that forced a person to confess all. I was usually immune, but today it worked on me.

"Okay, I'm a hot mess. Jeanie, my daddy's wife, is stumbling around like a zombie. And something is off with Ryder. She's hiding something from me. Whenever I call, she's in a rush to get off the phone."

Roland massaged my shoulders. "People deal with grief differently. Maybe you remind her of your father?"

I shook my head and leaned against his chest. "No, I don't think that's it. The girl has been my shadow since she was three years old and they moved in with us. We usually talk every day. No." I shook my head again. "Something's up. But I'll see them for the reading of the will on Thursday."

Maybe I shouldn't wait until then, I thought. I could pop by unannounced. Like lover boy here. We had rules of engagement, and for the most part, we stuck to them. Rule number one, never go to his house. It was a rule I created because his neighbor is the father of the biggest gossip in our office: Katy, our paralegal. She didn't live with her parents but was at her parents' house often enough to know Roland's comings and goings. Not to mention she had the hots for him. One word whispered about our affair could mean the end of my chances to make partner.

Although fraternizing was technically allowed, it was generally frowned upon. Not to mention generally women tend to not come out on top when affairs are discovered.

Roland would get a slap on the wrist and a high five when no one was looking.

I would either be frozen out by my coworkers or blocked from any real promotions or exciting cases until I got the hint and resigned. The very same situation happened to a friend of mine from law school. I'd be damned if my career got iced because I couldn't control my hormones.

Roland rubbed my arms. "Why is it so cold in here?"

"No idea." No matter how many times I set my thermometer to seventy-five degrees, lately it seemed like it reset to fifty degrees.

"I'll check your thermostat." He stood and went to the wall that led to the kitchen.

"You know . . . my daddy used to say if you don't pay the bills, don't mess with the temperature."

"Mhmmm." Roland tapped on the gauge. "You need to call the management company. It says it's on seventy-five, but it feels like it's below freezing. You want me to call them?"

"Umm . . . no thanks." I snorted and shook my head.

Instead of coming back to the sofa, Roland scanned the ingredients on the island in my kitchen.

He picked up the bag of raisins. "Are you making me oatmeal-and-raisin cookies?"

"I'm baking, yes."

"For me?"

"For . . . for people." I licked my lips.

"You know oatmeal and raisins are my favorite."

"Really?" I shrugged. "Didn't know. Happy coincidence."

He chuckled, leaning against the counter. "You hate raisins."

I did, but how did he know? "Says who?"

"You pick the damn things out of the cookies, Princess."

"Ryder likes oatmeal-and-raisin cookies, too."

"Uh-huh," he said as he sat at the round breakfast table in my kitchen. Manilla folders, legal pads, and my iPad were scattered across the tabletop.

"Bringing work home?" He flipped through cases and I let him. Sometimes when one of us needed help with strategy, we bounced ideas off each other. He was brilliant, and though I didn't like asking for help, I did my best for my clients.

I shrugged. "Not exactly. I fell behind on some of our pro bonos."

"Sanjeeta Bahati?"

"She was passed over for a promotion. Boss straight up told her he didn't like her kind . . . Muslims. And he's been reprimanded in the past for saying some racist-ass comments."

"Any witnesses willing to go on record?" Roland asked, flipping through papers.

"I've got one brave soul."

"Still, it's going to be tough."

Roland knew the deal. It would seem like it would be a slam dunk, but companies, big and small, tended to put their heads in the sand. They only paid attention if they got bad press or found themselves in the middle of a social media war.

"It's a good thing she documented her clients' and peers' feedback," he added. "Otherwise it would be harder to prove."

"I've got a few more aces up my sleeve. He's an asshole: cheats on his wife, hits his kids. I'm going to see if we can add that to the discovery to question his character. And I'm going to slide his wife my business card and resources for a shelter while I'm at it."

"You always find a way, Warrior Princess."

"I can't change hearts, but I can make 'em pay." I rubbed my fingers together. The world was full of selfish, opportunistic assholes. Once, I had a guy who'd paid an old friend a shitload of money to seduce his soon-to-be ex-wife so he could get out of paying alimony. I knew people who orchestrated car accidents to get money from insurance companies. And sometimes people were just plain dumb. Someone had even called me to ask if they could sue a frozen food giant because they got a bad case of gas.

So, when a good person—a person who actually needs help—gets screwed, I'm all up in that ass. I especially take joy in going after insurance companies.

My phone vibrated on the table. I recognized the number from the gate and buzzed the visitor in. Which reminded me that I hadn't buzzed Roland in.

"Who's that?"

"Chinese food. And how did you get past the gate without me buzzing you in? As a matter of fact, you rarely call me from the gate when you're here." The luxury apartment complex had decent security. We usually had a guard on duty and, if not, a gate system. Daddy had made sure of it before I moved out of the house after I returned home from law school.

"I know your security guy, Stan the man."

"Stan the man?"

"Yep, his name is Stan and I call him 'the man.' Ever since then, he just buzzes me in. Tonight, I followed behind another vehicle."

"Jesus."

"So Chinese food, huh? I could eat."

"I only ordered enough for myself." It was a lie. I always ordered enough for two meals, but he needed to learn that popping by was not okay. Giving him food would be like giving tuna to a stray cat.

"Fine." He gave me a slow smile while reaching for his phone. "I'll just order something from Lenny's diner. They deliver, and hey, I'm sure Sheila, your aunt's friend, won't notice my name and the fact that the order's being delivered to your apartment." He typed a few numbers, but before he could press the button to call, I grabbed his cell.

"Fine. I can spare you some food. But next time, call me first." I tossed the phone back to him.

"Deal, Princess." He gathered me close in his lap. "But after we eat, I want my dessert."

Thursday evening, March 26th
18 days

Dell McManus—or, as I called him, Father Time—was stooped over his desk. His liver-spotted fingers gripped a quill—kidding—a pen as he quickly scratched something on unlined paper.

The quirky old man was my father's mentor, and I'd known him all my life. He was intelligent, kind, and it was hard to see him without my father by his side, slapping his shoulder and laughing at something he'd said.

Daddy's gone. He's really gone. From a damn heart attack. The man loved his cigars and brandy and sure, he went to town on my Aunt Clara Bell's infamous soul food Sundays, but otherwise, he was fit.

A few months ago, while he was alive, you couldn't pay me to admit that the man drove the ladies around town crazy. With his salt-and-pepper goatee and good looks, he could've been a ladies' man. Hell, I'd much prefer he had been than settle for Jeanie's woe-is-me-ass.

Dell put his pen down then stood. He walked from behind his desk and gave me a bear hug. "Hey, Tootsie Pop," Dell greeted me with the nickname he'd given me as a child. He said I was all hard on the outside, but on the inside, sweet as candy.

"Are you ready for this?" He guided me to the couch, pushed against the wall, and settled beside me.

"Heck, no." I shook my head.

"Me, either. When I drafted your father's will nearly a decade ago, I thought my younger partner would execute it. Not me." He took a deep breath. "But a deal's a deal. And I'm going to follow his words to the T." He flicked my nose. "You want a Jolly Rancher?" He pointed to his candy jar on the corner of his desk.

"No. I'd much prefer a scotch."

"And you shall have it." He got up, went to a cabinet behind his desk, and poured me a hefty portion.

"How's your heart? You've been taking your pills?"

He tapped his chest. "The old ticker's doing fine."

"Have you been keeping up with your appointments?" I took a sip. The alcohol stung my tongue.

"Mhmm."

"Really? Because I spoke to Tina on my way in and she said you missed your last two. Don't make me come to your appointments." I could hear the nag in my voice, but I couldn't help myself. I had a gooey spot for Dell. Not to mention Daddy's sudden heart attack shook me.

"Dell," Tina, his paralegal's disembodied voice boomed over the intercom. "Mrs. Donaldson just arrived."

"Send her to my office, please." His voice went tight.

"Is it going to be that bad?" I took another sip, fortifying myself for the will and for Jeanie's river of tears.

"Sharing someone's last wishes is never easy." He poured himself a drink and then settled into his black leather chair behind his desk.

"If you don't mind, I'll take a glass, too," a soft voice said behind me. I knew who the voice belonged to without turning around. The woman who'd taken my mother's place in my father's heart.

She was like hand-spun glass and antique teacups. You breathe too hard, and she'd fall apart. Daddy ate it up. He loved being someone's savior.

If the woman sneezed too hard, Dad scooped her in his arms and became a human handkerchief.

I remembered the day she moved in, plastic bags and suitcases. Strolling around the house, she made plans for "sprucing up" the decorations my mother, Renee, had done.

Getting rid of the picture of me, Mama, and Daddy, in the living room hit me like a shot to the heart.

Hell, she'd tried to move the urn from the front room, but I had a hissy fit. Daddy just sat there, a besotted look on his face, and let her get away with everything.

He never asked how I felt about Jeanie. How it felt to be ignored when she was around. How he'd abandoned the memory of my mother.

I had no love for Jeanie, and I knew she didn't love me either. She'd never tried.

But I couldn't help but feel something for the woman in front of me. She was delicate, yes, but she wasn't her typical glossed-up self.

A run in her stockings, flat shoes. No makeup and her usual golden-brown mane pulled into a messy bun.

There was no denying there had been stars in her eyes whenever Daddy was around, but I always wondered which aspect she loved most in Joseph Lee Donaldson: the man or the provider?

Something pricked my conscience. I clenched my hands before I could reach out and . . . I don't know what.

"Maya." Jeanie clutched a small purse and sat beside me. After she settled in her seat, she reached for the scotch Dell offered and slugged it down in one gulp.

"S-smooth," she hissed and pressed the back of her hand against her lips. With her other hand she gave him back the empty glass. "Another, please."

"I . . ." Dell looked at me, a helpless expression on his face.

I shrugged. Jeanie was an adult. She could make her own decisions.

While Dell poured her another round, a distinctly smaller portion, I asked, "What's with all the pomp and circumstance? We could've done this at the house. Or you could've just sent it over to us for review."

"With Ryder at the house, I thought it would be better to read it in the office." He looked down at a blue folder and took a deep breath. "Let's get started."

I gave him a nod. Jeanie gave him the same confirmation.

"I, Joseph Lee Donaldson, residing at Eighty-seven Meadow Ridge Lane, Hope Springs, Georgia, declare this to be my Will and I revoke any and all wills and codicils I previously made."

Dell bounced along with legal jargon. Daddy gave Ryder his car. Left all of us money, giving me the lion's share. Some old watch that he loved but never wore. Nothing too crazy until . . .

"I give my residence, subject to any mortgages or encumbrances thereon, and all policies and proceeds of insurance covering such property to my daughter, Maya." Dell glanced away from the will and zeroed in on me. "I will also allow my wife, Jeanie, to live in the house as long as she sees fit."

As long as she sees fit.

"What. In. The. Hell?" He wants her to live in the house. My house. Forever? Oh, hell no, Dell."

"Now, young lady, I need you to calm down."

Jeanie trembled beside me, melting like wet tissue.

Oh hell. Here comes the crying jag.

"Joseph!" she wailed. She covered her mouth, bending over until her knuckles touched her lap.

"You're telling *me* to calm down?" I pointed to my chest and jerked my head to Jeanie.

"Yes. Can't you see she's upset?"

Like I give a damn. I stretched my hand out. "Can I see the will?"

Dell nodded and handed me the documents.

"I mean . . . I'm fine with Jeanie staying until Ryder graduates, of course. Are you sure this is what Daddy meant?"

"Yes." Dell tapped his desk. "I've read everything of importance."

My hands shook around the thick stack of papers. How could he? He knew Jeanie and I didn't get along.

What was he thinking?

That he would live forever. I knew Dad. The heart attack had been sudden. He thought I would've moved on, barefoot and married before he died.

Now he'll never meet his grandchildren. If I have them.

I pressed my hands against my temples. Mama and Daddy built the house for *our* family—not for Wilting-Flower Barbie.

I shook my head. "This is not acceptable."

"Fine," Jeanie whispered beside me. Her brown eyes stark against her pale skin, she dabbed her face with a crisp handkerchief with my father's initials. "I'll just pack my things and leave. I have enough in my savings to get something appropriate for me and Ryder."

Ryder.

Her name was like a bucket of freezing water doused on my head. "No, it's . . . we'll figure something out."

I wouldn't kick Ryder out, but once she graduated, Jeanie had to get the hell out. With my father gone, she had no business staying in my mother's house.

She turned to face Dell. "I'm happy to forfeit my right to stay there after Ryder graduates from high school. She plans on going to Emory anyway, so just as soon as she's gone . . ." Her voice went hoarse and shaky. "Then I'll be gone. Maybe I'll move to Atlanta with her."

Dell shook his head. "Don't make a decision right now. Why don't both of you sleep on this?"

Jeanie nodded like one of those Atlanta Falcon bobbleheads in Daddy's office. "I'm tired." She grabbed her forehead, her eyes squeezed shut. She whispered, "Is there anything else to discuss?"

"No." Dell shook his head, his jowls flapping with the motion.

"Very well." She nodded and left the office without a goodbye.

I sat rooted in my chair. Dell jerked his head toward the door. "Close it, will you?"

I leaned over and tipped it shut.

"Maya, I know you and Jeanie have your differences." He paused, stroking his chin like I'd see him do in court. "But this is what your father wanted."

"Why?" I whispered. "It doesn't make sense."

"For what it's worth, Tootsie Pop, I did try to talk him out of this. But he insisted that *if* anything should happen, he wanted to make sure all his girls had a home."

"Dad left her a nest egg and she's only fifty years old. She can go back to work and find her own place. Hell, Ryder will be off to college soon."

"Do you even want to live back home?"

"Like you said, and as Daddy stipulated, it's *my home*. A house my mom and daddy built together, intent on growing a family. Then . . ." I sighed. "It's the only thing . . . the one thing I have from both of them. And I don't understand why Daddy would put in that clause. He just didn't get it." I threw my hands in the air.

The same ole shit but I can't argue with him because he's dead.

Dell leaned back, resting his hands on his stomach. "Tell me why you two never got on."

I shrugged and leaned back into the chair. "We're just oil and water."

"Do you think you would've felt that way about anyone your father remarried?"

"No. I'm not that self-absorbed. I just never liked Jeanie."

And apparently, it'd been since the day I met her. Even as a little girl I saw the hero worship in Jeanie's eyes. She wanted him, even then. And when Mama died, she slid right in, like it was her due. I couldn't tell Dell about my instincts. We lawyers focused on facts and logic.

"I just don't . . . I don't know if she ever *saw* Daddy, if you know what I mean. Just the power he had and what he provided."

"Well, that's not fair. Your father was shrewd. There are things you couldn't see as a child. Things your father shielded you from. But when your mother died, he grieved. *Deeply,* Tootsie Pop. And Jeanie was there."

"To take away his pain," I said with air quotes. "What in the hell did they have in common? There's a fifteen-year age gap." Anyone with a brain could tell that Jeanie had a classic case of daddy issues. Not to mention, an old black dude and a young white woman did not go over well in Hope Springs, Georgia. I kept my thoughts to myself. Dell was one of those guys who pretended like he didn't see color, but hell, he didn't have to acknowledge color. He was an old rich white man. I loved him, but those were facts.

"Joe wouldn't want you to contest the will."

"I won't."

"You won't?"

"No. You heard Jeanie. She's going to leave after Ryder graduates. I think that's fair."

"But—"

"I didn't force her, okay? You're a witness. She said she would leave."

"After your less-than-happy reaction."

"Look, stop acting like she's a victim. I didn't force her. She volunteered. And she hasn't been the best stepmother in the world. She hates the fact that I am closer than she is with her daughter, and that I was the apple of my father's eye."

"So, she's jealous?" he asked, curiosity in his voice. He seemed to be thinking about it.

I didn't have to think about it because her feelings were on the surface. The evidence lived in her actions and comments. Her passive-aggressive remarks about the way that I wore my hair. She called it *those braids*. She nearly had a heart attack when Ryder tried to copy me.

And when Daddy and I debated the outcomes of hotly covered cases in the media, she would get this sour look on her face and walk away. She was another person who didn't believe that people were racist. It was as if she didn't notice the blatant stares she received when she and Dad went out on dates or the nasty whispers from her little church friends or the parents at Ryder's school.

"Well," Dell sighed. "Let's just hope she doesn't change her mind."

I stood, leaned over, and gave him a kiss while *Hamilton*'s "Ten Duel Commandments" played in my head. "Then she'll have a battle on her hands. And I never lose."

CHAPTER 2

RYDER
NEW NORMAL

Monday morning, March 30th
22 days

I snuck into Mom and Dad's room and did the same routine I'd been doing for three weeks: collecting cups, dirty plates, used Kleenex, and whatever bottle Mom had downed from the night before.

I didn't need to check if she was breathing—her snores sounded like we were going through a wind tunnel. Still, I crept over to the bed and watched her chest rise and fall. With her hair spread over the pillow, she looked like a Disney Princess. But Disney princesses didn't go on drunken tirades, cry uncontrollably, or say nasty things to their daughters.

She doesn't mean it. She can't help it.

I left bottled water and two aspirins on her nightstand. Every morning she woke up with a huge migraine and a dry throat.

But I wouldn't be here to make sure she took her water and pills. Today was my first day back to school since he died.

I wanted to stay at home, but Maya wouldn't let me. "You know education was important to Daddy."

The thought of going back to school made my stomach teeter-totter with Mrs. Robertson's lasagna. My being at home was the only reason why Mom stumbled out of bed.

I couldn't tell Maya. It'd be another reason she and Mom would never get along. Besides, Mom's drinking wasn't permanent.

By the time I made it to Whitfield Academy, Mom was still heavy on my mind. But she'd have to suck it up and move on, just like me. Just like Maya. Just like everyone who loved Dad.

I shuffled down the hallway to homeroom. Funny, nothing had changed. The black and white checkered floors were still spotless. Mr. Blue, the custodian with hair that looked like clouds, waved as he buffed the already gleaming red lockers.

Banners decorated the halls. Pictures of famous alumni hung at the end of the hallway. Not Beyoncé famous. Famous in Hope Springs meant you owned a restaurant or served on the board of something.

Scents of florals and citrus filled the hallways—a combination of cleaning products and fresheners.

Everything was the same and as it should be.

I was not.

Dad was a good man, a wise man. A man who taught me the meaning of love—unconditional love. I thought about that a lot. He was the only father I had ever known. My biological father, Ricky, had been in and out of my life. I loved him but not the way I loved Dad.

Dad read me bedtime stories (and did all the different voices; Mom's voices all sounded the same) and tucked me in at night. If I had a nightmare, he'd be the first one in my room, ready to battle every monster hiding in my closet or under my bed. He was always there for me, his presence larger than life. And he gave me a sister—the best big sister in the world. She always let me into her room when I was little. She never got mad when I followed her around the house.

I rounded the corner and paused before I entered homeroom. I could hear voices through the door. The other students weren't unusually loud; Mrs. Donavan would not tolerate it, but their voices pounded on my ears like the thud of dirt on a coffin.

I pushed open the door. The chatter stalled, replaced by whispers and open-wide stares. Usually, I would've marched straight to my desk, put my headphones in, and listened to one of my podcasts.

But my feet were stuck in cement.

My attention swung to my desk. Notes and cards had been neatly stacked with a yellow ribbon tied around the pile.

My mouth popped open, and I couldn't breathe. I probably looked like one of those dead fish Dad and Maya brought home every Sunday from the lake.

"Ms. Bennett," my homeroom teacher said in a soft voice. Somehow, she stood next to me. A few seconds ago, I could've sworn she sat at her desk.

"Are you okay?" She placed a hand on my back.

The words wouldn't come to me. My head saved me with a nod.

"Judge Joe was a good man. You have my condolences." She rubbed my back.

My head did the nod thing again. My legs unlocked, and I walked to my desk.

My classmates stared. My cheeks blazed.

"Sorry for your loss," Josh Green whispered behind me, his breath hot on my neck.

I turned and smiled, then put on my headphones. I didn't want to hear it.

I didn't need this attention. I was never popular. And I never wanted to be. I didn't get teenagers, to be honest. What did we have to be upset about? Most of us, especially at my school, had a two-parent household, food in our bellies, and a more-than-adequate roof over our heads. We didn't have bills. We were just expected to go to school, learn, and be respectful. Big friggin' deal.

After homeroom period ended, the day sped by with sad looks from teachers and whispers from students. It was exhausting, pretending to be okay. By the time AP English, the last class for the day, rolled around, I was ready to go home.

I settled in the seat and removed my headphones. A few other students were settled at their desks. The bell had another few minutes until it rang, but like always, I arrived early to class.

Mrs. Frierson whisked from behind her desk and stood in front of mine. "I am so very sorry for your loss." She had the most beautiful green eyes, speckled with brown. They seemed to see straight through the soul. "Grieving is never easy. Here." She gave me a small book.

"*The Sun and Her Flowers*," I read the title out loud.

Mrs. Frierson nodded; her springy red curls bounced. "Something to read during this difficult time. Let me know what you think." She leaned down to give me a hug and floated back to her desk like a fairy caught at dusk.

"You're that poetry girl, right?" Dani Jones, the most popular guy at school, asked me. He settled in the desk beside me. Weird—it wasn't his assigned spot.

I smiled and tucked my hair behind my ear. He didn't say sorry or ask how Dad had died. He identified me with something I did.

I liked that he didn't ask intrusive questions, but I didn't like Dani. I didn't like that he introduced himself to other people as Dani with an "I." Who does that? And besides that, what was wrong with good ole-fashioned Danny—two N's and a Y?

Beyond his name, Dani was a ne'er-do-well, as Dad would

say. Last year, he asked if he could cheat off my notes. I promptly told him no. He was in advanced classes, which meant he was smart enough to do his own work.

But the worst offense was that he was a liar. He filled up pretty girls' heads with pretty lies and broke their pretty hearts.

No, I did not like Dani-with-an-I, but I liked that he didn't ask about Dad.

"So." He lifted an eyebrow. "You like poems?"

"Yes." I licked my lips. "I like poetry." *Brilliant, Ryder.*

"Cool. Maybe one day you can write something about me." *So long, Dani.*

"Maybe." I gave him a tight smile (I was good at them) and turned to face the front. I didn't want to miss today's lecture about Greek mythology. After an hour of dissecting "The Iliad" the bell rang to end class.

I jumped from my seat, ran to the bike rack, and peddled home from school. I should've taken my sweet time. Maybe biked around town, grabbed some froyo, or stayed at Maya's place.

Instead, I went home straight away. The blue and gray drapes that hung on the center window in our sitting room had been drawn.

Actually, all the windows in our home had been covered by blinds and curtains.

I walked to the kitchen at the back of the house.

"Oh, no."

Black construction paper covered the window, up to right around the height of my mother. It was like a DIY-Pinterest project gone wrong. The small table near the window had bits of dried glue stuck to the surface.

The long table in the center of the room was stacked with paper. Scraps of black construction paper littered the floor. I bent over, scooped them up, and dumped them into the bin. *Why didn't she just use the friggin' shade?*

Irritation floated around my head like a pesky fly. I wouldn't let it land. *There is no place for anger.* I closed my eyes and took a deep, fortifying breath, remembering my instructions from the daily meditation I listened to. I opened my eyes again, taking in the piles of massacred paper.

Mom had Dad install custom solar shades. I stomped to the cupboard to find the remote to control the shades.

"Where is it?" I searched the cupboards and the bowl where Dad put our miscellaneous remotes, loose screws, and knick-knacks. No dice. The keys weren't there, either.

Mom's not home!

An army of dancing leprechauns did a Riverdance on my chest. I rushed to the door that led to the garage.

No car. Just a workbench and old paint cans.

Mom shouldn't be driving.

God, Mom.

I couldn't protect Mom if she wouldn't protect herself. I grabbed my cell and scrolled to my favorites. *Maya.* My thumb shook over the button. I should call her. She would fix it.

But Maya plus Mom equals World War III and I'd be a casualty.

Plus, drinking and driving was a pet peeve of hers—mine, too. A drunk driver had killed Maya's friend from law school. Maya would kick Mom to the curb, and then who would protect her?

"I can fix this." I grabbed the step stool. Mom was five foot nine, and I was a few inches shorter. I peeled the paper off the windows, some of which had been glued. Mom abhorred filth. She liked a neat house. She hated crumbs and stains and dirt, and if cleaning were an Olympic sport, she'd be a ten-time gold medalist and her event would be vacuuming. The sound of the motor soothed her. As a matter of fact, anytime she had to make a big decision or if she was upset, she vacuumed. I'd lost count of how many times I saw perfect lines in the carpet that looked like mowed grass.

So even though Mom had made a mess, I took care to clean the windows the way she would like it, even if she wouldn't notice it now.

One day she'd be back to normal, fussing at me for leaving a glass on the table without a coaster.

I scrubbed the gunk off the window, squeegeed the panes, and then wiped the windows down with a terry cloth. My biceps felt like cooked noodles as I scraped the squeegee from side to side, the squawks and squeaks telling me I'd applied too much pressure.

Pressure. I knew that feeling.

Pressure to keep Mom's breakdown a secret.

Pressure to stay sane while my insides were ripped to shreds.

Pressure to keep up my grades. To make sure Maya and Dad were proud of me.

Even if he wasn't here, I still wanted to make him proud.

"Bunny ear laces, kisses on scraped knees. Words of wisdom near water and fire. Homegrown lessons learned, hard-lived wisdom earned. Father of mine, who isn't mine of blood. But of heart. Father of mine, who is not mine. Be mine. Of heart and mind and soul."

After Maya had left the Father's Day dinner—I think I was nine—I found him alone in his office. Mom made cranberry apple–stuffed pork loin. I remembered because I was so nervous, I wanted to upchuck and every time I swallowed down bile, it tasted of cranberry apple.

"What is it, Little One?" He waved to the seat in front of his desk. I shook my head and remained standing, just in case he

thought the poem was amateurish. I could just walk away, maybe cry by the lake or something. He liked my poetry. Maya loved it.

Anyway, I took a deep breath and recited the poem.

He'd given me the best smile. He smiled often, but it was the big one with crinkly eyes, the one dimple on his left cheek and a full set of white teeth. But there was something else there, too. His eyes were misty. Not full-on tears because he didn't really cry, but I could tell he felt something.

He walked from around the desk and gave me a hug.

"You are mine, Little One. From the day you were born. You grabbed my finger and made the sweetest sound. And I swore I heard you say Daddy. Blood is blood. We can't control who we're related to. But I chose you, and you chose me."

The soft growls from the engine of Mom's Range Rover cut the memory short.

I had to figure out a way to pull Mom out of the dark, though I didn't know how. She deserved time to grieve. Time to process her feelings. Time to understand what life after Dad meant. It had only been a few weeks, and honestly, I was still sorting myself out, too.

The garage door screeched. Dad used to spray it down with WD-40 every month, and it was time for another spray. I would carry on the tradition now.

A minute later, Mom walked in. "Hey, Chickadee."

I stopped cleaning, taking her in. She wore an oversized brown sweater, skinny jeans, and ballet slippers. She usually wore pumps, pencil skirts, and pearls, because, according to her, classy women wore pearls. Today she wore her hair curly. She usually straightened her hair—she didn't like curls. I loved her curls. It was the one thing I wish I'd inherited from Mom.

I sniffed the air. She didn't smell or look drunk, but she didn't look her best, either.

She dumped her keys on the counter, right by the key hook.

"Why'd you take the paper down?" She moved closer to me, closer to the window, and looked out.

"Why'd you put the paper on the window?" I resumed my side-to-side wipes. "With glue of all things."

"It's bright." She waved at the glass. "Too many windows."

"Well, then, next time you can pull the shade down."

"I couldn't find the . . ." She snapped her fingers. "Don't tell me . . . Ha! The ree-mote." She put an emphasis on the E and T.

I held my breath until my chest burned. She was definitely drunk.

I could tell because she took some *My Fair Lady*–type finishing school class when I was little and ever since she'd restrained her twang tighter than a dog on a steel leash.

But when she drank, the twang broke loose and anything with a-e-i-o-u became ayyy-eeey-iiiahhh-owww-yaawl.

"Can't find anything. Nothing's been right since . . ." She sighed.

"Then you should've kept the shades up, Mom." My voice went soft as did my irritation.

"Maya probably stole it."

"Stole what, Mom?"

"The ree-mote. She's a sneak, you know." She crossed her arms and rubbed them. "God, it's freezing in here."

I took another deep breath. Without Dad to act as a mediator, Maya and Mom were circling each other like the gangs from *West Side Story*.

"No, she didn't. Maya isn't like that."

"She is. She hates us, you know. She's going to take the house and kick us out."

"No, she isn't."

"Well, not you. But she's gonna have me livin' on the streets as soon as you leave. This is my house, too, you know."

If she says "you know" one more time . . .

Mom had told me about the reading of the will. Maya had agreed to let us stay until I graduated or left the house for good.

"Do you really want to stay in the same house as Maya? What happens when she gets married and raises a family?"

Mom laughed as she stared out the window. "Maya isn't getting married. She's going to be an old miserable hag."

"Mom!" I threw the squeegee in the bucket. Soap suds splashed on the floor. "Stop talking about her like that."

"She changes men more than she changes her clothes."

"Not true. She just hasn't found the right guy yet." And she hadn't. Maya needed an alpha guy. Someone to challenge her, someone who was her intellectual equal, yet a little bit of a bad boy. She hated goody two-shoes and thought good guys were boring. That's one thing we differed on. I loved good guys. Good guys didn't abandon or hurt you. "Maya just hasn't—"

"Maya this, Maya that. Maya, Maya, Maya," Mom said in a high-pitched voice.

"Whatever, Mom." I rolled my eyes. "You're drunk, and I'm not going to argue with you."

"I'm not—" she yelled and then grimaced. She lowered her voice. "I'm not drunk, young lady. I just have a headache." She massaged her temples. "I'm going to bed."

"Fine. Whatever." I dumped the water down the sink, opened the back door, and ran.

I could see Mom staring through the window, waving at me to come back. I turned away, grabbed my bike and helmet and hopped on my bike. I pedaled fast down the road, as if the Grim Reaper tailed me.

My lungs burned. My calves stretched like a rubber band. Still, I pedaled faster, determined to beat my best time. Determined to outrun Mama's grief and callousness.

After arriving at Maya's apartment, I slowed and crept up to the security box and dialed the code to get in. A long beep and then the guardrail lifted.

Stan gave me a chin nod. I waved and rode off, going toward the back of the complex until I spotted Maya's cherry red Lexus Coupe.

I leaned my bike against the brick wall near her door and then knocked. "Maya. Open up. It's me, Ryder." A minute passed by. There was some sort of noise coming from the other side of the door, but I couldn't make it out. It was probably one of those reality shows. She loved *The Bachelor* and *The Bachelorette*, though if anyone else found out, she'd deny it. "Probably can't hear me over the TV."

I patted my back pocket for my phone. Nothing but my keyring. "Crap." I smacked my forehead. I ran out so fast I'd forgot my cell. "Maya, I'm coming in." The keys jingled while I sorted through the ring. I opened the door and—

"Oh, God. Oh, God. Oh, God. Don't . . ." Gasp. "Stooooop."

All I could see was a firm muscular butt and my sister's legs wrapped around someone's waist.

"My eyes!" I yelled and slapped my hands over my face.

"What the—" a low male voice shouted.

"Ryder? What are you doing here?"

I spun away from the naked couple with my hands still covering my face. Zips and clinks and something else I couldn't make out was being dragged against the carpet. "Umm. I'll just come back later, and umm . . . next time I'll call."

"No, no," Maya said, out of breath. More clinking. "You can turn around now. We're dressed."

I turned.

"And uncover your eyes."

"You sure?"

"Girl, yes."

I took a deep breath. I shouldn't have. The smell of latex and sweat weighed down the room like a summer heat wave.

I opened my eyes. Maya had two wineglasses in one hand and a bottle of red wine in the other. I walked through the living room and took a seat at the kitchen table. Maya hurried past me and washed out the glasses.

"Roland, huh?" I reached for the orange in the fruit bowl.

Roland was kinda her boss at the law firm. I knew they dated. I'd met him a dozen or so times, but Maya made it seem like it wasn't serious. She hadn't mentioned him for the past few months. "Glad he's still around."

"What's that supposed to mean?" I heard a deep voice say from behind me. He ruffled my hair.

"Please tell me you washed your hands." I shuddered and ducked my head.

He chuckled. "You're a germaphobe. Just like your sister."

I ducked my head again, secretly pleased at any comparison to Maya. Even in a gross situation. "Sorry I crashed the party. It's Monday, and I figured that you'd be free." Maya and Roland's secret love affair had a strict schedule. Only twice a week. Tuesday and Friday with every other weekend if they decided to go out of town.

"Roland decided to surprise me . . . again." Maya shot a heated stare at him. Not the hot kind, the scary kind. "Besides, we're done."

"Are you sure? Because you told him not to stop, but then he stopped. I mean, it wasn't his fault because I kinda barged in and ruined things. So, I can just leave, or maybe I can wait outside until you're done . . . then you won't have to st-st-stooooop."

"Jesus Christ. I can't believe she just said that." Roland leaned forward and laughed into his hands.

"That's Ryder for ya." Maya shook her head. She put both hands on her hips. "Roland, you can leave now. Ryder and I need to catch up."

She turned around and pretended to wash already clean dishes.

"Okay, Princess. I know when I'm not wanted." Roland wrapped his arms around Maya's waist and whispered something in her ear. He kissed her neck and she squirmed, but it didn't seem like she wanted to get away from him.

"Later, Maya." He walked over to me, then leaned down and kissed my temple. It was kinda sweet and reminded me of Dad.

"Roland. What kind of car do you drive?"

"An Audi."

"Color, make?"

"Silver, A4. What? You planning to jack me?"

"No. Just . . . if I see your car, I won't barge in next time."

"There won't be a next time," Maya cut in. "He's sticking to the schedule. This is the third time in two weeks."

"Sure, I will. See you tomorrow, Princess."

"Wait up." She pulled a Tupperware bowl from the fridge "Here."

"Chili?"

Maya nodded, looking away as if embarrassed by something.

"You are so in love with me." He kissed her forehead.

Maya snorted and pulled away. "I don't want you to starve."

Roland shut the door, mumbling something under his breath that made him laugh again. I liked that he laughed. Maya needed someone funny in her life, especially now that Dad was gone.

Maya stopped pretending to wash clean dishes. "Are your eyes still bleeding?"

"I'm fine." I waved her off. "Now that the shock's rolled off, I can see the humor. At least he has a nice butt."

"And what do you know about a nice ass?"

"I'm seventeen." I shrugged. "I've seen male butts before."

Okay, I hadn't seen a naked male butt before, but as far as I could tell, it seemed like a nice one to see for my first time.

"Sure, you have." Maya gave me a knowing look and rolled her eyes. She crossed the kitchen and sat in front of me. "Haven't seen you in a while."

I spoke to her once or twice after the funeral, but for the past few weeks, I'd been busy with Mom.

"Sorry." I shrugged. "I figured you needed some time to catch up with work."

"Yeah. I went back last week. I'm fine. How's school?"

"School is school. I've been busy with stuff." My voice trembled. Maya's eyes sharpened, and she went stiff in the shoulders.

"Bullshit. What's going on?"

I couldn't get anything past her, so I opted for the truth. "It's just hard. I'm trying to get the hang of my new normal. You know, life without Dad. It's so weird . . . kids at school are staring at me and saying nice stuff . . ." I shrugged. "I don't like it."

"Has anyone said something mean to you?"

I shook my head. "No. Even Dani-with-an-I said something nice to me."

"That dumb fuck who tried to feel you up?"

"He didn't feel me up. He just wanted to cheat off my paper."

"Like I said . . . the dumb fuck. Anyway, ignore him."

"I will."

"And how's your mother?"

"She's just . . . sad, you know?"

Maya shook her head. "I know. But is she still taking care of you? She can't be falling apart."

"No, nothing like that. She doesn't need to cook because we have so many leftovers. And now I'll be busy with school stuff, so I don't really need anything." The lie fell from my lips to the pit of my stomach. I needed Mom. I needed someone. Maya was dad's biological daughter. I was just . . . the stepdaughter. Dad never treated me different but sometimes I felt my pain should matter less. "How do you feel?"

"I won't sugarcoat things. Losing a parent is . . ." Maya shuddered. "It's heartbreaking and sad, and it sucks. Now that Mom and Dad are gone, I feel like an orphan. Which is crazy, because I'm an adult, right? I should be satisfied that I had Daddy as long as I did."

"Doesn't matter if you're a kid or not. It still sucks."

Maya tapped the table and nodded. "Yeah, well, Jeanie and I may have our differences, but we are both here for you. You know that, right?"

"Yeah. I know it."

"Good." She stood. "Enough of the sad shit. I've got a few cases to work on tonight, but we can order takeout and watch TV. Or you can do some writing. I have one of your notebooks in my bedroom."

Usually, I didn't mind Maya working while I watched TV or journaled, but what was the use? The words weren't flowing.

"No." I shook my head. "I already ate. I should get going."

"It's getting dark out. Did you bike or drive? Why am I even asking? You never drive."

I hated driving. Dad had been taking me out to practice every Sunday. Mom was too nervous to teach me, and Maya had no patience.

"Yeah, I'll go ahead and get going—"

"No. I'm taking you home. You know these country bump-kins can't drive to save their asses around here."

"But—"

"No buts, Ryder. I'm taking you home." She grabbed her keys from a bowl near the door. "Bring your bike in and come get it later. Let's go." She waved at me.

I took a deep breath and sent a quick prayer—*please let Mom be passed out and please, God, don't let Maya come in.*

CHAPTER 3

JEANIE
RAINY DAYS AND MONDAYS

Monday evening, March 30th
22 days

Sandalwood and tobacco. I rolled over from my side of the bed, grabbed Joseph's pillow and sniffed, inhaling so hard my lungs burned. My nose already knew what my heart refused to acknowledge—my Joseph was fading away.

Joseph died on laundry day. And silly, eager me, I'd already washed his pajamas and undershirts and dropped his slacks and dress shirts off at the cleaners.

Now the only thing I had was this overstuffed king pillow to keep me company, along with his favorite drink. The expensive Cognac had helped me through the first week. It burned at first, but the fire blazing down my throat dried my tears.

They didn't sell Joseph's favorite drink at any of the liquor marts in town. He'd had it delivered every few months, along with specially made cigars. It was the last gift I gave him for Christmas. He lit up when I gave him a simple card and email that detailed his membership. I lit up right along with him.

I liked pleasing him because he'd done so much for me.

Every Christmas and Father's Day and birthday I went a little overboard.

Now I couldn't help wondering if I had a hand in his death. I hated those damn cigars, but I got them for him. The pillow grew damp under my cheeks. My body shook as emotions rolled over me like that boulder from the Indiana Jones movies.

I moved over to the edge of the bed, my hand swinging in the dark until it hit something solid. Something better than medicine.

Larissa, the clerk at the store, said the premixed stuff tasted good. And besides that, I didn't have to go into the kitchen and mix it up.

The alarm buzzed beside my bed. 8:00. "Huh . . . a.m. or p.m.?" The damn thing was smashed in. The screen cracked in a tiny million pieces.

I need to pee.

I skedaddled to the bathroom, pairs of jeans and shoes cluttered the way to the toilet. I fumbled around for the light switch and flicked it up.

After I did my business, I washed my hands and dared a quick look at the mirror, freezing at my reflection. "Oh . . . oh my." Mascara lined the trail of tears down my cheek. My eyes were brown and red. Mostly red. A pinkish crust that looked like a wart sat at the corner of my lips. I wet a cloth and scrubbed my face.

Old makeup gone, I splashed water on my face and smoothed the cool water over my neck. A loose curl dangled between my eyes. I twirled the tangled strand, chancing another look in the mirror. A wide-tooth comb sat on the corner of the vanity. I grabbed it and went to work on my hair, yanking it through until the tangles became waves.

My shoulders relaxed at my new and improved reflection.

No more crust, my hair passable, but my eyes looked like someone had poked them with needles.

"Visine. Visine." I opened the mirrored medicine cabinet, feeling around until I found the small plastic bottle.

My hand caught on a bottle, sending it crashing into the sink.

Joseph's cologne. Cracked glass plinked against the ceramic. Musk and sandalwood invaded my nostrils.

The smell was so heady, a pressure built in the center of my head.

I scanned the cabinet. I didn't see another bottle. I always bought double of his cologne.

"No, no, no."

My heart stuttered as I wiped the wasted cologne with my hands. Pieces of glass gathered under my fingernails and bit into my skin. Tiny dots of blood spread like fungi on my fingers. "I can buy more." I sniffed up the tears that gathered and continued wiping the sink. The cologne seeped into my cuts, but it didn't stop me. I liked the sting because I liked what came next: numbness. It was like a sip of alcohol; liquid fire that shot a path from my lips to my belly.

"All done." I put the chipped, empty bottle back on the shelf. Everything, his clippers, aftershave, and creams were neatly lined and intertwined with my perfumes and moisturizers.

They had to stay in place. Everything was changing. They were swearing in a new county judge to replace Joseph. The Piggly Wiggly, the place I first met Joseph, was going out of business. Lisa and Tom, the owners of the shake shack where we had our first date, were retiring to Florida. And my normally mature Chickadee had grown from sweet to sullen.

I didn't know how to connect with Ryder. Lord knows I've tried. One day I cooked her favorite meal: eggplant lasagna with lots of Parmesan cheese. Momma said apologies should always start with a hot, delicious meal and a warm cherry pie. And this meal was my way of apologizing for ignoring her the past few weeks. I had everything set up, but she walked past me without saying a word and stomped upstairs.

Then I went back inward where no one else could hurt me, like one of those little turtles in a shell. And now, being surrounded by his scent made the memories rush in. I smelled smiles and tender kisses. Brandy and cigars, jazz and dancing in the rain. Whispered promises of love, everlasting. We had a love of a lifetime. Something that no one understood, even our friends and families.

Folks on both sides were uneasy because of our race and our age gap. They either thought he was taking advantage of my youth or that I was a gold digger. I did not give one flip about those lies. I didn't care much about anyone else's opinions, including those sisters of his.

The truth of the matter was that I fell in love with Joseph. He saw that I was more than a high school dropout who worked at the Piggly Wiggly.

The day I met him our one and only cash register had broken. I had to manually ring up groceries and calculate the change. I'd rung up Joseph—pull-up diapers, wipes, formula, and chocolates. He shot me a wink so smooth, I just knew he practiced in the mirror. He said the chocolates were for his wife.

I smiled and gave him the correct change. He said that I was impressive—the way I worked so quickly to help frustrated customers, that I could charm the scales off a snake. I didn't really know what that meant, but I knew it was a compliment.

He said, "Keep it up, and you'll be running this store one day." It was the first time a stranger had said something nice to me, and not about my looks but about my brains.

I laughed and said, "Thanks, Judge Joe." Everybody knew Judge Joe in town. He was the first black man who held a position as judge for our county. Daddy said a few choice words about him the time Joe took his license for drinkin' and drivin'.

I didn't fall in love with him that day. He was married and just a nice man, but the way he smiled at me, so kind and honest—it made me feel special.

Somehow his words motivated me. A year later, I became the assistant manager. It was easy—keep inventory, keep the store clean, and make sure everything balanced out.

After the manager was caught with a sex worker in town, he moved away, and I became the manager. A few years after that, I saw Joseph's advertisement for a secretary. I applied, but I didn't get the job. Joseph took me to the side and told me he couldn't hire me because I didn't have any clerical experience. He said to me that if I wanted to work as a secretary or even a paralegal, to try a few courses at the nearby community college.

I finished the courses and a few more to boot. A year or so later, his secretary got pregnant and quit. I applied again and got the job.

And shortly afterward, the poor man lost his wife. He wasn't eatin' or sleepin', that's for sure. So, I cooked him my famous pot pie and made him eat it in front of me. He had the biggest grin, pure gratitude. He needed me and I . . . I shot clean one hundred feet into the sky, landed on cloud nine, and fell in love.

I wasn't some hussy like his sisters said. I didn't have designs on him when his wife was alive. I even checked out a book at the library on how long to wait to ask a widower out for a date. The book said to wait until the person had properly grieved and that there wasn't a time limit. I waited two years. It was only right. And I liked his first wife. She was very kind the few times I met her.

"Are you up there with her, Joseph?" I tilted my head toward the ceiling. "Sitting there at peace with her, hugging and kissing and loving her while I'm . . ." I hiccupped.

"Why'd you have to leave me?" I put both hands over my face, breathing in his cologne as the tears poured out. "I shouldn't have let you out of my sight that day. I knew something was wrong. Everything was breaking around the house. That stupid coo-coo clock. My flat tire."

I shuddered. Hindsight was twenty-twenty, and that day had been filled with bad omens. I should've listened to the signs. "I could've saved you, you know. You should've taken me with you to go golfing, and I could've done CPR. I took that class a few years ago, you remember? And you would've stayed with me because I wouldn't have let you go."

It wasn't fair.

It wasn't fair that the only man I'd ever loved had left me. And now his daughter was trying to kick me out of the one place I'd made a home.

Ryder would probably side with her. She always did. I didn't understand my Chickadee. So quiet and clever, nothing like me. And though she was pretty, with her big blue eyes and straight blond hair, she didn't resemble me. She looked just like Ricky Bennett, her no-good father. The day I found out I was pregnant, I was determined he wouldn't do the same thing to our child. I would fight him tooth and nail to make sure of it.

I read all the baby books and ate the right things. I even did prenatal yoga at the Y. I sang to her and said those positive affirmations. Turns out I didn't need to fight. Babies were permanent and Ricky never stuck around for anything serious.

The alarm system chirped. "Ryder?" What was she doing home so early? Or late. Still hadn't figured out the time yet.

"She's got a lot of nerve, slinking in here." I rushed out of the room to meet her. Stumbling over more clothes and some sort of papers along the way. "I'll clean tomorrow." I always kept a clean home whether it was the double-wide trailer that Daddy was determined to make smell like piss and beer, or my modest apartment I had for a few years after I gave birth to Ryder.

"Ryder. What are you doing here at . . . at this hour?" I rounded the corner, meeting her near the door. Chickadee's head hung low as she fiddled with the strings on her jacket.

But she wasn't the only person in our home. Maya stood near Ryder, her arm stretched out in front of my daughter as if she needed to protect her from me.

She wore her usual scowl. Her braids were twisted up in some sort of intricate knots that looked cool and if we were friends, I'd give her the compliment.

"What the hell is going on?" Maya's voice was low. Her eyes darted around the foyer.

There was a basket of dirty laundry in front of the guest bathroom that I'd planned to wash soon. A few pairs of shoes were tossed by the door. I'd been in a rush, and I hadn't had time to put them in the closet.

Magazine cutouts for a vision-board party lay scattered on the table. Linda at church was doing it for her fiftieth birthday. I'd overheard her say it when I was at the store the other day. She hadn't invited me yet, but I knew she would soon. Besides, I'd never done a vision board before, and I wanted to practice.

"Nothing's going on, Maya." My tone was just as hard as hers. I even crossed my arms over my chest and swerved my neck like she used to do as a teenager. I didn't have to explain myself to her. She may be the lady of the manor now, but she didn't lord over my life. "What're you doing here?"

"What. The. Fuck?" Maya snapped. "Ryder, why didn't you tell me?" She waved in my direction.

I stepped closer to Maya. "Tell you what?"

Maya closed the short distance between us. "That you're sloppy and losing your shit."

"Language, young lady. Now, I may not be your mother—"

"That's for damn sure."

"But I deserve respect."

"Re . . . respect? You're walking around in fuzzy boots and panties, smelling like straight-up moonshine and cologne." Maya paced the floor, her attention jumping between me and Ryder.

I looked down, just realizing I did indeed have on panties and nothing more on my bottom half. No, that's not right. I had on a pair of UGGs. *When did I put those on?*

"Tell me she isn't doing this every day?"

A rosy tint spread over Ryder's cheeks. "Mom has her bad days, but it's been fine. We're fine."

"Are you?" Maya's voice went high. "Who are *we?*"

"The Wonder Twins."

"Right, the Wonder Twins. And we don't keep secrets from each other, Ryder. Ever."

I hated when they did this—acting like twins with their own language and inside sayings and jokes.

"Maya." Ryder's voice dropped low. "Daddy's passing hit us hard. We all grieve in different ways. It hasn't been that long since he passed."

"Twenty-two days," I answered. I glanced out the windows. It was dark outside. Which meant it was 8 p.m. "And four hours," I added.

Maya shook her head. "Okay." She clasped her hands together and stopped pacing. She was quiet for a while. I didn't move, mainly because the floor started spinning. Ryder was doing a two-foot shuffle in her dirty black-and-white tomboy shoes.

"Fine." Maya moved into action. Picking up the basket and

placing it in the laundry room. Then cleaning up the scraps of paper on the floor and on the table.

"Stop." I tried to snatch the trash out of her hands. "This is *my* house. I'll clean it later."

Maya balled her hands around the paper. "Your house? Let me tell you something, my father and mother built this home. Mom chose the windows, the wood, the color that you decided to change to this godawful blue and pink. Had my Daddy living in a place that looks like Barbie's silly-ass dream home. FYI, I'm changing it back to my mother's green when you get your ass out of here."

"Maya." Ryder stood by the front door, hugging herself. "Don't say that."

My lips quivered. *Did Joseph hate it?* I'd tried keeping the color the same, but the unique color was out of stock.

There was no point telling Maya what happened. She always assumed the worst. "Go ahead." I shrugged. "It doesn't matter, because, at the end of the day, there is nothing you can do about it. Joseph wants me to stay here, and that's what I'm gonna do . . ."

Going. I promised myself when I became Joseph's wife that I would speak right.

Speak well.

"Uh-oh. She's got some whiskey courage."

"I'm not drunk." I shook my head. "The law is on my side."

"Sure it is." Maya bent over and lined my shoes. "This is the last time I'm picking up your shit, Jeanie."

She then turned to Ryder. "Pack some clothes. You're coming home with me."

Ryder shook her head. "I . . . I want to stay home." She looked down at her shoes.

Maya put her hands on her hips. "I don't care. You need to come with me. Clearly, Jeanie is still—"

"I'm fine." I cut her off. "She's my daughter. I'll take care of her."

"Look at you." Maya looked me up and down like I wasn't any better than dirt on her shoes. "You can't even take care of yourself. You—"

"Maya, Mom, stop it, okay?" Ryder raised her voice, her hands balled into fists by her sides. "I'm capable of handling myself. It's getting late, I'm going to bed. My *own* bed, okay?" Ryder gave Maya one of those hidden looks they'd shared over the years. I knew they were communicating something. They always did. Ryder raising her eyebrows, a reluctant smile from Maya or sometimes both would break out into a fit of giggles. Laughter should bring people closer, but theirs made me lonely.

Maya's shoulders relaxed. "Fine. You better call me before you go to school tomorrow."

"I will."

"Promise?" Her voice was thin and stressed like an enormous pressure sat on her vocal cords.

"I promise." Ryder walked over to Maya and held out her pinky. After a few beats, Maya hooked her pinky around Ryder's.

My heart deflated like a balloon losing helium. Ryder and I didn't have anything like that.

"Fine." Maya turned to face me. "I'll be watching you."

"You know where I *live*."

Maya rolled her eyes, stomped out of the door and slammed it shut.

"I do not get her." I sighed.

"Mom?" Ryder's eyes shimmered.

It tugged at my heart, and I wanted to do anything and everything to wipe away her pain. "What's up, Buttercup?" I pepped up my voice.

"Just . . . just stop it, okay?"

I nodded, though I didn't know what the "it" that I was stopping. I kept nodding when she turned away and ran up the stairs.

Stop it? Stop what?

Stop crying? Stop wanting the world to slow down so I could just catch my breath? Stop wanting love and affection and just a small morsel of human kindness? Stop wanting to numb my pain?

I lifted my still bloody hands to my face. My head sank into my hands, and I breathed in his scent again. Pretending it was just another night, and I was wrapped tight in his arms, with my nose pressed against his chest. He was reading a John Grisham novel, an old beat-up copy he'd probably read a few hundred times.

And for one simulated moment, everything was perfect.

CHAPTER 4

MAYA
WHAT'S GOING ON?

Sunday afternoon, April 5th
28 days

"Oh, nearer. Nearer, my God to thee." Aunt Lisa's sweet, alto voice filled the kitchen. Aunt Eloisa tried to harmonize in a shrill soprano.

Aunt Lisa was in her element. The whisk clinked against her favorite blue and yellow ceramic bowl that Leonard Jr., her son, had given her when he was in elementary school.

Every Sunday Aunt Lisa sifted, whisked and beat cornmeal and eggs and butter together, a delicious skillet cornbread that I couldn't wait to devour.

Her charm bracelet jangled as she stirred the mixture. The silver bracelet was adorned with a Bible, a cross, a bird and her birthstone. Leonard Sr., her husband, didn't get a chance to fill it up. He'd died four years ago.

Meal and butter stuck to her thick, capable fingers. Fingers that had a gentle touch when she'd wiped my tears when Mama died.

Fingers that thumped me when I was up to no good. And when I was little, I was very often up to no good.

And fingers that pointed in someone's direction when she was pissed off, which was a lot.

As I filled my aunts in on the latest drama about Jeanie, Aunt Lisa clacked the whisk against the bowl and shook her head, along with her curly wig. "I told you that woman wasn't good for Judge. Now she goin' 'round trying to steal folk's homes. Like she can't up and get another man."

Her words stung just a little bit. I'd like to think Daddy was irreplaceable. And Jeanie, for all her faults, did feel something for Daddy. I just wasn't sure if it was romantic love or daddy issues.

"Now, we aren't going to sit here and talk about someone who ain't here." Aunt Clara Bell shuffled into the kitchen with her walking cane. I didn't bother to help her. Last time I did it, she tried to bop me with her cane.

"Hmm." Aunt Eloisa, who was stirring greens in the pot, turned around with a dramatic eye roll. "Since when?" She covered the pot and bent over to check on the baked chicken in the oven.

"Since now." Aunt Clara Bell's voice was sharp. "We got a new pair of ears 'round here, and I don't wanna hear no complaints."

"Whose ears?" Aunt Lisa asked, pouring the batter into the skillet.

"We'll get to that after supper." Aunt Clara Bell shuffled over to Aunt Eloisa and lifted the pot. "Girl, why you put all this fatback in the pot? You trying to kill me or, better yet, Lisa?"

"Kill me?" Aunt Lisa scrunched her nose. "What're you talking about?"

"You know you got high blood pressure."

Aunt Lisa put her hands on her hips. "Now, Aunt Clara Bell, you know I eat healthy on the weekdays. But Sundays are different. I like fatback."

"Turkey's better," Aunt Clara Bell snapped back.

Aunt Lisa slapped my shoulder with the back of her hand, her wide brown eyes growing wider. "You like fatback, don't 'cha, Maya?"

I agreed with Aunt Clara Bell, for once. It was less greasy and salty. However, I made a promise to myself not to get involved in my aunts' and my great-aunt's affairs. As per usual, I raised my hand and said, "I'm calling Switzerland. I'm neutral."

"Lord, I wish you'd stop saying that," Aunt Clara Bell mumbled as she pulled out a chair at the kitchenette table. "How are you an attorney and use that Switzerland nonsense?"

"Mhmm." Aunt Eloisa was munching on the topic at hand. The juice from the pork greased her lips better than a glob of Vaseline.

"The court of law provides structure. There is a judge. Two opposing parties that argue within an organized construct. Y'all"—I pointed to all three of them—"will throw a hissy fit if I side with the other." I snatched a cooling skillet cornbread. Aunt Lisa pretended to swat my hand, but the little curve of a smile dotted by a deep dimple gave her away.

Aunt Clara Bell finally sat down at the breakfast table and continued her rant. " 'Sides, I don't see the big deal in wanting to *be* in Switzerland. It's expensive as all hell to live there and there ain't no black folks."

"Fine, I won't use Switzerland again."

Damn, if my coworkers could see me now, they'd know my weaknesses were ornery yet loveable aunts.

Aunt Clara Bell nodded once. I guess she was happy to get her way.

"Is Ryder coming over?"

"She said she might pop by."

My aunts were just half a mile down from our lake house. Daddy had built Aunt Clara Bell a smaller property by the lake. Aunt Clara Bell had always loved Ryder and quickly accepted her into the fold. It'd taken Aunt Eloisa and Aunt Lisa some time to accept her, but eventually she became part of the family. It was Jeanie they'd never warmed up to.

"I'm thinking about visiting Jeanie," Aunt Clara Bell said slowly, her eyes on me. "Make sure she's doing good."

"It's a free country." I shrugged. Aunt Clara Bell would do what she wanted.

Aunt Lisa snorted. "And who's taking you?"

"You." Aunt Clara Bell tapped her cane and stared at Aunt Lisa.

Aunt Lisa shook her head. "Eloisa can do it."

"Nah-uh. I've got yoga."

Aunt Lisa rolled her eyes. "She hasn't even said when."

"Don't matter." Aunt Eloisa shrugged.

"Lisa, you're gonna take me to Judge's house. We are going to be good Christians and check on her. Judge wants us to do it. He told me."

I couldn't hold back the sigh. I wasn't in the mood for Aunt Clara Bell's ghost stories.

Aunt Clara Bell stared at me for a moment. She was noodling over something. Her eyes seemed to jump with information. She worked her jaw, her bottom lip shifting from side to side.

"Well, go on and tell us." Aunt Eloisa stopped her bumblebee flight around the kitchen and settled in the seat across from her.

"It's a message from beyond the grave. From your daddy. It's up to Maya if she wants me to share it with everyone."

I let out a breath, my concern replaced with good ole-fashioned irritation. I loved my aunt to the moon and back, but she was bat-shit crazy.

"Aunt Clara—"

"Now don't pull that highfalutin tone on me, young lady. I

know what I heard, and your daddy has been worrying himself sick over you, Ryder and Jeanie. Now . . . would you prefer that I tell you by yourself or with your aunts?"

"Well, I don't want to hear it." Aunt Eloisa stood. She raised her eyebrows and shot me a commiserating look. "You need to leave well enough alone, Aunt Clara Bell. Don't be digging up fresh wounds for our Maya."

Aunt Lisa was surprisingly quiet. She didn't mumble and grumble like she usually did when someone said something foolish, and it wasn't because her beloved aunt said it. She stood, frozen by the oven, her arms crossed and her eyes wide.

Aunt Clara Bell folded her hands one across the other. Her veiny fingers smoothed over the peeling laminate table.

I wasn't fooled by Aunt Clara Bell's breezy attitude. Whether or not I gave her permission, she was still going to tell it.

"By all means, Aunt Clara Bell. What does Daddy want you to tell me?"

"Well, now. I'll paraphrase it, 'cause honestly, I think he was a little high-handed with his opinions. Easy to tell folks how to live when you're dead."

"Go on," Aunt Lisa said, her voice impatient yet soft.

"He says to stop harassing Jeannie about that will. That he said what he said. Also, he wants to know what you're doing out and about with that young man."

"Who?"

"Mr. Tall, Dark and Handsome." Aunt Clara Bell smiled.

"You can tell Daddy he's no one." I shivered a bit. I know Aunt Clara Bell was talking out of her ass, but a part of me was freaked out at the thought of Daddy watching me get my freak on. I rolled my eyes. "Anything else?"

"He's sorry he left you. He's sorry he broke the penny promise."

My heart full-on stopped. What. The. Hell. She must've already known. Air rushed back into my lungs. My chin wobbled, but I powered through and pasted a smile on my face. Aunt Clara Bell waited for a reaction. A validation by her family that she was gifted.

"Yep. Sounds good. You tell Daddy that instead of telling me what to do, that he should be worrying about his alcoholic widow."

"Judge got a message for her, too, mmhmm." She nodded. "Don't you worry. I'll be making my rounds."

"That's enough of that crazy talk," Aunt Eloisa cut in. "Now we cooked this nice meal together. Be a shame to ruin it with your ghost stories."

No one said anything after that. Aunt Eloisa buzzed about the kitchen.

Aunt Lisa finished the last batch of skillet cakes, then settled in the living room. I sat across from her, then leaned over and whispered, "Why didn't you tell Aunt Clara Bell to be quiet?"

A weird look crossed her face. "Be quiet? Why?"

"Umm, I don't know. Maybe because she's pretending to be Whoopi Goldberg's character from *Ghost*."

Aunt Lisa huffed and looked up at the ceiling. "Remember when Leonard Sr. died?"

"Yeah . . . of course."

"I was a mess, baby. Hid it from you, hid it from Judge Joe and Eloisa. But I couldn't hide it from Aunt Clara Bell. She knew what I was going through and she soothed me. She told me Leonard was at peace and pain-free. Told me things that only he and I knew about."

I leaned even closer and looked around. The house was small, and voices carried. "Has it occurred to you that she's just observant? A good listener and an even better gossip?"

Aunt Lisa sighed. "You know I used to say the same thing but . . . whatever it is, she just knows."

"Well I don't want to—" I cut myself off when Aunt Clara Bell walked into the living room.

Aunt Clara Bell sat beside me, patting my knee.

The doorbell rang.

"I'll get it." I stood and turned to Aunt Clara Bell. "Look, don't say anything to Ryder about what you said to me. It'll scare her."

"Scare her? He won't hurt her. He can't. He's dead."

"Aunt Clara Bell. I love you, but not everyone believes in ghosts. She's just a kid. Don't scare her."

"I'll just make it seem like it's coming from me and not Joe."

The doorbell rang again. "Fine." I hurried to the door.

Ryder fidgeted at the door in her usual attire: jean shorts cut off at her knees and a plaid shirt, and underneath that some teenager snarky T-shirt. Busted-up Converses that I replaced every Christmas and birthday. She was due for another pair.

"Thank God you're here." I pulled her in the house.

"Why? What's up? Why are you sweating?"

"It's hot in here. Isn't it hot to you?"

"I guess." Ryder gave me a weird look, shook her head and then went to the kitchen.

"Well, hello there, young lady." Aunt Clara Bell beamed a pearly white smile at Ryder. Sometimes I forgot how beautiful Aunt Clara Bell was—I'd inherited her smooth dark skin, light brown eyes and penchant for bold lipsticks.

"How have you been?"

Ryder's shoulders relaxed, though she fidgeted with the bottom of her shirt. I sat beside her and patted her shoulder.

"I've been well, thank you. How are you, Aunt Clara Bell?" she replied, her voice soft and respectful. Ryder was a unicorn—she was one of the few teenagers who still had the respect gene. I sure as hell didn't have it at her age, which is why I got so many pops on my mouth from my aunts.

"Oh, I've been good, thanks for asking. Outside of *somebody* who's been bugging me to talk to you."

"Aunt Clara Bell." My voice held warning. I shook my head.

"Who's that?" Ryder wound the string around her finger, looking back and forth between me and my aunt.

"Oh, nobody," Aunt Clara Bell said in a singsongy voice. "Heard you've been hanging out and coming home late."

A red flush spread from her neck to her cheeks. "Wh-what?"

"You came home late. Then you said some words to your mother."

"I . . . don't know what you're talking about." Ryder chewed her lip, her face as red as an apple.

My attention swung from Aunt Clara Bell to Ryder. Now I didn't believe in any of the ghost bullshit that she'd spill, but Ryder was obviously hiding something.

"You don't?" Aunt Clara Bell said, her voice dripping with disbelief. " 'Cause let Jo—*folks* tell it, you were stomping in well past midnight and on a school night."

"Is it time to eat yet?" I yelled.

Ryder tilted her head. "What folks?"

"Joe said you've been stomping in well past midnight and on a school night. Now I'm not going to relay all the other stuff he said because it was bordering on mi-sogy-nistic," she broke out the word.

"Aunt Clara Bell." I slapped the table. "Stop it."

Ryder shook her head, her mouth clamped. "I'm really not comfortable talking about Dad this way. He's no longer with us . . . and I'm sure . . . I'm sure if he were here, he wouldn't want you s-saying those things."

"What things?" Aunt Clara Bell leaned back, gripping her cane. "The truth?"

Ryder stood, nearly toppling over her chair. "I've got to go." She marched out of the kitchen, through the living room and out the door.

"Now wait a minute!" Aunt Eloisa yelled.

"I've got it." I waved her off before she could pursue Ryder.

"Best you talk to her." Aunt Clara Bell nodded. "You've got that way with her."

I paused at the doorway of the kitchen. "I love you, Aunt Clara Bell, I do. But I don't want to hear anything else about Daddy. He's dead and . . . and every day is a struggle. You bringing him up is like pouring a vat of salt on an open wound. I can take it, but Ryder can't. So, no more ghost stories, okay?"

"Okay. You're not ready . . . yet."

I didn't respond to my aunt but hurried after Ryder. As I opened the door, Ryder kicked up the bike stand, her legs straddled on the bike.

"Hold up." I walked toward her, unhurried.

Ryder rested her feet on the grass, her eyes focused on the ground.

"I'm sorry about back there. I should've protected you from all of that. Aunt Clara Bell won't mention it again, all right? You can come back in, eat some dinner."

Ryder shook her head. "It's getting late."

"It's four o'clock, Ryder."

"Homework," she said, still staring at the patchwork of browns and greens on the spotty lawn. "Do you . . ." She finally looked up, her blue eyes misting. "Do you think Dad is in heaven?"

"Yeah. I'd like to think he's with my mom, Gran and Pop-pop."

Ryder nodded, tucking a stray blond curl behind her ear. "Because it sounds like . . ." She took a breath. "I know Aunt Clara Bell thinks she can talk to spirits. Do you think Dad can see us?"

I sighed, crossing my arms across my chest. I looked back at the tiny cottage with the pointy roof, blue shutters and robin's egg–colored doors. Potted flowers littered the porch, bird feeders perched on the rails. The house was quirky, like its owner.

"Aunt Clara Bell is . . . complicated. I don't think she means any harm. I think a part of her hears something . . . or rather, she convinces herself that she hears it."

"Well, I don't like it. I don't like how she pretends that he's still here."

"Yeah, well, me neither. It's kinda creepy thinking about the possibility of Daddy seeing everything."

Ryder smiled, looking off at the house. "It's not just that. I don't like the idea of Daddy being . . . stuck here. Watching us do things without him. Watching us be sad and struggle." She swallowed, her breathing shaky. "That's the part I don't like."

"Are you okay? I mean, outside of being sad about Daddy."

"Yes, I'm fine—well no, not fine-fine. But things are okay. School is school. Everyone's being nice to me, which is weird, but I guess that's not a bad thing." She looked down at the grass again, her hair curtained around her face, blocking me out.

"No, it's not," I replied softly. Yes, she was definitely lying, and I would make it my business to find out.

"I do need to get going. Tell the aunts I'm sorry to rush off."

"That's okay. Do your homework and get some rest."

She put her feet to the pedal. "I will."

"See you soon, Ryder."

She looked back, her eyes panicked. She nodded and sped off.

Monday at noon, April 6th
29 days

Standing by the microwave in the office's breakroom, I warmed up my lentil soup with curry. I'd taken pity and made Roland a batch, but only after he promised he wouldn't bring it to work.

"Please tell me you're taking an actual lunch break?" Chelsea, one of the new associates, asked.

"Why?" I pulled my soup from the microwave. "You miss my excellent conversation skills?"

"Yeah," she said in her usual chirpy voice. "The only other people who take lunch right at noon are Thing One and Thing Two." She scrunched her nose. "Yesterday they were talking shit about a client who couldn't pay. Poor guy just lost his job. Instead of seeing if he qualified for pro bono work, they just dismissed him. I hate that."

Irritation pricked my skin like porcupine quills. I wasn't surprised. David was a pompous, privileged ass. Katy was willing to do anything to get rich.

"Did you catch the guy's name?"

Chelsea shook her head, her chestnut curls swishing with the motion. "No, but Katy has it. Maybe Mary Anne," she referenced the other paralegal.

"I'll look into it. See what he needs."

"Aww." Chelsea dabbed the corners of her lips. "You may have all the other associates running scared, but you don't fool me. You're a softy underneath all that hard core."

I shook my head, swallowed my soup and my annoyance at Chelsea's comment.

I shrugged. "It's not a state secret that I care about people. I'm not sure why I scare people."

Chelsea paused mid-bite from her salad. "I . . ." She cleared her throat. "You know, I'm not sure. I guess . . . I guess it's because you aren't afraid to speak your mind. You're direct."

"Yeah." I shrugged. "But so are Karrie and Darlene, Roland for the matter, and everyone else at the firm. That's what makes a good lawyer. Communication."

"You're right," she said. "I bet if you were a man, no one would think that." As Chelsea spoke, Katy and Roland walked into the breakroom.

"What's this about Maya being a man?" Katy laughed. "You certainly do act like one."

"Really?" Roland walked to the refrigerator and opened the door. "Maya doesn't remind me of a man at all."

My dark skin camouflaged the blush triggered by his comment.

"No, no." Chelsea waved. "I wasn't saying anything like that. I was just saying that Maya wasn't afraid to speak her mind, and . . . oh, never mind." She stuffed her salad into her mouth.

I bet it tasted better than her foot.

"Hey, Roland." Katy smiled at him. "I know you like those Marvel movies . . ."

My stomach clenched, and I didn't hear the rest. I knew what she would ask. I was afraid that one of these days he would say yes.

It was no secret Katy had the hots for Roland. David had the hots for Katy. Her voice was muted while I took her in. Katy leaned against the counter, decked out in a navy-blue pencil skirt, a thin, leopard print belt and a cream blouse.

Katy was beauty queen material. Perfectly dyed brown hair that swept her shoulders. Smooth brown skin and pert . . . everything.

"No, thank you. I already have plans."

"You seem to always have plans." Katy gave him a practiced, playful pout. "One of these days I'm going to be too busy for you."

"Sorry." Roland unwrapped his sandwich and sat across from Chelsea and me at the small bistro table. "I'm in the middle of a major case, working with this crazy client. She only meets me on Tuesdays and Saturdays. Stubborn woman won't budge for anything." Roland's gaze clashed with mine. I kicked his shin under the table.

Shut up, fool. I swear the man didn't give a damn who found out about us.

"She's stupid." Katy scooted a chair next to him, despite the table being at max capacity. "I don't care if I was just a client. I would love any time I could spend with you. You should drop her if she isn't listening to you."

"And you should mind your business," I snapped. "I think Roland knows what he's got himself into with his . . . client."

Katy sucked her teeth while she smoothed her perfectly coifed bob.

I shoveled soup into my mouth before I could say anything else messy.

"Mhmmm, Maya." Roland put his nose near my bowl and sniffed. "That smells good."

"It's delicious."

"Oh, I bet." His nose was still near my bowl. "Can I have some?"

"No. I'm hungry."

"Just a little taste. C'mon. Don't be stingy." He gave me a wicked smile.

I shook my head and kept eating.

"Fine." He grabbed the spoon from me.

"Hey. Get your own spoon. I don't know where your mouth has been."

He lifted an eyebrow. "If you're implying I have the cooties, I assure you I don't. The only time I put in these days is with my prickly client." He dipped the spoon into the soup and lifted it, pausing right before his mouth. Everyone stared at him.

Chelsea glanced between Roland and me, a look of horror on her face. I'm pretty sure she knew I wanted to kill him.

Katy's expression was a cross between woeful and jealousy. Like he was the last glass of water for a hundred miles in a desert. And she desperately wanted a drink.

Roland closed his lips around the spoon, right into his waiting mouth. He took his time pulling the spoon out of his mouth as if he were savoring a scoop of ice cream. "Very good." He returned the plastic spoon to me. A daring look in his eyes.

I grabbed the spoon, marched to the trash. I turned around, looked him square in the eyes, and chucked it.

Chelsea clutched her stomach and laughed. "And that's why I love lunch with you, Maya. Never a dull moment."

"That's what I'm here for." I put a lid on the soup and packed up my lunch bag. "Well, I've got work to do."

"So do I." Chelsea stood and grabbed her things. "I'll walk out with you."

"You two have fun." I waved without looking back, though I wanted to shoot Katy the evil eye.

I didn't know what to do with Roland. The man scared me. Pushed me. Tested me, inch by inch, making me give up more and more of myself. And if I wasn't too careful, he'd take a big chunk of my heart. I couldn't afford to give away any more pieces of me. There wasn't much left after Daddy.

Monday evening, April 6th
29 days

I passed by my apartment complex on a mission. There would be no jogging three miles around my complex or eating veggie stir-fry to stay in line with my meatless Mondays.

Nope, not today. I left work a little earlier than I'd intended. Something wasn't right. Ryder seemed more than a little spooked by Aunt Clara Bell's assertion that she was getting home late. So, if she wasn't back by eight p.m. and on a school night, something was up.

She didn't have extracurricular activities outside of the poetry club she'd founded. And that sad little club only had her favorite English teacher and three other kids. One had been forced to join by her parents, according to Ryder. Their meetings were usually done before five and they had meetings every other Friday. I shook my head. Who in the hell had meetings on a Friday?

I pulled into the curved driveway of my old home, parking at the top of the curve. The lights were on, so someone was home. I opened the door. My mouth popped open.

Jeanie clutched a bottle of cheap whiskey. There was a bucket between her legs.

Ryder rushed into the living room with a wet cloth in her hand. "Mom, you really have to stop this . . ." Her voice trailed off when she saw me.

"Maya." Jeanie's head popped up. "G-get outta my house." She hiccupped and then vomited. Chunks splashed in the bucket and dribbled down her chin.

"What in the hell is going on?" I yelled.

CHAPTER 5

RYDER
REBEL WITHOUT A CAUSE

Monday evening, April 6th
29 days

A chunk of something I didn't want to examine too closely hung from Mom's chin. She wiped it off with the back of her hand, her hard eyes on Maya.

Maya stared right back at her, her mouth wide open—and then just as quickly, she snapped it shut. The smell of beer and alcohol, of days without a shower and old food—food I'd tried to get Mom to eat that she took one bite of and told me it was shit—littered the wood and glass table.

"Oh, hell no." Maya rushed through the doorway.

"Maya." I finally found my voice.

She put up a hand. "Hush, Ryder."

"Get up!" she yelled, clapping her hands in front of Mom's face.

Mom stuck a chipped manicured finger in the air. "No. I belong here, you know. For as long as I shall live." She pushed the bucket to the side.

"And you won't live long if your sloppy ass keeps at it. Now, get up."

Mom struggled to stand.

I rushed to her side, hooking my hands under her armpits.

"Stop it." Mom wiggled like a toddler. "I don't need your help, God." She flopped back to the floor. "Oweee. My butt." She rolled over to rub her sore spot and giggled.

Heat hit my cheeks. "C'mon, Mom. Stop it."

"C'mon, Mom," she parroted. "Stop it," she said in a high-pitched voice that sounded nothing like me. Dang it, I was hoping I had more time. When Mom sobered up in the morning, I'd planned to sit her down and talk. Until today, she'd woken up sober, sad, and a little shocked at the mess. She would get up, shower, pick up a little, but not her usual deep cleaning. She was too tired and wrecked to do much else.

But in the quiet of morning, there'd be nothing to block her from the newness of the day. The war in her eyes calmed, and I think her mind cleared. She would give me those looks she always gave me when Dad was alive—a soft smile paired with a look of endless curiosity, a puzzle she couldn't solve. A puzzle she was determined to solve, no matter how long it took because I was worth the effort. And then, a look of pride washed over her features. I'd like to think it's because I'm hers and she's mine and the sum of our differences didn't matter.

Mornings were a blessing and a curse. A blessing because in that small sliver of time, Mom was back. A curse because I had to go to school, and I couldn't be there when loneliness clouded her sensibilities. When she couldn't see past the light and couldn't process there could be a life after Dad. Darkness transformed my mom into a drunken beast.

Maya rubbed her temples with both hands. "Jeanie. I will not repeat myself again. Get your drunk ass up."

Mom managed to roll over, grabbed the table leg, and propped herself up. "I'll go to my room. 'Cause I don't wanna see your ugly faces. You're probably just . . . talking about me. You always do." She pointed at both of us.

The cruel words were like a shot to my heart. I wrapped my arms around my center.

"Jeanie," Maya's voice was oddly low and a little scary. "You speak to Ryder like that again, I will drag your ass to your room and lock you in until you get your shit together."

"I'm sleepy anyway." She wiggled her fingers at us and then staggered away.

I headed in the opposite direction toward the laundry room.

"Hold up." Maya grabbed my arm. "Where are you going?"

"I'm going to clean up this mess." I waved at the bucket and bottle and blankets Mom had left.

She shook her head. "No, you aren't. When Jeanie wakes up, she'll do it. She needs to face the ugly truth."

"It stinks, Maya."

"It sure does, but I don't care." She dragged me to the kitchen. "The last time I came here your mom was in her panties. I asked you what was going on with her and you played it off. Now, she's going around snapping and saying horrible things to you. She's clearly abusing alcohol. She needs help."

No. She needs me. She needs time. Maya wouldn't give her what she needed. I stared out the window. The peaceful lake did nothing to calm the storm in my mind.

I licked my lips and pushed myself back and forth against the countertop. "She struggles sometimes, okay? But Mom and I talked, and she is going to therapy."

"She is?" Maya furrowed her eyebrows.

"Yes." Lying wasn't easy, but it was better than the alternative of having Mom shipped away to strangers.

"Mom is going to feel bad in the morning. You can ask her yourself. It's only been a little over a month since Daddy died. I don't think it would be fair to put her into some program when it's not even a habit."

"Fine," Maya whispered. She took a deep breath. "I'm staying tonight."

"It's not necessary." I needed to talk to Mom. Tomorrow would be a good time to get into her head, have her read the material I'd printed from the grief counseling website. There was a counselor just outside of town. He had good ratings and was board certified. Maya tearing her down the one time she was okay in the morning wouldn't help.

"Oh, I think it is necessary."

I crossed my arms and leaned against the counter. "Seriously, Maya, we're fine. You're busy at work, so you should focus on that. If anything pops up, I can handle it."

"It's not up for you to handle this. You're just a kid."

"No, I'm not." I slapped the counter. My palm stung against the marble. Maya had always treated me fairly, like my voice counted. Now she was trying to ruin everything. "Just . . . back off, okay?" I pushed off the counter. "I've got this."

"You can't control someone's actions, Ryder. And yes, in the legal sense, you are a child. And since your mother—"

"Whatever, Maya. Do what you want." I fled upstairs to my room.

God, I hated this. Hated running off like a little girl, but I was so tired of being *treated* like a child.

When Dad was alive, he called me his little girl. Mama calls me her Chickadee. If she could have her way, she'd pick out my clothes and dress me as her twin for the rest of my life.

Maya was the one person who had never treated me that way. Hearing her call me a kid felt like a harsh slap to my face.

I made sure Mom paid the bills on time. I cleaned the house, wiping down the sticky soda, the sickly-sweet daiquiri mix from the counters. I made perfect dinners only to have it thrown up or thrown out by Mom. I did my homework and braved the hallways of my school with a fake smile on my face to hide my fear.

She thinks I'm a kid?

Fine, then I'd *be* a kid.

Tuesday morning, April 7th
30 days

I woke up early, ready to be a rebel. At school, we had three options for skirts: plaid, khaki, or navy blue. The shortest skirt had been my khaki because it was three years old. I had to shimmy into the pleated skirt, with the hem resting just above my knees.

After that, I scoured the drawers for a push-up bra Mom got me for my sixteenth birthday. I never wore it. Not after Mom squealed and winked at me the one time I wore it out to a classmate's birthday party. The Oxford white shirt was easy, I just wore the one from last year. Though it wasn't super tight, last summer I'd grown some curves and the shirt accentuated my boobs.

The last part of my rebel makeover was makeup. I stared down at the drawer with two years' worth of foundations, blush, pencils, moisturizers and tons of eye makeup. It looked like one of those overstuffed dollar bins at the pharmacy. All courtesy of Mom, of course. I never cared about being girlie.

I picked up the eyeliner pencil. The first thing I think I needed was definition, according to the makeup bible I downloaded to my e-reader last night. I took the dark kohl, steadied my hand and traced around my eyes.

My hand slipped, and the sharpened pencil went straight into my eyeball.

"Holy shit." I covered my throbbing and tearing eye. Heat and pain pulsed beneath my closed lid. "Why do women do this?" The pencil rolled into the sink.

" 'Cause we want to be pretty," someone said from behind me.

I looked up into the mirror with my one good eye. Mom's eyes were a bit glazed, yet she focused on me. She laughed, a full belly, un-self-conscious laugh. To me, it was the most beautiful thing about her, the one thing she hadn't snipped, trimmed, or tucked away.

"What're you doing, Chickadee?" She had a wide smile on her face, her hand in her tousled hair, leaning against the door jam.

Eye still covered, I waved my hand around toward the vanity. "Makeup." I twisted the nozzle and wet a cloth.

"Uh-huh." She pushed off from the door. "Scoot." She opened the drawer. "Ah-hah."

She lifted a clear bottle and cotton pads. "I got you makeup remover as a stocking stuffer. Don't put water on them. It's only going to give you raccoon eyes."

I lowered my hand, looking in the mirror. "I already look like a raccoon."

Mom gave me another smile through the mirror. "Don't worry. We can fix it," she whispered. She put the makeup remover on the cotton. "Turn around. Face me." She wiped around my eye. The smell of makeup remover wafted. But I didn't complain, I just let Mom handle it.

"There. Fixed." She tossed the used pad in the trash can near the door. "Let me show you how to apply it."

"Okay," I agreed and for the next few minutes Mom was being . . . Mom. Warmth hit my chest. Maybe she didn't need those pamphlets, maybe she just needed time to come back to herself. But I'd told Maya that she was getting help, so I needed to say something, in case Maya followed up.

Mom grabbed my shoulders and turned me to face the mirror. "Beautiful."

The smile dropped from my face. "Just last night, you couldn't stand looking at me." I looked down at the sink.

Her fingers sank into my flesh. It didn't hurt, but it got my attention. "I'm sorry, Chickadee. I hope you know I didn't mean what I said."

I shook my head. "I know, I know . . . it's just that . . ." I licked my lips. "Maybe you could talk to someone?"

"We're talking now." She wrapped her arms across her chest. "I'm owning up to my sins and telling you I'm sorry. I slipped up."

Slipped up? She'd been slipping up for a month now.

"And besides all that, who would I talk to?" Her lips curved down. "My so-called friends at church are too busy."

"Not a friend, but someone professional, like a grief counselor."

Mom shook her head. "Oh, no. I'm not letting some stranger worm around in my head." She whirled her finger in circle, by her head. "Like I'm some coo-coo crazy person."

"Taking care of your mental health doesn't make you a cuckoo. It's like going to the doctor when you're ill."

"You think I'm mentally ill?"

"No!" I yelled. I took a deep breath, drawing on patience. "No," I repeated, softening my tone. "But I do think you should speak to someone."

"Like I said, there isn't anyone here. I don't want to go to a doctor in town. Everyone would find out."

True. There weren't many secrets in our town. "Then we go to the next town over. I can do some research, find someone who's under our insurance."

"Chickadee, I appreciate you. But I don't need your help. I'll . . . I'll cut back on the drinking. I'll do lots of prayer and throw everything out. I'll even tell Larissa at the liquor mart to stop selling me things for a while, okay?"

I nodded. It was better than nothing. *At least she's trying.*

But I had a feeling prayer wasn't going to be enough. I wanted to give her a smile, but my lips wouldn't move.

"How about this?" Mom rubbed my shoulders "If I need someone to talk to, I'll come to you."

"Promise?" I whispered.

"Promise." She gave me a firm headshake.

I smiled. Suddenly I felt dumb doing this whole rebel thing. Mom would get better and we'd talk more. Daddy had been great, he was easy to talk to and I missed him, but maybe Mom and I could talk like that, too.

Mom leaned over, hesitated and then kissed my forehead. "I'm going to take a shower, clean this house and then shower again."

That sounded more like Mom. "That's great."

I had a bounce in my step when I walked around school. Life was hard without Dad, but we would make it through.

Tuesday afternoon, April 7th
30 days

"Something is different about you." Dani-with-an-I slid into the desk next to mine.

"That's not your seat."

"It's not?" He frowned, somehow achieving both an adorable and confused look.

"Nope. You're one seat back. Roger sits there."

"Well, I'm sitting here now. I'm sure he won't mind."

Roger wouldn't mind because he desperately wanted to be Dani's friend. A few minutes later, my theory was proven true when Dani said, "Dude, switch seats."

"Sure, bro. No probs." Roger tipped his chin and slung his backpack into Dani's former seat.

Sure, *brother*. No *problem*. What was it with people chopping up words?

Dani leaned forward, his legs crossed at the ankles. He stared at me openly. Did I have something on my face? Lunch had been sloppy joes. Despite my greatest effort I always got sauce on my face, shirt or hair.

"What is it?" I narrowed my eyes at him.

"You look different, I'm trying to figure it out."

So, it wasn't food on my face. That meant my makeup. I rolled my eyes and flashed a thin smile. Boys were so vain. "It's called makeup."

I cracked open my English Lit book and then turned my body to face the front.

"No. It's not the makeup. That's nice and all, but it's your smile or something. You're different." He shrugged. "Whatever it is, keep doing it."

Maybe he was right, maybe it was relief. Mom had a plan to get back on track. Maya had driven me to school, and she seemed less stressed once she looked Mom over.

"Yeah. Things are looking up."

"So . . . my parents are out of town."

I rolled my eyes—I couldn't put it off this time. *C'mon Mrs. Frierson. Start class.*

"I'm not like that." I flipped a page, pretending to read. Even when Aunt Clara Bell said those things about me being out late, I was at a guidance counselor meeting. After the heavy conversation I went to Lenny's Diner and ordered a milkshake.

"I know that." He chuckled.

I ignored him.

"Hey," he said, his voice soft. "Look at me."

I did. He had big brown eyes with little specks of green. Maybe they were hazel. Either way, his eyes were exceptional, one of the many things attractive about Dani. Despite my brave words, my heart zipped. Something about him, the way he looked at me made me wish I had followed through on being a rebel today.

"I'm having a get-together tonight."

"Tonight? B-but . . . it's Tuesday."

"Why yes, it is," he whispered back in a scandalized voice.

"I don't think so." I shook my head. "I need at least eight hours of sleep."

"Aww, c'mon. Live a little."

I shook my head, my decision made. Parties during a school night is how kids let their grades slip. I had dreams: go to Emory University, major in English with a minor in education. Teach during the school year and write during the summers. The county gave full scholarships to the valedictorian and salutatorian. The only other requirement is no criminal record, easy criteria for someone like me. Someone who didn't have a social life. Someone who actively avoided trouble. And Dani was **TROUBLE**—all caps, underlined and bold. I just knew it.

"Fine. I'll text you my address." He grabbed his phone and typed something.

"You don't have my number."

Ding.

"How?" I grabbed my phone and frowned at the screen. Sure enough, he'd sent his address.

"I have my ways."

The bell rang, signaling it was time to start class. Mrs. Frierson wrote something on the whiteboard—again, nothing out of the ordinary.

"I hope everyone completed last night's homework assignment."

Everyone nodded and Mrs. Frierson beamed. "Excellent. Can someone tell me the elements of the epic hero cycle?"

No one raised their hand or volunteered. The bright smile on Mrs. Frierson's face waned. I waited ten seconds, so as to avoid the teacher's pet rep.

I shot my hand in the air.

She pointed to me, her smile returning. "Yes, Ryder?"

"A main element of an epic hero cycle is a quest."

"Exactly. A quest." Mrs. Frierson pointed her finger at me. "They're in search for something. In Greek mythology it's a difficult journey toward a goal."

Dani raised his hand, his eyes on me. "Mrs. Frierson?"

"Yes, Dani?"

"A quest requires bravery, right?" He looked at me, then returned his attention to Mrs. Frierson. "They have to try new things. Otherwise, how else will they grow?"

Mrs. Frierson nodded. "Not the element that I'm looking for, but yes, the hero must move forward and overcome great odds."

Dani lowered his hand, his lips twisted into a cute smirk. "Exactly what I meant." He winked at me and mouthed, *Call me.*

I jerked my head to the front, listening to Mrs. Frierson beg the class for more hero-cycle elements.

I didn't agree with Dani's definition of bravery, but as each day had passed since Dad was gone, I felt like I'd been sucked into the twelve labors of Hercules. Taking care of Mom, diffusing her and Maya's hatred. I felt stuck. Dad used to be the peacemaker . . . well, kinda. "One of these days, my girls are going to get along," he'd always said. Well, they didn't. And his will stipulations made it worse.

I sighed. Still, I couldn't help but think Dad would want me to wade in, and I would, but I was way out of my depth.

Tuesday afternoon, April 7th
30 days

When I got home, the house in the same state—dirty dishes, and pillows here and there, old food, stale beer and cheap liquor—I wanted to run back to school, go back to AP English and tell Dani yes.

My heart weighed ten tons. It took up so much space and was so heavy that all I could do was go upstairs to my room. I didn't check on Mom. I didn't have enough space in my heart to try.

Tears rolled down my cheeks. That, I could do. I slammed the door and sank into the purple carpet I'd begged my mom to get when I was ten because it was mine and Maya's favorite color.

Another ding. A text from Dani.

Party starts at 7.

I texted him back.

I'll be there.

I grabbed a Kleenex from my desk and dabbed away tears to preserve my makeup. Mom was too wasted to help me re-apply. I rushed to my closet. My private school uniforms were front and center. I yanked the string to turn on the light and pushed the skirts and shirts out of the way; the plastic hangers squeaked against the metal bar.

At the back of the closet were T-shirts of my favorite bands, and slashed-up skinny jeans. I wanted something different, I didn't want to be the same old Ryder. I snapped my fingers, pivoting to my trunk. Mom had stuffed girlie clothes down my throat over the years.

After twisting the lock, the lid popped open. A stale, mothy smell wafted in the room. It wasn't overpowering, but it could use a few squirts of Febreze.

"Thank you, Mom," I said, rifling through clothes. Cropped T-shirts, off-the-shoulder sweatshirts, there was even a tutu skirt, pink tulle that would totally work with the black crop top.

It was only five thirty. I sprayed down my outfit, ironed my shirt and brushed my hair. Every five minutes I glanced down at my phone. Time crawled by and I wished it would speed up—just in case Mom crashed into my room or Maya popped by unannounced. For once, I wanted to do something fun.

And I liked how Dani made me feel—interesting and special and pretty.

Gah. I didn't need some guy's approval. I pulled out my phone again, this time determined to screw my head back on. I listened to meditative music and a compilation of my favorite English poetry. I thumbed through dog-eared pages until I landed on my favorite William Wordsworth poem. He was one of my favorites, though after a healthy debate with Maya I now understood he had stodgy beliefs when it came to gender-based roles. So now I stuck to his nature poems. I liked the way he critiqued the wastefulness of mankind. And the way he basked in the serenity and majesty of the outdoors. I liked nature, that's why I biked. You couldn't taste the wind if you're stuck in the car. You can't smell the birth and death of spring if you're glued to the house. It wasn't a popular opinion among my age group. To them, I was the weird girl who walked outside without shoes. I was the girl who didn't know about the latest TV show, but I could quote my favorite lines from the latest children's books to thriller novels.

I know I'm weird. Mom thought I was shy. Dad thought I was too smart to deal with kids my age. But Maya understood that I'm just an awkward introvert. There were people I liked to talk to at school, but I wasn't so close that we hung out over the weekends. Weekend times were meant for family. *Until Dad died.*

But now it was time to find my new normal. And maybe I could make friends with Dani.

After the sounds of pan flutes and poetry soothed my nerves, I put on my clothes, smoothed my hair and stared at myself in the mirror. I looked good. Really good. I walked carefully downstairs. Not that it had mattered. Mom had passed out on the couch, her mouth agape. A part of me wanted to shut her mouth and wrap her in a blanket. The other part of me—a big part—wanted to smack her.

Instead, I told her good night and used the car Dad had given me in his will, an Acura RLX. It was too much. The car was only a year old, black exterior with white leather seats. I slid my hands over the butter-smooth steering wheel, my eyes tearing up. Dad loved his car and kept it in tip-top shape. He even washed it himself every two weeks in our front yard.

"Don't worry. I'll treat you right," I promised the car. I plugged Dani's address into the navigation system and seven minutes of heavy and sudden braking, jumping curbs and turtle-slow driving later, I arrived right on time.

"Oh, God. I'm here." I tried swallowing but my throat was like a sand dune. I pulled the Acura up to the three-car garage. There weren't any other cars in his driveway.

A light flipped on at the front door. Dani stepped out in a blue polo shirt and dark jeans. He tapped on the passenger window. "Hey, Poetry Girl."

"Hey, Dani-with-an-I," I said back to him.

"Dani with an I?" He screwed up his face, confused.

Oh, shoot. "Never mind." I looked around, noticing no other cars in the driveway or near the curb. "Why am I the only person here?"

"No one is here yet and my friends never park their cars at my house." He looked at the house beside his for a few seconds and then swung his attention back to me. "Can you unlock your door? I'll show you where to park."

I nodded and pressed the button. When Dani slid into the passenger seat, I noticed he didn't have any shoes.

"Don't you want to get your shoes?"

"Nah. We aren't going too far." Dani had me make a few turns and park at the back of the subdivision, near a cul-de-sac.

"Why do we have to park so far away?" I asked him as we stepped out of the car.

"My nosy old-broad neighbor, Mrs. Smith, likes to keep tabs on me."

I shook my head. "Well, isn't she going to hear us talking? Or if you play loud music?"

"Ten steps ahead of you. Mrs. Smith can't hear worth a damn, so on the nights I have people over I sneak into her house and take the batteries out of her hearing aids." He chuckled, winked, then looked straight ahead.

I stopped walking. Dani kept going until he noticed I wasn't moving.

"What?"

"That's a crappy thing to do."

"What?"

"Remove batteries from her hearing aids. What if a fire alarm goes off or . . . or if someone breaks in? Not to mention you're breaking into her house in the middle of the night. She could have a gun and shoot you on sight. And it'd be within her rights because you're trespassing."

Dani turned around and put his hands on my shoulders. "Wow. You've got a lot going in your head, don't you?" He gave me a toe-curling smile.

"I just . . . it's against the law," I whispered. "And if something happens to her—"

"Then I'll save her," he replied, his voice softer than mine. "I would never put Mrs. Smith in harm's way. She's been my neighbor since I was six years old. She's like a grandmother to me. I have a key to her house, and sometimes I'll house sit when she's out of town visiting her grandkids. When her cat runs up the tree, I'm the first person she calls. We're good, okay?"

I licked my lips. "You really saved her cat?"

He smiled. "Every other week, it seems."

"Well, that is nice. But stealing her hearing aid batteries is still a jerky thing to do."

He lifted his face toward the sky and smiled. "You've got to lighten up, Poetry Girl. Live a little."

My cheeks heated. I tucked my chin to my chest, letting my hair fall in front of my face. I knew he was teasing but his words rang true. I always did the right thing, followed the rules, colored within the lines—and what happened?

Dad died, Mom is a mess, and Maya wanted to ship Mom away. It was time to change my set of rules. I didn't have to be a full-on rebel, but like Dani said, I could live a little.

I lifted my head. "Fine. I'll loosen up. But you'll have to show me, because I don't know how. I go to school and come home. Every Saturday morning my sister, Maya, and I get breakfast at Lenny's—you know the big waffles? And a milkshake, too. Mostly vanilla but sometimes I like to mix it up with strawberry and—"

Dani stopped walking, clutched his stomach, and laughed.

"Stop laughing," I hissed. "I told you I don't know what I'm doing."

"No, it's not that, it's . . . you ramble. It's cute. Really cute. I like that you're shy."

"Cute?"

I wasn't shy, per se. I just didn't like talking to people and in front of people.

Okay, maybe I was a little shy.

"No, I mean, yeah it is but . . . you're nervous, right?"

I nodded. "Of course. A lot of things could go wrong. What if Mrs. Smith calls the police? What if your friends don't like me? What if—"

"It'll be fine. What I'm trying to say is that I'm nervous, too. Not about all of that, but about you. It's nice that we're on even ground."

"Oh." I blew out a breath. "Okay. Whatever works. Do you have food? I could eat."

"Yeah, our cook froze a bunch of meals for me. I thawed out

a casserole. You can heat it up. After that, I'll show you how to live."

"A little," I corrected, as my mind flashed to my mom, who went way on the opposite of living on the wild side.

An hour later, I was certainly doing that. No one arrived until about eight thirty. Apparently, if you were a cool kid, you never arrived to anything on time. So noted.

There were six of us: Coraline Stewart, a senior and the school's resident mean girl. Blond and blue-eyed Malibu Barbie. Well, she desperately wanted to be. There was only so much Malibu you could channel in Hope Springs, Georgia.

Her boyfriend, Eric Frasier—I think he was her boyfriend, his tongue was constantly down her throat—was another senior in the group. Football god, attractive, with the body of Thor.

Then there were the fraternal twins, Kaitlyn and Kayden Murphy, who were both juniors like me and Dani. Kaitlyn was funny—like *Saturday Night Live* comedienne funny. She was great at impressions and she made me laugh when she mimicked Coraline putting on lip gloss. Kayden, the more serious twin, sat back, watching his sister, and occasionally adding a dry remark here or there. They were both redheads, though Kayden's hair was more of an auburn and Kaitlyn's hair was the color of a carrot.

Dani and his friends drank, while I sipped a Coke. I couldn't stomach the taste of alcohol with Mom drinking every night. When I said no, Dani gave me a look and I gave him one right back.

Coraline looked me up and down. I don't know what she found, but there was something cautious in her eyes. "So, what's your story, Riley?"

"Ryder." I sipped my Coke, giving her a bland look. How could she expect me to share "my story" when she couldn't bother to remember my name?

"Yeah, whatever. What's your story?" Coraline asked again.

"It's still being written."

She rolled her eyes. "What does that even mean?"

"I just turned seventeen. It means I haven't lived long enough to have a story." And I sure as heck wasn't sharing anything that had happened so far with strangers.

"We should have a party." Kaitlyn clapped her hands and squealed.

"No thank you. I'm not really up for one."

"Oh . . ." Her eyes went big. "Oh," she said again, her voice slow and exaggerated. "Your dad just passed away, didn't he? I'm sorry about that."

"Who's your dad?" Coraline leaned in, her eyes sparkling like we were gossiping instead of discussing death.

"Joe Donaldson. He was an attorney and a county judge."

"Hey . . . I know him. The big black guy?" Coraline tilted her head.

The big black guy? Dad was a lot of things—kind and smart and handsome. Big and black wouldn't be my first choice of words. I didn't know how to respond to that, so I didn't. I just knew if Maya heard it, she would've ripped Coraline a new asshole.

"So, he's your stepdad, then. Because he's, like, black." Coraline smacked gum in between asking a deeply personal question.

Kaitlyn smacked Coraline's shoulder, and Eric snickered behind his hand.

My eyes went wide. "Oh, my God. He's, like, black? I had no idea." I shot to my feet, looking down at Dani and the others. "Dani, did you know?"

Dani laughed and shook his head. "Nope. Thought he was white this entire time."

"Kayden? What about you?"

"I always thought he had a nice tan."

"I've gotta go home and tell my mom. My God, this entire time!"

Coraline rolled her eyes. "Sorry, sheesh, I get it."

I sat back down. Kaitlyn laughed then gave me a high five. "Nice threads, by the way. Where did you get them?"

I shrugged. I didn't want to admit that my mom shopped for all my "cool" clothes. "Probably online or at Northshore Mall." We didn't have much of a mall. Just a few boutique stores, a Macy's and Dillard's at the dismal mall the county over.

"You paid for it?" Kaitlyn laughed.

"Yeah."

"Seriously?"

"Seriously. How else am I supposed to get clothes? You give currency and you receive goods."

Kaitlyn pointed to her watch. "Got this at Macy's." She pointed to her leather jacket. "Got this from a store in Atlanta." She finally pointed to her Gucci bag. "Boutique shop downtown." She smiled, biting her lip. "Ask me how much."

"How much?"

"Zilch. Nada. Nothing."

"Do you mean you . . . you stole them?"

"I liberated them from the store. I'm like a superhero or something. My powers are sticky fingers." Kaitlyn sipped something, a mixed drink I think, out of a red Solo cup.

"But why do you steal? Your parents have money."

Her dad was a dentist who specialized in something. Her mom was a neurosurgeon, I think she flew around the country to give trainings and speeches.

Kaitlyn shrugged. "Because I can."

I folded my arms across my chest, thinking of an excuse to leave. I mean, I wanted to live a little, but this was foolish. Besides that, Dad had always taught me to be honest, to never lie or cheat or steal. If Maya were here, she'd shake her head and say something about bored white rich kids. I couldn't help but think she was right.

Everyone's eyes were on me, studying me, waiting for me to say something or bolt; it made me feel weird. I wanted to be cool, to be liked, but I didn't agree with stealing. This conversation made me feel like I was standing naked in a stadium full of people and I hadn't shaved my legs.

Dani's eyes were on mine. He looked worried.

"It's all good, Poetry Girl. If you don't want to do it, you don't have to."

"Do you . . ." I licked my lips, ". . . do it?"

Dani shrugged and gave me a sheepish smile. "Umm . . . Yeah."

"Why?"

He put down his beer. "So, check it. I watched a documentary the other day about child labor in India. They get, like, a quarter a day and work from sunup to sundown. Then some other dude sells it to stores, and then they jack it up by about two hundred percent from what they paid for it. Then they charge the consumer for something made by a child that costs nothing." He took another sip of beer. "Now, I'm not saying stealing is the right thing to do. I'm not that stupid. But I'm saying that these big corporations won't miss it. They are the real thieves. And I'm sorry, but I'm not going to get mad about taking something from them when they've done so much to third-world countries, not to mention our environment."

"Yeah." Kaitlyn snorted in her cup. "What he said." She rolled her eyes. "So anyway . . ." She put her cup on the table. "Why does Dani call you Poetry Girl? Are you a writer or something?"

"Or something." I smiled at Dani.

Thankfully, for the rest of the night we talked about school, with Coraline supplying the latest gossip about students and teachers. We talked about television shows—I recognized a few of them—and some of the guys talked sports. It was fun.

When I finally got up to leave, Dani walked me to the door. He grabbed my hands and I knew right then he was going to kiss me

He didn't rush in and just take, like I'd seen a lot of boys do around school. He didn't ask outright, but he hesitated, licking his lips as his chest rose up and down. He stared into my eyes before he lowered his mouth to mine. I liked the curve of lips when he closed in on me, inch by inch on a slow exhale. The taste of cool mint and a hint of beer was unexpected and nice. It was the soothe I didn't know I needed.

It was a good first kiss. Until I started thinking, that is. Did this mean we were together, kinda together or just friends? Maybe I could send him a text: **Do you like me? Why did you kiss me?**

But, wait. Should the girl text first? I thought Maya said guys need to text first after a hookup because . . . I don't know. Hetero dating rules were so stupid.

"I mean he has to like me, right?" I asked as I drove back home. Scratch that, it was a series of stop and starts. I was so freaked out, I pulled over to the Pump and Go.

A silver Audi pulled up beside me. All the innards in my stomach dropped when I recognized the driver.

"R-Roland." My eyes went wide.

He mimed me to roll down the window. God, it was midnight. He would for sure rat me out to Maya.

He turned off his car. I opened the door and scrambled out.

"Roland, what are you—"

"Just leaving your sister's apartment. What are you doing out?"

"Hanging with friends." I tried for casual; I was so not casual. I was a big fat scaredy cat.

Roland crossed his arms and leaned against his car. "Is that right?"

"Y-yeah. That's right. I'm not lying, you know. I was hanging out. I didn't do anything bad. I didn't drink. You can smell my breath, it'll smell like cola, or have me walk a straight line or—"

"Oh, I believe you. But I bet your sister would be pissed if she knew you were out late and on a school night. Your mom, too."

Mom's too drunk to care.

"Are you going to tell Maya?"

"Depends. Are you going to sneak out again?"

"No," I quickly promised. "If I tell Maya she'll be okay with it. As long as I call her when I arrive and when I leave."

"Good." He nodded. "You do that. Please. Otherwise, your sister will have my balls if I don't tell her." He smiled like he wanted to give Maya his balls on a platter or something.

"Do you like my sister?"

"Of course."

"Do you . . . do you love her?"

He took a deep breath. His eyes didn't look away, and he didn't flinch when he said, "Of course."

"But she doesn't know."

He shook his head. "I haven't said it yet."

"Don't."

He cocked his head. "Interesting. Why shouldn't I?"

"Maya has to realize she loves you on her own. If you tell her, then the thrill of sneaking around will be gone. Then she'll feel guilty and responsible for your feelings. Then she'll want to stop, even if deep down she loves you, too. She feels like she isn't ready to settle down. Especially now that Dad is gone."

"But shouldn't I tell her? She needs to know that she's loved now more than ever."

"Show her through your actions. Let her say the words first. Let her feel like she's pulling you in."

He chuckled, shaking his head.

"What?"

"That's what Judge Joe said. He told me to let her reel me in."

"Dad was the wisest man I've ever known. You should follow his advice."

He tapped the car roof with his knuckles. "Yeah, I . . . It doesn't feel right, but okay."

"Good. And another word of advice: don't give up on her."

"I won't," he said, too quickly, too confidently. He didn't know my sister, not as good as he thought he did.

"I mean it. She'll push you away. But don't give up. She's worth it."

"I know she is. Don't worry. I've got this."

No, you don't.

"Promise me you won't give up on her."

"I promise."

"Good." I offered him my hand. "We have a deal. I'll tell Maya next time I step out late. I won't spill your feelings, and neither will you."

"This is weird as hell but . . . you've got yourself a deal." He grinned, shaking my hand.

"I'm going to fill up my tank." He pointed to his car. "Then I'm following you home."

"I'm, umm . . . not the best driver."

"I've heard. Which is why I'm tailing you."

When I arrived home, right after midnight, I tucked myself in and closed my eyes. For once, I didn't feel the dark or the loneliness. For once, I didn't say a little prayer for Dad or worry about Mom or wonder when the bottom would drop.

I was just a girl, who kinda sorta liked a bad boy and his

merry band of thieves. Most of them liked me, I think. Kaitlyn for sure. Dani and Kayden talked to me most of the night. Eric was too busy with Coraline. But even with Coraline being a little frosty toward me, she still wanted to know my story.

They were by no means perfect. They were privileged, misguided and spoiled. But they weren't bad, and I liked them.

CHAPTER 6

JEANIE
SPIDERWEBS

Thursday morning, April 30th
53 days

The ungreased wheel on the shopping cart swiveled around like a fish out of water. The Piggly Wiggly had gone way down in quality since I quit some twenty years ago. Today I wasn't looking for cheap wine. Joseph's aunt Clara had asked to come over and I'd planned to cook up a few appetizers.

A burp pressed against my throat. Ladies didn't belch in public, but this one was building up. I grabbed a Gatorade out of the small fridge near the cash register, twisted the cap off then gulped the drink down.

The Gatorade helped me swallow the belch.

"Hey, now, Jeanie," Dollie, the manager, yelled from the front.

I dropped the bottle into the cart and waved her off. "Ring it up later. You know I'm good for it."

Dollie twisted her thin lips and then shook her head. "Bet you are," she muttered as she swiped a package of discounted meat for Vita, the secretary at my church. Clarissa, her little girl, danced around her mother.

"Ms. Jee-Jee." The six-year-old ran over and hugged me around my knees.

"Hey, Pretty Girl."

She tilted her head up, her eyes wide. "Are you a spider?"

"Am I a spider?" I looked over to her mother, Vita. Vita's mouth had formed a perfect O.

I smiled and lowered myself to the floor.

I wiggled my fingers and went for her belly. She laughed, wrapping her little arms around my neck. I picked her up and walked toward Vita. Clarissa giggled, tossing her head back, and snorting like a little piggy. I smoothed a blond curl stuck to her sweaty forehead. I missed these moments. The pure innocence of a little one. I breathed deeply and took in her cotton candy scent, my heart aching for the olden days when Ryder let me hold her.

I bopped Clarissa's nose. "Now why would you think I'm a spider, you silly goose?"

"Lissa, leave Ms. Jeanie alone. I'm sure she's busy." Vita snapped her fingers. I was surprised she could do it with her long acrylic nails.

Clarissa shrugged. "Mommy says you're a black window. And teacher says that black windows are poison-sis." She leaned back, her brown eyes widening. "You aren't poison-sis, are you?"

My attention swerved from Clarissa to Vita. "You think I'm poisonous?" The accusation rattled me. Heat prickled on the top of my head and traveled at the speed of light through my body.

"I . . ." Vita shook her head as red spread from her forehead to her neck. "I didn't say that." She pulled Clarissa from my arms. "Now what I have told you about going around telling tales?"

"I ain't tell no tales, Mommy. That is what you says. Remember Daddy said Ms. Jee-Jee looked sad and you said she shouldn't be 'cause she was sitting high on a hog." She looked around the store. "I don't see no hog."

My mouth popped open. This vile lie, this gossip came from the church secretary. When her husband was out of work, I gave him a recommendation for a security guard job at the courthouse. When Clarissa fell ill and neither Vita nor her husband could afford to take off work, I was the one who watched their daughter.

When Vita's mom died, I helped organize the funeral when she fell apart. My lips quivered. No matter what I did, how I helped, I was either poor white trash or a gold digger. No one ever saw *me*.

It was just like when I first started dating Joseph and he introduced me as his girlfriend to his family.

"You really gonna date that white girl?"

"You robbin' the cradle, aren't you?"

And the worst, the one that almost made him break up with me. *"Renee's turning in her grave. You think she'd want that young girl up in the house y'all built, raising her baby?"*

His aunt Clara Bell just floated to the center of the room. Joseph moved to stand in front of me.

She slapped him upside his head. *"Move. That's a grown woman behind you."*

Joseph stepped to the side. I shivered a little, not quite sure what to expect.

Her eyes stared into mine. She lifted her hand and I flinched. I don't know why I was so afraid of the old woman, but I was.

"She's got kind eyes. She's a 'fraidy cat but she'll find her footing one day, sure enough." She smiled and then turned to face his sisters. *"They're meant to be. Don't question it."*

But those memories were no help to me today.

Vita at least had the decency to look ashamed. Her eyes were aimed just above my shoulder. "Jeanie, I don't know what she—"

"People like you give Christians a bad name." I jerked the shopping cart around and tried to storm away, but the defective wheel made the darn thing more of a raging bull than a metal cart.

Before I could even turn down the aisle, Dollie's and Vita's heads were bent, hands around their lips as if their loud voices didn't carry.

"Why is she getting upset? She knows it's true," Dollie said.

Gossiping hens. They had no idea. No friggin' idea how much I loved Joseph. I never poisoned him. If I were guilty of anything it would be nagging him about his health. I hid his cigars. Sunday meals at Aunt Clara Bell's had been restricted to once a month.

I flew down the grocery aisle, throwing food into my cart at record speed. I was buying groceries for Aunt Clara Bell's visit. She liked my meatballs and cheese balls, though she could usually only have one. They were too rich for her.

Five minutes later I crept back up to the checkout. Dollie still manned the only open lane.

She avoided my gaze, not attempting to make small talk. *Good.*

I waited until she bagged my items and then handed her my credit card. "Twenty-seven dollars and fifty-two cents." She swiped my card and frowned. "Hmm. It's not going through."

"What?" I asked her as she continued to swipe.

"Says it's declined. Look, if you want, I can put you down for—"

"No." My voice came out curt. I knew what she was going to suggest. Once a month, the Piggly Wiggly gave a temporary store credit to a family in need. It was a program I'd created. I wasn't in need. I didn't know what the hell was going on, but I would get to the bottom of it.

"Just try this card." I handed her my debit, trying to remember what happened to the credit card. It came out automati-

cally from our joint account. Unless . . . unless Maya somehow
froze the card.

The other day Maya called me to ask if I was "taking care of
business." I told her I was.

And then she said in the snootiest voice ever, "Good. 'Cause
if you aren't, I'll step in and handle it myself."

My chest heaved. After Clara left, I would give Maya a piece
of my mind. I still didn't understand how someone as loving as
Joseph had raised a shrew.

When the debit went through, the knot in my chest loos-
ened.

She wouldn't push me out of my home and my means of sur-
vival. If she wanted a war, then I would give her one.

Thursday afternoon, April 30th
53 days

The meatballs were a little dry and the cheese balls were
soggy. I wasn't sure what I'd done wrong, but Aunt Clara took
a small plate I offered her, nibbled like a little mouse and then
frowned. She sniffed and put the plate down on the side table
near the chair. We were in the sitting room. The chairs were
firmer than our deep sofas in the living room and I knew she
needed something sturdy for her back.

Aunt Clara stared at me for a full minute. It was like those
old brown eyes could see into my soul.

If she could, then she wouldn't see anything. I had nothing
left. Joseph had taken that six feet under, along with my heart.
I bounced my knees, my plate nearly falling off my lap. I caught
the plate before it fell and with shaky hands put it on the table.

How long does she plan on staying?

"I thought you didn't drive?" It was more question than
statement. Her nieces were usually flanked around her. I was
thankful it was just her visiting.

"I don't."

I reached over for my glass of wine and took a deep gulp. "So, uh, how did you get here?"

"Lisa. She's outside waiting in the car."

"Huh." My Southern manners nearly did me in, compelling me to invite her inside. But Lisa and Eloisa were always mean to me, unlike Aunt Clara.

So, when she called and informed me she would be over at noon sharp today, I tried to make her feel welcome.

Clara raised an eyebrow. Her lips ticked up suddenly like it was jerked by puppet strings.

"How are you doing?" she asked me.

"Oh, you know. I'm just getting by."

"Oh, yes, I *do* know. I'm sure you've heard the family talking. Heck, maybe Joe even told you. But I have a gift. A *special* gift."

"A gift? What kind?"

She looked me straight in the eye. "I can speak to the dead."

The room got still, quiet. So quiet you could hear the scuttle of a beetle bug.

She was pulling my leg. I laughed.

Clara laughed along with me. Her laughter was warm and light. I laughed even more. I hadn't realized the old woman had much of a sense of humor.

I drank another gulp of my wine. "Oh, you . . . you had me worried for a second." I pointed to her.

Clara stopped laughing and dropped her smile. "Now that you've gotten that out of your system, I'll say it again. I commune with the dead. Not often, but enough. Usually it's someone I know. The ones I don't know, I tell 'em to get the hell out of my house. I can't just be having strangers pop in and out of my home, ghost or not. You invite one in and you'll be overrun, I tell ya," she said in a conversational tone as if she were giving me advice about gardening.

"Anyway . . . Joe is concerned with how you, Maya and Ryder are getting on. I've shared his messages with the girls. Judge says you've been hitting the bottle a little too hard, if you know what I mean."

"No." I dropped the warmth from my voice. "I don't." I plopped the wineglass on the table.

"Really? The way Judge tells it, you drink every night and not that little wine you've got there, drinkin' like it's water. He says liquor, and it's hard. Now, I'm not one to judge, but—"

"Did Maya put you up to this?"

"No." Clara shook her head.

"Oh, I bet she did. Now, I've done nothing to you. But you come here, in my home, and tease me about my dead husband coming to visit you? Do you hate me that much?"

"No, sweetie. I don't. But Judge can't move on until you move on. His soul isn't at rest."

"Enough!" I jumped from my seat. "It's one thing to disrespect me. But do not bring Joseph into this. He doesn't deserve it." I rubbed at the dots sprouting along my arms. The room had gone cold again. The A/C was on the fritz. Nothing had gone right since Joseph died.

"But he needs—"

"I said, s-stop," I hissed. "You need to leave."

Clara nodded. She took her time getting up from the seat and shuffled toward the door.

I'm done with this family. I had no ties. I grabbed the glass and dumped the wine. Then I hit up my secret stash, high up in the cabinets, pulling out rum with a splash of Coke.

I paced the floor, fuming about Maya's latest antics. "How dare she? How. Dare. She?" Using an old woman in her crazy mind games. Invading my space. "She thinks she can just drive me out? Oh, I don't think so." I gulped down the drink and made another.

And another.
And another.
And another.
I ran out of Coke and shot the brown liquid, straight.

"Thinks she can scare me." I jutted the glass toward the sky. The drink spilled over on my hand. "Screw her. Just 'cause she's a lawyer doesn't mean she knows everything."

Another burp rose in my throat, but this time I chased it away with my rum.

"Freeze my account. My account." I slapped my chest and then slammed my drink on the kitchen counter. "You know what? I'm gonna tell her just where she can go and where she can put it." I marched to my car and pressed the ignition and swung out of the garage onto the road.

The Rover jumped up and hopped on the curb. I hit the brakes then rolled down the window. "Thank you, Jesus." I crossed myself, glad it was a curb and not a child. "They need to widen these streets."

The Rover tilted up and slammed back on the pavement. The green from the traffic light blurred. "They need to get that fixed, too."

Beep! Beep! Hooonk!

I looked in the rearview mirror. An older fellow shook his fist out of the window. "Gooooo."

"All right. Cool your jets." I lifted my foot from the brake and gassed it. The law firm sat on the corner of town, near the courthouse. There were only two firms and a smattering of attorneys. "Cockroaches, the lot of 'em . . . except for Joseph, of course. Joseph is an angel. He's my angel." I sang to myself. Angel Joseph. I kind of liked it.

"Dickerson, Hill and Sanders?" I snapped my fingers and bopped to my new angel song. I turned into the tidy parking lot with bright white parallel lines. "Right in the middle." I parked between the two spaces. No one was there anyway. I swung open the car door. "Maya, you dunno who you're messing with."

My shoe heel got caught between the door and seat. My hands stopped me from falling on the ground but the pebbles in my palm stung a little.

I straightened myself up and took a deep breath. "I am a good person and I deserve to be treated . . . good." After repeating the mantra a few times, I marched up the two steps and knocked on the door. I knocked for at least a minute, maybe ten.

"Hey, is this place open?" I yelled at the door.

The door swung open. A young slender black woman answered the door. Her lips were as tight as her skirt.

I mean, I liked her skirt, but it left nothing to the imagination, if you know what I mean.

"Madam, the door is unlocked." She pulled down the handle a few times. "See?"

Or maybe she just unlocked it. I decided to keep that conspiracy theory to myself. I'd save my arguing for Maya. "Okay, then."

I moved past her into the main reception area. My heels clacked against the hardwood floor. I pivoted on my feet and went to the front desk.

The woman who answered the door followed me.

I leaned over and eyed the nameplate. "Hey, Dawn."

"Umm, hi?" The petite brunette looked uneasy.

I turned my head toward to the lounge area. A man with a long tie gripped his briefcase to his chest. An older lady glanced away from me and back to her upside-down magazine. I sighed and turned around. What was the big deal? So, I banged on the door. And if the door had really been open, they should put up a sign or something.

I turned back to face the receptionist. Her shaking hand

inched toward the phone. "Good gracious, I ain't . . ." I stopped myself. "Excuse me." I cleared my throat. "I'm *not* gonna— excuse me again—*going* to hurt ya . . . I mean, hurt *you*." I smiled at myself. There was nothing wrong with correcting yourself in front of people.

A tap on my shoulder made me turn around. It was the young lady with the tight skirt.

"I'm Katy Hicks, the paralegal here. Do you have an appointment?"

"No, I do not, but I demand to see Maya Donaldson."

"Maya?" The woman tilted her head and crossed her arms. "Why do you want to see her?"

"Because she's trying to kick me outta my home and take my money, that's why!" I pointed a finger in the air.

"Sounds like a good enough reason. Excuse me, Mrs. . . . ?" She trailed off, arching an eyebrow.

"Oh. I'm Mrs. Donaldson, Maya's stepmama, and like I said, I want to see her. Right away."

"Oh, I know you. I'd be happy to fetch Maya." Katy gave me a bright smile. My, she was polite. Maya and Ryder could take a few pointers from her. "You just stand right there. I'll give her a call."

"Thank you very much, Katy."

"Oh, it's my pleasure." She sashayed behind the desk and pressed an intercom button. "Maya." Her sweet voice seemed to be everywhere. "Your stepmother is here to see you, and she seems very adamant. She may be a little . . . inebriated?"

"Hey! I'm not drunk." I shook my head.

A few seconds later, a cold blast chased up my spine. The hairs on my arms stood up. Maya blew into the room, the Wicked Witch of the West.

Maya grabbed my elbow and jerked me around. The tips of her nails dug into my skin.

"Ahhh! Let me go, you . . . you monster." I swung away from her, slapping her hand away.

"Stop it. What in the hell do you think you're doing?" Maya hiss-whispered. But she didn't grab me again, so that was a plus.

"What am I doing?" I repeated as a few more people gathered in the lobby. From the looks of it, smartly dressed attorneys. "You froze my asses."

"Your what?" she asked, darting looks behind her.

"Assets. I can't use my credit card anymore."

"Jeanie. Let's go outside. Now is not the time or the place to get into personal matters."

"No. No!" I repeated, picking up steam. "Everyone should know how much of a . . . witch you are."

Someone gasped. I think it was Dawn.

"Excuse me?" Maya's voice went up an octave.

"You're kicking me out of my home and taking my money . . . and . . . and . . . you got your crazy aunt to tell me spooky stories about Joseph."

Maya just stood there, her fists and jaw clenched, her nostrils flared and something . . . was it something in her eyes? It couldn't be tears. She never cried. Not ever. Not even after Joseph died.

"That. Is. Enough." A young man with dark chocolate skin slid in between me and Maya. It was Roland. He'd come by the house once to talk to Joseph. I bet her fancy-schmancy office didn't know they were sexing each other. I'd heard rumors and Joseph had a hunch, too.

He blocked my view and whispered, "You are clearly drunk."

"No, I'm not. And by the way I know all about—"

"Yes, ma'am, you are." His eyes narrowed, and he stepped closer. "You are just ten steps from the county jail and surrounded by attorneys. Please step outside. I will arrange a ride for you."

"I've got a car."

"Lady, if you get in that car, I will call the cops. Take my offer and"—he leaned closer—"do not test me." He leaned back, towering over me. "Do you think Judge Joe would appreciate you coming to his daughter's job, yelling, screaming and carrying on?"

My shoulders deflated. My mood deflated. He'd hate what I was doing. Even if his daughter was evil. "No. No, he wouldn't."

"Then come with me."

"Okay." He walked us outside. The glare of the sun made my eyes tear up. The chill lifted once I stepped outside, but coldness remained inside me. No amount of sun or alcohol could chase the freeze away.

I chewed my bottom lip and looked at Roland. He was typing something into his phone. He looked up. "I'm getting you a car service. It'll be here in a few minutes."

I nodded, wrapping my arms around my middle. After a few minutes I asked, "Do you think she'll kick me out of the house?" I couldn't help the whine in my voice.

His eyes lifted to mine. He watched me for a bit, like he was trying to figure me out.

"I think you've got bigger problems to address." He nodded toward the street. "The driver is around the corner. I'll wait until you get in the car."

The car pulled into the parking lot. He placed a hand on the small of my back and guided me into the backseat of the car I didn't recognize and held open the passenger door. Right before he closed the door, he leaned in and whispered, "Please don't come back here again."

"I won't." I couldn't say more. A hiccup grew in my throat. I took a deep breath and held it.

He nodded, and then went to the passenger side to whisper something to the driver. The driver grunted, and then pulled off.

"Fifty bucks extra if you blow your shit, lady. I don't care what that guy said." He flipped up his blinkers and muttered, "Don't have time to clean up anyone's puke."

The hiccup escaped. "I won't."

CHAPTER 7

MAYA
WELCOME TO THE SHIT SHOW

Friday morning, May 1ˢᵗ
54 days

Wind chimes woke me from my sleep.

I wasn't much of a morning person. I needed to be eased out of sleep, and the soft harps going up and down the musical scale made waking up a little less horrible.

I rolled over, grabbed my phone and glanced at the screen. "Shit." I didn't need to get up at six a.m. after Jeanie's attempt to ruin my career. Marc had come into my office and told me to take the day off to settle my affairs. Jeanie wasn't an affair. She was a hundred-and-ten-pound monkey strapped to my back.

The only reasons why Jeanie was still among the living were because one, I couldn't practice law in jail; and two, Ryder.

That still didn't mean I couldn't kick her drunk ass.

I bet she was still asleep without a care in the world, even though she fucked up my life. It was Friday, so Ryder should be getting ready for school. After an hour of piddling around my apartment, I got dressed, drove to the house—*my* house—then busted through the door.

Jeanie's body was sprawled on the couch, but her head and one arm were on the floor. She snored louder than a 500-lb trucker.

I aimed three fingers at her, my thumb overlapping my pinkie, and gave her the Celie-till-you-do-right-by-me fingers. "Everything you do, Jeanie. Everything you muthafuckin' do."

I marched to the kitchen, grabbed a pot and a wooden spoon. Smacking the spoon against the pot was going to be satisfying, but . . . no, not yet. I tossed the pot on the counter. First, I needed to throw away everything.

I opened the cabinet doors under the sink and grabbed a few garbage bags. I went into the master bedroom, next to the living room.

"Dammit." Clothes, half-eaten fast food and empty bottles littered the floor, TV stand and dresser tops.

My fingers itched to clean. I shook my head and exhaled. "Nope. Destroy the stash."

I gathered bottles. Lots of bottles. Pints and 750-ml, liters and a half, and 40-ounce malt liquors. "She really is scraping the bottle of the barrel."

The only people I knew who drank malt liquors were Billy Dee Williams and my great-uncle Charles.

I chucked the empties into the garbage bag and then made my way to the bathroom. Clothes, shoes and towels cluttered the tile floor.

I poured the bottles down the bathroom sink. The combination of sweet liquors and booze tensed my stomach muscles. I kept pouring until I noticed a blood streak stained the porcelain. "What in the . . . ?"

Did she try to kill herself? Was this an accident?

I grabbed a sponge and Lysol from underneath the cabinet and then scrubbed. This time, I would clean behind her—bloodstains were a different story.

I finished up the rest of the house. A mixture of old burgers, lavender from the scented garbage bags and alcohol stung my nose.

While I stuffed trash into the garbage bag, my blood pressure soared. It had been years of her Helpless Hattie act. Meanwhile, Daddy pushed me to be strong, to never cry or show weakness in public. He'd drilled that message into me since I was seven years old. I'd come home crying when Mrs. Donavan gave class president to Jefferson Duke, a little jerk in my homeroom who had wealthy parents and a mom who was ever present with cupcakes and treats for the students.

"Why did he get it over me? I always volunteer to help the class pet, and when someone needs help, they always come to me, not Jefferson."

I'll never forget what Daddy said. He sat me on his lap and listened to me, but the moment the tears gathered, he dashed them away.

"Did you cry at school?" His voice sounded weird, like I'd done something wrong.

"No. I came straight home."

"Good. Never let them see you cry. They'll think you're weak. They'll think they broke you, but you aren't breakable, you hear me?"

"Yes, Daddy."

"You are so strong. So, what if Jefferson is the class president? You just work harder and smarter and one day, he'll be working for you."

"Okay, Daddy," I replied, though at the time I had no idea what he meant. The only thing that stuck out to me from the conversation was to always be strong.

Be strong and never let them see you cry became my mantra. I had a steel spine, even in elementary school. Then here comes Jeanie, who cried over sad movies and birthday cards. And what did Daddy do? He just smiled and let the tears fall, no admonishment and no judgment.

"He treats Jeanie like fine china but I'm unbreakable." I snorted. "Bullshit."

Bitterness wormed a tunnel through my stomach. Anger, the second stage in grieving. But I wasn't just mad at God or the universe for taking away my father. No, I had to be honest, I was spitfire mad at Daddy. He left me to deal with his widow's issues. Issues *he* enabled. *Doesn't matter.* My new goal was to get her on her feet so she could get the hell out of my house.

I dumped the trash outside and then returned. Now it was time to snoop on Ryder. She was a good kid, but since Jeanie was falling down on the job, I had to be the authority figure.

I stepped into her room. Everything seemed tidy and in place. No wrinkled clothes, no food. The gray, plush carpet had been vacuumed. Her books were perfectly lined on her small bookcase. Even her desk gleamed with wood polish. A glossy magazine on her desk caught my eye. A pink flag stuck out from one of the pages. Flipping through the pages, I found the flagged page.

"'Morning Glory,' by Ryder Bennett." I read the poem, once, twice. "Damn, this is really good." I flipped back to the magazine cover, *Poet Magazine.*

"That's amazing, Ryder." I sighed. "But why didn't you tell me?" Something wasn't right with my girl. *You won't figure it out if you don't move in.*

But moving in meant daily encounters with Jeanie.

Nah. I would literally kill Jeanie if we lived together. And I liked my space. If anything, I could have Ryder stay in my apartment until Jeanie got her shit together. Speaking of, it was time for her to wake the hell up.

I marched downstairs and grabbed the pot and spoon.

Thwack! Thwack! Thwack!

"Wake up," I sang.

Clank! Clank! Clank!

"Get your drunk, trailer-park-Barbie, silly, life-ruining ass up."

Jeanie fell off the couch. "Wha—?" She wiped the slobber off her mouth, her eyes wide open.

"Oh, good. You're awake." I put down my pot and spoon, a wide grin on my face. Daddy used to call it my shark-smile.

Jeanie must've recognized it because her eyes darted away from me. "What are you doing here?" She gripped the blanket pooled around her feet. "Aren't you supposed to be at work?"

"I would love to be at work right about now. But since you accused me of stealing, I'm on temporary leave."

She slow-blinked. The fog seemed to have cleared and her eyes grew wide.

"Ah. It's all coming back to you."

She licked her lips. "Listen, Maya. I don't know what I was thinking but I'm so sorry."

"Yes, you are." I clasped my hands behind my back. "I've had a lot of time to think about what you did. But you know, since I'm a Christian woman, I'm willing to give you a chance to get it together."

Jeanie scrambled to her feet. "I swear, I will. I've just been so sad and—"

"Nope. I am one hundred percent not interested in how *you* feel."

Jeanie nibbled her bottom lip and looked away. Head hanging low, she rubbed her arms, looking like the loneliest woman on the planet.

She wasn't looking pathetic when she was calling you names at your job.

The anger mounted again. I had a stockpile and not just from her tirade yesterday.

"Jeanie, you can't afford to have a breakdown. You have a daughter who depends on you and bills that must be paid. Sure, Daddy left you a nice nest egg, but you're fifty years old. You can't live off that if you live past sixty-five."

She snapped her attention back to me, fire in her eyes. "I've worked hard all my life, and I don't mind going back to work. But your father wanted me to stay at home. That's the only reason why I resigned."

"So, you wanted to work?"

"Yes. Of course. It kept me busy. That's why I started volunteering for the church and babysitting around town."

"Then why did you stop?"

"Like I said, Joseph wanted—"

"Grow a pair, Jeanie. If you want to do something, then do it. Except for drinking. That is clearly out of control."

"I'll get a job."

"Oh, no. Don't worry about a job right now. Word has spread around town and no one is giving you a job within thirty miles of here. For now, you need to focus on bettering yourself." I clapped my hands. "You're going on a PIP."

"I'm a pimp?"

"No. A P-I-P. A Performance Improvement Plan, but for your life."

"Huh?" Jeanie scrunched her nose. "What does that mean?"

"You will have ninety days to get it together. You slip up in any way, that includes driving drunk, insulting me or your daughter, drinking a drop of alcohol, I'm sending you straight to rehab."

Jeanie crossed her arms. "I may not be some lawyer with a fancy degree, but I know my rights. You can't force me to go."

"You're right." I nodded. "I can't make you. But the police may have to be called because you're causing a domestic disturbance. Or maybe you're driving drunk or you're intoxicated in public, then you know, maybe a judge—a judge I happen to know—orders you to go to rehab for your own good. Tell me, Jeanie . . . can a *judge* order you to go?"

"I can't believe you're doing this to me." She slumped onto the couch.

"Oh, I can't take credit for this hot mess. This is all on you. Regardless, you owe it to Ryder to get yourself back on track."

"Don't go bringing Ryder into this. You're just . . . just building a case so you can kick me out. You want me out of the way so you can fill up my girl's head with lies." She waved her arm.

I groaned to the sky. What in the hell did Daddy see in this woman? Sure, she was attractive, but she had no substance. Self-absorbed and unaware of anything outside of Daddy and sometimes Ryder. Hell, her daughter was a freaking genius.

"Did you know that your daughter's poem was published in *Poet Magazine*?"

Jeanie wrapped her arms around her torso. "When?"

"I found last month's issue on her desk. She didn't tell me, and she didn't tell you. Now, I know our girl is humble, but this is a big freakin' deal, and she said nothing. Probably because she feels neglected." Thank goodness Ryder had common sense. She could be doing all sorts of crazy things.

"Oh. And the great Maya Donaldson didn't read her mind to figure it out?"

"No. The Great Maya has been too busy cleaning up your shit, grieving and focusing on her career. Now, I love Ryder more than anyone else in this world, but you are her mother. Our little rivalry can wait. She needs us."

Jeanie blew a shaky breath. "You're right."

"Glad you agree." *You didn't have a choice anyway.* "Now I think the first thing you need to do is clean this house."

"Fine, I'll do it after my headache clears up."

"It's called a hangover, and it's not going away anytime soon. Take two aspirins, suck it up and clean."

I turned to walk away.

"And where are you going?" she asked.

"Don't worry. I'm not going anywhere. I'll be here all day."

"Great," Jeanie muttered.

I went upstairs, did some research on substance abuse, and then worked on pro bonos. Roland called five times. I sent every call to voicemail. What could I say? Jeanie embarrassed the hell out of me, and Roland stepped in to save the day. And sure, Roland had seen me naked, but having him witness the fabric of my life unraveling was too much.

My phone rang. I glanced at the screen. This one I would answer. We had her employers on the ropes, and it was just a matter of time before they offered a settlement.

"Maya!" Sanjeeta Bahati yelled into the phone. Sanjeeta wasn't a yeller. Despite the shitty things her boss had done to her, she kept it together. I wasn't surprised by her strength. It was a common thing for women of color to have a mask for work. I'd worn mine daily.

"Sanjeeta? What's with the yelling? Everything okay?"

Everything is absolutely perfect!" She rolled her R's and her accent became thicker. "Guess who turned in his resignation?"

"Racist Richard?"

"Yes! The one and only."

"Was he forced? Or did he volunteer?"

"Oh . . . I don't know. I did not ask. Am I allowed?"

"It's not considered *professional*, but what's the word on the street?"

"I haven't heard any words on the street. I just know he was mad when he packed his bags and he shot me the vilest of looks. But he left, and I am happy."

"Good for you."

"Wait! There's more good news."

"Go on." I laughed, happy that Sanjeeta was happy.

"Mr. Connelly, the senior director, offered me Richard's job. With a twenty-five percent raise."

"Damn, girl. That's nice. But wait . . . are you dropping the case? Did they tell you to?"

"No, no. They haven't mentioned the case. But . . . I think I should drop it now, wouldn't you agree? Richard is gone and I'll be compensated. I skipped two levels, you know."

I nodded. "Okay, but if you take this promotion, they may not say it, but they will expect you to drop it. And to be honest, you can make a lot more money from the settlement."

Sanjeeta sighed. "It was never about the money, Maya. It was about standing up for myself. And thanks to your work, it shined a light on discrimination at my company. I just wanted to be judged fairly. Not because I look different, or I speak proper English." She chuckled at her joke. "Or because I don't have a Southern accent. You made them see, Maya. You made them see me. Everything is resolved. So, yes, I want to drop the suit."

"I get it." I tugged at my braids. "I understand and I support you. Just . . . just make sure they treat you right, okay? And if they don't, call me."

"I will. In fact, I am going to strongly suggest our company invest in classes to address unconscious biases. And that we have someone write up a code of conduct."

"Good. I'm seriously happy for you."

"Thank you, Maya. Thank you. Thank you. Thank you."

"You are so welcome, Sanjeeta. You made a terrible day less terrible."

"May you have many less terrible days. May God shine a light on all that you do."

"Amen. You take care now."

"I will. Goodbye, Maya."

"Goodbye, Sanjeeta. Take care of yourself."

I sighed and flopped back on my bed and wiggled my toes in the air. This was the type of work that gave me a happy buzz. Daddy said to listen for the buzz, the thing that made your soul sing. I enjoyed my work, taking down insurance companies, giving people their fair share, even though I could not help them reclaim what they'd lost. But fighting for someone's rights, well, it was what pushed me out of bed.

Sanjeeta's win was the good news I needed. For one moment, I forgot about the crap Jeanie pulled. The forced leave of absence. The fucking will and the mess Daddy left for me to fix. I just wish I could have held on to the feeling for longer.

Friday night, May 1st
54 days

I paced the carpeted floor in the living room, fuming, as I glanced down at the watch on my wrist. "See what I mean?" I waved at the door and then back at Jeanie.

She'd done as we agreed, and the house was now spotless. Everything had been cleaned right around the time Ryder was due to be back from school. Yes, it was a Friday, but still. It was nine p.m. and she hadn't answered any of my calls. They'd gone straight to voicemail. If she didn't get her ass home in the next thirty, I would send Dale at the sheriff's office on her tail.

Headlights illuminated the window. "This better be her." I yanked open the curtains. Jeanie flipped on the porch light. A white cruiser pulled into the driveway. Red and blue lights blinked from the driveway.

"Oh, God." I clutched my stomach and rushed toward the door. "Please, please, please."

I rushed past the doorway, while a deputy languidly walked to the front of the house. He took off his hat and rubbed a hand over his buzz cut.

"Hey," I said, impatient. I didn't know this guy. He must be new. I knew all the officers in town.

Jeanie came up behind me. "O-Officer. Is everything okay?"

"Are you Jeanie Donaldson?" He directed his hawkish eyes at her.

"Yes," she whispered.

"Your daughter is fine, so to speak. But we found her along with a few others attempting to break into a building. They also had alcohol. We gave her a breathalyzer, but she didn't blow on the register. She hadn't been drinking."

"Where is she now?" I peered over his shoulder.

The officer looked me up and down. "And you are?"

"Maya Donaldson, daughter of the recently deceased Judge Joseph Donaldson and owner of the home Ryder resides in," I snapped.

There was some recognition in his dark eyes. "In the car, ma'am."

"Is she arrested?"

"No. A slap on the hand as a warning. But for delinquent stuff like this, the judge—the *new* judge—wants to see the kids in his chambers on Monday morning."

"Fine. Tell Judge Bryant we'll be there. Thank you, Officer." I didn't know much about the interim judge who replaced Daddy, but I knew small-town judges tended to lean on the fair side.

"My job, ma'am." He tipped his hat and went to the car. He opened the back passenger door and pulled out a handcuffed Ryder. I clasped my hands behind my back so I wouldn't wring her neck.

What was she thinking? She'd better be glad she's a young white girl. If she were any other race, she may not have been given a second chance.

He uncuffed her. She rubbed her wrists. When she looked up, she stumbled over her feet when she saw me at the door.

Good. She should *be scared.*

CHAPTER 8

RYDER
BAD GIRLS CLUB

Monday morning, May 4ᵗʰ
57 days

Maya had raged at me all weekend. If it were possible, I think she would've chained me to the bed. Friday night she'd followed me upstairs to my room, yelling at the top of her lungs about my stupidity. She'd never called me stupid, and it hurt.

So, I yelled back.

Mom had come upstairs, too. Instead of yelling, she just sat on my bed, wringing her hands, crying, probably wondering where she'd gone wrong.

If she only asked, I'd tell her. She wasn't there. No one was. Not even Maya. The only time we hung out was when we went to Lenny's Diner on Saturdays. For the past few weekends, she'd been too busy with work.

This morning, she banged on my bedroom door and ordered me to hurry up so we can meet the judge before his court sessions began.

Right before we entered his chambers, Maya turned to face me. "Be quiet. Only speak when spoken to and say 'yes, sir' when he addresses you. Got it?"

I nodded, pulling the strings to tighten the hoodie on my head.

Maya pushed the hood off my head. "Let's go."

As soon as we stepped into his office, Maya turned on the charm. She even gave him a copy of my transcript.

I looped the cotton string around my finger, twisting it until my knuckles turned red. I did this while Maya sweet-talked the new judge. He was nothing like Dad.

New judge was all round and soft, Daddy was muscular and hard. Daddy went to the gym, golfed and swam regularly.

Dad's voice thundered like a preacher, but this judge's voice was soft. It was like he was afraid that if he spoke too loudly, something would break.

His eyes focused on me. His mouth moved, saying something to me but I didn't tune in. I didn't need Judge whoever his name was . . . I looked at the nameplate on his desk, gold, black and permanent: Judge Bryant.

My stomach bounced. It'd only been two months, and they'd already erased Daddy's name.

Pictures of me and Maya and Mama were replaced by photos of what I assumed where his wife, kids and grandkids. The law degree from Daddy's alma mater, Emory, had been swapped with the University of Georgia. This guy apparently loved the bulldogs. The school colors, red and black, were splashed in every nook and cranny.

"Ryder?" Maya nudged my side. "Judge Bryant is speaking to you." Her voice was sickly sweet. So sweet I knew I was going to get an earful as soon as we got to the car.

I looked at his eyes. They were green. Not spring green like the rolling hills in Ireland but faded.

There was something in them that reminded me of Dad. Kindness. "Y-yes, sir?"

"Your stepfather was a good man. I've got big shoes to fill."

"Dad," I corrected, even though he was technically my step-father since my biological one refused to give up his parental rights.

"Right." Judge Bryant gave a curt nod. "Your father always gave second chances, and based off your step . . . excuse me, your sister's impassioned testimony and your grades and general good behavior, I'm giving you a pass."

"Thank you, Judge Bryant." Maya sighed.

"Don't thank me yet." He raised a finger. "Something else Judge Joe was good at doing was making sure lessons were learned. Since you are quite the writer—"

"How do you know?"

His bushy eyebrows that reminded me of caterpillars wiggled up and down. "Your sister said you were published in *Poet Magazine*."

I hadn't told anyone about that. There was no way she knew unless she snooped around my room. "Really, Maya?"

Maya leaned closer to my chair and pinched my side.

"Ow."

Maya shot me a shut-the-heck-up look. "I was telling Judge Bryant about your scholarship. We need to keep your record clean."

"Whatever," I mumbled under my breath.

"My sister-in-law is a drama teacher." Judge Bryant folded his hands over his belly. "Each summer she does a performing arts camp—acting, singing, dancing and whatnot. They perform a few times throughout the summer." He tapped a finger on his desk. "Since the school year will be ending in two weeks, you will participate in the summer camp."

"What? C'mon. I didn't even steal anything, I was just—"

"Quiet, Ryder." Maya's voice rose over my protest. "Thank you, Judge Bryant. This is more than fair. Anything else we should know?"

"Enroll by the end of this week. I'm sure the camp can use someone as talented as you."

"Oh, God." I dropped my head into my hands. "Are my friends forced to do this, too?"

"No. I've given them other things they can do to give back."

"But—"

"Young lady, you are fortunate I held your father in high esteem. You are lucky your sister cares enough to take time from her job to make sure you don't have anything on your record. And you are darn lucky that this is a nonprofit that you can put on your college application. Because right now, according to your transcripts and activities list, it doesn't seem you have any volunteer hours."

"I founded the Poetry club and I—"

"If you interrupt me again or disrespect your sister, or if you don't turn up for your volunteer station, your luck will run out. Do you understand me?" he asked, all business and no-nonsense.

"Yes, sir."

"Good. I'm giving your sister paperwork. Orientation is June first. All other information"—he gave Maya the stack of papers—"is here." He turned to Maya. "Make sure she doesn't squander this second chance, yes?"

"Oh, don't worry. I'll drop her off every day."

"Good." He nodded and lifted his UGA mug to his lips. "Have a nice day."

Sure, I will.

When Maya stood, I followed. She was eerily quiet, saying nothing from the walk from the judge's chambers to her car. She did something on the passenger side before she let me in the car. She held the door for me, her eyes focused on the street.

I was annoyed. This wasn't us, this distrust.

You did it. It's your fault.

She didn't say anything the entire ten-minute drive to school. She just gripped the steering wheel, sometimes sighing, sometimes shooting me dirty looks.

We finally pulled into the parking lot at school. The judge was nice enough to meet me before my first class started, though I already missed homeroom. She shifted the gears into park, and I reached for the door handle, ready to hop out and get through the rest of this craptastic day.

"Wait," Maya said, her voice oddly dull.

"The bell is about to ring." I gripped the handle and tried to open the door. It wouldn't budge. "Child lock? Really?" I slammed my back against the seat.

"Listen, Ryder. I know that you're hurting. I know that I haven't been there for you, but I'm not doing that anymore. I'm moving back into the house."

"That's not necessary. I made one mistake." I pointed a finger in the air. "One. It doesn't mean it'll happen again." My voice was loud and defensive.

"You know how fortunate you are? Kids with a different skin tone don't usually get second chances. You know that, Ryder. You are well-informed and smart. But today you talked back to a judge. A judge, Ryder. Someone who has the power to impact your future. You didn't listen, and you gave major attitude. I'm terrified." Her voice shook. "Terrified that I've lost you. This attitude, this stealing—"

"I didn't steal. I was the lookout."

"There it is," Maya's voice finally found passion. "You haven't accepted responsibility. You *know* better. Never in a million years would you have let Dani's delinquent ass convince you to do something so reckless. Never in a million years. I . . ." She took a deep breath and lowered the volume of her voice. "Like I said, I'm moving in. I've already settled my lease. Roland is helping me move in tonight."

"Glad to hear he's still around," I said in the nastiest voice I could conjure. God, what was wrong with me?

A familiar look passed over Maya's face. Her lips were stretched thin. Her eyes were on fire as she ground her teeth. It was a look I'd seen her give my mom. Creepy crawlers slid over my skin. The few spoons of oatmeal I'd eaten for breakfast sat like lead in my stomach. Tears pressed against my eyelids.

"You're free to go." She clicked the lock open. "School is out at 3:45, and I expect your butt home by 4:15."

"I don't have my bike."

"Ride the bus."

She twisted the ignition and pulled back the clutch to reverse, though her feet remained on the brake.

"Fine." I shoved the door open and then stomped to class.

Monday morning, May 4th
57 days

"Hey. Hey, you." Dani sat in Roger's old seat beside mine. The bell was about to ring any second. And as much as Mom and Maya thought I hadn't learned my lesson, I kinda did. What they hadn't realized is that Dani and his band of merry thieves had taken off and ditched me when I told them someone was coming.

They ran off and split in different directions and then later met at Dani's house. Apparently, they had a plan, a plan they hadn't told me.

The police had caught me and Coraline, who snitched out everyone involved.

I hadn't said a word.

When the gang found out that Coraline had been the one to snitch, they called and praised me. I said no problem, but inside I was seething.

Weren't they embarrassed to be arrested? Hadn't the cuffs

dug into their wrists? Hadn't their faces heated when their Miranda rights had been given? Didn't they feel as low as worms when the officer pushed their heads down to get into the cruiser?

The snick and click of the handcuffs, the strain and scrape of the shackles around my wrists had been more than enough to deter me from a life of crime.

Meanwhile, I had to figure out a way to not be such a brat to Maya. It was just that every time we talked, it's like we couldn't hear each other.

"Hey . . . so you're not talking to me?" Dani gave me a smile, slightly chagrined and all the way roguish.

"No, Dani, I'm not." I flipped through a book.

"Aww, c'mon, Ry."

That was another thing I hated. He called me Ry. I wasn't a grain with the potential to transform into whiskey.

The bell rang and I continued to ignore him. It was easy to do, because we were studying poetry and I couldn't wait to dissect the iambic pentameters. And hey, maybe that could be the antidote to the venom in my veins that made me such a brat.

The bell rang again, signaling the end of the school day. I grabbed my books, determined to hustle to the bus area so I could get home in time. Earlier that day I'd gotten the bus number from the administrator. I didn't want another heated conversation with Maya.

"Ry, wait up."

"No." I shouldered my backpack and jetted out of class.

"Seriously, what is up with you?"

I turned around to face him. He nearly crashed into me. He steadied himself and then grabbed my shoulders.

I shrugged off his hands. "I don't want to hang out with you anymore."

"But . . . why?"

"I got into trouble. Big trouble. So much trouble that I was in the judge's chambers this morning. I have to perform at a camp all freaking summer."

"That sucks."

"Yeah, it does." I didn't read my poetry to anyone outside of my family. Ever. This was the worst sort of punishment.

"It sucks but it doesn't mean we can't be friends."

"Friends don't let friends get in trouble. Friends don't encourage each other to do bad things."

I didn't have a lot of friends, but even I knew this.

He folded his arms across his chest. "Did I ever ask you to join us? Did I ever order you to be the lookout?"

I thought about it, and he hadn't. But he hadn't exactly discouraged me, either. He just gave me one of his goofy little grins. A few days ago, I thought his grins were cute.

"Look, Dani. I plan to leave this town and graduate with honors next year. I want to . . . I want to major in English. I want to write poetry for a living and maybe I'll be an English teacher, too. I want a small house in the city, in a nice neighborhood where everyone knows my name. A place where people look out for each other, unlike *this* town."

"O-okay?"

"I'm telling you this, Dani, because I have a plan. And hanging out with you and Coraline and Kaitlyn and Kayden and Eric jeopardizes that plan. And yeah, what I just told you, even to my ears sounds a little lame, but it's also heaven to me."

He still looked a little confused. Something in his eyes softened my anger. He looked like a little boy who'd been rejected.

"I don't think you're a bad person. But I have to look out for me."

"Sure." He nodded. "Just . . . just don't count me out, okay? I can respect the fact that you want to do something different. If you get bored, or maybe you just want to hang out, I'm here. I don't care how long it takes you to come back."

"Yeah, sure." I stepped away from him.

"You will?" he yelled over the crowd.

"Yes." I lied, feeling just a teensy bit sad. Though I hadn't known Dani for long, he still made things bearable. But I had to get back to being me, and the common denominator, outside of Dad's death, was to stop hanging with Dani.

Monday morning, June 1st
85 days

School had ended and I had nowhere to run to or hide.

I still hadn't figured out a way to bridge the gap. Maya had been living with us for a month and we had a weird routine. Either she or Mom cooked. Mom was still shaky and wasn't doing all that well with the dry-out. I think she even snuck a few drinks in every now and again but not enough to get her into trouble with Maya.

Sometimes we all sat in the living room to watch television, but we never spoke, nothing of substance anyway.

After weeks of awkwardness, I welcomed a change. Even if it was court-ordered.

"Be good." Maya dropped me off at the community center and sped away. I stepped through the double doors and signed my name at the front office. I picked up a packet and then settled at the back of the darkened auditorium. A few others filed in, some waved at each other, some chatted away with each other. I, the cheese, sat alone.

"Welcome, you bright, young performers!" A woman who was probably Mom's age with raven-black hair and purple lipstick addressed us. There was a dozen of us teenagers and some people who looked a little older, probably college-aged.

"My name is Dianne Bryant, the founder of this fine-arts camp. You may call me Mrs. Bryant. We are so happy you decided to spend the summer with us. How many of you have been to the website?" Everyone raised their hands, including me.

She clapped. "Wonderful. Then you know our mission is to bring joy and light to those who are unable to go out into the world. Think of us as a fine-art traveling troupe. We will sing and dance and act."

Oh no. I slouched down in my seat. I was not a performer. The last time I was in a stage play, I was a tree in *The Wizard of Oz.* I'd been cast initially as a flying monkey, but my drama teacher said my performance was unconvincing and lackluster. I was twelve. What the heck did she expect? No one wants to be a monkey.

"Now, I have everyone's list of talents here." She tapped on the clipboard. "You have been grouped with some of our wonderful assistant directors. Oh, yes, I should introduce them." She put her hand over her chest and laughed. "Please stand and wave when I call your name.

"Nadia Winthrop." A girl with black hair that went past her butt shot out of her seat, smiled and waved. "Nadia is our choreographer. She attends Valdosta State and is volunteering her talents to help us."

Did she really volunteer or was she here because she got in trouble, like me? But from her sweet smile and high energy, I doubted it. Then again, I'm sure I didn't look like a trouble-maker, either.

"Evan Gilroy." A lean guy with dirty blond hair stood and waved. His other hand was stuffed in his pocket. "Evan will oversee drama and performance. He is a junior at Georgia State University.

"And finally, Alston Wolf is overseeing poetry. He is a sophomore at Emory University. Alston will also assist Evan, when needed, in drama." A guy stood and I gasped. Like legitimately gasped so loudly he turned around and saw me. He smiled a little, very slowly, and I stared, transfixed. It was like watching a flower bloom. He was beautiful. No, that was too common a word.

His eyes, from what I could tell two rows away, were a hazel brown. His hair curled this way and that. One curl teased against his forehead but wasn't quite long enough to cover it. His forehead protruded a bit. Something that edged him away from being labeled as devastatingly handsome, but still magnetic. His hair rested just below his ears. His jaw was square, and his face clean shaven.

I swore he winked at me. Something zinged and zanged in my chest. My hands gripped around my moleskine notebook.

Mrs. Bryant clapped her hands. "Okay, everyone. Let's introduce ourselves. Tell us your age, the school you attend, your talent and why you're here."

Uh-oh. I racked my brain while other students stood and gave their life stories. I couldn't tell them I was court-ordered. It was my turn. I knew it was because everyone stared at me.

I stood and cleared my throat. "Hi." My voice sounded surprisingly strong.

I looked around the room. My attention snagged on Alston. He dipped his chin and gave me another smile and, dang it, another wink.

"I'm Ryder." Something flittered across Alston's face. Maybe he didn't like my name or hated my voice?

"I'm uh, here because . . . because I like poetry. I'll be a senior next school year and I'm looking forward to building my college application and, you know . . . helping people."

I slumped down in my seat.

"Excellent. I think that's everyone. Now review the list posted on the wall near the stage. Please review it and meet your group leader. For those of you who are a triple threat, i.e. have multiple talents, we've assigned you in two different groups and you'll be dividing your time, unless you want to stick to one group. We're flexible here and just happy that you're joining us this summer."

I didn't need to look at the list. Alston would be my leader.

I pretended to peek at the list, scanning until I saw my name listed under Alston's. There were only two other people, three of us in total.

Alston had squared away some tables in the back of the room. I was the first to arrive.

"H-hi, Alston, right?"

He sighed and tilted his head. "Do you actually like poetry?"

I furrowed my eyebrows. One, because his tone was snotty and two, didn't he hear what I'd said?

"Yeah. I do."

"Favorite poet?"

"Langston Hughes."

"Why?"

"Because no matter what, he portrayed a realistic life for black people in America. He didn't make it pretty or palatable for others. His words, the language he used to paint a story was raw, and sometimes difficult to take but that was life for a lot of people who were often ignored." I'd discovered Langston Hughes after one of Maya's high school assignments years ago. I'd been practicing my reading and I did so through poetry.

"And you like writing poetry?"

"Yes," I hissed. This beautiful man was starting to tick me off. Didn't I fill out the darn application? What did he want, a sample?

"That remains to be seen." He looked up. The other two students were coming toward us. "Find me at the end of the day and I'll sign your paper."

"Paper?"

"The *court-ordered* paper. The one that proves you showed up."

My face burned bright. I didn't have anything to say. I took my seat and remained quiet. I snuffed out the spark I'd felt from Alston. The look in his eyes, like I was the village idiot, told me enough.

That's it. Back to meek and mild Ryder, only responding when spoken to. The courage he'd given me with a simple nod, wink and smile had vanished.

CHAPTER 9

JEANIE
OVER MY HEAD

Friday morning, June 19th
103 Days

I want to see my girl.

My palms were puddles of sweat. I didn't need this from Ricky. Not today, not ever. Ricky was Ryder's father, and once upon a time, I thought myself in love with him. That was before I learned the real meaning of love.

I threw my phone onto the bed, pacing the fluffy carpet in my room. We only heard from Ricky a few times a year. One, when it was Ryder's birthday. Sometimes he'd call on whatever phone he'd stolen from some poor woman who had the misfortune to fall for his charm. Most times, he sent a Dollar Store card filled with dirt, grease and not much else.

The other couple of times he went back and forth with Joseph, dangling the carrot of giving up his parental rights to Ryder so that she could take Joseph's last name.

Another ping—the sound so jubilant and upbeat, nothing that foreshadowed whatever dirtbag remark that would follow. And best believe Ricky Bennett, meaner than snake spit, had something awful to say.

Still, I couldn't duck my head in the sand. That's something Maya would expect me to do, and with her breathing down my neck, I had to keep everything together. It hadn't been easy. Drinking had settled my nerves, and a glass or two of wine never hurt anyone. But last time I snuck out to get a drink while Maya was at work and Ryder at school, Linda, the bartender at Bruno's, told me that Maya had eyes on the place and I'd better hustle back home. Bruno's and Finnegan's were the only bars in town. I would've gone out of town, but Maya checked my darn mileage, too. If anything exceeded the radius of town, she would know. So, I snuck to the Chili's and got a Long Island iced tea.

Anger spread like a rash throughout my body. I was her stepmother. I didn't need someone who wasn't even thirty years old to tell me what to do. The only thing that kept me in check was her threat. Just as sure as poop stinks, she'd get a court order.

And even more, I didn't want to tarnish Joseph's legacy. I didn't want to be known as a black widow and a drunk.

Be brave, Jeanie. I took a deep breath and read the message.

Momma says you killed your old man and now you're walking 'round town drunk. I'm coming back and I'm taking Rider.

How dare he? How dare his momma? She wasn't around, heck, she barely even acknowledged us when she saw us, especially after I'd gotten married. And he misspelled his daughter's name.

I pressed Ricky's stupid name and clicked the phone icon. "He's got some freakin' nerve."

The phone only rang once.

"Jeanie, darlin'."

"Oh, you . . . you shut up!"

"You're the one that rang me up, darlin'."

"You aren't taking my daughter."

"Correction. *Our* daughter."

I paced the floor. "Oh, really? You can't even spell her name correctly. Ryder is spelled with a Y, you . . . you dick."

"Uh-oh. I've gone and made you mad."

"I'm not doing this, Ricky. I'm not going back and forth with you. Ryder is happy and thriving. She's going to make something out of herself, despite having a shitty father. Correction: *biological* father."

"I am her father by the law and every other way that counts. I never gave rights away to that darkie you married."

"You shut your mouth. You shut your filthy mouth, Ricky. I will not tolerate you speaking ill of my husband. He is ten times the man you'll ever be."

"He can't be ten times anything. He's a hotel for worms right about now."

"H-he . . . he may be gone, but his legacy lives on. You know who came to his funeral? The mayor and the governor. They even lowered the flags for him at city hall. You know what'll happen if you drop dead right now?"

"What?" Ricky asked, humor in his voice.

"Nothing. Life would go on. No one would miss you, not even *my* daughter. Because you are *nothing.*"

"Well, now you're just being nasty." There wasn't any humor in his voice anymore. It'd turned to the same kind of nasty he accused me of being.

He shut up for a moment. Probably thinking of something to tear me down.

"I've got a job now. I drive trucks, been doing it a while. I make fifty-K a year."

"So what, Ricky?"

"That's more than you make. You haven't worked in years. You ain't got no skills, except for painting, and well . . . we both know you aren't good at anything."

My mouth went dry. It was true, I hadn't worked in five

years, but I could figure something out. "You'll be gone all the time. No way the courts will choose you over me."

A few tick-tick-ticks sounded from the phone. "Hmmm. Says here a child who is fourteen and older can choose which parent they want to live with. Just need a little affidavit from Ryder, and I'm clear."

"You can't take her away," I whispered.

"Your black knight is gone. And it's just me and you, Jeanie. Unless, well . . . we'll talk later."

"Ricky, listen." My throat ached, but I pushed past the pain. "Ryder doesn't need the stress of a custody battle. She's already lost . . ." I took a deep breath. Ricky didn't care about Joseph. I switched gears. "She'll be a senior next year and she needs a stable environment."

"And she's getting it from you?"

"From me . . . from . . . from Maya. Despite this . . . hard time she's making good grades. She's a good girl."

"And she'll be even better with me. I'll be seeing you soon."

My heartbeat pounded in my head as seventeen years with my girl flashed before my eyes. Her tiny wrinkled hands and the little tuft of hair. A lone piece, always sticking up like a lightning rod.

Kissing the boo-boos on her skinned knees. The *World's Greatest Mom* mug she got me for Mother's Day. They'd made a little ceramic cup in grade school.

"Don't . . . don't take her away. I don't have much, but I love her. I've cared for her for seventeen years. You just can't do this to me."

"I've been pushed to the back because of him."

"You were never around, Ricky, I—"

"He's dead now and I'm her daddy. So you can just fuck off if you think I'm not getting my girl." He clicked off.

Tears stung my eyes. I slumped to the floor so hard my tailbone throbbed.

"He's not taking her away. He can't. He won't." I put my head on my knees, wishing Joseph was here to hold me and tell me that Ricky was ridiculous and that he'd make sure everything would be okay.

"I miss you so much, baby." I hiccupped as a single tear rolled down my cheek. Its twin quickly followed. "I can't do this."

Another chirpy ping.

Running late at the office. Need you to pick up Ryder from the community center. They'll be done with practice at four.

My breathing steadied. I had something to do, something to take my mind off Ricky. I set my alarm to 3:45 since it was just up the street. I wouldn't be late, and I'd show Maya that I could take care of myself and my daughter. "I'll show you. I'll show Ricky, too."

But it was only noon. And I could use something, anything to get my mind off my ex's threats.

I could go to the Piggly Wiggly. Get one bottle of wine. That's it. It wouldn't hurt anyone. No hard liquor, just something light like . . . like Riesling or something.

Decision made, I went to the Piggly Wiggly, incognito. That gossip Dollie wasn't there, thank the Lord. It was someone who couldn't have been older than Ryder. I didn't know her, which meant she didn't know me. Still, I kept on my oversized glasses and Joseph's old fishing hat in place.

"Might as well get a couple." I could stock up and stuff it in my lingerie drawer.

I packed away four bottles of rosé, Merlot, Riesling, and Pinot. I stared at the bottles, guilt attacking me like a school of piranhas.

"No. Just one. Just . . ." My hands shook as I placed all but one bottle back on the shelf. I licked my lips, still salty from my tears. I hustled from the aisle and rushed home.

I opened the Riesling, filled up my wineglass with ice to chill it and drank it at the same time.

She doesn't love him. She'll stay with me. Of course she will.

But I wouldn't blame her if she didn't. I gripped the stem on my chilled glass, pacing the floor. "Ricky will be on the road and she'll get away with practically anything." And then her grades would slip. She'd go off with some no-good boy and repeat the same mistakes I'd made.

"Be smarter than me, Chickadee." After the golden liquid hit my lips, my shoulders relaxed. "God. This is what I needed."

I drained the glass and poured more. "Just one more glass," I promised myself. The first glass had been filled with ice anyway.

The next one went by just as quickly as the first one. After a little while, the wine disappeared, along with my worries.

My stomach and chest were warm and fuzzy.

Beep! Beep! Beep!

My phone blinked and buzzed with the little reminder I'd set to pick up Ryder. I stumbled over to the couch. "Keys, keys."

I patted my pants and looked at the counters. I snapped my fingers. "Keyring." I went to the door and, sure enough, they were hanging from the lock, just as free as you please.

"I'm coming, Chickadee!" I hurried out the door and slipped into the driver's side.

There were a few bumps in the road, but I made it in time, with a few minutes to spare. No one was outside yet. I parked the car at the very front of the center, right by the door.

I wouldn't mind seeing what she's up to. I got out of the car and tripped on the curb. Honestly, this town needed to fix the sidewalks. If Joseph were still here, I'd tell him to mention it to his city council buddy. They used to golf together. Richard was his name. Sometimes Richard looked at me funny, like a thirsty man stranded in the desert. He gave me the heebie jeebies.

I pressed the bar on the door. It swung open. A bunch of teenagers were spread all over the theater. There were small, brown, stadium-looking seats that faced the stage. All eyes were on me. I scanned the crowd and finally spotted Ryder. I could barely see her since she was slouched down in the chair. "Hey, Chickadee." I waved. "It's your momma. Come to pick you up and I'm right on time." I beamed at everyone, waving as I made my way down the slight decline. I almost tumbled, but I caught myself on one of the chairs. "Oops. Two left feet." I laughed a little, nervous as all heck in front of so many eyes.

"Oh. Em. Gee," someone whispered.

I rolled my eyes. Everyone tripped a time or two in their lives. I held my head high, though it was kind of spinning.

Ryder rushed over to meet me. "Mom, are you okay?" There was a young man behind her. He was a cutie pie. Pouty lips and serious eyes. The way that Ryder darted her eyes between me and him, I could tell she had a little thing for him. That, and she was blushing like all get out.

"I'm fine, precious. I just . . ." My stomach lurched. The spinning was starting up again. Wine and worry swirling faster than a washer on the high-spin cycle. I waved away the young man who tried to help me.

My stomach squeezed like someone was trying to choke the life out of it. Spinning around, I sprayed vomit over the wall. My stomach muscles relaxed. "I don't feel so good."

"Oh, my God, Mom." Ryder stepped away from the pile of puke.

As I stumbled to a seat, my feet slipped on the mess I'd made. Finally, I made it to a chair, but I couldn't sit down. Closing my eyes, I tried to block out the noise around me.

"Did she . . . did she get you?" Ryder's voice was apologetic.

"Yeah . . ." Someone sighed. "It's all good. It'll wash off."

"I'm so, so sorry. I'll clean up."

"No. You should probably make sure your mom is okay and gets her rest."

"Mom." Ryder lifted me up and grabbed my hands. "Let's go." She rushed me out and opened the door.

The bright sun broke the darkness of the theater. "Really, Mom? You parked here?"

"What's wrong with—"

"Keys?"

"Pocket." I dug them out and handed them over.

"I can drive, you know. I'm not that sick. Must've been something I ate."

"Or drank." She shook her head. "Just get in the car."

She started the car, her face all twisted and ugly with something I was too ashamed to figure out.

"I'll never forgive you. Never." Ryder's voice was sharp as tears streamed down her face.

Friday night, June 19ᵗʰ
103 days

Maya yanked the door open to my room and slammed it shut. "Can I get one week of peace? Just one week when Ryder isn't a moody-ass teenager and you aren't acting like a hot dumpster-fire mess."

A sliver of moonlight seeped between the blinds. Maya flipped on the lights. I shot up in bed.

"What's wrong with you, Jeanie? Do you not care about Ryder? About yourself?"

My skin grew cold and my bones turned to Jell-O. Not from Maya's yelling or Ricky's threats. No, I wasn't scared of that. I was scared because I remembered everything.

Driving while drunk.

Risking Ryder's life.

Showing up buzzed and throwing up at her court-ordered volunteer service.

The embarrassment, the utter look of devastation on my Chickadee's face.

"I'll never forgive you. Never."

This wasn't me, not the real Jeanie. But Jeanie didn't live here anymore, and I didn't know how to get her back.

"I'm sorry it's just that something happened and I . . ." I considered telling her about Ricky's threats. But Maya looked on edge and I wasn't sure she'd care about my excuse. I should've been able to handle myself better.

"What?" Maya asked. "What was so awful that it drove you to compromise your daughter's life?"

The pounding was coming back, right smack in the center of my forehead. The steel hammer was relentlessly dinging up everything in its path.

"Nothing."

"That's what I thought." She sat in the recliner on the opposite side of the room. "Listen. As much as you think I want to get rid of you, and I do, I don't want to do it like this. But we had a deal. You stay clean and take care of your daughter, real basic-ass shit."

Maya crossed her legs, her fingertips drumming her lips. "Alcoholism is real. And I honest to God think you need help."

"You're right. I do." I nodded, my hand gripping the comforter. "M-maybe I . . ." I sniffed away the stinging in my nose. "M-maybe I can go to a few AA meetings around town? I can stay here with Ryder and . . . and with you?" I looked up at Maya. A mass of emotions crossed her pretty brown face. In that moment, I realized she looked just like her daddy. Serious brown eyes spaced the same width as Joseph's with a cleft in her chin.

I'd noticed it before but now . . . now it was like seeing his legacy in the flesh. And seeing the pain he would feel if he were here. Suddenly I knew ... I just knew what I had to do, though I didn't want to.

"No, Jeanie. I'm sorry, but no." She shook her head. "You're a danger to Ryder and a danger to yourself. We can do this the easy way and you sign yourself in. Or I can march into Judge Bryant's chambers and get a court order. How do you want to play it?"

How do I want to play it? This wasn't a freaking game. This was my life. I knew what I needed to do but I didn't like it. And I still didn't like her.

I pinched the bridge of my nose. "Ricky is going to try to take Ryder if I leave."

"He called you?"

"Yes."

"Today?"

I nodded.

"Hmm." Maya's eyes glittered with something dangerous. "I'll handle Ricky."

"But what if—"

"I said, I'll handle that dirty, lying dog. If he so much as comes near Ryder or this house, I'll spay him with a rusted spoon. You just handle yourself."

"Fine. I'll look into some programs."

"Don't worry about that. I've already found something for you. It's just outside of Atlanta, right by a farm. You can dry yourself out and pet animals."

"Do you think this is a joke?" I snapped. "And of course, you already picked something out. You were just waiting for me to fail."

"I wasn't waiting, but I prepared."

"Just admit it," I hissed. "You wanted me out and you were just waiting for me to screw up. Well La-de-da, I did it, didn't I?"

"Yes, Jeanie. *You* did it. And here I am, breaking a promise to myself not to fix your issues." Maya bent over and reached for her purse. She pulled out printed pages and slammed them on the side table. "Read it. It's the best there is in this area, and it's a twenty-eight-day program. I've called them and they have an opening in a week."

My eyes filled. "Get. Out."

"With pleasure."

She opened the door and slammed it.

I wrapped the comforter around my body, chilled to the bone. My teeth chattered and maybe there were remnants of being drunk, but I could see my breath puffed like clouds in the air. "What have I done?"

Sunday morning, June 28th
112 days

I stared out the window. Cows and rolling green pastures sped past. Smooth jazz played in the background while Maya drove us to Straight Arrow Recovery Center.

I checked the navigation dash in the center of the console. The purple line that led us to the location got shorter. The star on the monitor that marked the location blinked. We were two miles away. My stomach clenched with every mile that bought us closer. I'd read all the literature, spoken to the program director and looked at the online videos. After watching the testimonials I'd felt a little optimistic, that is until the program director said, "Don't worry, Mrs. Donaldson. We're going to help you get your life back."

I would never get my life back. Normal life meant Joseph was alive, my daughter didn't hate me and the town didn't revile me. I didn't tell her all that. I just wanted to end the clutter in my house and in my mind. I tried to stop the jitters from taking over. I needed to be free of my sweaty nightmares.

What I didn't want, or need, were empty promises.

And after I got out of this godforsaken place, I'd bide my time, find a nice job near town and save up to get my own place. Somewhere nice with a little land. It wouldn't be anything as palatial as home, but I could find some sort of normal.

"We're here," Maya said unnecessarily, pulling into the graveled parking lot. The SUV bounced over the rocks. I pressed my purse to my chest, while my stomach twisted into infinity knots.

Maya parked. Someone was already waiting at the front. A woman stood on the porch. She looked to be in her mid-forties. A few strands of white poked through the bush of wheat-colored hair. Her purple sleeves fluttered as she waved at us. She looked . . . kind. I guess that sort of thing was important at a place like this.

A man, who had to be in his early twenties, walked toward the car. Maya opened the door and stepped out. I didn't, but I could hear the muted conversation.

"Can I get the bags, ma'am?"

"Sure. In the trunk." She pressed a button on the key fob.

I looked away from Maya and the guy, focusing on the woman.

The lady from the porch approached, coming straight for me. "Oh, God, oh, God. I can't do this." I locked the doors.

Maya shot me a murderous look through the windows from the driver's side and then, with a dramatic flair of her hand in the air, clicked the unlock button on the key fob.

The kind-looking woman knocked on my window. "Hello." She smiled. Up close I could see her pale pink lipstick.

She stepped away from the door, her hands clasped in front of her. I finally opened the door and slid out of the vehicle.

"Welcome, Jeanie." She rocked back on the heels of her sporty black shoes. "I'm Lydia Collins, the clinical liaison. We're going to take good care of you."

"Thanks, Lydia," I muttered as I wrapped the long strap of my purse around my shoulder.

"You have a few options. I know the first day can be over-whelming. We can give you a tour now or you can go straight to your room, and we can show you around tomorrow. What will it be?"

"Tomorrow." I cleared my throat. "Please."

"Absolutely. Good choice. I can show you to your room."

She waved for me to step in front of her. Maya followed us as we walked toward the building.

"I know you don't want the grand tour, but I'll point out some things as we go. In the middle of the room, we have the rec area, foosball, and air hockey." A man and a woman were spinning the metal rods on the foosball table. The woman grunted as if she were actually kicking the ball instead of the little figurine she controlled on a stick.

"We have games," Lydia continued, "anything you can think of—Monopoly, Taboo, Scrabble." She pointed to the other side of a room with three full bookcases. "We have a library. Well, not a full library. Most of the titles are donated, but we have fiction, business, inspirational. But no self-help. That's where we come in."

Her shoes squeaked against the linoleum. Maya's heels clicked, brisk and impatient. I didn't make any noise. Walking down the hall was like walking the Green Mile. There was a se-ries of brown doors, likely patient rooms. Lydia slowed her pace.

She took out a key and gave it to me. "Go on, open it." I took it and slid the key into the lock. I paused for a second, taking a fortifying breath, and opened the door.

Three walls were a light gray, save for one lime green accent wall. On the wall, in vinyl letters, was the Serenity Prayer: *God, grant me the serenity to accept the things I cannot change.*

Courage to change the things I can. And wisdom to know the difference.

"On your application, you marked that you were Christian, so I thought this room would be good for you. However, if there's an issue we can move you around or cover it."

"No, no." I shook my head. "It's fine. I like it, I think."

The prayer I was fine with. The color was too loud. You can't ignore lime green.

The young man put my bags just past the kitchen, into the living room. Maya reached into her purse, pulling out a twenty-dollar-bill. The young man and Lydia both shook their heads.

What did she think this was? A hotel?

Lydia showed me how to control the AC and television channels, and waxed poetic about having my own bathroom and fresh linen.

She pointed at a closed door on the other side of the living room. "There's another room. It's locked and vacant for now, but you may have a roommate. Just depends on how things shake out." She snapped her fingers. "Oh, your schedule is on the fridge and your vitamin pack is on the counter there. You'll need that to help you stabilize and stay healthy and strong." She pointed to a small pill box. "Go ahead and take that now. We'll give you your dailies at breakfast. Tomorrow you have individual counseling with Dr. Mitra. After that, we'll give you some time to explore campus. A map of the grounds is on the back of the schedule, everything is available, including horse riding. You and Dr. Mitra can discuss the plan for group counseling."

My teeth snapped together as I gave her a wordless nod. I didn't want or need to confide in a group of strangers.

"Don't worry," she said, lowering her voice to a soothing murmur. "You can share as much or as little as you want. There will be no judgment, and remember, everyone in the

room, including some of our counselors, are going through or
have gone through recovery."

Lydia stepped back. "Okay, then. I'm sure this is all very
overwhelming, Jeanie, but if you want to beat this, we can
help you."

She turned toward Maya, who sat at the kitchen table.
"Maya, I'll give you both a few minutes and then we'll need
you to leave the premises." Lydia ended the statement with a
smile, but her voice held firm.

Good.

Maya nodded. "Understood. I won't be long."

Lydia closed the door behind her.

I settled on the love seat, pulling the gray and blue checkered pillow to my chest. "Well," I sighed. "You did it. You finally got what you wanted. Are you happy now?"

Maya tugged on the bill on her Atlanta Falcons' hat. She
sighed. "I haven't been happy since Daddy died."

I hiccupped as salt and sorrow stung my eyes. Tears splat-
tered like rain from my cheeks and onto my lips. "If he were
here, this wouldn't have happened. E-everything would be
okay. I'd be home cooking while you and Joseph fished on the
lake. Joseph wouldn't want me here."

"Believe me . . ." Maya shook her head. "I don't want you
here, either."

"Yes, you do," I whispered.

"What?" Maya asked.

"I said"—this time I shouted—"yes, you do!"

"Trust me when I say, Jeanie, I'd rather take door number
two—the option where my father is still alive, treating you like
a princess, while you continue to be the living embodiment of
daddy issues."

"What?" I snapped my head back.

"Everyone knows your father never said a kind word to you
or your mama. And while that's unfortunate, I don't appreciate

that my father, who was fifteen years older than you, had to be the father you never had."

My body jerked back as Maya shot words as piercing as bullets. All I could hear were insults. And suddenly I wasn't at Straight Arrow, I was back at my childhood home in my double-wide. Daddy just got home after a shift at the gas station's garage. Grease caked under his nails. As soon as he stepped across the threshold, he went straight for the fridge, yanked it open and pulled out a Bud.

Momma had better have dinner ready: either burgers and fries, fried chicken or pot pie, or she'd get a smack across the face. While Momma set the table, and after two-point-five beers, Daddy yelled for me. He'd said, *"Jeanie girl, if you flunk another test I'mma sock you."* I didn't start failing tests until Daddy started hitting me. That hadn't been a problem for him until one of his coworkers at the garage bragged about his genius son.

Then he'd said to me, *"God blessed you with looks, but you've got shit for brains."*

And all I could do was sit there and cry. It wouldn't do any good running off. Daddy liked to see his victims bleed—whether by his fist or his words.

And though Maya never hit me, her words pounded just as hard.

I shot up from the couch and marched over to Maya. "Is that what you think? Is that what . . . what everyone thinks? My God . . . I loved the man not only because he was incredibly kind . . . he was sexy and smart, a good father and a wonderful, wonderful man. And you stand there"—I pointed to her—"judging me, just like everyone else. Poor white trash can't find love anywhere and she'll take it from anyone. But that's not true. I loved your father. I won't have you take away my life while you go back home and wait for me to fail again. I know you. Oh, I know your game. I've Googled it. You want to declare me incompetent. So, don't tell me this isn't unfolding the way you'd planned it."

Maya snorted. "Let me get this straight. You think it was written in my evil master plan to have an alcoholic stepmother who endangers her daughter and has damn near ruined my career?" She glanced at the door and then lowered her voice. "Spoiler alert: my driving you two hours away, touring a rehab center and leaving Ryder at home with the aunts isn't my ideal Sunday."

Didn't she see I was trying? I didn't want to be this way, but it was like she was rubbing my mistakes in my face. More tears rolled down my cheeks. "Why are you so mean to me, Maya? I'm not a tough girl like you, okay? The love of my life died, and I don't know what to do. I honestly don't know what to do. I'm sorry I'm falling apart. I'm sorry I failed my daughter. But I'll get better. Just stop it. Stop being so damn mean to me!" I walked back to the living room and swiped at the hot tears that splashed onto my cheeks with my sleeves.

"And here it is." Maya waved toward me. "Classic Jeanie."

"What are you talking about?" I grabbed a Kleenex from the side table and then dabbed my eyes.

"How am I the mean one in this situation? Did I come to your job and insult you? We've had words but that's been in the privacy of my own home, not out and about where anyone can hear. I'm *devastated*." She patted her chest. "Do you hear me? Devastated about Daddy. But have you once thought about anyone else's pain? Have you asked Ryder or, I don't know . . . me, his daughter, how we feel?"

I shook my head. "Y-you never cried. Not when we first found out or during the arrangements or even at his funeral."

"Let me let you in on a little secret." Maya stood and crossed her arms. "You want to know why I'm such a . . . what did you call me . . . a 'tough girl'?" she asked with air quotes. "It's because I have to be. Daddy made sure I didn't show weakness, But for you? Oh, he laid out the red carpet, he never told you to suck it up."

"What are you talking about? Your father was always there for you. He was a good man."

"I didn't say that he wasn't a good man, but the way that he dealt with your emotions compared to mine—night and day, Jeanie. Night and day." She slapped the back of her hand on her palm. "Like when I came home past curfew back in high school."

"Yes." I nodded, remembering Joseph's reaction. He was furious and scared out of his mind. Just as I'd been when Ryder came home late. "He screamed at you . . . now I admit he was a little over the top, but he was—"

"It's not about him being upset. I get that, now. But I started sniffling. My tears were barely welling in my eyes when he told me to dry them up. He told me to stop being weak."

She squeezed her eyes shut. "And the very next day, you dropped a hot, steamy casserole dish. You were upset and crying. Daddy hugs you close, wipes away your tears and then mops up the stain."

"No," I whispered, my mind refusing to believe her thoughtless characterization of my husband, her father. "You were in trouble and he was upset. He said something mean, but he didn't mean it."

"Okay, fine, I'll give you another example. Remember when I was in eighth grade and my pet hamster died?"

I nodded my head, remembering Squeakers.

"Daddy told me he died while I was at school and he buried him for me. I burst out crying and he gets this little frown on his face. Like he can't believe I loved Squeakers enough to cry. So . . . he takes me out back, near the lake. He says he's sorry, but life goes on. He told me that I should be tough, because Squeakers would want me to be happy and not to cry. But you . . ." She threw up her hand. "Hell, you cry over one of those sad pet infomercials and Daddy just pulled you close and kissed your forehead."

She paced the floor, crossing her arms over her chest. "I am so tired of you walking around like Scarlett O'Hara, wanting someone to carry around your bucket of tears. You need to get a fucking spine and save yourself. My father isn't here to do it for you anymore." She uncrossed her arms and waved them. "Dig deep, Jeanie. You have a daughter to raise and you can't melt like tissue paper every time something bad happens. I love Ryder more than I love anyone else in this world, but I am *not* her mother and I don't want to be. You are." She pointed at me. "If you fall, people rush to your side and offer help and . . . and bandage your scraped knees and kiss away your hurt. Me? I don't get a damn thing. I'm expected to be strong. But guess what? I hurt. I bleed. My heart is broken. My mother died before I really got to know her and now Daddy is gone. The world doesn't hug and protect me. The world doesn't care about my tears."

Maya blinked over and over, moisture building. She scrubbed her face with her hands and rubbed the wet on her ripped jeans. "Would you look at that," she laughed. It wasn't a ha-ha laugh, it was a tired laugh. "See there? I wiped them myself." She pivoted on her heels and fled out the door, as if the hounds of hell were at her feet.

I sniffed, my body quaked and my lips trembled. But I didn't cry.

Monday morning, June 29th
113 days

If the cold shower didn't wake me up, all the orange, blues and yellows in the cafeteria would. Over the omelet station, hung a framed quote: I WILL BE A BETTER ME!

I just wanted eggs, toast and a mimosa. I ordered a veggie

omelet and sat at a vacant table. It was six a.m. and there were three other early risers. I sat at a square table with lime green chairs that sat lower than I expected.

I bowed my head and whispered my prayer. It wasn't long and drawn out. Just enough to bless the food and a request for someone to bail me out. A small miracle considering God's track record.

I yawned as I forked my eggs. Last night had been riddled with nightmares and I hadn't gotten much sleep. I was on stage in an auditorium. A spotlight had been suspended above me and pointed in my direction. I sat alone on a chair until Ryder came in and told me she hated me and never wanted to speak to me again. I cried and told her I loved her and promised I would get better. She told me she didn't believe me and left the room.

Then, Maya came in shouting at me to stop being a crybaby (to which I cried even more).

But the cherry on my nightmare sundae was Joseph. He came in. I jumped from my seat and ran to him. I tried to jump on him, like I used to, but he shook his head and pushed me away. He didn't speak, but he looked so disappointed. Like he couldn't believe the person I'd become. He turned around without a word and left. I woke up, hot and sweaty, heart poundin' faster than a jackrabbit on a hot date. I tossed off the bed cover and ransacked the cupboards for anything, *anything,* that could ease my anxiety.

"I'm Samantha." A manicured hand hovered over my breakfast.

I wasn't ready to speak to anyone, but manners quickly replaced irritation. I put down my fork and offered her my hand. "Jeanie."

"Hi, Jeanie." She shook my hand and then settled in the seat in front of me.

"I'm one of the counselors here. I lead the group therapy

sessions. I'm so glad you've decided to take charge of your recovery."

"Yeah . . . umm . . . me, too." It sounded more like a question. I mean, who in their right minds would be excited about rehab?

She laughed. "I get it. You don't want to be here but trust me, it goes by fast. I took the program myself ten years ago."

"You did?" I blurted. I mean, the woman was the definition of blue blood with full makeup at six in the morning, pearls, a matching blue blazer and skirt. Her hair had been styled in a chic bob like Jacqueline Kennedy Onassis. She looked more like a mayor's wife than a recovering alcoholic.

"Mhmm. And if you stick to the plan, it works." She nodded once and slapped her thigh. "I'm going to grab some breakfast. You want coffee?"

"I . . . yeah . . . sure, I want some."

"How do you take it?"

"One sugar, half a cream."

"Half? Of the miniature cup?"

I nodded. Every little calorie counted.

Samantha laughed. "Oh, honey, a full cup won't hurt you. How about this, I'll bring you the pack and you can pour it yourself."

I nodded again.

"And maybe one day I'll convince you to take the whole darn thing."

Now that I thought about it, half of the little creamer was ridiculous. I bit my lip, attempting and failing to stop the laughter from bubbling up.

"Success!" She pumped two fists in the air. "I made you smile. Okay, off I go."

She came back with coffee. She shared pictures of her children and grandchildren from their vacation in Destin, Florida.

She was a retired teacher but would sometimes substitute. She loved it because children gave her energy. A few people stopped by and introduced themselves. I couldn't recall their names. I was starting to get a headache and my hands were shaking. Per my schedule, I swung by the clinic and got my vitals taken.

"Good morning." A young nurse wrapped a Velcro cuff around my arm. Her big blue eyes reminded me of Ryder's. The cuff squeezed my arm. My heart squeezed, too. I knew it was only the first day, but I was at a loss on how I would bridge the gap between me and Ryder.

"Hmm. Blood pressure is a little high," the nurse muttered as she looked at a small screen with my numbers.

She did a few other things, listened to my heart. Asked me if I experienced tremors and anxiety. I told her the truth—I was a little shaky but not bad. And sure, I was anxious. She made me take a few pills that I couldn't pronounce even if held at gunpoint.

"Open your mouth."

Heat hit my cheeks, and I avoided the woman's gaze. She had to be at least half my age. But I did as she asked.

"Please let me or any of the staff know if you experience hallucinations or tremors."

"Ha-hallucinations?"

I was an alcoholic, not a drug addict.

She nodded, her wide eyes serious. "Some patients experience hallucinations as a side effect of alcohol withdrawals."

"Sure. I'll be on the lookout."

Even if I started seeing things, there was no way in heck I would tell them. They'd surely make me stay for longer or put me in a straitjacket.

An hour later it was time for my meeting with Dr. Mitra.

He didn't look like a shrink. He had on a Hawaiian shirt, khakis and sneakers. His skin was light brown and he had a head full of silky black hair that sat on his shoulders. The only thing that made him look official were his glasses, but then again, the wireframes were green.

"Hi, Jeanie. I'm Dr. Mitra. Please take a seat." He waved toward the couch.

I sat down, picking at the cotton balls that'd gathered on my slacks.

"Jeanie, hey." Dr. Mitra greeted again.

"Oh, sorry, I . . . sorry," I finished on a whisper.

"Hey, no need to apologize. I just wanted to let you know something." He pointed to a sign above his head that read: JUDGMENT-FREE ZONE.

"First let's take a deep breath." I did as he said, inhaled deep and let it go.

"Again," he instructed. "Let's take three more deep breaths." He closed his eyes and breathed deep with me.

"How do you feel now?"

"I . . . honestly? I don't know. I guess I'm okay. I met Lydia and a few other folks. They seem real nice."

He nodded. "Have you had a chance to read about our program? We left a pamphlet in your room."

"Yes, I did. And I already did some research online."

"Excellent." He bobbed his head. "So, you know this is a twelve-step program. Right now, you've elected to participate for a month. However, if we feel you may benefit for a longer stay, we will let you know."

I shook my head. "I'm sure I'll be fine in a month." If I stayed any longer, Maya would auction all my worldly possessions before I returned.

"For now, we're taking it day by day," Dr. Mitra continued. "No need for us to jump ahead. But right now, Jeanie, we want you to take time to reconnect with yourself. There's a spiritual aspect to all of this. You relied on alcohol and we want to identify and address the root cause. Now, I see from the question-naire you filled out, that your husband recently passed away, which triggered you to drink."

"Yes." I licked my dry lips. "I never really drank before then. Daddy—I mean, my father—is a heavy drinker, and I never wanted to be like him but, well . . ." I shrugged. "Here I am. Fifty years of good behavior and then I turned into this . . . monster."

"You are not a monster. You're human, and you need help. We all do."

I gripped my knees, staring down at my chipped nails. God, they looked horrible, like I'd stuck them in an electric pencil sharpener. I usually had the girls at the nail shop paint them a pale pink, but I'd forgotten all about my standing appointment. I wondered if they forgot about me. Or maybe they were gossiping about my downfall, just like everyone else in town.

"Let me tell you a story, maybe it'll change your perspective."

I returned my attention to Dr. Mitra. His deep brown eyes drew me in.

"All right."

"There was this man who got into this awful car accident. Broke his ribs and fractured his legs. It was a miracle he made it out alive."

I winced.

"Yes. As you can imagine he was in an extreme amount of pain. Doctors prescribed medicine to make him feel better and boy, did it." He chuckled. It was same dry laugh Joseph used to do all the time when he saw bad things on the news.

"The drugs worked all too well. He got addicted to the meds, and after he recovered from his injuries, his body and mind couldn't shake the dependence. He lied and stole from family and friends. A lot of people wrote him off as a lost

cause. He wanted to get better, and he found this program."
He pointed to a Straight Arrow Poster with their logo and the
words: BE POSITIVE.

They sure did love their affirmations. If only saying the
words were as easy as doing it.

Dr. Mitra smiled. "It took the full ninety days and then some
for the aftercare, but he succeeded. Does he sound like a monster?"

"No." I shook my head and I meant it. "He just had some
bad luck and made bad choices."

"Correct. Addiction is overwhelming. You need to focus on
aligning your mind, body and spirit to overcome. And that is
what we are going to do together. You are capable of accom-
plishing amazing things."

"Yes, sure. Th-that's fine." My voice was as dutiful as a student.

Dr. Mitra cracked a small smile. "It's okay if you don't believe it now. We will show you. But do me a favor, okay?"

"Yes?"

"When you call yourself a monster, you're labeling everyone
here a monster, too. The one thing that you can control right
now, in this moment, is your attitude. Can you change your attitude?"

"Yes."

"Can you love and forgive yourself?"

I thought about embarrassing my Chickadee. The look on
her face when she said was done with me. My heart plopped
right between my feet. She didn't even say goodbye. My lips
quivered, I felt the familiar sting in my eyes and nose.

You have a daughter to raise and you can't melt like tissue
paper every time something bad happens. Shame and anger skittered like spiders on my skin. No. I would not cry. I wouldn't
give Maya the satisfaction of being right. Even if she couldn't
see me.

Deep down, I knew there was some truth to it. I certainly didn't cry for attention. Crying didn't spare me from getting my head knocked through the walls at home. Crying didn't get Momma to comfort me when Daddy demanded she come to bed. I cried because . . . because I'd always done it. Because it made me feel better to get it all out.

"Jeanie?" Dr. Mitra pulled my attention back to him, his voice as soft and velvety as rose petals. "Can you forgive and love yourself?"

"I . . . yes. I can try."

"Do you want to get better?"

Ryder's face popped into my mind's eye. "Desperately."

"Then let's begin."

And we talked. A whole lot. He asked me about my childhood, and I told him about Daddy. He asked me if I'd been abused and I said yes to physically and no to sexually. Daddy was a bastard, but he wasn't a perverted bastard. I told him I dropped out of school. He asked me if that impacted my self-esteem and I said, "I don't think so." Then he asked if I thought I was smart. I laughed and said no.

"Why not?"

"I'm a high school dropout."

"And that makes you unintelligent? Based on a decision when you were a teenager?"

"Uhh, yeah. Doesn't take much to run the register at the Piggy Wiggly. If it weren't for Joseph, I would've worked there forever. I'm not smart like Joseph or Ryder or Maya. Joseph was the county judge and Maya's an attorney. And get this: Ryder writes poetry and she's been published."

Dr. Mitra shook his head. "That's all very admirable, but that doesn't take away from your accomplishments. You escaped an abusive home. You worked your way up in the grocery store and you went back to school, got your GED and so on to become a paralegal. I think that makes you not only smart, but hardworking."

I shrugged. I wasn't going to argue with the man about my intelligence. I didn't know him from Adam anyway. We moved on to a different topic. We talked a lot about Ryder and even Maya. He scribbled a lot when I spoke of Maya. He looked up from his pad. "You and your step-daughter don't get on?"

"No, we don't." And I left it at that.

An hour and a half later we were through. I was exhausted but it felt good for someone to listen to me. Then again, he was getting paid to do this.

He stood from behind his desk and then walked me to the front. "You're on to a great first day." He smiled at me as he hobbled to the door of his office. One leg kicked out while the other stood straight.

"There was this man who got into this awful car accident. Broke his ribs and fractured his legs."

I gasped. "Dr. Mitra." I stopped just before the door. "Were you the guy . . . the man who broke his legs and ribs?"

"We all have a story." He opened the door. "And mine ended happy. Yours will too, if you stick to the program."

I stepped through the door and said goodbye. That seemed to be a theme. Stick to the program. He almost had me believing until he mentioned happy endings. My prince died, and I was all alone in the tower covered with poison ivy and thorns. I didn't believe in happily ever after.

Not anymore.

CHAPTER 10

MAYA
SO MUCH FOR MY HAPPY ENDING

Wednesday morning, July 1ˢᵗ
115 days

Three days had passed since I dropped Jeanie off at rehab. Forty-three hours since Ryder told me she'd never forgive me.

Work had been my only salvation. Well, not the personal injury cases, but the pro bonos. The firm allowed us to do up to twenty hours a month. I'd already logged in fifteen for the month. But I was still handling the moneymakers so the partners shouldn't complain. Tonight, I'd planned to take a long bubble bath and watch re-runs of *The Bachelorette*. The latest season was bananas.

"Psst." Something clinked against my bedroom window. "Hey!" Another plink.

What in the hell? I hurried to the front window, lifted it up, and stuck my head out. Roland stood below. Suddenly, his curious questions about the layout of the lake house made sense, what floor and which side of the house my room was located.

"What are you doing here?" I whisper-hissed. My heart pitter-pattered in my chest. Though we worked together, we'd all but stopped our weekly rendezvous since I moved back home.

"I needed to see you."

"You see me at work."

"You know what I mean, Maya."

I rolled my eyes and shook my head. "I already told you now isn't a good time."

He shrugged. "I'll be quiet."

I snorted. The man did nothing quiet. He didn't sleep quiet, he rolled around, coughed and talked in his sleep if he had something on his mind. He sang in the shower and hummed when he put on his clothes.

"Yeah, right."

"Okay. I didn't want to bust this out until the last minute but . . . I come bearing gifts."

"Gifts?" I leaned forward, my upper body now fully out the window.

He nodded and pulled something out of his backpack. "I cooked your favorite—baked chicken and rice."

"You can't cook, Roland. Also, sushi is my favorite."

"Well, I can't cook sushi and all the restaurants in town are shit."

"True." I nodded, one of many things I missed since I moved from Atlanta. A little grin started to push its way through.

"Chocolate pudding for dessert."

"Hmmm . . ."

"Yeah, I know, I know. Your favorite is chocolate cake, but I can't bake a cake. And the bakery was closed by the time I thought of dessert."

I snorted. "So far you're two for two . . . in the hole."

"That's okay, because this last thing is going to blow everything out of the water."

"Sure, it will." I waved at him to bring out the next terrible gift.

He grabbed his phone and pressed something. I heard a ding from my phone. "Got you something online. Go ahead. Check it."

I moved away from the window to the dresser where I'd left my phone. I opened my email app and saw the gift from Roland. All seasons of the *Real Housewives of Orange County* and *Courage the Cowardly Dog*.

I laughed and ran back to the window.

"You didn't."

"I did." He nodded. "We can watch our favorite episode with Ramses. No way in hell I'm watching *Real Housewives*, though."

An owner's father often came up to the law firm to complain about anything—the damn weather, the damn president, the damn country and the damn world. He was the quintessential grumpy old man. With his thick round glasses, lanky stature and bald head, he reminded me of Eustace, the cantankerous old man in *Courage the Cowardly Dog*. One day I cracked a joke that Eustace was in the office and Roland was the only person who got the joke.

After that day, we both discovered that we loved all things '90s and early 2000s, and sex. Lots and lots of sex.

"Well, since you already sent it to me, I really don't need your burnt chicken and chocolate pudding."

Roland grinned and lifted a few small bottles. I couldn't make out the labels.

"Okay, last but not least, you get a one hundred percent free massage with a happy ending."

"A . . . a what?"

"Happy." He pointed to his chest. "Ending." He lowered his finger toward his pants.

"Oh, my gawd, please just let him in!" Ryder yelled from her own window, just fifteen feet away from mine.

"R-Ryder?" I leaned out the window and turned my head in

her direction. Shock rolled over my body. One because she was talking to me, and two . . . because damn, I hadn't noticed that Roland and I had stopped whispering.

"Did you hear . . . ?"

"Yes. Everything. Besides that, Roland threw rocks at my window first."

Roland shrugged and called out, "Hey, you just broke the cool-kid code. I thought we were keeping that to ourselves?"

Ryder sighed. "That was the plan until you propositioned my sister with a happy ending." She sounded like a disgruntled, recently retired librarian. "And P.S., I do know what that means."

I slapped my hand over my mouth to stifle giggles, half-delirious from this conversation and half-elated that Ryder was joking with us. Maybe the alien that had body-snatched my sister had gone back to space.

"The door's unlocked," Ryder continued.

"Good looking out." He packed his stuff and walked toward the front door.

"Hey!" I protested. "I didn't say you could come in."

Ryder sighed. "I'm going to put on my headphones and go to sleep. Good night." She slammed her window shut.

So much for sweet Ryder.

I shook my head and rushed to put on my yoga pants and a bra, since I'd only been wearing a T-shirt. I hurried out of my room and slowed down when I hit the top of the stairs. I couldn't have him thinking I was flustered.

I took a deep breath and walked down the stairs. The alarm beeped. Guess Ryder took care of disarming the alarm, too.

"Hey, you," Roland said as he watched me descend the stairs.

"Hey, yourself."

He opened his arms and I walked into his ready hug. I stood

on my toes and nipped his earlobe. "You really don't respect any of my rules, do you?"

He grabbed my waist and lifted me in his arms. "I missed you."

"Well, I can't say the same—"

He devoured my lips and my lie. The man didn't do anything half-assed, and kissing was one of the many things he'd mastered. He tasted me, licked my lips, and explored. Probing, demanding, leaving no room for thoughts or arguments, just feelings.

But he kissed me longer and deeper, like a man starved. Maybe he really did miss me. After a few minutes of heart-pounding, soul-stirring kisses, he patted my ass and lowered me onto the ground.

"Have you eaten?" he asked as he reached for his backpack-o'-things.

"No."

"Good." He pulled out two containers of food.

I lifted the lid and saw what I'd already suspected: over-cooked chicken, dried out rice and soupy green beans. "You cooked this yourself, huh?"

"Sure did," he answered, a wide smile on his face.

I sighed. "What are you in the mood for?"

"I really liked that chicken marsala you cooked me a few months ago."

"I was thinking more in the line of grilled cheese sandwiches."

He gave me the saddest puppy eyes.

I rolled my eyes and sighed. "I suppose I can whip it up for you. C'mon." I grabbed his hand, leading him to the kitchen. "You're in luck. I thawed out some chicken for the slow cooker tomorrow."

"Excellent. While you cook, I'll prep the dessert."

"You mean lift up the lid for the pudding."

"Yep. And I'll set up cartoons and pour the wine."

"You, sir, are too kind."

"I spoil you."

"Mhmmm."

After an hour, we sat in the living room with our bellies full, laughing at Courage's shenanigans. Roland massaged my feet, which were propped on his lap.

Roland stood and stretched. It was getting late and I knew he had to leave. Disappointment bloomed in my core.

"Ready for bed?" He looked down at me.

"Yeah . . . I . . . I guess so. Thanks for coming by. It was fun."

"Did Maya Donaldson admit to having fun with me?"

"I have to admit . . . you're a good date."

He pulled me into his arms and carried me upstairs. The bed had already been turned down. He lifted the covers, tucked me in. Then he shrugged off his jogging pants and shirt. He stood in front of me, in his boxer briefs, looking like a fantasy. Ripped muscles, thick, muscular thighs. His eight-pack abs were sculpted to perfection.

He lifted the covers and moved in behind me. After that, he didn't make a move. I thought he would, but no. He just pressed his lips to my neck and whispered, "How are you feeling?"

"I'm good. Great, even."

"Maya," he said on a sigh. "It's just us."

My shoulders went tight. My nose tingled. I was thankful that he spooned me and couldn't see my face. I didn't answer him.

"Princess, you know I think every inch of you is delectable, but you're losing weight."

"I've been busy."

Roland tightened his arms around my waist. "You've been withdrawn. You don't socialize at work. And baby, I know you're an amazing attorney, but those cases . . . they aren't fulfilling you. The only time you light up is when you do pro bono, civil rights work."

"Do the partners . . . is it being noticed at work?" Since I'd been living at home for the past few weeks, I hadn't stayed late at work. I was out of the door by five thirty.

"Your job is safe, Maya."

"But what about partner? They're making a decision soon, right?"

"Right." His voice went tight. "But I want to know how you *feel*. There's more to life than making partner."

"What else do you want to know?" My tone went granite. "I said I was fine."

"No, Princess, you aren't. Your father died a few months ago. Your stepmother is in rehab and your stepsister—"

"Sister," I cut in.

"Sister," he amended, "has gotten herself into trouble. Not to mention work. You've got a lot on your plate. I want to ease your load."

"It's kind of you to offer, but there really isn't anything you can do."

"That's not true."

"Really? Can you . . . can you make Jeanie stop drinking herself to death?"

He sighed. "Maya, baby . . ."

The tingle in my nose became a sharp sting. "Can you make my sister not look at me like I'm the vilest creature on Earth? Can you make her understand that I'm not trying to take her mother away, that I just want her to get better? Can you bring my father back to life? My mother? Of course, you can't, you aren't God or a necromancer." I turned to face him, sniffing back tears and stuffing down emotions. "So, you see, there is nothing you can do to help. I'm all alone in this."

He stroked my cheek. "I'm telling you that you aren't alone.

If you let me, I can help. I can be your sounding board, a shoulder for you to cry on. I can be your man if you let me."

"Roland," I groaned over my skipping heartbeat. "I told you, things are too busy right now. I don't have time for a relationship."

He closed his eyes, sighing. He pulled me closer, his lips on my forehead. "Woman, you are killing me, you know that?"

"Let's just get over this partner hump and see how Jeanie does in rehab. And then we can talk."

"Really?" I could feel the smile on his lips against my forehead.

"Really."

He bear-hugged me. "I want to come over tomorrow."

"Okay," I agreed, knowing that, in the end, he would come over anyway.

"I want to spend the weekend here, too."

"You, sir, are getting very ballsy."

"I mean I've got 'em."

I snorted. "In spades."

"Promise me you'll let me stay the weekend. I can grill hot dogs and burgers for the holiday."

"Holiday? What . . . ?" I stopped myself when I remembered the Fourth of July.

"Fine, okay," I agreed. It was easier to give in, for now. He would just creep over and throw rocks at my window or yet again, piss off Ryder or wake her up. "Ring the doorbell next time."

He kissed my forehead again. "You promise, right? No matter what?"

"I never go back on my word, Roland. You know that."

"I know." He sighed. "Let's go to sleep."

He burrowed his face into my neck. He was getting mighty comfortable.

"So, you're sleeping over?"

"Go to sleep, Maya."

I smiled and, for once, did what I was told.

Friday, July 3rd
117 days

I was in my office, knee-deep into drafting questions for my trial next week, when my office phone blinked and buzzed. I'd planned on scooting out early. It was Friday and Roland had planned to stay the weekend. I had a pot roast in the slow cooker, and I needed to grab a nice Merlot from the store. I hadn't kept any alcohol in the house once I discovered Jeanie's abuse.

"Maya," Katy called, her voice unnervingly sweet. So sweet I paused mid-type.

"Yes?" I answered, staring at the phone.

"Meeting with the partners in ten."

"What?"

"Meeting with the partners in ten minutes. Conference room."

"Okay." My heartbeat rattled my chest. I was so tempted to text Roland, my fingers tingled.

When we first began our affair, we both agreed that I wouldn't ask him about the partners, even when I decided to go for partner. It wouldn't be fair to him. Besides that, I didn't want him to feel like I was using him for information. I wanted to earn it all on my own.

Instead of giving in to temptation, I opened my compact mirror to check my appearance. I reapplied my coral lipstick and readied myself for the news.

An army of dragonflies attacked my stomach. I pressed a hand against my abdomen. "I can do this." I strode to the conference room, passing by a smiling Katy with David all in her face.

"Hey, there, Maya." David smiled. He looked down at Katy. They shared a cheesy grin. I rolled my eyes. Apparently, love was in the air.

Love? I tripped, righting myself on the wall. *You don't love him.*

I shook my head as I turned the corner. I saw the *him* in question, along with Marc Sanders and Fred Dickerson.

"Maya, please, take a seat." Marc and Roland stood when I entered the room. The other partner, Fred, remained seated.

"Water?" Marc offered.

"No, thank you." I shook my head and settled in the chair across from the attorneys.

"So . . ." Marc thumped the oak table with his fingers. "We've come to a decision for our next partner, and we have decided to go with David."

I squared my shoulders, determined not to show the impact of the news. I took a deep breath.

"Please know that you're a valuable asset to our team . . ." Marc continued talking. I looked up but not at him. My eyes found Roland. Cool hand Luke had been calm, hands clasped in front of him; even his eyes were blank. I stared at him a little longer. His breathing pattern changed, and something flashed in his eyes—a little give to the steel he displayed.

"Marc," I interrupted, "can you tell me what . . . what I've done to miss this opportunity?"

Marc shook his head. "You're a great attorney, passionate and talented. We just decided that David's a better fit for partner."

"If you don't mind, I'd like to hear feedback from everyone. This is the only way I can improve."

"Fine," Marc sighed. "You seem a bit . . . preoccupied. Understandably so, with your father's passing and stepmother's health."

The other partner agreed with the bullshit Marc spouted. Now, it was on Roland.

"Mr. Hill." I nodded. "Please tell me what makes David a better candidate for partner?"

Roland cleared his throat. "You've been a great asset to our firm, however, I am of the opinion that you don't have a passion for personal injury." Funny, he sounded like a passionless bot while he delivered the news. *I'm in the Twilight Zone.* This couldn't be the man who held me while I slept last night.

"Excuse me?" I gripped the arms of my chair.

"That's true," Marc added. "Your billable hours haven't been as extensive as David's. You seem to really enjoy pro bono, which is commendable, but it's not billable. Not to mention you've been cutting out early."

"By early you mean five thirty. My goodness, I get here at six a.m. most days. I rarely take lunch breaks, and I bring my work home. And okay," I said, clearing my throat. "Maybe my billable hours haven't been as high this past month, but before my father's death I had the highest billable hours while maintaining pro bono cases."

"Yes," Fred agreed, "but we had to consider the entire year and the recent . . . events in your life. Perhaps you should focus on personal issues for now."

"So, let me get this straight . . . if my father hadn't died or my stepmother hadn't barged in drunk, I could be partner."

The temperature of the room dropped, but there was a fire in me that was stoked by every unfair assessment. I looked each man in the eye. Fred didn't have skin in the game. He'd treated me fairly in the past, but he was the one whose vote I found the least surprising.

Marc's was like a stab to the gut. Roland's, a stab to the back.

And from the way Marc fidgeted with his Rolex, and the way Roland's intense eyes pleaded with me to understand, they knew this was bullshit. David was not partner material. He was just a product of the good-ole-boys network. His father and Fred were fishing buddies.

The clock on the opposite end of the room painfully ticked away seconds. I didn't need the reminder that my time had been wasted.

"Know your worth, Baby Girl. And if any man makes you feel less than what you are, get the hell out of there and then call your daddy. I'll set him straight." I was pretty sure Daddy was talking about a relationship, but like all the other advice he'd given me over the years, this was evergreen.

"Maya," Marc cut into the silence. "Believe me when I say that we are truly sorry. This is one of the hardest decisions the firm has had to make. I'll personally make sure we get you plugged into bigger, high-profile cases."

"No." I waved him off. "I respect you, Marc. And I appreciate you hiring me. But I have to say that going with David is utter bullshit. I've had more wins, and not only that, I've made this firm more money, including billable hours that you've accused me of skimping. So I had two, maybe three less-than-stellar months. But for the past four years, I've kicked ass. I've worked twice as hard, have had harder cases and come out on top—every time. As a matter of fact, I have more cases than any other associate in this firm. And let's be honest, if David's father died and his family needed him, you'd have given him time off *and* partner."

The partners were silent. They just stared, looking at me like I was the crazy one. Like I wasn't usually the last to leave the office, outside of the partners, and definitely including David. Like I wasn't the one who took the risky cases and turned them into gold. And here they sat. Two of them married with stay-at-home wives who made their lives easier. Two of them had kids, again, being taken care of at home. Someone to dry clean their suits. Someone to keep their houses clean and their kids fed. Someone to keep up with bills, to rub their shoulders when life became too heavy. Not a single one of these men who'd judged me for having shitty luck could relate.

Not even Roland. I glared at him. He'd talked about passion for the job. I would show him passion.

Promise me you'll let me stay the weekend.

Ahh. It all made sense now.

I took a deep breath. "Gentlemen. Thank you for the candid feedback. While I don't agree or respect your opinions, you've clearly thought it through. As such, I must verbally give you my resignation."

"Maya." Roland shook his head. "There's no need to leave. Take a few hours, cool off."

"What? And then have you guys track my hours and use it against me? No thanks. I need to quit everything within this law firm."

Including you.

"Maya, you can't just quit because we didn't make you partner," Fred said.

"Actually, I can. But that's not the only reason. I'm quitting for self-preservation. I can no longer give you my time, my youth, sixty- to seventy-hour weeks, knowing that I'm the best damn associate at this firm, while you give partner to a mediocre attorney."

I raised my voice over their protests. "And you know it." I stood. "I'll follow up with a formal resignation and have it on your desks before I leave. Out of respect, I will give you two weeks. Any other cases and trials can be transferred to your newest *partner* or however you see fit. Good day, gentlemen, and best of luck."

You're gonna need it.

I marched to my office, past the receptionist and paralegal desks, opened my door and shut it.

Then I grabbed a stapler and chucked it across the room. "Shit!"

I'd just quit my job, but I had plenty of savings. Daddy made us more than comfortable and I wouldn't have to work for three to four years if I managed my finances well. Still, I wanted to work. And I had no idea what to do. I either had to pray they had openings at the two other law firms in town or commute at least thirty miles out to the next largest cities, Macon or Warner Robins.

I slumped into my chair, clicked my music app and played my neo-soul playlist. I had two uninterrupted hours. Thankfully no one came after me. Not even Roland. I took that time to draft a resignation letter.

Dear Misogynist Pigs who don't know how to identify talent if it spanked you on your collective doughy asses, go screw yourselves.

I deleted it, Googled resignation letters and downloaded a template.

My door opened and Roland stepped in.

"Get out." I pointed to the door.

"What the hell happened back there?" Roland closed the door behind him. "Why did you act like a damn brat and quit?"

"A brat?" I threw my hands in the air. "David making partner over me? That was bullshit and you know it. I'm tired of working twice as hard, getting paid either less or the same as any man. Why? Because I'm a woman. A *black* woman. You think they would've treated David like that if all of this happened to him? Nope. But me"—I pointed to my chest—"I don't get the benefit of the doubt."

Roland shook his head. "You're right. And look, I fought

for you. I really did but the decision has been made and you need to respect it."

"No." I shook my head. "I'm not giving this company my energy. Hell, I can start my own law firm and take on cases I'm *passionate* about." I threw his earlier words in his face.

"Maya—"

"How could you say that about me? And in front of them. You know I love being an attorney. I put in the hours."

"But your heart's not in it. Not in this area of law."

"So. Fucking. What?" I yelled. "So what? I still do a damn good job. So, what, I don't love P.I. cases? I still get the work fucking done."

"But you're going to burn out. Trust me, I know."

"Oh, so you're burned out?"

"Yes, Maya, I am. You know the hours I put in, and like you, I prefer the cases where people really need help. The ones who can't afford us. But it doesn't pay the bills. I just don't want you to end up like me."

"End up like you? What? A partner? To have the respect of your colleagues and to be fairly compensated? Which part, Roland?"

"Being a partner here isn't all that it's cracked up to be."

"And that would've been my decision to make. Mine to experience. But you planted seeds of doubt."

"No, I did not. You pressured us to tell you why, so I told you the truth."

I shook my head. "You knew this would happen. That's why you made me promise to have you over for the weekend. I rescind the offer."

"Maya, c'mon, don't do this." He leaned against the door and banged his head against it.

"And what's more, we are over."

He rushed to my side, tried grabbing my hand. "You don't mean that."

I jerked it away. "I do."

"I'll give you the weekend to calm down."

"Don't."

"I'm not giving you up."

"If you don't leave me alone, I'll consider this harassment and let the other partners know. We're done. Now, get out."

"Don't do this. Don't choose anger over love."

"Love?"

He leaned over my desk, crowding my space, confusing my senses. "I love you."

"Stop it."

"I do. I've been in love with you for a while."

"We've only been together for a year."

"And I loved you then. I fell in love when you offered our client a tissue when he lost his daughter in a car accident. You told him that it would be okay, and that although you couldn't bring her back, you would get her justice and you did just that."

"That was three years ago."

"I know." He lifted my hand and brought it to his lips. "Let us be more. Let me be your man. Let me share your load."

"Roland." I looked away before the pain in his eyes slashed at my resolve.

"The thing is I know you love me, too. It's written all over your face." He cupped my jaw and turned my face toward him. "You feel it here." He pointed to my heart. "Look me in my eyes, and tell me, convince me that you don't love me, and I'll walk away. I'll let you go."

"I'm . . . I'm flattered that you love me. And I have really enjoyed this past year of us hanging out."

"Hanging out, Maya?" He chuckled, but it held no humor. "C'mon, stop it."

"I have. You're a wonderful man, but I'm not in the market for love. I'm too busy. And honestly, after this whole partner experience, I just . . . can't look at you the same." I shook my head. "You don't have my back. You want me to fall back and support you."

"I've never said that." He looked confused.

"Both of us can't be the chiefs, right? We both can't be partners."

"Maya—"

I raised my hand, swallowing down the grief that hit my heart. Another loss for me, first Daddy and now Roland. I blew a stream of breath. Readying myself for the hurt my words would cause to both of us. "I don't love you, Roland. I never did. I liked you, respected you, but not loved."

He shook his head. "You really are cold." He turned around, yanked open the door and let it slam behind him. My framed law degree shook.

"You did the right thing." My head was convinced. My heart would take some work. Good thing is, I had the time now.

Chapter 11

Ryder
My Milkshake Brings All the Boys to the Yard

Monday morning, July 6th
120 days

The sun beat down on my back. It was like someone had a magnifying glass focused on me like a bug. I rolled the bottled water over my neck, seeking coolness from the muggy heat.

There were only three people in the poetry group: me, a pretty sophomore named Gina and an upcoming junior, Craig. Both attended the public school in town.

Alston had made us walk half a mile down the road to the rec center's baseball fields. There were four different fields; two were being used for actual baseball practice. With each step away from the community center, Alston seemed to relax. The wrinkles in his forehead smoothed. He even grinned and waved at some of the ballplayers on the field. Maybe being in the dark theater sucked all his energy. Maybe he wasn't a judgmental jerk.

"Is this a volunteer program or are we on probation?" Gina moaned as we trekked to center field.

Alston snorted. "For some of you," he mumbled under his breath.

Never mind. He's a judgmental jerk.

My face blazed. This time, it wasn't the from the sun. My crush on Alston had been crushed before it started. The first week, I caught him staring at me a few times. When I looked at him, he either averted his eyes or shook his head like I was an extreme disappointment to the human race.

Then after Mom threw up on his shoes, he seemed to soften around me, just a fraction. Instead of ignoring my raised hand, he looked at me and then called someone else. That was something, at least.

It was like I didn't exist for him. No, that wasn't it. It was like he didn't want me to exist.

Today was the start of the fourth week. We hadn't written anything yet; we just studied other poets and broke down thematic meaning and structure. It was like being in school. I loved school, but I didn't like my teacher.

For some reason I'd thought Alston would be cool. But everything he said was robotic, like he was reciting things line-by-line from a textbook. This week, we were auditioning for *Grease*. I love the musical, but I wasn't what you'd call talented. I was a triple threat to people's eyes, ears and emotions.

Alston walked over to the pitcher's plate and waved his hands. "Everyone gather around." We did as we were told and formed a semicircle around him. I was the farthest away and I'd positioned myself there on purpose.

He cleared his throat. "Today's lesson: Spoken Word.

"Have any of you written a poem, specifically to be performed?" He pulled a towel from his backpack and tossed it over his head to block out the sun.

I shook my head. Everything I'd written had been scribbled in my journal. I'd had no intention of sharing until my English teacher, Mrs. Frierson, made me submit my poem to *Poet Magazine*.

"Spoken word is just poetry that's written to be performed,

to be heard. When you perform you want to pull the audience into your point of view. Pull them into the world you've created. It's like reading a book, but your words and your voice guides and hypnotizes them until they are embedded deep into your fictive dream. Does anyone know what 'fictive dream' means?"

My hand shot up. He pointed at me.

Oh my God, he chose me.

"Tell us, then." Alston waved at me.

"Oh yeah." I lowered my hand. "It's when you take the reader, or in the case of spoken word, the audience out of their everyday reality and pull them into your word picture."

Alston nodded, taking a quick swig of his water. "That's the perfect definition of a fictive dream. You want everything else for the audience to disappear. You want them to focus on you, your words. If they're thinking about their laundry or their jobs, you've failed them."

Gina nudged me with her elbow and whispered, "I'd like to be *his* fictive dream."

I didn't respond. Though, I wouldn't mind it, either.

"When you think of spoken word, who or what do you think of?" Alston asked the group.

Craig tipped his chin. I guess it was his way of raising his hand. "I think of some dude with a goatee and a beanie performing at a local coffee shop. Somebody's playing jazz in the background. And when he's done, people snap instead of clap."

Alston laughed. "All right. That sounds like something out of a movie. Gina, what about you?"

"I think about some angry girl who just broke up with her boyfriend. And she's like . . . screaming into the mic, letting it all hang out."

Alston tilted his head. "God, what are you kids looking at these days?"

"YouTube." Craig shrugged.

"What about you?" He didn't say my name, he just pointed at me again. His blazing hazel eyes held my gaze.

"I don't think of one thing. There are so many forms. I guess when I was younger, I always associated rap with spoken word."

"Really? A rap song?"

"Yeah. Or . . . like a cypher or freestyle battle. Artists like Dead Prez, who use rap for social commentary, or Nas, who raps about his life experiences and growing up in Queensbridge."

"Exactly." Alston smiled, the most beautiful smile I'd ever seen. "How do you know about that?"

"About spoken word or the artists?"

"Both." He crossed his arms.

"Maybe it's because I don't live under a rock?" I shrugged. *Did he think he was an authority on rap or something?*

"When I was younger, I was a part of the Big Brother program. My Big Brother, Tim, got me into rap and poetry." He waved at me as if to say, *now you share.*

"My sister, Maya. She loves rap and freestyles."

"Is she the one who drops you off and picks you up?"

"Yeah. She's the reason why I love poetry. It all started with rap and Langston Hughes."

He shook his head, his eyes going a little dreamy.

Does he like Maya? Bricks stacked in my stomach. Of course, he does. She's smart, beautiful. A law-abiding citizen.

His eyes cleared as if he were jerking himself out of a daydream. God, I hope it wasn't about Maya.

"I want to share something I wrote, is that cool?"

I *think* I nodded my head, my eyes glued on him. I was anxious, hungry to see the real guy behind the boring lectures.

He cleared his throat and took a few steps back.

"Rich boy meets poor girl. Two forces collide. Does he love her or love her not?" Alston mimed plucking petals.

"Is it love or lust? Turns out wedding vows sketched in chalk and papier-mâché hearts with glue that never dries can rot and rot and rot from the inside out, when Rich Boy takes his daddy's check . . . and checks out."

Alston pointed to his chest. "And Poor Girl's life is turned upside down when *Me*, the product of the union and *Me*, the reminder of failure and *Me*, the boy, the *man* Mom can't stand with Rich Boy's looks and Poor Girl's pockets." Alston's strong voice went low into a whisper.

"Turns out stone hearts can't love. And not even the birth of a child, and the love from her little boy can bring her joy. And his toys become his friends and books become his way to escape this . . . so-called 'wonderful life,'" he said with air quotes.

"Books have no shelf-life and within those immortal pages he becomes a knight, the slayer of dragons. Though . . ." He shook his head, eyes closed as he swayed to the rhythm of his words.

"Though in the real world there's no way a young boy can fight demons larger than life. Demons who brought drugs into his home and made Poor Girl feel like she had no one. So, she shot, snorted and sniffed and let men *in* who did her *in*. And here I stand on sand, desperate to be a man, learning what *not* to do from Tin Men too stiff to let anyone in and . . . cowards preying on women like 'lions and tigers and bears, oh my!' and . . . scarecrows that ran at the first sign of trouble. There's no place like home. There's no place like home. There's no place like *my* home where . . . wizards were pimps and pushers and Baby Boy was caught up in Poor Girl's tornado of needles and crackpipes. The dark clouds powered by nightmares, powered by broken dreams and broken people laid out, unrepaired."

He stopped, speaking, his chest heaving. He opened his eyes again and I swore he stared right at me.

"But the twister's got no agenda. He upends and destroys and tosses around Baby Boy. Boy meets world. World breaks boy's heart. Despite it all, Baby Boy tries to become a man. I think I can. I think I can. I think . . ." He tapped his temple and shook his head.

"Rich Boy meets Poor Girl. Two forces collide. Does he love her or love her not? Stop!" He raised his hand. "The cycle ends. I am not the product of failure. I am love. Boy becomes man."

Alston stepped back and bowed.

"Holy shit," I whispered. My curse was swallowed by the sound of clapping from me and the others. Gina whistled, like he was a stage actor taking his final bow.

Goose bumps broke over my skin. I clapped so hard that my palms were stinging.

"What was that?" Gina asked.

"That is spoken word. And today, we are going to learn to write and then, later, perform it."

"Thank God," I blurted out loud.

Alston smiled. "I know some of you were bored to death by what I was teaching you. But that's why we walked so far. I had to get away from Mrs. Bryant. She's a traditionalist and my kind of poetry isn't her speed. I figure we write the poems, recite them all calm-like and then . . . bam!" He smacked his hands together. "We perform it how we want to. How it's meant to be performed."

"Yeah." I snorted. "Those senior citizens won't know what hit them."

"Hell, yeah they won't." Alston smirked and shook his head at me. "All right, Grasshoppers. Take out your notebooks and listen up. We're going to dissect my poem and then you're going to reconstruct it and do it yourselves. Sound good to you?"

"Yes!" we all agreed.

"All right. Let's go hit the shade"—he pointed to the covered bleachers—"and we'll get started."

We went to the bleachers, and for an hour listened to Alston break down his poem. From his backpack, he took out a few pieces of paper. "Here are copies of the poem. Read it and then compare reading it to how I performed it. I'll give you all five minutes." He took out his phone and touched his screen a few times. "Time starts now."

My heart slammed against my chest as I read his words, experienced his childhood. Energy hummed beneath my skin. My fingers trembled. I wanted to write him back, respond to his hurt, and comfort the young boy caught in his mother's storm. God, did I ever understand. When he described the twister, a spark of electricity hit me. Mom's addiction was like an erupting volcano. For years, she'd been dormant, until she wasn't.

I blamed myself for not helping her sooner. Each time I passed by her room, ignoring the stench, ignoring the sound of the freezer door opening and shutting. Ignoring the clink of ice against the glass.

Ignoring the way Mom teeter-tottered around the house, eyes hazy with pain. All those times magma had been building up and then . . . eruptions. At Maya's job, at the community center. And when Mom erupted and oozed on everything in her path, she incinerated us.

Monday afternoon, July 6th
120 days

I kicked up the stand on my bike and eased it out of the rack.

"Hey, you." Alston's arms were crossed as he leaned against the brick wall of the community center.

"Hey, you . . . too."

Smooth, Ryder.

"It's hot out here."

"Yeah." I shrugged. From the sheen of sweat that covered my legs and dripped from my forehead, I'd have to agree. "Heard on the radio that it's a heat wave."

"Why are you riding your bike? Where's your sister?"

"I told her I'm riding my bike today." More like begged. But I bet she wouldn't have let me if she'd realize there was a heat wave. She seemed out of it lately.

"You don't know how to drive?"

"I do. Just not good enough for when there are other cars or buildings or people around." I shrugged. "Why do *you* care anyway?" My tone just a wee defensive, but what was it to him?

"Because driving is a practical skill that you need to have."

"My dad died before I could learn. Everyone else is too . . . it's not a good time, okay?"

Alston's eyes softened a bit. They were greener than brown right now.

He pushed his back from the wall and then walked toward me. "I know how to drive."

"No surprise, as you stated earlier, it's a practical skill."

He stopped walking and laughed. He had a good laugh, deep and rich. "I have a car, too." There's a twinkle of humor in his eyes.

"I've seen it," I said, walking my bike toward him. "You should slow down in parking lots, you know." The other day he'd swung into the lot like he was in the middle of a high-speed police chase.

"Do you want me to teach you or not, Ryder?"

"I . . . what? You will? When? Why?"

"Yeah. Today if you have the time, and it's no big deal."

"Are you sure? Also, do you have insurance? Because I

don't want to be liable for any car crashes. Also, do you have proper seat belts and air bags? Your car is a bit old, nice, but old and sometimes if you're not careful, you can get a car without the—"

"Yes, Ryder."

He grabbed my shoulder and guided me to his car. "I'll lock your bike up. You get in."

"Cool." I bit my lips, hoping to keep them shut and stop my rambling. And that hot summer day, the hottest of the summer, the hottest boy I'd ever met gave me a driving lesson.

Friday afternoon, July 10th
124 days

After a few days and more lessons from Alston at the community center parking lot, I could confidently say that I hadn't improved by much.

"Okay, move the gear into Drive."

I clutched the stick, pressed the brake and pulled it back to Drive.

"Good, now slow and steady."

My foot slammed down on the gas pedal. The car jerked forward. We barreled forward in the parking lot toward a curb.

"Hit the brakes! Hit the brakes!"

I slammed my foot on the gas. The car went faster.

"Brake, the brakes. Other pedal."

I slammed the other one. The car halted. My head bumped my hands gripping the steering wheel.

"Oh, my God," Alston whispered. His olive-colored skin had turned pale.

My hands shook. I buried my face into the steering wheel. I couldn't look him in the eyes.

"I'm so sorry. I can't . . . I'm not good at driving."

"No shit."

"S-sorry." Oh no. I could feel it coming on. It was like a torch to my skin and onions under my eyes.

"I should go." I unbuckled my seat belt. "Thanks for the lesson."

"Hey." He put his hands over mine, stopping me from unstrapping the belt. That fire torch that burned my face went into overdrive. Tingles of heat dashed up my hand. "Wait. Don't be embarrassed."

"I'm not," I lied.

"Then why are you crying?"

"I'm not crying."

"Really?" He gave me a slow, lazy grin. "Then your eyes must be sweating."

"No. It's the smell in your car. Have you been eating onions in here?"

"I had a burger at lunch."

"Must be that."

"No onions, though." He grinned, a wide grin. "I hate onions."

"Well, the smell in your car suggests otherwise." I licked my lips.

His eyes settled on my lips. He leaned in closer, so close my tongue could trace the seam of his lips if he wanted me to. And boy, did I want to do it. When he swallowed, his Adam's apple bobbed. He leaned a fraction of an inch closer. *This is it. It's happening. Be cool, Ryder.*

"How old are you?"

"I . . . uh . . ."

"Don't lie. I can check the records," he said, backing away.

"I wasn't going to lie." My voice went sharp. "I'm seventeen."

A pained look passed over his face. Just as soon as I noticed it, the look vanished. "Damn. Jailbait."

"Huh?"

"Nothing. Let's get you out of this car." He unstrapped himself and opened the door.

"How old are you?" I asked, scrambling behind him.

"Too old for you," I heard him mutter.

"That's not an age."

"Twenty."

"Okay, three years, and perfectly legal. That's not—"

"Going to happen. Look. I know what almost just happened in the car. I acknowledge it. But we can't do stuff like that. I'm your teacher."

"It's a volunteer program. This isn't school, and I'm not some silly schoolgirl lusting after my professor."

"Fine. I'm twenty, you're seventeen. What's more, you're in high school."

"I'll be a senior next school year."

A red Lexus coupe sped into the parking lot.

"That'll be your sister."

"Yep."

"See you later." He took three big, cowardly steps away from me.

"Really?" I cocked my head. "You're acting like I've got the cooties."

Alston spun on his heels and strode toward his car. Maya pulled closer to the curb, where I stood.

"Later, Jailbait." He opened his door and cranked the car.

"I'm not jailbait. I'm legal."

He rolled up his windows, as if to shut out my protest.

"Whatever." I stomped to Maya's coupe.

"Who's the cutie?" She jerked her head toward Alston's car.

"Alston. He's a poet."

"Nice." She wiggled her brows.

I snorted and turned toward the passenger window.

"What? We don't like him?"

"Meh. He's just a dumb boy."

"A dumb boy who writes poetry?"

"Yep. Exactly."

"His eyes look soulful."

I snorted. "He's fifty feet away. You can't see his eyes."

"Oh, I've seen them."

I didn't answer. Maya knew me too well. Besides that, we still weren't one hundred percent yet.

"Alrighty, then," Maya broke the silence, her voice light, despite her death grip around the steering wheel. "If you don't like him, then I don't either."

I sighed. "Good."

Okay, so I liked him. Deep down, I kind of liked that he was thoughtful enough to care about our difference in age. I had ten more months until I graduated. I could wait. But I wouldn't be making it easy for him.

"So . . . change of plans." Maya switched gears and sped toward the stoplight near the entrance. "Do you want to go to Lenny's tonight?"

"Really? But it's a Tuesday." My voice took on a little more enthusiasm than I was willing to give. Before we had our falling out, we always ate at the diner on Saturday mornings.

Maya shrugged. "Let's switch it up."

I wanted to pump my fist and yell *hell yeah!*

"Yeah, I could go for some greasy food."

Anything was better than Maya's healthy cooking kick. Every few years she'd claimed that she needed to detox or lose weight. And for six months straight it was baked chicken, broiled fish and the most tasteless steamed veggies known to man.

"I'm guessing you're not enjoying my recent cooking selections."

I shrugged and looked out the window, taking in the brilliant views of cow pastures and faded red fences.

Dad hated when Maya went on diets. She went on a diet late

last year so she wouldn't gain the "Holiday Ten," as she called them.

Last year Maya slapped a cookie out of Dad's hand when he offered it to her. He looked at her as if she'd sprouted horns and wings.

"Sorry, Daddy."

"Go in the kitchen and get a sandwich, Maya."

Maya shook her head. *"Ten more pounds and I'll quit."*

"And you'll look like a damned lollipop if you keep it up. The only thing you have left to lose is your goddamn mind. So quit the diet and let us enjoy the holidays in peace, for goodness' sake."

Suffice it to say, she quit that very night. I laughed out loud. I couldn't help it. Dad and Maya had epic arguments.

"What are you laughing about?" Maya's question brought me to the present. She had an uneasy smile on her face.

"Nothing." I shook my head and dropped the laughter.

Maya's smile dropped, too. I knew I was being unfair, but I just didn't know what to do and how to feel.

No, I knew how I felt. Angry. Angry at Mom for numbing her feelings and drinking away her pain. Angry at Dani and his band of merry thieves for pulling me into an illegal situation. And angry at Maya. Mom already felt alone. Dropping her off to rehab sure as heck wouldn't help her grieve.

I balled my fists. Most of all, I was mad at Dad for leaving us in this mess. For pitting Mom and Maya against each other. He had to know Maya wouldn't react well to his will stipulations. He had to know Mom would crumble without him.

Five minutes later, we'd arrived at Lenny's.

"Found a good spot." Maya swung her car into the open space.

I opened the passenger door and shimmied out. We were parked dangerously close to a silver Audi.

"I'm getting one of everything on the menu," Maya said as

she clicked the car alarm. She rushed toward the double doors with a bounce in her step like a kid entering the gates of Disney World.

I rolled my eyes. Maya was nearing the final stages of her diet, where she ate everything in sight, therefore negating at least a month's worth of dieting. Like Dad said, she really didn't need to lose weight.

Maya stopped at the entrance. I ran into her back.

"What the heck, Maya?"

Her shoulders were stiff, her attention at the back booth, our favorite spot.

Roland sat there with some other woman. I stood on my tip-toes to peak over Maya's shoulder. *Katy.* I'd met her at the last company picnic two years ago. Short shorts and a plaid cowboy shirt that stopped just above her navel and high heels.

There were two things I'd learned on that hot summer day: One, she had killer legs. Two, she absolutely hated Maya. Or maybe it was jealousy. She insulted Maya's hair. She had it curly and natural that day. She looked gorgeous. She told Maya she looked positively adorable, like Curly Sue, whoever she is.

"Hey, Maya, hey, Ryder." Franny's loud voice carried in the small restaurant.

Roland's attention snapped to us. He looked at Maya, something fierce in his eyes. Katy literally took one of her impossibly long claws on his chin and turned his head back. She whispered something and he said something back. She laughed. "Roland, you are just so silly." But silly sounded like sexy. And the way she crossed her legs and licked her lips, it was more than implied.

Maya didn't say a word. I couldn't see her face.

Franny looked at me, a worried look that made the lines on her face crease deeper. "Here you go, Ryder. Pick a spot. Any spot," she said unnecessarily.

"Let's go, Maya." I pulled at her elbow and guided her to

the front of the diner near the high-top counters. It was the only table available but not far enough away from Roland and Katy.

I dragged Maya and guided her to sit with her back toward the couple.

I sat facing them. Katy wiggled her fingers at me. I rolled my eyes and focused on my sister.

Maya's fingers were gripped around the large plastic menu on the table.

She cleared her throat. "What are you getting?"

"Let's just go home. We can get fast food."

"No. I don't want fast food."

"Okay, then." I blew a breath. "Let's get something to go. Or go to the steakhouse?"

"No. You don't like steak." She finally lifted her eyes to meet mine. My heart clenched, witnessing the hurt plastered on her face.

Her lips quivered and she blinked a few times. She swallowed. "It's okay. It's fine. I forgot to mention it, but Roland and I broke up."

"You broke up?" I squeaked.

"Shush." Maya shook her head. "We had a difference of opinion."

"What difference?" Roland loved my sister. He told me so and I believed him. Did he not listen to anything I'd said? God, adults could be so dumb.

"You know that promotion I was going for?"

"Yes." I nodded slowly. *Oh, God, please tell me she didn't get passed over.*

"I didn't get it. David was awarded junior partner."

"What?" I shouted.

"Lower. Your. Voice. Ryder," Maya said between clenched teeth. "Anyway, I quit my job."

"What? You did? When?"

"Last Friday."

"What the freak, Maya? Why didn't you tell me?" I leaned closer, my arms crossed. "I thought we were the freaking Wonder Twins? We"—I waved my finger between us—"don't keep secrets."

"Well. What does a Wonder Twin do when the other one refuses to speak? Talking to you is like talking to a wall. You're hot and cold and I'm . . ." She sighed. "God, I'm so damn tired." She massaged her forehead. "I'm tired of being run over. I'm tired of being taken for granted. And I . . . I was mad at Roland for not giving me the heads-up. He knew what was coming and he didn't warn me. He didn't protect me." She firmed her lips. Her eyes went hard. "People think because I'm this ballbuster, that I don't have feelings. But I do. And to be honest, between Jeanie's drunken tirades, your rebellion and losing out on a promotion that I more than deserved, I need a break."

"Hey, darlin's," Sweetie, our favorite waitress, smacked her gum. "What can I do ya for? The usual?"

Maya lowered her menu. "One of everything."

"What?" Sweetie smacked her gum, her eyebrows near her hairline.

I smiled at Sweetie. "She'll have the usual. Western omelet, but with egg whites. House fries and whole wheat toast. I'll have the short stack with a side of bacon."

"I want pancakes," Maya protested. "And bacon."

"Upgrade it to a full stack." I said to Sweetie. "We can split the pancakes and bacon."

"Two sweet teas?" Sweetie asked. "And a vanilla shake for you, Ryder?"

"You got it." I gave her a thumbs-up. Sweetie hurried away, yelling the order to Marty, the cook.

"I'm sorry, Maya. I've been kind of a brat."

Maya snorted. "Kind of?"

"Okay, a full-on brat. I didn't think about you and I'm sorry. Things are just . . ."

"Crazy. Sad. Fucked up."

"Yes. All of the above." I put up three fingers. "Girl Scout's honor, no more delinquent acts."

Maya crossed herself. "I would greatly appreciate it."

Sweetie returned with our sweet teas and my milkshake.

"Girl. Where do all of those calories go?"

I slurped down the milky-sugary goodness and burped a little. "I bike." Roland's eyes caught my attention. I stuck out my tongue and focused back on my sister.

"Roland keeps peeking over."

"I don't care," Maya said, lying straight through her teeth.

"Are you going to say something to him?"

"Hell, fuck no."

"I guess you're firm in that decision?"

"As firm as a rock."

"I thought it was solid as a rock?"

"Solid, firm." Maya shrugged. "The point is, I wouldn't talk to him, even if there was a guarantee to cure the common cold."

"Really? If you had a chance to cure the cold, you wouldn't do it? For the world? You would be forgoing, like, a Nobel Peace Prize."

"I said the cold, not freaking cancer." She cracked a smile.

I gave her a wide grin. I was happy to get that kicked-my-puppy look off her face. It didn't suit her, and I hated Katy and Roland for doing that to Maya.

Speaking of the she-devil, Katy sashayed our way.

"Oh, hey, Maya." She stopped in front of our table.

Maya sipped on her tea, looking straight at me.

"We miss you at the office. It's a shame you quit because you didn't make partner."

Maya stopped drinking her tea. "You need something, Katy?"

"Nope. I've got everything I want and could possibly need." Roland walked toward the table.

Holy crap.

"Maya." Roland stuffed his hands into his pockets.

I held my breath, waiting for Maya's reaction.

Her face became as placid as a windless day on the lake, but she didn't fool me. I could feel the strain it took to keep it together. They needed to leave, pronto.

"So anyway, snookums and I were just finishing up dinner. Then back to his place."

"That right?" Maya's voice went up a few octaves.

Katy's eyes lit. She knew she hit the jackpot. She must've known about Roland and Maya's relationship.

Katy turned to completely face Roland. She grabbed his shirt and pulled him in for a hot kiss. They kissed for five full seconds before he pulled his head away.

"Katy?" he said, his voice shaky.

"Let me freshen up for you, baby." She patted his chest and slithered like the snake she was toward the restroom.

My eyes swung to my sister. Her lips were quivering, her fists shaking.

Damn Roland and damn him for using Katy. From the way he swiped the pink lipstick smudges from his mouth, it was obvious he wasn't into her.

"Didn't take long for you to replace me." Maya's voice had turned subzero cold.

"There was nothing to replace. We were nothing, remember?"

"If you say so." Her voice sounded smooth and confident on the surface, with a hint of anger. But the way her chest heaved, the flare of her nose, all said barely suppressed rage.

But her eyes held no life, no anger, no joy.

My sister wasn't mad. She'd passed that emotion miles ago.

She was tipping over the edge of anger into angst. And if Roland and Katy stuck around for a few seconds longer, the mask would crumble.

I grabbed my milkshake and hurled it at Roland. Splatters of sticky white goop dripped from his face. He looked like a young, angry Santa Claus.

"Hey!" he yelled at me, wiping at the milkshake with his hands.

The restaurant went quiet.

"You're an idiot," I hissed at him.

He stopped his fruitless wiping. "She broke up with me."

I stood from my seat and leaned toward him. "I don't care. If you love someone, you don't give up. Maya lost our father, a promotion she richly deserved and she's taking care of me and my mom. She deserves someone to champion her. I thought you were the one." I thumped the back of my hand on his chest; a bit of shake clung to my fingers. "But obviously you weren't."

"That's enough, Ryder." Maya stood and tossed bills on the table. "Let's go."

I followed her and stopped near the door. Katy came out of the bathroom, gasping when she saw Roland.

Roland grabbed the napkins from the stand at our old table.

"Baby, what happened?" She looked between Roland and me and Maya.

Maya pushed opened the door. She hurried out.

I put up three fingers, like Celie from *The Color Purple*. "Till you do right by Maya, everything you do will fail."

"Are you putting some kind of voodoo curse on me?" Katy clutched her chest.

I rolled my eyes. She didn't even get *The Color Purple* movie reference. God, she sucked. "Have fun with your empty, boring girlfriend who doesn't get pop culture references to freaking classic movies, Roland." I stomped out the door.

Maya waved at me from the car. "Hurry up."

I got in and slammed the door shut.

Maya didn't speed off like I thought she would. "Did you . . . did I see you just pull a Celie on Katy?"

"Sure did. She thought I was cursing her with voodoo."

Maya threw her head back and laughed. "I should take away her black card." She sighed, shaking her head. "So apparently you aren't done with your delinquent acts."

I wouldn't apologize for the milkshake incident. I was happy to finally have Maya's back. She'd done so much for me. "That's the last time, I promise." I leaned over and gave her a quick hug. "We're in this together."

"Damn right, we are." Maya put out her fist and I bumped hers with mine.

We said the catchphrase together. "Wonder Twin powers, activate!"

CHAPTER 12

JEANIE
TOILET HUMOR

Friday morning, July 10th
124 days

I'd found the art studio on the second day of rehab. It was after hours and the door had been cracked, propped open by a toy troll. I left the hideous, pink-haired doll at the door.

When I stepped into the room, I took a deep breath. The smell of paint had been faint. After strolling about the room and checking out the materials on the shelf, I discovered it was acrylic paint. Acrylics were fine, but they weren't my paint of choice. My first love had been oils.

But paint was paint and I hadn't done anything in a long time, not since Ricky sank his hooks into me. So, on that day, I squeezed different colors onto the flimsy paper plate. Gold and green, purple and black and blue and orange. Before I dropped out of school, I painted in the art room. Sometimes, my art teacher, Mrs. Radley, managed to get her hands on oils. Even when I stopped going to school, she'd stash away paints for me, dropping them by the Piggly Wiggly just before closing.

I got to work. My hands guided the paintbrush across the

canvas. There was a little smile on my face as I painted the colorful feathers on my mystical creature.

Hours later, I stepped back to admire a Phoenix with its wings spread on top of his cage.

"That's a damn good picture. Especially with acrylics." Someone had snuck up on me. I glanced away from my picture and stared up into the face of a beautiful woman. She looked to be about my age, with tight, springy curls that rested just above her eyebrows.

"Name's Victoria but everyone calls me Vic." She stuck out her hand.

I glanced down at my paint-splattered hand. "Oh, umm . . . I don't want to get your hands dirty. But my name is Jeanie." I waved at her with my free hand.

Vic rolled her eyes. "I'm about to get started myself so go on, shake it."

I clasped her hands and shook.

"Nice to meet a fellow artist."

"Noooooo, no." I shook my head. "I'm no artist."

Vic snorted and rooted around her purse. "Your picture says otherwise, honey. That's good stuff."

I looked back at my Phoenix. Pride swelled inside my chest, knocking my heart a clean two inches to the side. It'd been fifteen years since I picked up a paintbrush. When I painted, I'd forgotten all sense of space and time. Doubt disappeared.

Vic took out a small basket with tiny tubes.

I took a peek and gasped. My fingers inched to touch the precious treasures. "I didn't know we had oils."

Vic snorted and snatched the basket away, placing it on the other side—away from me.

"*We* don't. Oils aren't allowed here." Vic rolled her eyes. "Dumbasses around here get high off anything. Now we have to use these lame-ass acrylics."

When she untwisted the cap, I could already smell the nutty aroma.

"How did you get them in here?"

"I know people." She narrowed her eyes. "You aren't going to tell anyone, are you?"

I shook my head. "Of course not. But . . . they'll probably smell it."

"Mhmmm." She squeezed a few dabs onto a plate and then swiped her brush in one. "It's like perfume, isn't it?"

She sniffed it a little *too* hard, if you ask me.

"What are you in here for?" I asked.

"I took the phrase 'It's five o'clock somewhere' a little too seriously."

"Huh?"

"I like cocktails." She shrugged. "So, sue me." She busied herself with setting up her station. Her eyes darting here and there, but not at me.

"Is it all right for me to smell the oils, at least?" I joked, hoping to cut the tension.

"Smells are free. Oils are not. Speaking of which . . ." She grabbed her purse and moved some things around. She shook a can. "Coffee beans." She pulled out a few cotton balls, and two small bottles of peppermint and vanilla extracts.

"Do you mind dabbing the peppermint and vanilla on the cotton balls? You can place them around the room to cut the fumes."

"Sure." This was the most action I'd had in days. I placed cotton balls throughout the room. "We aren't going to get in trouble, are we?"

Vic looked up from her canvas. She'd already started mixing. "Most of the residents are sleeping. Counselors have locked up. I propped Orlando, the troll doll, at the door, while Carl distracted Lydia."

I didn't know of a Carl. Lydia was the clinical liaison who

stayed on campus, but it didn't seem too complicated to sneak into the art studio at night. And what could they do if I got caught? Kick me out?

"Would it be all right if I stuck around?" I was missing home and I wanted to paint a picture of our lake.

"Fine by me." She smoothed her hand over the canvas and flicked the surface. "God, these are cheap. Needs more weight, more structure."

We painted, me just a few more hours before I finished up. Vic was about a third of the way finished.

"You really are a nice artist." Vic broke our companionable silence. "I love the golds of the tree and how the path leading to the lake kind of meanders. Really nice composition. And it's a nice proportion from the boat to the lake."

I had no idea what she was talking about, but I shook my head. "Thanks. That's what I was going for. Strong composition and proportions."

She smirked. "You don't know what the hell I'm talking about, do you?"

"No idea. But like I told you, I'm not an artist. This used to be a hobby until . . ."

"Until?"

"Until it wasn't." I cleared my throat and blocked out memories of Ricky.

"Uh-huh."

"How long have you been an artist?" I asked Vic.

"I've been painting for thirty years." She didn't offer any other information.

"Well, okay." I stretched my hands over my head and arched my back. "I'll see you around."

She nodded. "Come to class tomorrow. You get the choice between a beach or an affirmation."

"I could paint a beach."

"Eh. Go for the affirmation, you get more freedom that way.

The beach one is one of those paint-by-numbers deals. An artist like you—and you *are* an artist—will shrivel up and die from boredom."

I nodded and agreed. Listening to someone telling me what to do wasn't something I'd want. I had enough of that at home.

"Okay. I'll see you tomorrow."

"Four o'clock," Vic said, still focused on her canvas.

"Four o'clock," I repeated.

Saturday afternoon, July 11th
125 days

The next day, I was back in class and seated in the back row. The setup seemed more formal compared to last night. The paints were nicely proportioned on the plates. There was an easel up front, where I assumed the instructor would show us what to do.

I hummed along to Queen, one of my favorite songs, "The Show Must Go On," that blasted through the speakers. I went with the affirmation painting. They gave us a few thought starters and I chose the affirmation: *I like the person I'm becoming.* I snorted. Maybe one day I'd believe it. Truth was, I hated myself. I hated looking at myself in the mirror. I hated the bags under my eyes and my pasty skin and dull, dank hair. I hated this place, and I hated Maya for forcing me into this zoo for freaks who failed at life.

The only thing I didn't hate, at the moment, was painting.

This morning, I put more care into my appearance. A white apron with paint splotches covered my chinos and silk shirt. I pretended that instead of completing ten days of rehab, I was at a girl's night out at the Fizzy Paint—a place where you could bring in bottles of wine and snacks, and paint with friends. Trixie and I were joking about our husbands. My friends gossiped about folks around town.

"You're here." Vic slung her purse, a much smaller one, on the open table in the back of the room.

"I said I'd come."

"Yeah, but four o'clock has horseback riding and I'd figured you might want to do that."

I wrinkled my nose. "Why on earth would I want to ride a horse?"

"No reason." She scanned me. "I just took you for a horse person."

"Because white people love horses?"

Vic kind of shrugged her thin shoulders. She didn't seem all that embarrassed by her assumption.

"That's a stereotype," I pressed on. "Besides, my late husband loved to go horseback riding."

I smiled at the memory. He looked like a sexy cowboy.

"Which supports my point . . ." Vic waved a hand.

"My husband was black." I rolled my eyes.

"Oh, well, my bad. You like painting and hate horses. Got it, girl."

"Welcome, welcome. I see some new faces out there. My name is Dina and I'll be your instructor for tonight."

Vic leaned over to me and whispered, "Dina's got zero talent, but lots of enthusiasm."

Dina continued, unaware of Vic's insult. "You have the choice to paint your affirmation. If you look along the wall, you'll see some examples I've painted."

I looked at colorful paintings like "*You can do it, stronger than yesterday, everyday I'm better.*"

"But if you want to paint a picture, today's theme is *Life's a beach.*"

"More like a bitch," Vic muttered.

I covered my mouth and smothered my laugh. "Shut. Up." I whispered back to her.

"Who's ready to have fun?" Dina shouted as she clapped.

There were a few sad attempts at clapping with her. Mine included.

Vic placed her hand over mine and shook her head. "Don't do that."

After paint class, I said my goodbyes to Vic and walked around campus. Someone invited me to play Scrabble, but I declined. One, it reminded me of Joseph and Ryder. It was their favorite game. And two, I was terrible at Scrabble. I wasn't good at figuring out a way to compound words and get a larger score. It made me feel dumb, though Judge and Ryder never made me feel that way.

Instead of joining the game, I sat in front of the television, on the far end of a large couch that someone else occupied.

A man clicked the remote and looked at me. "Going back and forth between the games. You mind?"

I shrugged. I watched football but I never could get into it. I hated the violence. But since I told the stranger that I didn't mind it, I watched for fifteen minutes and then headed to my room.

I rounded the corner and paused at the door, key in hand. Someone was singing in my apartment.

The program director said there was a possibility for me to have a roommate. Looked like it happened.

I took a deep breath. *Here goes nothing.* After twisting the key into the lock, I pushed the door open.

"Well, hey there." Vic snapped to the music and bobbed her head. Music drifted from the television from a woman singing on stage.

"Vic . . . wh-what . . ." I licked my lips. "What are you doing here?"

Vic grabbed the remote and muted the TV. "Apparently I have a drinking problem."

"I . . . yeah, I know that, but what are you doing here . . . in my apartment?"

Vic snorted. "Is that what you're calling this li'l box?" She waved her hand about. "An apartment?"

"What I'm saying is, I just met you last night, so I'm assuming you were assigned to a different room." I walked into the kitchen to grab a bottled water.

"Bingo." Vic pointed at me. "But me and Delilah, we go way back, and girl, let me tell you, we have *never* gotten along. So, I asked to be switched to the room with the sad, quiet white girl."

I rolled my eyes. "I'm not the sad, quiet white girl."

"Sure, you are. But hey, we've all got our ghosts. I figured me and you . . . we can help each other out. Do some group therapy. Tell the counselors what they want to hear, and we can get out sooner rather than later."

"We can get out sooner?"

"You can always sign yourself out. The goal is to show them and your family you're good, but not stay here longer than necessary."

She seemed to know a lot about this process. Too much. And why should I take the advice from someone who obviously couldn't get it together?

I swallowed my water as I thought through my next words. "You seem to know a lot about this stuff . . . how many times have you been here?"

Vic's cocky smile dropped. "A few times. But don't worry about me. I've got a feeling this'll be my last time." She winked. "Wanna sneak out of here and paint?"

"Oils?" I asked, my voice hopeful.

"I've gotcha back, girl. Perks of being my roomie." She hopped from the couch and pressed the record button. "You like *Pride and Prejudice*? It's coming on at eight."

"Yeah." I nodded like a well-behaved puppy. Ryder and I used to curl up and watch it every time it came on cable. Or if one of us had a bad day, we'd pull out the DVD. "Which version?"

"Which one is your favorite?" she quickly countered, hands on her hips, like my answer meant the beginning or end of our fledging friendship.

"The one with Colin Firth. I like that it's a series, too."

"Hmm." She relaxed her stance. "You love to paint, and you like the Colin Firth version the best. You might just be best friend material."

Sunday evening, July 12th
126 days

I woke up early and put on a full face. Joseph used to call my makeup war paint. Moisturize and on top of that, primer, and on top of that, concealer and foundation, bronzer and two shades from my nude eyeshadow palette.

Makeup gave me the boost and protection I so desperately needed for group therapy.

I'd avoided it for about a week, but Dr. Mitra strongly suggested to take advantage of all resources available. But it'd been Vic's advice about showing progress that stuck with me. Group therapy would show Ryder and Maya that I put in the work to get better.

I'd passed by the group therapy room a few times. It seemed like an ordinary office. There were two big sofas and a desk, but right dab in the center of the room were several seats set up in a circle.

A few days ago, I sat outside of the room, waiting for the group to file out.

I studied their faces. Did they look happy, sad? Did it help, were they really changed? I'd notice a range of emotions—deep pain or stark relief; one of the women even skipped out of the room.

God, I had no desire to discuss my shameful mistakes. No one would understand putting your daughter's life in danger, embarrassing her in front of a court-ordered volunteer service, no less.

There were only six people today, including me. A tall woman named Charlene. I'd met her on my first day at lunch. A squat man, balding with a rat tail. I'd seen him and his rat tail around, but I didn't know his name. Someone else passing by said, "Hey, Dodger," so I guess that was his name. The other person was a young man with intense blue eyes. His gray V-neck shirt stuck to his hairy chest. His knees jumped as much as his eyes darted around the room. Another guy, middle aged, who reminded me of Daddy, had stick-thin arms and legs, with a potbelly. Last but not least, Vic whirled in, her clothes and makeup flawless and fabulous.

"Hey, girl." She waved and sat beside me.

I couldn't get away from her. But the way she grinned at me, all sunshine and hope, maybe I didn't really want to get away.

"Welcome, welcome, everyone," the man with the potbelly greeted. "I'm Ray Freemont, and I'll be leading group today."

The young man in the gray T-shirt raised his hand, though his head hung low. "I-I want to share something, share my s-stuff today."

The room went silent. Vic folded her hands across her lap. Ray, whose legs were crossed, leaned forward after a few tense and awkward seconds. "Go ahead and share with us, James."

James took deep breaths. He swallowed so hard it was like he'd gulped down a gallon of water.

"My mom's my best friend. I-I know it sounds silly. That a twenty-three-year-old guy is best friends with his mom, but it's true. I-I've got other friends. Girls and guys my age, but Mom is the best."

"It's not silly." Vic shook her head and smiled. "My two girls are my world. I would love it if they considered me their best friend. I think that's really sweet."

James didn't seem affected by Vic's praise. He just bounced his knees and wrung his hands together.

"She, umm . . . she got injured on the job. Hurt her back and was in a lot of pain. I took care of her. Got her around, got her meds, made sure she had food and a clean home. She did it for me when I was young, and I didn't mind. But . . . what she didn't know was that I was already an addict. It started off slow but then ramped up to heroin, coke, anything that got me high. And so, I . . . I took them, the drugs. Her drugs. One day she ran out, before the next refill. She was in so much pain. Her eyes were glazed over. She was sweaty all over and scream-ing, 'Help me! Help me, baby.'"

He took a ragged breath, his nose squeaked like a toy duck. "I . . . I took them all. The only thing I could give her was Tylenol." He swiped at the tears with the heel of his hand. "God, I'm such a jerk. I'm a bad son."

"Hey, now," Charlene said, her voice maternal and soothing. "We've all done things we aren't proud of." She tucked her hair behind her ears. "When I was drinking, I stole things from my job, I forgot to pick up my daughter from swim lessons while my husband was out of town. I was so drunk I didn't pick up the phone. My mother, who lived two hours away, had to get my daughter."

My skin prickled as I took in Charlene. She was just like me—too busy drinking to look after her daughter. I uncurled my fingers and smoothed them against my chinos.

"Yeah, but you didn't steal the one thing that brought your family relief."

"I've stolen before," Vic admitted. "If you think about it, we all have." James stopped bouncing his knees and, for a brief moment, he looked up at Vic.

Vic continued. "I robbed my family of their time, time taking care of me, picking up the broken pieces of whatever distraction I caused. I've robbed them of their peace of mind. One time my daughter told me her biggest fear is coming home and finding me dead in my own vomit. So yeah, maybe I didn't steal a pill. But I took away from my family. I know how you feel, James. Likely, we all do." She looked at everyone in the group. A few of us nodded. I didn't.

"It's really awesome you're sharing with us," Ray cut in. "What made you share today?"

James shrugged, and rocked back and forth.

"Come now. What changed? What you did today was incredible."

"I . . ." He sighed. "I guess I'm tired of feeling so wound up. I come here and it's good to hear what everyone else shares. But sometimes I don't feel better. Anyway, the last time I was here my stomach was hurting and, umm . . . yeah, well, I took a dump."

"A what?" Vic asked.

"A dump. You know, drop a load, chop a log? Anyway, I felt better. So, it occurred to me that if I dropped a load on you guys, like I did after my stomach hurt, I could feel better emotionally, too."

"Umm, excuse me." Vic raised her hand. "Can you never, in your entire life, say that you took a dump on us?"

Oh, my Lord. I cupped both hands over my mouth and hunched over. My shoulders shook.

James looked at me, the corners of his intense eyes crinkled, and he laughed right along with me.

Vic finally cracked and laughed, and soon others joined us.

"There has to be a better way to say it," Charlene said between fits of giggles.

I raised my hand. "I prefer to call it the royal squat."

The room erupted in more laughter. Vic gave me a high five.

Ray shook his head. "You guys are something else."

I laughed, looking at the group. They were in the trenches with me, struggling to overcome and recover our old lives. Maybe, just maybe I could give this group thing a real chance.

CHAPTER 13

MAYA
THE SOUTH RISES AGAIN

Monday morning, July 13th
127 days

I sat at my dad's old desk in his home office, staring at my unfinished biography on my new website. When I'd swiped the one off the firm's website, I was surprised they hadn't already removed me, nor had they added David as partner.

I'd managed to write that my seven years of experience, undergrad and law degrees, and my passion for pro bono civil rights cases led me to open Maya Donaldson and Associates. Ha. There were no associates. I couldn't afford to rent office space without a steady salary, and after I created my bio, I had an ever-growing to-do list like registering my business and making sure I had all the rules and regulations for practicing law out of my home.

There was no way in hell I could use the house now. I could just imagine Jeanie barging into a client meeting with a pint clutched in her hands.

"One thing at a time."

"Talking to yourself again?" Ryder hopped onto the overstuffed love seat across from the desk.

"Always."

"Whatcha doing?"

"Updating my bio. I just hired someone to do my website."

"The person who did the website for your friend from law school?"

"Yes. Her templates are simple and easy to use and she's a good copywriter, too. She said something about optimizing the website for SEO to make it searchable."

Ryder nodded. "Yeah, I liked her, too. Just thought she was too expensive."

"Don't worry about me, young Padawan. I talked her down. Besides that, we aren't in the poor house. Dad set us up nice. And I have a decent savings."

"I know . . . I'm just . . . I'm sorry you didn't make partner. I can't help but think it's Mom's fault."

Oh, it is. I sighed, burying my frustrations. "The firm made their choice. I'm the one who decided to quit."

"Do you regret it?"

"No." I shook my head. "I know my worth. They'll figure it out once David screws something up."

Ryder fiddled with the strings on her jacket. When she started chewing on her lip, I knew something was up.

"What's going on? And stop gnawing on your lip."

"Nothing." She looked over my head, focusing on Daddy's law degree. "Did Roland text you again?"

Something painful swirled in my chest.

"Yep." I pretended to type something important. It was a bunch of gibberish.

"What did he want?"

"If you're worried about him being mad about the milk-shake—"

"No. I stand behind my decision."

"You're telling me you thought about the consequences of throwing your vanilla shake in his face?"

She shook her head, her eyes now on me. "Yes, I did. The pros: He learns to not be a jerk-face. The cons: He presses charges." Ryder bent over and knocked on the wood desk. "So far, no cops have been by."

Lately. I kept the snarky thought to myself. We were just getting over the hump of our relationship.

"Anyway . . . what did he say?"

"He reiterated that he did nothing wrong and he doesn't understand why I'm so upset." I went back to typing more gibberish.

"What else?" Ryder asked.

I sighed, reached for my phone and pressed my thumb against the button to open it. After it scanned my thumbprint, I tossed it to her. "Here. Read it yourself."

Ryder scrolled through my phone. "Mhmmm."

"Mhmm, what?"

"Did you really tell him that you didn't love him?"

"I did."

"Why?"

"Because I don't."

"Maya . . ." Ryder groaned.

I continued typing.

"Stop it," Ryder snapped. "You usually have a little wrinkle between your eyebrows when you're working. It's not there, you big faker."

"Fine." I pushed away from the desk. "He caught feelings. He knew what the deal was, and I don't owe him anything. I told him I wasn't looking for anything serious. He agreed and then continued to press me about it. I'm not the monster here. He lied to me."

"He didn't lie." Ryder shook her head. "Maybe the arrangement worked out before but then he fell in love. We're all human and it's our right to change our opinions and feelings.

Maybe you should reach out? Maybe you should face your feelings?"

"And maybe you should drop the Iyanla Vanzant act and stop trying to *fix my life*, ma'am. I've got this. Now, enough about me." I closed my laptop. Nothing was happening today, anyway. I waved my fingers. "C'mon, now. I know something is up with you. Save me the ten-thousand what's-wrongs and just tell me already."

"I . . . umm . . . Grandma Sarah wants me to come over."

I took a deep breath and massaged my temples. "Grandma Sarah *and* Grandpa Jim." They were founding fathers–type racists. And I was pretty sure Grandpa Jim owned a few white sheets with eye- and mouth-hole cutouts.

"Y-yeah."

"To their house?"

House was a loose term. There was nothing wrong with trailers, but that damn trailer was a health hazard—nothing but a pile of Pabst beer cans and cigarette butts.

Ryder nodded again. "I know you don't like them—"

"I don't like them because they hate me and hated my father because we're black."

"I know, but—"

"Need I remind you that they cut your mom off? And they refused to go to the wedding and then went about spreading rumors about how my father blackmailed their precious daughter into marrying him."

Ryder flinched. "I know they aren't good people . . ."

"But you still love them."

"Yeah. Grandma Sarah isn't all that bad. Mom never told me much about her childhood, but I think . . . I think Grandpa hit them."

I leaned forward, a pinprick of sympathy blooming in my gut for Jeanie. "That may be true, but now you want me to be okay with letting you go to your grandparents' house?" I shook my head. "I'm sorry, but I can't. As your temporary guardian, I say no."

"Maya . . ." Ryder rubbed her forehead. "I'm trying to be honest with you. But I do intend to see my grandparents. They have questions about Mom, and my father's parents are spreading rumors around town. If you keep hiding me, things will get even more out of hand."

"If you think for a second I'll allow Ricky's parents to take you, then you are sorely mistaken."

"I know, but . . . I just want to talk to them. Hey, maybe we can just ask both sets to come here? Then they'll see how I am and that you're taking good care of me."

"Oh sure." I gave Ryder a fake smile. "Let's host a tea party for your racist-ass grandparents."

"Maya—"

"We'll have the 'I Wish I Was in Dixie' blasting in the background."

"Maya—"

"I'll hang a little Confederate flag in the front. That should make them feel right at home."

"Maya!" Ryder jumped from her seat. "I realize what I'm asking for is difficult. But I'm trying my best to manage the situation. I . . ." She sighed. "I went through Mom's phone. My father had been texting her the day she went off the deep end and came to the community center. He said . . . he said some mean things. Taunted Mom about taking me away. I think she got scared. Now suddenly Grandma Sarah calls me every day about meeting up with them and my other grands. I think they got to her."

"Got to whom?"

"Grandma Sarah. I think she's worried about me and Mom. Anyway, I want to show them that we are fine."

"And what do we say about your missing mother?"

"She's on vacation, a sabbatical or whatever like *Eat, Pray, Love*. She loved that book, you know."

I leaned back, still shaking my head. "Daddy's probably rolling in his grave. Do you know, do you even realize the shit those four put Daddy through?"

They'd even contacted the state bar, lying about things he'd done. Thankfully everything had been cleared up.

I'd heard my dad go off about them a few times when he thought I wasn't around. But looking at Ryder, her thin lips in a straight line and her jaw set, I realized if they didn't come here, then she would go over there. And there was no way in hell I'd allow her to go to that rat trap.

"Fine. They can come over. No more than an hour. However, I reserve the right to kick them out if they do anything to piss me off."

"Yes. Thank you!" Ryder walked to the desk. I know she wanted to give me a hug. I shook my head. "Nope. I need time." I waved her off. "Set up the details and keep me in the loop." And while she did that, I would figure out the *real* reason her grandparents were trying to slide their way into her gullible heart. I had a feeling I already knew the answer: Money.

Saturday afternoon, July 18th
132 days

Ryder flitted around as she prepared for her Tea Party with the Mussolinis. I sat on the couch with a bag of potato chips in hand. I'd been binge eating ever since we decided to bring Ryder's grandparents to my father's house. There was a hole in my stomach and nothing I did could fill it.

Ryder had made a charcuterie and cheese board, small sandwiches, tea and lemonade. The doorbell rang. My stomach dropped to my feet.

Ryder snapped up from her bent position. "They're here."

"Joy."

"I'm going to get the door."

"Go ahead." I dug into the bag of chips and shoveled more into my mouth. "I'll be here," I said, munching on my chips.

I grabbed a cocktail napkin and wiped at the grease on my palm.

"Hey, Grandma." I heard Ryder greet one of her grand-mothers. "Thank you for coming."

I rolled my eyes, mentally gearing up for battle. Steps grew closer and voices louder. "This is nice," Sarah said, coming into the dining room.

"Oh." The older woman jumped when she noticed me, clutching her fake pearls with her dingy white gloves. Her long cotton dress swished about her ankles when she turned away from me to face Ryder.

Jim Billy had on a faded black shirt with a woman in a bikini stretched out on a race car. He took off his trucker hat, folded and stuffed it into his back pocket. "What is she doin' here?" he asked, his beady brown eyes focused on me.

I looked him dead in the eyes. "She owns this house, Jim Bob."

"It's Jim Billy."

"Whatever." I waved toward the couch. "Take a seat. Or don't."

"Have an hors d'oeuvre, Grandma." Ryder sat on the oppo-site side. She wore a dress, too, a yellow sundress, but she still had on her favorite black Chucks.

Sarah leaned over, grabbed a small plate and started stack-ing meat and cheese on the plates. "This looks so good. Umm . . . wh-who made it?" She shot me a nervous glance.

Really?

"I did." Ryder smiled.

Jim Billy rubbed his stomach. "You got any beer?"

"No, sir." Ryder placed the tray on the center of the table, ignoring the daggers I was shooting at her back.

"Goddamn. Sarah," his voice boomed. "Go get my six-pack out of the car."

"Sit down, Sarah." I shook my head. "I don't allow beer in my home."

Jim Billy cursed under his breath. He hadn't said anything racist *yet,* so I kept my peace.

"Where's my baby girl?" Jim Billy's loud voice robbed the forced serenity in the room.

"She's on vacation," I answered, before Ryder could tumble over a lie.

"Huh. Where'd she go?" He didn't ask me. He had his attention on Ryder.

"To Jamaica," I cut in again. "She's trying to get her groove back. But don't worry, this time he'll be younger." I winked.

"My lord." Sarah put down her plate.

The doorbell rang again. "Oh, joy. Must be your other grandparents. I'll go get them."

I hopped from my seat before anyone could argue. I opened the door and found Ricky. I could see why young Jeanie fell for him. He had beautiful blue eyes, like his daughter. But instead of being soulful, they were soulless. His dirty blond hair was shaggy, hanging just below his ears.

"Why are you here, Ricky?"

"I've come to see my baby girl."

"Sure, you have." I opened the door. "You've got twenty minutes and then you're out of here."

"I know my rights."

"And I've got the right to kick your raggedy, no-good ass out of my home."

Ricky sucked his teeth and leaned inside the doorframe. "Ah, them's fightin' words, Hoss," he said, quoting a country song I hated.

"And I've got friends in low places. And those friends I've got are bounty hunters. Last I checked, you're wanted in Georgia, Colorado and Florida."

A cop siren whooped behind him. Ricky jumped. I waved at one of my deputy friends who'd agreed to drive around the neighborhood until the sons and daughters of the Confederacy were gone.

"You've got pigs circling the neighborhood?"

"Of course. And if I don't answer my phone or step outside every ten minutes they're coming inside. Just in case you get ideas. Now do please come in." I waved him inside.

"Father." Ryder stood with a tray in her hand. "I didn't know you were coming."

"Yeah. Your grandpa invited me. My folks can't make it, though. Something came up."

I bet.

"Sweet tea, Father?" Ryder offered him a glass.

"Hell, no, I want a beer. And what's with that funny stuff? Give your *daddy* a hug."

Ryder looked down at her shoes.

"C'mon, girl."

"Remember our chat, Ricky," I warned, wagging a finger in his direction. "Friends in low places. And we won't be serving beer. You won't be here long enough to drink, anyway."

"Fine."

Ryder settled into her chair and grabbed a glass of lemonade.

"So again, what brings everyone here? Perhaps it's my daddy's money that's got you sniffing around. I know none of you give a damn about Jeanie."

Jim Billy finally acknowledged me. "I done heard the rumors 'round town. Can't believe I raised a little whore who can't hold her liquor."

Ryder slammed down her glass of lemonade.

Jeanie couldn't hold her liquor, but she wasn't sexing anyone in town. That, I knew for sure. She didn't deserve her father's vicious lies.

"Don't." Ryder's voice went cold. "Don't talk about Mom that way."

"Jim Billy." I straightened my spine. "She is your daughter and she deserves respect."

"Shee-it!" Jim Billy yelled.

Come to think of it, he always yelled.

"That girl has been a pain in my ass since the day she was born. Always needing something. Always thinking her shit don't stink. Telling me that I was a drunk. Now look at her." He snorted. "Now she's got overpaid crackpots blowing sunshine up her ass. Waste of money if you ask me. Always knew she was a loser."

"I told you. She's in Jamaica, getting her groove back."

"What in the Sam hell does that mean? Is that some black talk?"

"*Black* talk?"

"Grandpa," Ryder admonished.

"Black talk." He grinned, a yellowed tooth on display. "You know, that slang stuff."

"It's a cultural reference. Getting her groove back means she's getting her freak on."

"Gross, Maya." Ryder groaned, her face turning beet red.

Jim Billy snorted. "Huh, yeah. Guess she can't help herself. Once a nig—"

"Don't you dare!" I stormed over to his seat. I leaned down and got close to his face. So close, I could smell cheap beer on his breath.

"My father, Joseph Ennis Donaldson, was a great man. So great, you don't even deserve to utter his name, sit on his chairs, be in his home and breathe the same air that he once breathed. He saved lives. You've ruined them. He gave young people of all colors opportunities to reach their dreams. Have you ever had a dream? His legacy will live on, through me, and despite your best intentions, Ryder. He was her father. And if you think coming over here, sniffing around my house and asking about your daughter, and thinking you're getting custody of Ryder or possession of what my father left me or Ryder or Jeanie, you've got another thing coming." I returned to my seat.

Jim Billy twisted his lips into an ugly grimace. "You don't know a damn thing about me."

"Yes, I do, Jimmy. I know you go down to the Slippery Frog on Fridays and Saturdays. I know you've got a side piece and give her that extra check you got when you messed up your hand during your short stint at the factory."

Sarah went stiff. Bet she knew about the side piece.

"I also know what happened on Thursday, March fifth, of last year. I know whose got your balls in a bind. And I know you *think* my daddy's money is going to buy you out of it, but no. No, no, no, Jim Billy."

"Fuck you, you stupid bitch."

"I may be a bitch, but I'm a smart one. Now, show's over. Get the hell out of my house. You've got two minutes or I'm asking Officer Jones to take you all to jail for trespassing. Ryder, please escort your grandparents and sperm donor out of my house."

A look of pure gratitude slid over her face. She exhaled and waved at her guests. "Let's go. Maya isn't playing games about having you arrested."

Ricky shot out of his seat. "See you later, baby girl."

"Go on." I shooed Jim and Sarah. "Our little tea party is over."

Monday morning, July 20th
134 days

"May I speak to Maya Donaldson?"

"Speaking." I didn't ask who was calling. I had the number saved.

"I'm Lydia Collins, calling on behalf of Jeanie Donaldson, your . . . stepmother, correct?"

Technically.

"She's my late father's wife, yes. Is she okay?"

"Yes, yes. She's stepping through recovery well and she's participating in group and one-on-one therapy. I'm calling because of therapy. One of the last steps we take, and it's totally optional, but we allow our patients to bring in friends and family. Those who've been impacted by their choices."

"Like an intervention?"

"No. At this point an intervention isn't needed since they're already in the program. Think of this as family therapy. We listen to each other, get an understanding of what led Jeanie to her decisions, get her point of view and some of the strides she's taking to get better. It can be very helpful, but it can also be very . . . stressful. We want to create a kind and supportive environment."

"Are you telling me you don't want me to tell her how I truly feel?"

"No. Jeanie . . . only wants to speak to Ryder."

"Now you want me to put my sister in an emotionally painful situation to make Jeanie feel better?"

I could see it now. Jeanie crying, asking for forgiveness. Ryder feeling guilty and sad. Then the cycle repeats again.

Jeanie has a weak moment and goes back to alcohol. And after meeting her horrible-ass parents, I could see what drove her to the bottle.

"Listen, Maya. I know this is a tough decision, but, either way, a conversation will happen between the two of them. And it should happen. This isn't something that should be swept under the rug."

"I know that, but—"

"Wouldn't you rather it be in a controlled environment with professionals equipped to help?"

"I . . . let me speak to Ryder. See what she says."

"Thank you, Maya. I'd appreciate it, and I'm sure Jeanie does, too."

I live for her approval.

"I'll give you a call later this week. When will this conversation take place, should Ryder agree?"

"In a few weeks. The week before she returns home."

"Okay, I'll let you know."

"Thank you. I look forward to your call."

"Mhmm. Bye now."

I clicked off the phone and slung myself back on the pillows. Thankfully, Ryder was at the community center. I needed space. I needed to think.

There were two places that made me happy. Target and the boat.

"I'll do both." We needed cleaning supplies and soap, and I'd planned to clean out Daddy's office. It was time.

Plan in place, I threw on sweats, a tank top, and a hat to cover my head. When the Target opened a few years ago it had been received with fanfare in our small little town. There was a coffee shop attached, great hot dogs and the colorful setup always made me happy. You had to find the little things living in a small town. Back in Atlanta, you could practically trip over fun things to do.

After the short drive to the store, I grabbed a bright red cart and pushed it down the aisle. There wasn't a lot of foot traffic around the store—just as I expected on a lazy Monday morning. I had just rounded the corner when I noticed a familiar tight ass in a pair of fitted blue slacks.

Shit. Shit. Shit. Turn around. Be quiet. I turned, the cart squeaked.

"Maya."

I looked up to the ceiling for strength. One thing's for sure: this town was too small, and I needed to get the hell out of dodge. I lowered my eyes and took in my ex . . . boss. Yes, that was it.

"Roland."

He moved closer, a plastic basket in hand. I stole a peek at the goods. Deodorant, socks, a bag of lettuce. No condoms but candles. What in the hell did he need candles for?

Katy probably loves candles.

"How are you?" He gave me a once-over.

I tugged at my hat and fidgeted with my tank top. This might have been the first time he'd seen me dressed like a bum. I tried to shrug it off, but I couldn't. I wanted to look my best. I bet Katy never wore sweats and T-shirts.

"Oh, I'm fine. I'm great. You?"

"Fine. Have you found something else?"

"Something else?"

He raised an eyebrow. "A job."

"Oh, no. I'm doing my own thing."

"Really?" He smiled. "Are you going to give us a run for our money?"

"No." I shook my head. "Civil rights. I decided to *follow my heart.*"

"Follow your heart." His smile disappeared. "Glad to hear it." His voice went from soft to sarcastic.

"And how's Katy?" I matched his bitchy tone. *God, why did I ask? Why, why, why?*

"Do you really want to know?" His voice went deep. Cold.

No. Yes. Maybe? God, he was still with her. Touching her and holding her and doing all the things he used to do with me. Was I that replaceable? Did I mean so little to him?

You pushed him away.

"Good seeing you, Roland." I maneuvered my cart around him, dashing away before I said something else. Before he could see my regret.

Do not cry. Do not break down in the middle of Target.

I abandoned the cart and jogged to my car. Tears threatened to burst forth. I could smell the salt of my tears, like the eve of a storm at sea. *Not here, not now.* I ground my teeth every time tears clogged my throat. For the angry bursts that sped my pulse, I smashed the gas pedal. My baby purred. She wasn't used to the speed, but she could handle it.

In seven minutes flat, I made it home. But still, I couldn't relax. Not yet.

I pulled the dingy from the dock, untied the rope and pushed myself off with the oar. I don't know how long I paddled.

Each stroke pushed me further away from my problems. No one could hurt me, no one could pierce through the peaceful mists over the lake.

"Sorry, Maya. You're just not partner material."

My heart clanged like an old church bell.

"Did you let them see you cry?"

"No, Daddy."

"Good. Be a shark, Baby Girl. Otherwise, the world will eat you whole."

The muscles in my biceps stretched like a rubber band ready to pop. I couldn't stop moving. I needed distance away from everyone and everything that embarrassed me, hurt me, ripped my heart away.

"Everyone should know how much of a witch you are."

A breeze caressed my cheeks. Soft trickles of rain plopped against the water and slid over me. It cooled the fire inside. I usually ran away from the storm, but today I was running from something much more dangerous than nature.

I needed the cool, the clean, the freedom.

The drops bounced from the lake, growing from a soft touch to a barreling force. My vision blurred, forcing me to close my eyes. Raindrops thumped against my forehead.

I lifted the paddle and placed it inside the boat. Tilting my head back, I let the rain blend with my tears. Why did Daddy have to die? Why did he leave me with this mess?

"What do you want from me?" I yelled. No one could hear me. Water hit the back of my throat. I pushed up and coughed out the water in my lungs.

God sends rain to the just and unjust. Daddy's familiar voice flooded my senses.

Who am I? Just or unjust? The shark or the prey?

God sends rain to the just and unjust, his voice said again in that patient way of his.

"I don't know what that means, Daddy," I whispered to him. The rain let up, leaving as quickly as it came.

CHAPTER 14

RYDER
A DREAM DEFERRED

Monday afternoon, July 20ᵗʰ
134 days

I twisted the key and turned off the ignition of Alston's Camry. I looked over at him; my breath hitched as I took in his handsome profile. The strength in his forearms when he grabbed the wheel before I hit a curb. His smile—sometimes it was easy, a light boyishness that I imagined he had before his parents' issues smothered him. Or maybe he found his smile after he left his home. Then there was the smile he reserved when he found a lovely line in my poetry.

My poetry. It wasn't healthy, but I became a little possessive over his smile.

Sometimes, it was harder to pull a smile from him, sometimes his shoulders stooped forward, like the weight of the world rested on them. On those days, I tossed out a topic for him to freestyle. Freestyles made him happy, free. It was my way of releasing him from the demons that roamed.

The thing is, I knew I could make him happy. I knew how to make him smile, and I figured that was at least a start.

He smiled easy today. *Perfect.* Because today was K-Day, the day I kissed him. I'd circled the date in my planner with heart stickers, and a line of poetry from Pablo Neruda: "If nothing saves us from death, at least love should save us from life." I had it all planned. My lips were slick with Cherry Chapstick and I'd been chewing mints like I was trying to break a Guinness World Record. Dani's kiss had been nice, but even as special as first kisses can go, it didn't set me on fire. So, I practiced on the mirror, my hand, the pillow—on any available surface. I'd even practiced his reaction.

"I know. I feel it, too." I give him a soulful stare.

"Yes, I'll go out on a date with you." I gently move his curl away from his forehead just a centimeter to the right.

And the one that replayed in my mind all the time. *"Yes, I'll be your girlfriend! College is right around the corner and I can visit you on the weekends."* Hand squeeze, sweet kisses and it's raining, of course. My feet kicks back like Anne Hathaway in The Princess Diaries *because our kisses are perfection.*

No time like the present to make my fantasy a reality.

"Hey. I think I'm getting better." I leaned forward. I arched my eyebrow. Another tip I found online about the art of flirt. Lean over casually. Laugh, throw your head back and touch your neck, because it makes him think of touching you. Skim your fingers, don't grab. I did that once and it looked like I was trying to choke myself. That's not the type of sexy I'm going for.

And finally, stare deeply into his eyes. That, I could easily do. No practice necessary.

And I did just that. "Don't you think I'm getting better?" The whispered question, the quake in my voice wasn't practice, just nerves.

"Yeah, Jailbait. You know what you're doing."

The jailbait insult sailed by. "I do?" My heart fluttered like a hummingbird.

He turned his head, eyes now focused on the community center straight ahead.

"When I first met you . . . when I read why you were here, I was disappointed."

The flutters stopped. I gripped the wheel and looked away. "It was a mistake. I—"

"Like I said, I misjudged you. I thought you were like one of those spoiled rich kids who gave me shit growing up. The ones who pointed out the holes in my shoes and laughed at my dirty clothes. I put my insecurities on you. All based on a piece of paper and I'm sorry," he finished on a whisper. "Which is crazy because I've done a lot of dumb things, too. I don't have a record, but I could have. It was by the grace of God. The grace of your father."

Father? It couldn't be my biological one. "Dad?"

He nodded. "Yeah. He gave me a chance. He wasn't even my judge, by the way. I lived a county over in Tulston. He was visiting our judge, overheard the conversation, and then he knocked on the door, stepped in and told my judge about a great program for fine arts. And here I am in this very program. I owe a lot to Judge Joe."

It felt like a frigid wind blew up my spine. *What are the odds?*

"Look . . . you're smart. You're beautiful and insightful. You have a bright future."

"But . . ." I prompted.

"You're seventeen. I'm twenty."

"Three years apart. That's not so bad. And totally legal, by the way."

"Legal, yes, but is it right? I . . . three years in theory doesn't seem like much. But at this age, *your* age, it's something different. I don't want to harm you or corrupt you or make you feel pressured in any way."

"I don't. I won't." I shook my head.

"We're long distance. I live in Atlanta."

"And I plan to go to school up there. One more year, no big deal."

God, this wasn't happening. He was supposed to grab my neck, kiss me back and tell me that's he's crazy for me. And where's the rain? The soulful stares? "I have a girlfriend."

"You have a girlfriend?"

"Nadia."

"The choreographer?"

"Yes."

"Since when? You guys don't act like you're into each other." And I would know. My eyes were always on Alston.

"We hooked up last weekend."

"H-hooked up?" I turned to face him. "Like kissing?"

"Yes." His voice as sharp as shears. "Kissing."

"This doesn't make sense. I . . . I've seen the way you look at me. I know you like me, too."

He looked up at the roof and sighed. "You should be with a guy your age anyway. Like the guy you were telling me about. Dani, right?"

"Dani is the reason why I got in trouble in the first place."

"You can't blame him. We all make our own choices. He didn't force you, right?"

"No." I shook my head. "Of course not. But he's not a great influence, either."

Alston turned away, pulling on his seat strap. He didn't say a word. He put his hands on his forehead, as if bracing himself from a headache.

"The other day he sent me a poem," I said.

"He writes you poetry?" His voice boomed in the car. "Sorry. I mean, it's a free country." He seemed to let the tension ease out of his voice. "He any good?"

"Let me read it to you." I shifted my butt to pull out the phone in my back pocket. I scrolled down the screen and clicked the message. "Roses are red. Violets are blue. How is my Poetry Girl? I'm thinking about you." I glanced at Alston, who grabbed his head. He seriously looked pained.

"See what I mean?" I waved my phone in front of his face. "You want me to hook up with Dani, just because we're the same age?" I gave him an unimpressed laugh. "That doesn't make any sense."

"I'm in college—"

"And I'll be there *next year*. Is this what I have to look forward to in college? My God, I'm not a toddler, a middle schooler. You just happen to be born a few years ahead of me. That's it, stop making this such a big friggin' deal!"

"Most kids your age don't have the emotional or mental capacity to have a relationship with an adult. And by all standard definitions, I am an adult. I think of you and I—" He raked his fingers through his hair. The sun highlighted the chestnut tones in his curly locks. "This is the last driving lesson. Summer's ending, anyway." He grabbed the keys from the ignition. I grabbed his hand to stop him from starting the engine and running away. His hand remained there, though he hissed, as if my touch were torturous.

His eyes are fire and I'm the virgin on the pyre.

One that consumed me, and those flutters are no longer flutters, but a raging inferno that incinerated everything in its path.

I leaned forward and pressed my lips against his. He froze. And just as I was about to pull back, he cupped my cheeks and kissed me.

His tongue licked my lips, gently parting them open. He slowly sucked my lips, focusing on the bottom, then both and then . . . and then . . . and then . . .

Perfection. Everything is perfection.

He broke away, both of us of breathing as if we'd run a hundred-mile dash. I missed the heat of his lips, the warmth of his breath.

His eyes cooled and so did I. Still, my chest heaved from the kissing marathon.

"You don't have a girlfriend."

He wouldn't have kissed me like that otherwise. He wasn't like that.

"Like I said, you know what you're doing. Last lesson." He leaned over my seat and opened the door. "Goodbye, Ryder."

"Coward," I whispered, before I got out of the car.

Monday evening, July 20th
134 days

Clicking the top of my pen over and over, I was determined to write a poem about Alston's wishy-washy behavior.

Two knocks on my door interrupted my brainstorm.

Maya entered my room. "Hey."

I stuffed my notebook under my pillow and rolled to my side. "Hey."

"What do you have under there?" She nodded toward my pillow.

I shrugged. "Angsty teenagey stuff."

Maya sat at the foot of the bed. "Is that why you've been blasting My Chemical Romance?" The bed dipped and the springs creaked. "You need a new mattress." Maya bounced on the bed, making the springs squeal. "No, you need a new frame." Maya rolled her neck and patted her thighs. "So . . . I've got an update about Jeanie."

"Really?" I sat up. "Is Mom okay?"

"Yes. The clinic liaison says she's doing well. She'll be out in a few weeks and, well . . . she wants you to come see her. Do some sort of family therapy."

I was glad Mom was doing better, but what if I said something that upset her? "I . . ." I chewed my bottom lip. "Will they tell us what to talk about?"

"I've never tried therapy, but I don't think it works like that. The director said something about creating a safe space for your mom to talk things out. I think they'll guide the conversation, so it'll stay on track."

"Okay. So, if I . . . if I say something to upset Mom, they'll stop me?"

Maya scooted closer to me and squeezed my hand. "Oh, Ryder. I'm glad you're thinking about your mom, but this is for you, too. I think she has some things to own up to, don't you think?"

The drunk driving. The vomit on me and Alston. When she came to Maya's job, drunk and sabotaging her chances at making partner.

"Yeah, she does," I conceded. "Will you be there, too?"

Maya shook her head. "I'll hang out in the lobby or something."

"Really? I want you there."

"Not a good idea."

"She needs to apologize to you."

"She doesn't want to speak to me." Maya shrugged. "She only wants you."

"Then no." I folded my legs under me.

"Ryder, I don't need you to—"

"I know, I know. I'm not your savior. I'm not trying to be." I waved her off.

Maya twisted her lips. "Seems to be that way, Wonder Twin. I love you to the moon and back. But I'm good. Besides, I'm not family."

A heated arrow struck my heart. "Is that how you really feel? That I'm not your family?"

"Of course, you're my family, Ryder. But the world doesn't see that. In the court of law—"

"Screw the court of law. Screw the world if they can't see it. You are family and I'm your sister. You've listened to every poem I've written, even the ones I've stuffed under my bed because I know you nose around my room. You protect me. I know you gave Kevin twenty bucks to knock out Devin Lockhart for touching my butt."

"And they say violence is not the answer." Maya snorted, looking not at all bothered that I knew the things she'd done to watch my back.

I sighed, holding back a smile. "What I'm saying, Maya, is that if Mom is trying to get better, if she's truly sorry, then she'll want to right all of her wrongs. Her excluding you from *our* family session tells me she hasn't learned much. And if she can't treat you with respect . . ." I let out a long breath. "If she can't own up to her sins, I'm not interested." I shrugged. "Sorry, not sorry."

Maya mumbled something under her breath, looked at me and then shook her head. "Fine. Okay. I'll let them know. However, let the record show that I am fine with you speaking to your mom . . . without me."

"So noted." I pulled my notebook from under my pillow.

"Okay. I'll let you write about how Alston's eyes makes your soul soar." She waved her arms as if she were flying.

And well, yeah, he kind of did make my soul soar. I wouldn't tell Maya that. "Yeah, well, not much flying will take place. He says I'm too young."

"Too young? How old is he?"

"Twenty."

She nodded. "I can respect that. As an older guy, I suspect he's trying to be careful with you."

"What?" I scrunched my nose. "Didn't you date a really old guy when you were eighteen?"

"Eighteen is legal. And he was only thirty."

"But you were in high school. It's still creepy."

"Apparently you and Daddy thought it was creepy."

"Dad found out?"

"Yeah. Some old biddy in town told him I was banging an old guy. Daddy lost his mind. Next thing I know, I received a very respectful email from Charles dissolving our relationship." Maya shrugged. "We didn't even have sex."

"And that's why dear old Charles still lives."

"Maybe." Maya sighed. "Look, I know I'm not the best person to ask for advice when it comes to matters of the heart."

I snorted. "You don't say?"

Maya grabbed the pillow from underneath my elbow and smacked it against my head.

"Oww, you psycho."

"Yeah, well you could have said, 'Maya, oh wise one, I appreciate any advice you can give me.'"

I put my hands together and bowed my head. "Maya, oh wise one. Goddess of advice, mother of slaying all day, please bless my ears with your wondrous advice."

Maya narrowed her eyes to slits. "You're a smart-ass and I both hate and love it." She tucked the weaponized pillow into her lap. "But . . . look. You have to respect what dude is trying to do. You're only seventeen and yes . . . I know pot meet kettle but play it cool. Be his friend, keep the lines of communication open and next year when you're in college—and if you're still feeling him—then go for it."

"Really?" I clasped my hands together under my chin. "What would you do in my situation? Would you wait even if you knew he's your soul mate?"

"Soul mate?" She rolled her eyes. "Really?"

"Fine, let me rephrase. If you really liked a guy would you wait? If you were in my shoes, what would you do?"

"I don't chase after men." She twirled her manicured fingers.

"And how's that working out for you?"

Maya shot up from the bed, whopping me with the pillow again. This time I saw stars. "Owww, that hurt. Like, for real this time."

"Good." Maya stomped out the room. "I really do love and hate your smart mouth," she yelled through the close door.

"Love you, too." I grinned and put the pen back to paper. I was feeling inspired. I would make Alston eat his words.

Friday afternoon, July 24th
138 days

I stomped out of the auditorium. The double doors slammed behind me. The thump of the doors hadn't adequately conveyed my rage. I wanted to stuff him into one of those protective-gear outfits that they used in self-defense classes, and karate kick the heck out of him. Or maybe forgo the suit and kick him in the shin with steel-toed cowboy boots.

Deep breaths, Ryder. I couldn't allow myself to tumble down a dark path. Surely there was something redeemable about the infuriating man.

These days, there weren't many nice things I could say about Alston, but one thing was for sure: he was a man of his word.

The day after he proclaimed lessons were over, he dashed out right after camp let out. When I shouted for him to wait up, he jogged away right next to Na-di-a. That's how I said her name in my head. Stupid, gorgeous, Na-di-a.

Same story throughout the week. He wouldn't call on me unless it was painfully obvious to others that he was ignoring me. And from the sly looks from Gina and the curious looks from Craig, the ignoring-me thing was going from awkwardly weird to *Twilight Zone.*

To make matters worse, Dani found out details about my

community service. Turned out Craig hooked up with Kaitlyn. So then Dani began turning up the heat. I never answered his calls or texts. The last message he sent said that if I kept ignoring him, he was going to come by the community center.

I texted him back, telling him I'd meet him over the weekend. It was a lie, a stalling tactic, but I didn't want another unwanted visitor at my volunteer service. Mom had wreaked enough damage.

Today it was too hot outside, so we all stayed in one of the breakout rooms in the community center. Alston pulled out a chair and flipped it around, his back to the dry erase board. A few more kids, mostly girls, joined our group after Alston made us perform for them a few weeks ago.

Apparently, poetry was cool. I suspected it was because Alston was good-looking and his tragic poem (a different one), had stolen the hearts of some of the kids at camp.

We sat at the desks that faced the front of the classroom.

"We've got the end of summer showcase." He leaned back and tilted his head. "I've got some good and bad news. Which first?"

I turned my head toward the window. He wasn't going to look or listen to me anyway.

"Good news!" Craig shouted from his seat.

"Good news is that Mrs. Bryant is going to let us perform freestyle poetry."

A few of us cheered, even me, though I was still pissed off.

"And the bad news?" I asked. Everyone quieted. Alston had no choice but to answer.

"The bad news is that we only have two slots." He addressed the group, still refusing to look in my direction. "You all have to audition."

"And who's judging?" I leaned forward, my eyes narrowing.

"Me. Auditions are next week."

236 / SHARINA HARRIS

Groans and excited whispers filled the room.

"Practice. Go find a corner. I'll rotate the room and help where I can."

For the next four hours he circled the room. He helped the new guy, Jake, who joined us last week, three times. He helped Gina and Craig twice, and another new girl, who obviously had the hots for him, once.

He never came to me.

I wanted to yell or raise my hand. But then I thought of Maya and what she would do in this situation.

I don't chase men.

Why did I fight for a guy who didn't want me? We weren't soul mates, we couldn't be. The session ended. This time, Alston didn't run away from me, I ran away from him.

I power-walked to my bike. Black clouds quickly moved in, darkening the sky. Lightning skittered across the heavens, a flash of white fire that lit my gloomy mood. I had to hurry. If I didn't leave soon, I'd get drenched. My phone dinged. I glanced down, knowing it was Maya before I read the message.

Storm's coming. I'll come get you.

I wouldn't mind biking in the rain, I needed to cool off. But Maya would lose her mind.

No need. I've got a ride. See you soon.

I heard another ding follow up, but before I could read the message someone yelled from me.

"Ryder!"

The voice came from across the parking lot.

Tall, dark, delinquent. He waved, leaning against the side of his car, looking James Dean cool in a simple white T-shirt and jeans.

Other students were starting to file out, but no Alston. Maybe he was waiting me out—waiting for me to bike away. *Coward.* Energized by anger, I grabbed my bike and marched— no, I sashayed over to Dani.

"Hey." He straightened from his slouched position. His mouth curved into a smile.

I kicked out my stand to prop up my bike. "Hey, Dani. What are you doing here?" I stuffed my hands into my cutoffs that skimmed just above my knee.

"You look nice." He picked at the frills on my lace white shirt. Maya told me I looked like a flower child.

"Thanks." I stretched up to my tiptoes and flopped back down to the soles of my feet. My eyes still on his, I repeated my question, this time a bit sterner. "What are you doing here?"

"I figured you were going to blow me off, so I made good on my promise."

"Why?"

"I wanted to see you," he said, but it sounded like a question.

"Why?" I asked again, determined to drill down to the real reason he *seemed* so into me. Boys lied. I knew that now.

He sighed. "Ry."

"—Der." I completed. "Ryder. Not Ry."

"Fine, Ryder." He rolled his eyes. "I like you and I miss you, okay?"

The back of my neck prickled. I turned around. Alston watched us from the front entrance. He was talking to a volunteer, but his eyes were on us.

"Who's the guy?" Dani's voice pulled my attention back to him.

"My teacher. Well, kinda. He teaches poetry."

"Oh . . . oh," he whispered again, more to himself.

"There's nothing there, Dani."

Thunder boomed.

"If you say so . . . *Poetry* Girl."

"I've gotta go."

"Why don't I take you home?"

"Maya's home."

"Your sister, right?"

"Right."

"That's fine. I'd like to meet her."

I shook my head. "Not a good idea."

"I know I screwed up. I know what I'm doing with my friends is wrong but give me a chance. People deserve second chances, right?"

My heart flipped a little when I thought of Mom. She was literally in the middle of her second chance. Maybe I wasn't being fair to Dani. Maybe he wasn't such a bad guy. And the guy I thought was good literally stood there, staring and willing to let me bike in the rain.

"What about my bike?"

"I've got a rack." He pointed to the roof on his black SUV. "Hop in the car and I'll strap it in."

Dani popped open his trunk and pulled out two bungee-looking ropes. "Get in, Poetry Girl."

I dove into the car. Raindrops pinged on the windshield. I looked out of the passenger-side window. The rain distorted my vision, but I could still make out Alston, standing out in front.

I turned away. This is what he wanted. He didn't deserve to stare. Or maybe he wasn't staring. Maybe he'd been trapped by the rain.

Whatever.

After another minute, Dani slid into the driver's seat, his wet shirt plastered against his chest.

"My address is—"

"I know where you live."

"Stalker." I snorted.

"Everyone knows you live at the big lake house." Dani pushed a button to turn on the car. "My dad was so jealous of your dad."

"Why? It's not like there aren't other houses out there."

"Your dad had the best view, the best plot. So . . . my dad didn't want anything else. He doesn't like anyone or anything that's second best." His tone was the definition of sour grapes.

Dani pulled up to the light and then navigated us to my home.

"Are you and your dad close?"

Dani shook his head. "He's gone most of the time. He does a lot of business in Atlanta, acquisitions and mergers."

"And your mom?"

He shrugged. "I think she's so afraid of dad doing something . . . dumb . . . she doesn't like to leave him alone."

So they leave their son alone. Dani gripped his hand around the steering wheel.

"How . . . how is your mom?" he asked.

I realized I was tapping my knee. I stopped and stared at him, licking my lips. "You know?"

"Yeah." He bobbed his head. "I've heard."

I sighed. Mom wasn't going to like that. She hated being the center of attention, but it was hard to keep secrets in Hope Springs. Now that I thought about it, it was probably my grandparents who started the gossip.

"She's okay, I guess? I don't know really. But she wants to speak to me but not my sister, and it makes me mad, you know? Like, if you really want to say you're sorry, tell that to everyone. Mom came to Maya's job. Totally screwed her over and messed up her chances for a promotion."

"Yeah, I . . . I heard about that, too. But my mom says Maya can have a lot of attitude, so maybe that's the reason why?"

"Your mom . . ." I snorted and looked out the window. "Does your mom have examples of Maya getting an attitude?"

Dani swallowed and stole a quick glance in my direction. "I . . . well . . . no. Now that I think about it, she only said that she came off high and mighty."

"Right." I rolled my eyes. "Maya's accomplished, has never

lost a case at her firm, has a good rapport with her clients, and volunteers her time for people who can't afford to hire a lawyer, but yeah," I sucked my teeth. "High and mighty."

Dani laughed, but it sounded nervous. Like he didn't know what to do with me.

"Yeah, guess my mom was being over the top. But for what it's worth, I think she means well. Maybe they just had a run-in."

"I think if your mom had a run-in with Maya, she would've told you. Instead she decided to hate on a young, confident black woman. And FYI, a lot of people 'mean well,'" I said with air quotes, "yet they spread lies to ruin the reputations of others."

"Whoa, whoa, whoa." Dani pulled up to the driveway. "How did we get here? Mom said something uncool, but that doesn't mean she's vicious."

I huffed a breath. "Yeah, you're right." And he was, sort of. I still thought his mom's words were crappy, but the source of my anger was Alston, not Dani. "Sorry."

We arrived at my house. Dani shrugged and turned off the car. "Can I come in?" His eyes were soulful and hopeful, and I couldn't say no. Not after the word vomit I'd just spewed.

"Sure. But like I said, Maya's probably home."

Dani smiled. "There's an umbrella in the back somewhere."

"That's okay." I grabbed the door handle. "I'll just run to the front. I'll meet you inside." I dashed out of the car before he could respond. Sheets of rain attacked me during my short sprint to the door. I keyed in the entry code and hurried inside, leaving the door open for Dani.

"Maya!" I yelled.

"Kitchen."

I rushed toward her voice and found Maya cutting carrots and celery. A can of low-sodium chicken stock sat on the counter, next to a steaming pot of water.

Oh, God, I hope it's not another diet.

"So really quick, I kinda have company."

"You can't 'kinda have' company. You do or you don't."

"Maya."

She stopped cutting the carrots. "Fine. Who is it?"

"Dani."

"Dani-with-an-I Dani? The little asshole that got you in trouble?" She raised the knife in the air.

"I got myself in trouble. But yes, him. Look, I know it sounds strange, but he's nice."

"Just because someone's nice, doesn't mean you have to bring them to your home."

I shrugged. "Can he hang out here for a few minutes?"

Maya sighed and looked at me. "Is Alston still giving you the silent treatment?"

"Yeah."

"Is this your way of getting back at him?"

The door shut. I glanced over my shoulder, confirming Dani was not behind me.

"No," I whispered. "Dani just showed up. He apologized and offered me a ride. I'm not being stupid, Maya, I'm just trying to—"

"Figure him out."

"Yeah."

"Okay."

"Okay?"

"Don't sound so surprised. I was a teenager once."

"Thanks, Maya. He umm, wants to meet you."

A wide, dangerous smile spread across her face. "Well, bring the young man in here."

"Be nice."

"Sure will." Maya turned to the sink and washed her hands.

"Dani, in here," I yelled.

Dani walked into the kitchen, with a sure, long-limbed stride. "Maya." He offered his hand. "I've heard a lot about you."

"And I you." Maya shook and squeezed his hand. "From both Ryder and the judge."

"Oh, I . . ."

"Kidding." Maya dropped the scary mask and became a big sister. "So . . . you're stalking my sister?"

"Maya!"

Dani laughed. "It's okay. I know I screwed up. Your sis is really nice and cool, you know? Like . . . she doesn't care about what other people think."

Maya gave him a hmmm. Hmmm in Maya speak meant *I don't know about you.*

"Well, nice to meet you, Dani." Maya stepped back to her cutting board.

"What are you making?" I asked.

"Chicken noodle soup. Trying a new recipe."

No, a new diet. Wonder what set her off? I'd ask later.

"Okay." I shot her a weird look while she focused on the carrots. "Dani and I will be upstairs in my room."

She leveled a stern stare at me. "Keep the door open. And you"—she grabbed a long carrot, focusing her attention on Dani—"don't try anything. I will be patrolling the hallways every so often and I have a shotgun. Understand?"

Dani bobbed his head.

"Good." Maya slammed the carrot back to the cutting board and whacked it.

Dani took a small step back.

"Have fun, you two."

I grabbed Dani's elbow and pulled him toward the stairs. He was still facing Maya and backing away, as if she were going to launch a sneak attack.

"C'mon, it's fine." I marched him upstairs and showed him to my room.

His shoulders relaxed.

"It's fine. Maya's just teasing you." *I think.*

"So, she's not going to check on us every so often like we're kids?"

"Yeah, she's definitely going to do that. And we *are* kids. We live in our parents' houses and are underaged." I inwardly cringed at my teacher's pet tone. God, no wonder I didn't have friends my age.

Dani looked around. "Nice bed." He fingered the lace on the canopy. It was the only girlie thing in my room, the only thing Mom and I had agreed on over the years. Other failed arguments included clothes, shoes, makeup and decorations.

We both saw the canopy and fell in love. I didn't remember much before our time with Dad and Maya, but I did remember Mom and me building forts with sheets over the long post bed. I wondered if the canopy reminded Mom of that time, too.

"Can I sit down?"

"Yeah, uh, sure."

"Are *you* going to relax? Sit down beside me?" he teased.

"S-sure. Sorry I . . . I've never had a guy in my room."

"Really?" His voice got deep. "Happy to be your first."

I narrowed my eyes. "Smooth, Dani. Anyway, how's the gang been doing?"

"Fine. We're still hanging out. Coraline's parents have a house not too far from here, so we go out and . . ." He cut himself off.

"Drink a few beers." I finished for him. "You can be who you are. I won't judge you."

"Okay, then yeah . . . we do that." He smiled and scooted closer to me. His tanned hand reached for my thigh. My heartbeat thumped like the drums in the marching band.

"Kaitlyn asks about you all the time. She's afraid you're mad at her. She wants your number."

"I . . . I'm not sure if I want that yet."

She was the one who'd convinced me to be the lookout. Like Alston said, it wasn't anyone's fault but mine, but the girl had a way with words. A way with making you want to feel like a part of the crew. She was a gateway drug and I wasn't sure if I was strong enough to withstand it.

"That's cool. I'll just tell her—"

"Don't tell her anything. Don't tell anyone you've been here."

"Why?"

"It's easier that way. I'm still not sure what to do with you, to be honest."

"I know what I want to do with you," he whispered and leaned closer and closer until his lips touched mine. He cupped my chin and swiped my tongue. I waited for it. The spark, the hammering heart, the feelings I'd felt with Alston.

Nothing.

Stupid, stupid girl. This guy wants you. This guy puts in the effort.

Why couldn't I like this guy? I pulled back. Dani's eyes were closed. His hands tracked up my shirt. He lifted it and pressed his palm against my stomach. My gut spasmed. I'd never been touched there or . . . or anywhere.

"Dani . . ." I pushed his hand away. "Maya could come by any minute."

"Well then, let's make the most of it."

"You promised to be good."

"Yeah." He shrugged. "I didn't want my dick to replace the carrot she was chopping." His lips grazed my neck.

I jerked away.

"Dani, stop." I shook my head. "This isn't going to work."

Dani sighed, running his fingers through his hair. "Is it that guy from the center?"

"No."

"Don't lie. I saw the way he looked at us in the parking lot. Then he followed you home. Like I was going to hurt you or something."

"H-he . . . he did?"

"Yeah. That's why it took me forever to come inside. I told him to leave you alone."

"Dani . . ." I sighed. "You had no right to speak for me."

"I'm sorry, Ryder. I didn't mean it like that. But it was weird him doing that."

Weird, but sweet.

"I'm sorry, Ryder. Let's start over. Look." He scooted away. "Lots of space between us." He gave me another winning smile.

Dani was dangerous. Not from a mortal standpoint and not to my heart. But he was the just-good-enough guy. The guy that would do just enough to make do, just enough to keep his friends, just enough to make his girlfriend not leave, just enough to not make waves.

He just wasn't good enough for me. No, that wasn't it. He just wasn't the guy for me.

He must've seen something in my eyes. "No, huh?"

I shook my head. "I'm sorry," I whispered. And I was. I didn't mean to hurt his feelings.

"No . . ." he sighed, ". . . problem. You're just not into me." He stood. "I'll go."

I nodded and watched him leave. In a few minutes, I would text him to make sure he returned home safe. Maya and Dani muttered something to each other downstairs. I couldn't make it out, and I didn't care to.

I stood at my window. He paused and looked up. He didn't smile, but he didn't look mad. He knocked his hand on the roof of the car and then opened the door and left.

"Bye, Dani," I whispered. My phone buzzed in my pocket. It was Alston.

Can I come over? Parked a few houses up.

I shoved the curtains to the side. Sure enough, his white Camry was just down the road.

I stuffed my phone in my pocket and rushed downstairs.

"Hey!" Maya yelled. "Where are you going?"

My hand gripped the doorknob. "Alston's outside. He wants to talk."

"Ohhh. Drama." Maya popped a carrot in her mouth. "You can invite him inside . . . if you want."

"Nope. He isn't invited. I'm making him leave."

"Sure you are." She waved at me. "Grab a jacket at least. It's still pouring out there."

I moved to the closet and grabbed a yellow raincoat and boots. I adjusted the buttons in the mirror, near the door.

The yellow hood and pink polka dot rainboots made me look like a middle schooler.

Great, now you really look like jailbait.

"Doesn't matter." I shook my head. "Be back in a few."

"Okay." She pretended to stir something in the pot. I knew it'd be only a few seconds before she plastered her face on the window to spy.

I marched to his car and knocked on the driver's window. He jumped, and then pulled up his seat. He cracked his window. "Get in."

"No." I shook my head. No more close quarters with him. I wouldn't give myself the opportunity to make a fool out of myself again.

"Fine. I'll come out."

I backed away as he opened the door.

Rain plastered his hair to his scalp and forehead. He didn't seem to mind.

"I came by to check on you."

"Why?"

"I don't like the look of Dani. He seems slick."

"It's easy to look slick when it's rainy."

"Yeah, maybe."

"I'm fine, as you can see."

He looked away. "I'm not with Nadia. Never was."

"And the sky is blue. I already knew."

His lips curved into a small smile. "I'm not a good liar."

"No. But it still hurts."

He looked back at me. His face wet and gorgeous from the rain.

"It hurts that you'd rather hurt me then face your fear."

"What do I fear?" His voice dangerously soft.

"I don't know what it is, but it's not my age. Maybe you fear what we could be. Maybe you fear what you feel in your heart. What you see in my eyes. Maybe something dark lodged inside of you when your mom's twister spun your life around."

"Ryder . . ." He grabbed me close, wrapping his arms around my jacket. His chest pressed against mine, his body warm and hard, his hands soft and firm. They didn't make my skin crawl like Dani's touch. He sought comfort, not a quick squeeze.

He didn't say anything more, just pressed his forehead against mine. The rain bounced off me and drenched him. "I like you," he whispered. "I really, really like you."

I closed my eyes, smiled. The apple of my cheeks ached, I smiled so hard.

"But you and me . . . we just . . . we don't make sense right now. I can't risk it."

My heart and smile dropped. "Risk what?" Raindrops caught on my lashes. I blink the drops away.

"When I was younger, I told myself I'd never end up like Mom. Or be a careless asshole like my dad. But somehow, I still ended up down that road. The break your dad gave me pivoted my path, and I don't want to squander my good fortune. Statistically, people with my upbringing don't make it out. Drugs, alcohol, abuse, you name it. So, I've got to stack the deck in my favor. I'm careful, I'm calculated and I don't make avoidable mistakes. You understand, right?"

A deep ache settled in my chest. Though I'd come down to send him away, a part of me, a big part of me, wanted him to fight for us. "When I first heard your poetry, the one you performed that day about your mom and dad, my world tilted. Because I'd found someone who understood me. It's not the romantic type of connection. It's the thread you feel with another human being. Kindness. Empathy. Pain."

"Thank you."

"But . . . but you live your life so carefully. Everyone is at an arm's distance. You don't hang out with the other instructors. They go to the bars in town, but you stay back, even before you taught me how to drive."

"I'm a bit of a loner."

"Loner, liar."

"What?"

He released me from his embrace. "What are you talking about?"

"Your spoken word is all about triumph, but in order to be triumphant, you have to live, go through the journey," I said, thinking about my lesson in school about the hero's journey. Ironically, of what Dani said. "There's no meaning behind your words if you don't live it."

I stepped away on to the curb. "I'm glad you like me. But I wonder if you'll do anything about it. I wonder if you'll be brave enough to withstand trials."

"I've been through enough trials. More than you can imagine."

"But you still got some living to do." I balled my fists. "I can't be the girl hanging on your every word, hoping that I'll be the one to inspire you to take a chance."

I moved away, up on the curb, but he didn't reach for me. He looked down at his shoes and whispered, "What about *your* journey?"

"I'm finding my own voice, my worth. I refuse to be ignored or treated like a child." And it wasn't just by him. By Mom and Maya.

"Keep your auditions, your professions of your feelings, your confusion, your wishy-washy behavior. I don't want it." I pivoted on my heel and stormed away.

Screw him and screw the end of summer performance. I was no longer the invisible girl.

CHAPTER 15

JEANIE
TEARS FOR FEARS

Monday afternoon, July 27th
141 days

I rubbed my sweaty hands against my khaki skirt, leaving a wet imprint on my thighs.

"Girl, chill out," Vic barked as she channel surfed. She sat beside me with her legs propped on the coffee table, waving one of those Asian paper fans. Sweat poured from her, too, but not for the same reason as me. She was still "drying out," as she liked to call it.

I was nervous as all get out because in T-minus four hours Ryder and Maya would arrive for family therapy.

"I . . ." I grabbed a glass of water and downed it. "This is dumb. I shouldn't have signed up. It's optional, anyway."

Vic shrugged, fanning so hard I could feel the little breeze from my seat. "It's no picnic, that's for damn sure. But Dr. Mitra's a good one, and he's been in our shoes. He'll make sure it won't go too far left."

I ran through scenarios in my head. "What if Ryder hates me?"

"She's a teenager, right? I'm sure she hates everything. Lord knows Lesha and Dana did at that age."

"No." I shook my head. "She's thoughtful and incredibly kind."

My face grew hot thinking about all the pain I'd caused my Chickadee. The danger I put her in. *God, she must hate me.* I thought I said that in my head, but I must've said it out loud, because Vic pressed the mute button and stopped fanning.

"Look. I'm not the best person to give you advice . . . if you hadn't noticed, this isn't my first rodeo." She pointed to her forehead, beading with sweat.

"But I guarantee your daughter wouldn't have agreed to come out here if there wasn't a part of her, even if it's just an itty-bitty part, that wants you to be okay. She may be hurt and angry, but you can't control her emotions. You just have to own up to what you've done and sort out the rest."

"Own up to what I've done." I snorted. That's the message Dr. Mitra told me that Ryder had sent. She didn't want to see me unless I apologized to Maya.

"Yes. Own it, girl."

"Maya will be here, too," I mumbled under my breath.

Vic nodded, her eyes now back on the TV though it was still on silent. She knew a portion of our troubled relationship. I'd shown her a picture of me, Ryder, Joseph and Maya. Ryder had been seven years old and Maya seventeen. It was the only family portrait we'd taken. Maya had refused all other times.

"Makes sense, if you're asking me. The consequences of your actions resulted in her taking care of your daughter." She said it in an easy-breezy way that bugged the heck out of me. She didn't have all the facts. She didn't know that Maya had tried to kick me out of my home—the home I'd lived in for the past decade. Vic didn't realize that Maya had made me feel alienated and, for the first few years, like a guest in my own home. I couldn't so much as move around a candle without Maya tensing up and running to Joseph.

"Yeah . . . well, things haven't exactly been peachy keen be-tween Maya and me."

Vic chuckled and turned her attention back to me. "Let me guess. She was the apple of her daddy's eye, and you were the evil stepmother."

"Bingo."

"Probably was a hard adjustment, too. Living in South Georgia, married to a black man."

"We don't live in the south of Georgia, it's just below mid-dle Georgia. And big deal! I married a black man, but he's just a man. It's not like I'm a freaking vampire or something."

Vic raised her hand. "All right. I'm not touching that with a ten-foot pole. Don't have the time or the energy." She sighed and stood. "I'm getting some juice. Want some?"

I nodded.

God, I was not ready for Maya. I wasn't ready for her atti-tude, for her rolling her eyes at everything I said. And what if she turned Ryder against me? I leaned my head into my hands and groaned.

"What a mess I've made." Tears pressed against my eyelids. Ever since my tête-à-tête with Maya I'd been too afraid of cry-ing. And what was that about? I should be able to cry. It was normal, healthy even, to cry. A catharsis, Dr. Mitra had said.

"Here, girl." Vic returned with a glass of orange juice and placed it in my hand.

I grabbed the glass like a lifeline. "Can I ask you some-thing?"

"Yep." Vic popped the P.

"The last conversation Maya and I had . . . it . . . it got ugly. And there's this one thing she said. Something that I can't get out of my head. I figured that since you're—" I waved toward her.

"Fabulous?"

"Yes, but—"

"Gorgeous, stunning, alarmingly intelligent." She batted her eyelashes.

I laughed. "Yes, all of the above. But black, too. I think . . . I want your perspective."

"Sure. Forty-five dollars an hour. In the invoice add the memo: Black girl whisperer."

"Vic," I groaned. "I really need your help."

She took a deep gulp of juice and waved, as if telling me to go ahead. I told her about my conversation with Maya. She didn't say a word. No mhmms, or really? Or no-she-didn't. Vic yelled that to the TV a lot.

"So." I took a deep breath. I was now standing, pacing the floor. "Isn't that crazy?"

Vic leaned back on the couch, examining a perfectly manicured nail. "Which part?"

"Wh-which part?" My voice went high. "All of it. Telling me to stop crying, *after* my husband died, mind you. That the world doesn't care about her tears. I mean, come on. That's crazy, right?"

Vic rubbed her temples and muttered, "I should've charged you."

"Be serious, Vic."

"All right, girl. Fine. Take a seat." She patted the space next to her.

I sat down, my heart thumping and my face heating up like water in a kettle. If she told me I was a racist or insensitive for crying, I'd march right out the door.

"Years ago, before I quit corporate America to paint, I was an account manager at an advertising agency. We were doing this campaign for a children's nonprofit org. Abigail, she was a coworker of mine. We're the same age and we were friendly."

She shook her head, as if convincing herself that they were. "We worked the ad together. It was my account, but she was passionate about the nonprofit and I allowed her to help. Anyway, we came up with a few ideas. We didn't have any photos of the kids at the nonprofit, so she decided to use stock. Anyway, Abigail comes back with a picture of . . . Lord . . . how do I put it?" She took a deep breath. "There were pictures of African kids. You know the ones where it looks like they're starving? It's basically poverty-porn, objectifying these kids for donations."

"W-was it a nonprofit for children in Africa?" I asked, knowing the answer.

"Hell, no. I mean, the nonprofit was basically an after-school program to promote literacy for inner-city children in metro-Atlanta. Children of all races, mind you. So . . . I very calmly informed Abigail that this picture wouldn't do. I explained why. And honestly, after the conversation I was frustrated and tired that I had to explain to a whole-ass, grown woman about how the ad spread was problematic. She takes it back, thanks me for telling her the truth and goes back to her desk crying."

I held my breath, waiting for Vic to finish the story. My body shook as the pent-up air burned in my chest. God, this wasn't me. I wasn't Abigail. She couldn't think that.

"Next thing I know, I'm in my boss's office and he's accusing me of being angry and not a team player. And he didn't understand why I wasn't gentle and constructive in my feedback. He . . ." She clenched and unclenched her hand. "He didn't ask me how I felt about the image. He didn't ask me what I'd said. He only saw her tears and forced me to apologize. And here's the kicker." Her voice wobbled. "When I cried because I was hurt by the lack of support, my boss asked me, 'What are *you* crying for? You're the one that hurt Abigail's feelings.' "

I gasped for breath. I couldn't hold it in.

Vic continued, "Do you know how it feels when . . . when

the world as a whole thinks you don't matter? I'm a . . . figure-head, a symbol. Sassy best friend. Stern mother. Surprisingly smart employee. Black girl whisperer." She nodded her head in my direction. "But not a person with my own feelings and emotions. If I have a bad day, I have an attitude. If I express my feelings, I'm aggressive. I'm not seen as a person, not really. I'm a representative of what the world thinks I should be. So, I have to make up these rules. Act a certain way. I've got to code switch."

"What's a code switch?"

"See?" she shouted, pointing to me. "You're telling me that you were married to a black man and helped raised his black child, but you don't know what code-switching means?" She rolled her eyes. "Lord have mercy, I really should charge you. Okay . . ." She patted her thighs and sighed like she hadn't ex-haled in years.

"You would call it a 'professional voice,' but to me, I have to put on airs to sound a certain way. I change the rhythm, the diction, pronunciation. Speak a certain way . . . not the way I speak to my friends and family. If there is a topic related to black stereotypes, I purposely steer the conversation in a dif-ferent way or pretend I don't know what the hell you're talking about. If someone wants to know about the latest dance craze, I tell them I have no idea. All of this to be 'acceptable,'" she said, making air quotes, "in your eyes."

"God, that sounds crazy and exhausting. Why do that?"

"It is. I used to do it because I didn't want to be passed over for an opportunity. I didn't want someone to subconsciously associate me with being not-the-right-fit for something. But I don't do it anymore, because I don't have to. Get it?"

I did, and yet I didn't. Daddy had made me feel so small, like a tiny little gnat that he could smash at any time. I carried those thoughts, that weight of feeling insignificant everywhere. But when I truly left my childhood home, when I got out from under my father's thumb, I could at least pretend. My skin, the way I looked, afforded me the opportunity. Though, on the inside, I was still that little girl, wanting approval from Daddy.

I licked my lips. "I'm sorry that happened to you. But I'm telling you, Maya is totally off base about Joseph treating her differently than me."

"Okay." Vic shrugged.

"I'm not a bad person."

"I didn't say you were. What I'm saying is that I understand what Maya said to you. And unfortunately, our experiences—hers and mine—are the norm."

"I should just stop crying?" I snapped.

She gave me a sharp look, lips in a straight line, looking me up and down, her patience so thin that if it were a frozen lake, there would be no way in heck I'd skate on it.

"Crying is normal. Yes, it can be therapeutic, and you shouldn't feel like you can't cry." She looked me in the eyes. "But you have to understand that your husband should've allowed his baby to simply be. He put his experiences as a black man growing up in the sixties and seventies on his child. I understand his logic but it sounds like it screwed her up."

"I just can't believe it," I whispered, shaking my head. "I never noticed the difference."

"Maya gave you examples. Hell, he should've let his thirteen-year-old daughter cry over a dead pet. He made her feel weak and that's not cool. Every child should be comfortable with expressing themselves in front of their parents."

I nodded. "You know . . . Daddy used to make me feel dumb and small and I . . . I could never relax around him."

"Exactly." She pointed at me. "You aren't Maya's mother, but you were her father's wife. And if you want to make things right . . . well . . . first step is to believe what she says and respect how she feels."

She patted my leg and stood. "Still might charge your ass."

"But how do I know—"

"Nope. No more questions. Session's over. Just sit and think on it."

Monday afternoon, July 27th
141 Days

Dr. Mitra's office was too small for a family therapy session, so we had to use the group therapy B Room.

I didn't like that room. It was too square—square chairs, square table, square pictures. The chairs were puke green and questionable-choices orange. It was like a pre-K setup retrofitted for adults. This wasn't the proper place to have a conversation about my progress. No way they'd take me seriously here.

Dr. Mitra sped into the room. The man was a ball of energy. He had an iPad in one hand and a mug of coffee in the other. His slouchy pants were held together by a braided leather belt. Bright green glasses sat perched on his nose. There were four vacant seats. He sat in the chair next to me. I wanted Ryder beside me. The other two chairs were spread farther apart at the corners of the table.

"Hmm. I don't like this setup." Dr. Mitra placed his coffee and iPad on his chair. "I'm going to move the table out of the way, if that's okay?"

I nodded so hard I strained my neck. When I first sat down, I had a nightmare that Maya would slide across the table to shake me, *Jerry Springer* style. "Do you need help?"

"No, thanks." He waved me off. "Besides, if the wife asks, I can tell her I exercised today." He pushed up his glasses and squinted. "It'll be fine, you know."

"I'm sure that's what Abraham Lincoln said to Mary Todd before they went to the fun stage show."

Dr. Mitra shook his head. "It's fine to be nervous, but Ray is wrapping up the meeting with them. They'll get an understanding of the recovery process. And they'll understand—"

"Just how messed up my brain is." As if I needed something else wrong with my noggin.

Dr. Mitra dragged the table and then propped it on the wall. He laughed. "It's important they understand your recovery process once you leave in a few days. That way you'll have some support, and they'll understand your experience."

"Sure, they will." I could see it now. Maya would tell me to suck it up. Ryder would tell me to stop embarrassing her. Yep. Sounded like fun. Why did I want to leave this place again? At least we were all recovering addicts here.

Dr. Mitra moved the table and rearranged the chairs in a circle. "Much better." He sighed.

I fidgeted with the fringe on my white linen shirt. No, it was *alabaster.* The saleswoman had told me the color when I bought it. She helped me pair it with turquoise cotton ankle-length pants. The girl in the store even found me a matching pair of earrings and necklace. Joseph said it made my eyes shine. And today, well, I could use a little shine.

The door swung open. Maya strode in first. She scanned the room until her gaze landed on me. She sized me up. Looking for what? If I had the shakes? If I sweated too much? If I was a raging, crying banshee?

I took a deep breath and gave her a cool nod, despite the steamy hot anxiety soup that sloshed around my stomach.

I clenched my stomach muscles and willed the fear away. Maya must've been okay with what she saw, because after a few seconds she stepped aside and let Ryder in the room.

Ryder's blond hair was pulled back in a ponytail. She never pulled her hair back. It always fanned across her face. She wore a striped, black and white horizontal shirt, a pleated black skirt and stockings. The stockings had holes in them.

The fashionable kind that the young celebrities on television wore when they knew paparazzi followed them.

I straightened in my chair, though my back was already as straight as an ironing board. *What else changed? What else had I missed?*

"Ryder." My voice squeaked like a newborn chick.

She gave me a smile as weak as days-old coffee. "Mom." She sat down across from me, right next to Maya. Dr. Mitra offered his hand to both Maya and Ryder. Once they settled, he asked for drink orders. Maya took water. Ryder, a Dr Pepper. He told one of the volunteers, who grabbed our drinks from the lobby.

"Let's get started, shall we?" Dr. Mitra clapped his hands. "Ray walked you through our program. Do you feel like you understand the recovery process?"

Ryder nodded. "Mr. Freemont said the alcohol overtook the prefrontal cortex, her reasoning and stuff, and made it hard for her to control her emotions." She twisted her hands together in her lap. "So, this caused Mom to become mean and angry and emotional."

"Yes. Now do you understand how difficult recovery can be?"

Ryder glanced at Maya and then at me. "Umm. Yeah. It's kind of fascinating. Seeing how jacked up your brain gets with alcohol. Not fascinating in a good way, right? I don't want Mom to have to struggle that way, but I'm kinda a nerd and anyway . . . yeah, it's informative." She took a deep breath and looked away. "Cool to know, not . . . you know . . . because it happened."

Dr. Mitra gave her a sympathetic smile. A smile I knew well. "Yes, I understand." He turned his attention to Maya. "Do you feel like you understand?"

"Yes, I do."

"What was your perspective before?" he asked.

"My perspective hasn't changed. I get it's hard to overcome alcohol abuse, but I guess I'm still salty about how she got to this place. She has a daughter who depends on her, yet she just dipped out."

"I didn't 'dip out' on purpose," I said with air quotes. "You dumped me here, remember?"

"When do we get to the accountability part?" Maya asked in a bored voice.

"Maya, you said you'd try," Ryder whispered, but the room was so small and awkwardly silent, everyone could hear.

"I want us to take a few steps back." Dr. Mitra steepled his hands. "There's clearly some opportunity to dig deeper and find healthy ways to interact. Now, I don't want to assume anything, but I want to get an understanding on family definition. Ryder, would you say your family is close or distant?"

Maya sighed as strong as a Chicago wind.

"I . . . yes. Just not in the traditional sense. Mom is still Mom and Maya's my sister. It's just that . . . not all of us get along. And it's been that way for as long as I can remember."

Dr. Mitra nodded. "Who, in your opinion, doesn't get along?"

Ryder blinked twice. "I think you know, Dr. Mitra."

"I don't want to assume."

"Maya and Mom."

"Maya, Jeanie, do you agree with Ryder's assessment?"

Maya and I said yes.

"Has it always been that way? Or did it start once your father died?" he asked, looking at Maya.

Why ask? He knew from our sessions that Maya has hated me since she was a child.

A flicker of anger crossed Maya's face. "She and Daddy dated since I was a preteen, though I suspect they'd dated for a lot longer."

"When was your first argument?"

"When she tried to move my mother's remains."

My head snapped back. "Wh-what? What are you talking about, Maya?"

She looked at me. "You remember. It was about a month after you moved in. I overheard you telling Daddy that you were moving *my* mother's remains. How are you surprised by this?"

"That's not . . . that's not what happened." I shook my head.

Ryder gnawed on her bottom lip. "I'm sure it was a misunderstanding—"

"It wasn't," Maya cut in. "One morning my mother's urn was on the table, and the same day I return from school and it's plopped above the kitchen cabinets, off to the side to be forgotten."

"Maya, no." I shook my head. "That was not my intention. Ryder was playing hide-and-go-seek with your father. She bumped into the table and nearly toppled Renee's remains. I put it up high to keep it safe."

I remembered talking to Joseph. Renee's ashes were encased in a beautiful emerald green urn. It sat on the side table, next to her picture. It was beautiful, but far too fragile for a curious and accident-prone child.

Maya crossed her arms. "Well, you . . . you redecorated the house."

"I like to decorate." I shrugged. "I . . . I wasn't trying to make you feel uncomfortable. But I realize now that I should've tried a little harder. You were a child and I was the adult. I should've made more of an effort, instead of chalking your feelings up to hormones. I'm sorry."

"Okay." She nodded. "Okay," she said again, this time in a softer tone.

"And while we're at it, I'm sorry about making you lose your promotion."

"Who told you I lost a promotion?" She re-crossed her

arms. She looked like Joseph, her brown eyes narrowed just a bit, determined to seek the truth.

"Ryder. That's why she insisted on you joining us and she was right. I do hope you can forgive me."

"It's fine." Her lips quivered and she closed her eyes shut. A deep wrinkle formed between her brows. "You don't have to worry about me."

"I don't have to, but I want to. I want to do better by you."

Maya's eyes flew open. Her eyes were so soft, so vulnerable, so raw. In that very moment I felt like the biggest fool. I never took the time to notice or care. Maya didn't say anything, but I could tell she listened. She leaned a bit into her chair, she was breathing, but then again, she wasn't. It was like air was caught in her throat, just waiting for release.

I took a deep breath of my own and continued. "Just so you know, your daddy didn't care about you making partner—he was so proud of the heart you put into your clients and your determination to use everything you had to help others. I'm sorry for being jealous of the connection between you and your daddy. And you and Ryder. As much as I love and appreciate that she has you, I've always been a little sad for me. And I'm sorry for not once considering, well, you."

"M-Mom." Ryder's voice nearly broke me, but I powered through.

"You lost your father, your last parent, and I was so focused on me that I didn't think that you might feel alone. Maybe because I don't see you that way. You know, lonely, vulnerable. I'm not your mother, Maya. Renee was. And from what I can remember, and from what I can see, she did an outstanding job. I'm not your mother," I repeated, "but I hope that one day I can work my way up to be your friend."

"I . . ." Maya sucked up air through her nose. "Th-thank you. But this day isn't about me. It's about you and Ryder."

Dr. Mitra cleared his throat. "Still, I think we made some

real progress here. Now, I have a question for you, Ryder. How has your mother and Maya's relationship impacted you?"

"It hasn't been a walk in the park." She tilted her head back, staring at the ceiling. "Dad, he was the peacemaker. When things got tense, he'd step in and make a joke about his girls needing to get along. I used to think it was funny, but now I wonder why he didn't say anything deeper about it. I don't know how he could stand their arguing."

Goose bumps chased my spine.

Ryder shivered. "Being in the middle of their conflict, I felt split in two. On one hand, I understood why Maya wanted Mom out of the house. They didn't get along and technically the house belongs to her. But on the other hand, sometimes . . ." Her voice trailed off. She snuck a look at Maya before she averted her gaze to the floor. "I was upset that Maya didn't give Mom a little grace. A little time to get on her feet. It hurts to see the people I love hurt each other."

Maya fidgeted in her seat. "Sorry, Ryder. But between your mom's drinking and you acting out with Dani, I was out of my element."

My drinking impacted so many things. It was my fault Ryder had rebelled and hooked up with that awful young man. "I'm sorry, Chickadee. It's my fault that you had to do community service. If only I had paid attention—"

"No, Mom." She shook her head. "It wasn't your fault. I made the choice. Just like you made the choice to drink. And right now, I don't want to root around in the past, I want to focus on the future." She lifted her eyes to meet mine. Her beautiful blue eyes sparkled. "Like it or not we're all family. And family takes care of each other. I think if we all embrace that, then maybe we can be better people."

My daughter, a freaking genius. How could this seventeen-year-old have life more figured out than two grown women?

Maya smiled at Ryder then looked at me. "I want you to succeed, Jeanie. That's why I put you here. And you may not have liked it but deep in your heart, you know Daddy would want you to be healthy and happy."

"He would." I nodded. "Thank you."

Dr. Mitra continued the session. We talked about Joseph, home life, and how to support each other. He then had us act out scenarios that would typically set one of us off.

The session ended. Ryder gave me a hug and said goodbye. No hugs from Maya, we weren't there yet. She did nod at me. I'd like to think it was progress. I think she did a lot of the stuff at the beginning for Ryder, but I'd like to think toward the end, some of the things we discussed helped her understand that my intentions were good. Misguided, but good. I walked back to my room with a smile on my face.

Vic was inside, rocking back and forth on the floor, her back against the sofa, a crumpled napkin clutched between her fingers. "I've gotta get out of here."

"Huh, what are you talking about? You just got here."

"Yeah, but it's been a few weeks. I'm fine." She wiped sweat off her eyebrows with the napkin. After she wiped, she shredded it into tiny little strips. "Anyway. I've done this before. I don't need help. I'll never drink again, easy."

A classic sign of withdrawal. *I need to call for help.* My eyes darted to the door.

"Don't do that."

"Do what?"

"Look like you're ready to bolt. You're in the same sinking-ass boat with me. I'm fine. I just want to go home. I want to go home. I. Want. To. Go. Home!"

I nodded, my gaze steady on hers, anchoring her back from the dark abyss. Something must've gotten through to her because the grooves in her forehead disappeared.

"My girls don't understand, just like yours. They told me to stay or they wouldn't take me back. How can they do that to their mama?" she hiccupped.

I sat on the recliner across from her. "Babe, when was the last time you had a drink?"

"Huh?"

I leaned forward, my elbows digging into my thighs. "When did you have your last drink? And how much?"

Her eyes blinked a few times as she tormented the napkin. "I dunno. A few weeks ago? A few drinks?"

"Okay." I nodded. "You've been here for two and a half weeks, so I'm guessing something happened right before. Maybe you had more than a few drinks?" I asked softly.

"Look, you don't know me." Her voice went hard as a paved road.

"I do and I don't. I know you are going through withdrawal. I know being away from your family hurts. I know you're equal parts frustrated and embarrassed you struggle with addiction. I know you've done things you aren't proud of. I know that alcohol is like the ex that won't die. Every time you wrangle with him, you tell yourself that it's the last time and it's over, but then he flashes a grin and you're right back there. Next thing you know you've got mascara running down your cheeks and holes in your memory."

She sniffed and stopped rocking. "Okay. Maybe you do know me."

My lips inched into a reluctant smile. "Like you said, we're in the same sinking a-s-s boat together."

"You can say 'ass,' you know." Vic dabbed scraps of napkin on her forehead.

"I know. I just don't."

She raised an eyebrow.

I answered her unspoken question. "Daddy used to curse up, down and sideways. And he was particularly creative with me." I shook my head, shaking away the memories, but it didn't work. Daddy's curses were like being slapped in the face with a weighted glove. The bruises might be invisible, but the pain never went away. The only time I cursed was when I drank. Just like Daddy. I never, ever wanted to be like him.

I took quick, shallow breaths. It felt like Daddy's fat fingers were closing around my throat.

"The food sucks here." Vic stood.

I gasped for air. Vic looked me over, but she didn't say anything.

I gave her a smile, grateful that she pulled me out of the dark just seconds after I'd helped her. "The food's not all that bad."

"They don't use any damn seasoning."

"It's fine. All you need is salt and pepper to taste."

"Girl, you're telling me you were married to a black man and he didn't ask you to use seasoning?"

"I'm a great cook!" And I was.

"Mhmm." She sighed. "You're leaving soon."

Not even a week. I was ready to go back home, yet terrified I'd be back again. Just like Vic.

"What am I going to do without you?" she whispered.

"Survive. Get better. This time, for good."

"But who will I talk to? I hate everyone else here."

She didn't. Everyone loved her, but I got where she was coming from. She was everyone else's cheerleader, but she needed someone to push and ground her, too.

"I don't know . . . I'll ask if I can call you."

"Nah, girl. You know it doesn't work like that here."

"Okay, what about email?"

She shook her head. "They only let us use laptops if we have critical work to do."

"Fine, we'll do it *Pride and Prejudice* style. We'll write each other."

She nodded. "Okay. Every week. Take a picture of your art,

too. You don't have to put that in the letter, but send me an email, and I'll check it out when I leave."

I shook my head. "You can write me weekly, but I'll write you every day."

"Really?"

"Yes, really. And we'll exchange numbers. Oh! And we can visit each other. You can come to my home and I'll cook you a nicely *seasoned* dinner."

"You want me to drive my black ass all the way from Atlanta to . . . where the hell are you from again? Warm Springs, Hope Floats?"

"Hope Springs." I snorted. Vic's smile finally appeared. We both laughed for a good long time. Tears streamed down our faces. It was a happy cry, a cleansing cry—two fractured souls, pulling and pushing and pivoting to get back to normal.

CHAPTER 16

MAYA
DADDY LESSONS

Sunday morning, August 2nd
147 days

To day, Ryder and I picked up Jeanie from rehab and brought her back home. She walked around, eyes big, touching and smiling at everything as if she couldn't believe she was back.

Now, she and Ryder were curled on the couch, watching their favorite Jane Austen movie. I gave them the space they needed and went back to work.

I had two clients. One had been a throwaway referral from an old law school buddy who couldn't take on more clients. Earlier in the month, I'd sent one of those desperate "I'm forming my own law firm (translation: going solo), and I'm open for referrals (translation: I need money. Send me clients because I'm tired of boxed mac and cheese.)" emails.

Okay, I wasn't poor just yet, but I didn't want to rely on Daddy's generosity and my savings. If I played my cards right, I could retire five to ten years early, or maybe invest in stocks.

My other client found me through an online ad on a law referral site. If things didn't turn around soon, I would have to go back to corporate life, maybe in Atlanta. I wouldn't dare beg for my old job back. Besides, I'd incinerated my bridges.

After I drafted a memo for one of my clients, I toggled over to my speech. The city had planned to posthumously give Daddy the key to Hope Springs next Friday. The only thing I'd written was "Thank you, fine citizens of Hope Springs."

"Ahhh. I give up." I slammed my laptop shut. How in the hell was I supposed to tell everyone how much Daddy meant to me? His legacy was impossible to replicate, his shoes too large and wide to fill. Not to mention everyone would be there. My old colleagues. Roland. No, maybe he wouldn't come. He was pretty pissed at me. The last run-in said as much.

I pushed away from my desk, ready to take out my little boat and row away my frustration. Maybe some creative entity would give me inspiration out on the water.

I power-walked through the living room.

"Hey!" Ryder chirped. Wrapped in a fuzzy gray blanket, a huge bowl of popcorn in her lap, Ryder looked snug as a bug. Jeanie was locked hip-to-hip with her.

"Want to join us?" Ryder tossed popcorn in her mouth.

I shook my head.

Jeanie fidgeted under the cover. "Are you sure?"

On the screen Elizabeth Bennet rolled her eyes at one of her sisters. I recognized Elizabeth Bennet. She was a master at giving her family the bitches-be-crazy look.

"I would but . . . I need to go on the lake. I'm trying to write Daddy's speech."

Jeanie paused the movie, her brown eyes warm and clear. "Thank you for doing that. Joseph would be so happy you're accepting the key on his behalf."

"Are you sure you don't want to give the speech?"

Jeanie waved a hand and shook her head. "No, thank you.

Joseph would want you up there for him, and you're so good at public speaking."

"Thanks, Jeanie." It was weird, her being nice and considerate and complimentary.

"You're welcome." She reached over and patted Ryder's knee. "Just standing near the podium with you and Ryder by my side is good enough for me."

Yeah, weird. It'd had been so long since I'd seen her sober.

Ryder was clearly excited about her mom's progress. I just hoped she wouldn't disappoint or disappear on Ryder.

She won't. I'll make sure of it.

"You've got this." Ryder gave me a thumbs-up. "Let me know if you want to practice what you have so far."

"Hello, and thank you, citizens of Hope Springs." I waved my arms in the air. "What do you think?"

Ryder snorted. "You'll figure it out. The lake always helps you like it did with Dad."

Anytime Daddy had a tough deliberation or in his earlier days, a tough case, he'd rowed on the lake. Sometimes he'd stay out there for hours. He used to say if you got quiet enough the lake would whisper its secrets, carried by the wind. I grabbed the keys from the hooks, opened the back door and stepped onto the deck. Like always, I jogged downstairs toward the ramp.

The dock looked wooden, but it'd been replaced by some aluminum decking and painted to mirror light wood. Daddy had just replaced the dock before he died. He'd said he had a bad dream about one of his girls falling through the old rotted wood. He wouldn't say who, but the way his glaze flitted up between me and the dock, I knew it'd been me. Hell, I was the only other person who went out on the lake by myself.

I didn't want to row on the lake today, I wanted something faster. The twenty-five-horsepower Mercury engine would give me the speed I needed.

I stepped into my boat, *Speedy* (no judgment, I'd named it as a child), and checked the fuel. After twisting the valve, the air hissed letting out air and fumes.

I put the keys into the ignition, pressed the button to lower the engine, squeezed the primer, and then turned the engine to let my baby purr.

Don't forget to undo the line, Baby Girl.

Once, when I was ten years old, my job had been to unhook the line and I'd forgotten. Even after decades of us going out on the lake, Daddy would still remind me to undo the hook.

"I won't forget, Daddy." I responded as I always did, but this time I didn't roll my eyes. I smiled, a little joy and a little sadness sat on my heart, as I walked to the back of the boat and unhooked the line.

The lake was semi-private—available only to residents of the quiet lake community. We were on the edge of fall and nature was turning. Small ripples in the lake reflected the army of green trees close to its banks. A light mist hovered just above the water. The Georgia humidity had vanished, leaving the morning air crisp. In a few months, it would bite.

It would be a good day to fish, but I hadn't brought my gear. I pulled the boat into a nook and turned off the engine.

I pulled my phone from my pocket and then swiped open the notes app. I breathed a deep breath. The clean air rush my lungs. "Okay, Daddy, I need your help."

A bird chirped. Water lapped against the boat's hull. But he didn't speak. I knew he wouldn't.

How did one boil down a lifetime to minutes? How could I express who he was and what he meant to so many in the community? Even before Daddy died, there'd been countless times someone came up to me, singing his praises. "They would've been under the jail, but he stepped in and offered a helping hand." Daddy didn't stop at the sentencing, he made damn sure to follow up and follow through. If someone needed a mentor, depending on their interest he'd set it up. If someone needed a job, he'd make sure to get them interviews, even if they were out of town.

But as wonderful as he was, he could be so very obtuse. He'd been raised by strong black women. Women who kept taking hits on the chin and never complained, never gave up. My aunts, his older sisters had a major hand in raising him and he had so much respect for them. He told me once that Aunt Lisa doubled down to raise her son by herself after Uncle Charlie died. She worked tirelessly, never complained. Aunt Clara Bell raised him and his siblings when their parents died. He told me similar stories of how she magically stretched money, how she made sure everyone had the opportunity to go to college.

"Samson had nothing on Aunt Clara Bell," he'd always say.

But did Aunt Clara Bell really feel that way? I had to know.

The matriarch's house was four miles away from us by boat. Daddy had built her a dock, too. Though she never went out on the lake, she loved our visits.

I sped the boat toward her house. My great-aunt sat on the dock, wrapped in a red blanket, her feet dangling just above the water.

"Hey, child." She pulled the blanket tight around her body. "Was wondering when you were coming for a visit."

"Sorry. I've been a little preoccupied."

"You've got a lot on your mind. Judge's speech, and you and your beau are on the rocks."

I sighed, turned around and secured the boat. I loved my aunt, but not the way she pretended to have some sort of psychic abilities. I couldn't deny she knew certain things, but I'm guessing it was the speed of small-town gossip and strong intuition.

"Anyway, I cooked your favorite and the coffee's warming."

She leaned over to push herself up, but I rushed to her side and helped. "Thank you, sweets. One day I'm just gonna roll right on over into this lake."

My heart rate spiked. I knew she was joking, but I didn't like the thought of my favorite aunt dying. "Well, then don't get so close." I guided her off the ramp that led right up to her house.

"Then how am I going to tease the little fishies with my toes? I've gotta be close to do that."

The smell of strong coffee hit my nose when we entered the house. Just as Aunt Clara Bell promised, my favorite food— French toast with peaches drowning in sugar and cinnamon. A rasher of bacon and stacks of sausage patties sat on a napkin near the stove.

"Anyone else coming over?" The spread could feed an army.

"Your other aunts will probably be by soon. But I cooked this for you." She put my plate together. Even if I insisted I could do it, she would have fixed my meal. Sometimes I think she still saw me in pigtails.

She put the plate in front of me. I didn't dare touch it. Not until my great-aunt fixed her own plate of grits, toast and scrambled eggs.

She grabbed her homemade whipped cream from the fridge. I greedily scooped a large glob and drizzled it on the sweet bread. Aunt Clara Bell leaned over and placed another peach on top of the whipped cream, just the way I liked it.

After she settled across from me at her little square table, she leaned over and grabbed my hand.

"Dear Heavenly Father. Thank you for allowing us another beautiful day to fellowship. Thank you for giving me the strength and foresight to cook this breakfast for my niece. And Lord, please give my niece the strength to tell me the truth, not waste my time and own up to the fact that she's still in love with her boyfriend, who she thought she was sneaking around town with, but Lord . . . everyone knew."

My eyes flew open. My aunt's eyes were still closed, though she had a little smirk on her mouth.

"In the name of Jesus, we pray, Amen."

I snatched my hand back.

"You betta say amen before you eat that food."

"Amen." I stabbed the fork into the fluffy bread. Syrup and cream oozed like melting ice caps on a mountain.

Aunt Clara Bell flicked a napkin onto her lap and then started to eat her food. She looked me over, as she chewed on her toast.

I continued shoveling food into my mouth. I'd come here to ask her about Daddy, but Aunt Clara Bell practically raised Daddy, and though she often cracked jokes at his expense, no one else could talk about her Joe.

I dropped my fork and backed away from my now empty plate.

"I've got a question about Daddy." I sighed and looked her in the eyes. "I'm struggling to write this speech about him. I don't know what's blocking me, but the words aren't coming."

Aunt Clara Bell dabbed the corner of her lips with a napkin. She tapped her long fingernails on the table. "That's because you've got some sour feelings towards your daddy. You wanna know why he put you and Jeanie in that situation with the will."

I nodded. "And it's just not that. It's . . . it's more. I don't think he meant to, but he treated us differently."

Aunt Clara Bell snorted. "Well, I should hope so. Jeanie was his wife and you were his daughter."

"No, it's . . ." I sighed, struggling to frame my question. "He raised me to be tough. He wanted me to be strong, take no shi—stuff." I amended my statement when I saw Aunt Clara Bell's eyebrows shoot to her hairline. "When I was in kindergarten there was a boy who bullied a lot of kids in class, especially the girls."

"Mhmm." Aunt Clara Bell nodded as she sipped her orange juice.

"Anyway, one day I came home crying about the boy. Daddy asked me if the boy hit me and I told him no. Then he asked if I cried in front of him and I said no, but I wanted to." I paused for a quick breath. "Daddy said, 'Good. Never let them see you cry, otherwise they'll hold the upper hand.' He said that . . . that you and Aunt Lisa and Aunt Eloisa were so strong. So ever since that day anytime I wanted to cry, I couldn't. I'd imagine the disappointed look on Daddy's face. I didn't want him to think I was weak—and then he goes and marries the human version of a weeping willow . . ." I shrugged. "I don't get it."

Aunt Clara Bell sucked her teeth. "I always knew that boy was dense."

"Aunt Clara Bell!"

"What? I'm telling the truth. I loved that boy like he was my own, but I cannot believe he told you that. And now look at you."

"What about me?"

"You don't know how to cry. Your best friend is a seventeen-year-old girl and you can't keep a man. Whew, chile. You need a vat of castor oil to flush out all that emotional constipation."

"You've got a way with words, Aunt Clara Bell."

She shrugged.

"You keep that up I'm gonna etch one of your little comments on your tombstone."

"And you won't hear a peep out of me because I'll be worm food. Now, honey . . ." She sighed. "Let's get back to the topic at hand. Your daddy was a great man, but you put him on a pedestal. He could do no wrong in yours or Jeanie's eyes. Heck, I think the only one who really saw him was Riley."

"Ryder."

"That's what I said," she snapped. "But what I'm saying is

that he was just a man. And he thought he was doing good by you to tell you that, because that's what he saw. Me and your aunts, maybe we went sideways on acting so tough around him. But hell, I was trying to raise a man. A *black* man in the Deep South, no less. But make no mistakes, we cried. With each other, with our men. The world"—she waved her hand— "can be cold. And you need someone to cover your soft side. Now, Joe covered all of Jeanie because she's sensitive, but that don't make her weak."

I snorted. I wanted to add a *shee-ittt*, but I liked my face without lumps.

"How many women would go toe-to-toe with me about giving Joe bad food after he found out he got a high cholesterol? Well, Jeanie did. And when you were younger, there was this nasty woman going around town spreading rumors about Joe. Jeanie told me and your aunts to let her handle it, and she did. Now, I don't know what she said to the lady, but she didn't so much as say a peep about her and Joe after that. She's not naturally a combative person, but she'll go to war to protect the ones she loves. She protected your dad's soft side, too."

I didn't understand. I thought the aunts didn't like Jeanie. Now Aunt Clara Bell never said anything bad around me, but I didn't get the impression that she liked Jeanie. I cleared my throat. "If you . . . if you saw those things about Jeanie and you knew how I felt . . . why didn't you say something then? Maybe I wouldn't have . . ." I sighed. "I don't know."

"Baby, you weren't in a state of reason. You hate that woman, plain and simple."

"Yeah, but this has been going on for over a decade. Surely you could've told me this."

"Have you met yourself?" Aunt Clara raised an eyebrow and folded her arms. "Girl, you can hold a grudge forever. Case in point, with your daddy and he's gone."

"It's not a grudge. I'm just . . . I'm just processing my feelings. I mean, I was a child when this all happened. I just wished Daddy would've made us address it instead of sweeping it under the rug."

"Like I said, your daddy could be dense. But he loved you, he loved all of us and he had a good heart. But he's not here, Sweets. The mess under the rug's been exposed and you're grown." She leaned over and squeezed my hand and gentled her voice. "It's you and Jeanie's mess to clean up now."

"Okay, yeah." I nodded. "I mean, I can do that or figure it out, but I should give Jeanie some time. She just got back from rehab and I don't want to say anything to set her off."

"That monkey is going to ride her back for a long time, so don't put it off. Just put on your big-girl panties and face the music."

"Okay, one last question. I was on the lake the other day, and it was raining. I kept hearing . . . this sounds crazy, but I heard Daddy say, 'God sends rain on the just and the unjust.' It's a Bible verse but what do you think it means?"

"What do *you* think?"

"Bad things happen to good and bad people? I don't know, that's why I asked you."

"Whew, chile."

I threw up my hands. "That's not an answer, Aunt Clara. What do you think?"

"I think you need to come on back to Bible study."

Before I could complain she held up a hand. "It means God wants you to love thy enemy. He wants you to do what he does. If your enemy is hungry, feed 'em. Be the better person and be like Him."

Damn. "You sure that's what it means?" I asked, knowing full well the mother of the church knew and understood her verses inside out.

Aunt Clara Bell rolled her eyes. "Very. Now tell me about Mr. Tall, Dark and Handsome you've been sneaking in and out of town with."

I dang near got whiplash from the topic change. "Who told you?" I'd thought we'd been discreet. No one threw us suspicious looks at the office. Well, except Katy, likely because she liked Roland.

"Oh, one of my spirit friends told me."

I wanted to ask if her spirit friend was Miss Jessie down at the gas station. The woman knew all the town's secrets. People brought drinks, gas, and gossip to the old woman. She and Aunt Clara Bell had been best friends since grade school.

"Tell your spirit friend they're nosy and need to get an afterlife." I shook my head. "I'll bite. What did they tell you?"

"That you got mad because he didn't tell you about not making partner. That you got into a hissy and broke up with him. Actually, no . . ." She looked up at the ceiling while my heart jumped out of my chest. "You didn't break up with him because you refused to get into a relationship. But he was wrong, too. He could've told you what was going on, but he was too afraid of losing you."

Aunt Clara Bell's sharp words ripped the air out of my lungs. Sometimes the old woman was scary as hell.

"You want my opinion?"

All I could do was nod.

"Take your time. You know, sometimes young ladies are so afraid of being alone, they accept whatever scraps are given to them. When my Henry died, there were a few suitors here and there who wanted me to settle down. And by settle down, I mean *settle down*. But I realized they weren't for me. And I like my own company. I like teasing the fishies with my toes. I like cooking for myself, I like sewing, and listening to my jazz records. I love going outside on the porch and dancing in the rain. Sometimes naked."

"God, gross."

"What I'm saying is be by yourself. See if you miss him. Ask yourself, does he make me better?"

"And if he does?"

"Then I suggest you get over there and snatch him up and fast, before that little heifer at the law firm does."

I stood. "Another option for the epitaph."

"Your choice," she said in a bored voice.

I leaned over and kissed her cheek. "Thank you."

"You're welcome. I'm glad you came over to talk to me about your man and your daddy. Makes an old lady feel useful."

"Of course, I need you. You're the wisest woman I know." I walked out the back door, but my aunt's voice stopped me before I cleared the threshold.

"Your daddy. He was an amazing man. He helped a lot of people, changed many lives. But he was never a saint. And he never wanted to be one. When you write that speech of yours, remind everyone that it's okay to be human. Give them hope that they can make a difference in their own way, too. Just like Joe."

Ideas sparked in my head. Joseph the comedian, the husband, the father, the brother and the son. The man who snuck cigars when his wife wasn't looking. The man who had a secret arch nemesis on the golf course.

I smiled as I trudged through the backyard and up the ramp. The words were jumping like fish now.

Thursday afternoon, August 6ᵗʰ
151 days

I stood near the podium at City Hall, a sweaty mess. Even the backs of my knees were drenched in sweat.

I adjusted the hemline of my dark blue dress as the mayor introduced me. Ryder stood beside me. Thankfully we didn't have to beat her into a dress, much to Jeanie's delight. However, the little sneak wore her Chucks.

Jeanie wore a bright yellow dress with yellow patent leather heels. The heel height wasn't as high as I usually rocked them, but the shoes were still cute. If we were best friends, I'd steal them. Her brown tresses flowed down her back. The dress was a little loose around her waist, but from the way Ryder shoveled food down her mother's throat, she'd gain back the weight in no time.

The mayor's loud voice snagged my attention. "Without further ado, I present the key to the city to Judge Joseph Donaldson's daughter, Maya."

Everyone clapped. The rhythm of my heart synched to the thunderous applause. I stepped to the podium and adjusted the mic to sit a little higher. With my stilettos, I towered over the short and portly mayor. He leaned over and whispered that he'd hand me the key once I finished my speech.

I noticed a sea of familiar faces. Old colleagues of Daddy. Even some of my old coworkers and bosses.

"Thank you, Mayor Franklin, for this honor. But I've got to tell you, if Daddy were here, he'd say, 'What am I gonna do with this big-ass key?'" I laughed with the audience.

"Excuse my language, but that's what he would say. Daddy, he wasn't one to accept praise gracefully. He liked working his magic behind the scenes, but if he were alive . . ." I licked my lips. "If he were alive, he'd be causing a fuss. Jeanie would make him put on his good tie, the one with the blue and maroon stripes. She'd make sure he got a haircut and used his beard cream." I looked at my stepmom as she blinked back tears. "Ryder would give Daddy a history about how keys to the city started in medieval times when you needed a key to the city after dark." Ryder grinned and nodded.

"And me. I'd tell Daddy to take the damn key because he

deserved it. I'd remind him of the many times scared parents called him in the middle of the night about legal advice for their kids. Or the times when someone sent him their résumé because they heard he had the magic touch in getting people jobs. I'd remind him of all the attorneys he's mentored, many of you who are here today. My father was an extraordinary man and with his position, he impacted many lives. A common theme I hear when people talk about my father's legacy is giving second chances."

My gaze clashed with Roland's. The intensity in his dark eyes was like a charger to my heart. I ripped my gaze from him and scanned the audience.

"It's not just about giving second chances but understanding the root cause to why something happened in the first place. To quote Victor Hugo: 'If the soul is left in darkness, sins will be committed. The guilty one is not he who commits the sin, but he who causes the darkness.' "

I waited a few beats to let the quote sink in. "For example, what happens when a young man steals bread for his family because his parents fell on hard times? Well, until something changes, he may do it again. Daddy understood that. He understood not being the sum of our mistakes. He peered into the soul of a person. He saw potential. He imagined the possibilities if an obstacle was removed. And I think . . . I think we all can do that, too. Now, I must admit, I didn't realize this lesson until he died."

A hot tear stung my eye. A cool hand slid into mine. The scruff of a hundred tiny diamonds encrusted around the band scraped against my finger. *Jeanie.*

I squeezed her hand.

"But I know he's smiling down on us, despite not wanting the hoopla and pomp and circumstance, because I finally learned."

I paused as the audience thundered with claps and praise.

I raised my index finger. "Now, I know sometimes, when we honor those who have gone before us, we get intimidated by their lives. We feel inspired, we want to leave a legacy, but at the same time, we feel so very overwhelmed."

A few heads nodded in the audience.

"Don't be. Let me give you a rundown on Daddy. He didn't have a lick of rhythm. He swore he was Barry White, but he couldn't sing at all. He left his socks on the floor and I'm sure I speak for me, Ryder and Jeanie when I say he drove us crazy calling us 'his girls.'" There were lots of grins and laughter.

"What I'm saying is, we all have our issues. Daddy was . . . a man. A living, breathing, fallible man. But he used his platform, his position, his knowledge to make life better for others. I challenge all of you to look into your hearts and figure out what you can do, because paying it forward is the highest honor you can give to my dad. Thank you, Mayor Franklin, and thank you, citizens of Hope Springs."

I stepped away from the podium. Ryder rushed me and pulled me into a bear hug. "Oh, my goodness, you rocked!"

Jeanie stood behind Ryder, beaming from ear to ear. "Joseph would be so proud of you. So proud." She sniffed and looked as if she were holding her breath.

"You can cry, you know." I gave her a smile and released Ryder from our embrace. "Sometimes it's okay to cry. I'm sorry if I ever made you feel . . ." I searched for the word and then Aunt Clara Bell's conversation popped in my head. "Emotionally constipated."

Jeanie barked a surprised laugh as she reached into her small clutch. She pulled out a wad of Kleenex. "G-good. Because I'm not going to make it."

She stepped closer as others began to crowd around us. She whispered, "I know I have the tendency to . . . to emote a lot.

But now I realize how my reactions can block out the voices of others."

I leaned away and said, "We'll just meet somewhere in the middle. I'll have a mind to let go and you have a mind to emote but not at the expense of others." I gave her my hand to shake. "Deal."

"Oh, yeah." She smiled at me through a glistening veil over her eyes. "Deal."

CHAPTER 17

RYDER
LET'S TALK ABOUT IT

Friday morning, August 7th
152 days

"I'm going to strangle your daughter." Maya paced back and forth while Mom and I sat at the kitchen table.

When I didn't attend yesterday's session, Alston had called Maya, who was listed as my next of kin. The showcase would go on tonight. Alston told Maya that he wouldn't mark me down as absent as long as I showed up and performed.

Mom sat beside me, rubbing her paint-stained hands raw. "I agree with Maya—not with the strangling, mind you." She glanced at Maya and then looked at me. "But you need to attend this showcase."

"You have no choice." Maya stopped pacing. "I will hog-tie your ass and plop you on stage."

I shrugged. "You can't make me speak."

"Ryder. What the hell? You will lose the opportunity for that scholarship if you have a record. And trust me, Judge Bryant meant what he said—you don't finish the community service, your future will be in jeopardy. Why are you doing this? It's your dream to go to Emory."

It was my dream, until stupid Alston ruined it. I hadn't toured the campus yet, but I'm sure it wasn't large enough to never run into him again.

"I don't have to go to Emory. I've got good enough grades to go other places. And I can get the state scholarship."

"But it doesn't cover room and board and all the books you need. Daddy left us a nest egg, but it's not forever."

"Then I'll get a job. I'll figure it out. It's no big deal."

"Having a misdemeanor on your record is a big fucking deal. Stop being silly. All of this is because you're butt hurt over a boy."

I averted my gaze to the wall and crossed my arms.

"You know what . . . ?" Maya sighed. "I thought we were over this rebellious bullshit. Jeanie, you're up." Maya stomped out of the room.

"Ryder—"

"Mom, I just . . . I know it sounds like I'm being dumb, but I'm not. Yes, I like Alston and yes it sucks that he's not willing to give us a chance, but the issue is that he's stunting me."

"Stunting you? Like, your growth?"

"Yes, as a poet. Like when we practice, he never helps me. He never calls on me to give an example. He avoids me like the plague. We're doing this group-dialogue thing but other than that there are only two spots for the poetry gig."

"Did he say who he's given those to?"

I shrugged. "I guess he announced it at the last meeting."

Her eyes widened, she shook her head and bit her lip. "That's why you didn't go."

"Yeah." Well, that was part of it. The other part I couldn't tell her.

"You know what? We should paint." She slapped her knee.

"Paint?"

"Yes." She smiled and bunny-hopped from her seat. "Let's pull out a few easels and paint outside."

"Mom I can't paint. I don't know how."

"I'll teach you. It'll be like one of those fancy sip-and-paint classes in town."

"O-okay, I guess." I was surprised. I thought Mom would stumble through a lecture about accountability. Or a low blow about how Dad would hate that I'd have a record.

"Great! Give me thirty minutes and then meet me outside." She clapped her hands and hurried away.

I met her on the porch. She had a tray with fruit, bite-sized sandwiches, Triscuits and cheese and Arnold Palmers—lemonade mixed with sweet tea.

Paint supplies were set in front of both easels. Mom pointed at a dirty apron. "Put on the smock and settle in. Today we are going to paint a theme. The theme choices are family or life."

"Mom," I groaned. "I can't paint people."

"And you don't have to, Chickadee." She held up a sketch. "I pre-sketched something for you. One with the word family or two, a quote from your favorite author."

I looked at the quote from Shel Silverstein.

> Underneath my outside face
> There's a face that none can see.
> A little less smiley
> A little less sure
> But a whole lot more like me

Mom had added swirls and smileys and a mask and stars.

"I love it."

"Good. There are your paints. Now get to work."

We painted for a few hours. Where I had zero talents, Mom's painting was stunning. She'd painted the swing on our front porch. There were three people on the swing.

"Is that us? Me, you and Maya?"

"Mhmm." She shook her head. "This is the Donaldson family. We laugh, we cry, we argue together. And maybe . . ." Mom sighed as she dipped her brush in bright yellow paint. "Maybe one day we can sit out on the porch and talk about our day." She stopped painting. Her bright eyes reflected the sun. No glaze or haze. They were clear and magnificent.

"I'd like that, too. And hey, we're kinda doing that now."

"Yes. Kinda." She smiled back. "So . . . when are you going to tell me what's bothering you?"

My back muscles stiffened. I slowed the sloppy streaky strokes on the canvas. "I already told you."

Mom dipped her brush into water and placed it on a tray near the easel. "I know I haven't been around, and the last thing I want to do is pressure you. But I can't help but wonder if you're avoiding this Alston boy for another reason."

I glanced at my phone that I'd propped against the railing. How could she know? Did he tell her?

"Chickadee . . . whatever it is, it's okay. No judgment, no pressure."

I nodded my head. "Alston and I got into a fight. At first because I felt like he was being childish and ignoring me. Then he told me he liked me but . . . I wasn't worth the risk. He's in college and I'm not. So, I told him to . . . I told him a lot of things. Things I don't want to rehash right now."

"Okay, I respect that. As long as he didn't threaten or hurt you."

"No, Mom. It's cool." I shook my head. "We haven't been talking but then he texted and said I was voted by the group to perform, and he agreed. But I can't now. It's too . . ." I took a breath. "I can't now."

"Why the heck not?" Mom frowned. "You're amazing and crazy talented. And you—"

"My poem. It's about you. It's about how you . . . how I felt about you. I wrote it for myself. But then I shared it with Alston, and he thought it was good and now he wants me to perform it and it was fine at first because I was so angry with you. But now I'm not. If I perform it, everyone will know it's about you and I don't want to embarrass you or hurt your feelings and—"

"Slow down." She shook her head. "Take a deep breath and just slow down." Mom grabbed a glass and gulped the iced tea down. "Whew. Okay." She shook her head as if she were gearing up for something. She took another gulp and sighed.

Creepy crawlers slithered over my skin. "See, I knew this was a bad idea."

"It's fine." She scrubbed her palms against her smock.

"No, it's not."

"Yes. Yes, it is. I'm glad you can be honest with me. And I have to be honest with you, too."

My toes curled into the soles of my shoes. I nodded and held my breath, waiting for the proverbial punch to land.

"You have every right to express yourself and you are entitled to your feelings. I have to own up to the fact that I embarrassed you. I endangered you. It's the greatest regret of my life. And right now, I'm equal parts ashamed and proud. Ashamed of what I did to you and proud—so proud that you are selfless enough to think about my feelings. But baby girl, this is your decision to perform the poem. This is your life. And I won't stand in the way of a great opportunity. I certainly will not stand in the way of you getting a scholarship. It's not worth it. My reputation is already tattered, and I did it to myself."

"But I don't want to do it, Mom. I wrote it for *me*. I've moved past those feelings."

"Have you?" She narrowed her eyes, assessing me like she used to when I was a little girl and had rolled around in the mud and pretended that I didn't know how I'd gotten dirty.

"Yes," I hissed. What was this? I wasn't the one who needed the intervention.

"Honey, I don't think so. You're so . . . stiff around me. You're so careful about everything."

"Like what?" I snapped.

"The clothes you wear. You've got on a maxi skirt and sandals. I thought you'd done it because of that boy." She shook her head. "But then I noticed how careful you are when you speak to me, right down to the word choice. It's as if you've Googled triggers and removed them from your vocabulary."

My head jerked away as if I'd been slapped. Yes, I'd done that very thing. Mom was sensitive and I wanted to be supportive.

But careful? That was the thing I'd accused Alston of being. Too cautious, too afraid to live. Was I the pot calling the kettle black?

"Maybe you're right. But I wanted to help. I want to support your journey. And, you know, dresses aren't so bad."

Her hands slid into mine. "Like you said, it's my journey. Mine to own. Mine to travel. Not yours. There is nothing you have done to make it difficult and it breaks my heart that you think this way. I may have cracked a little, but I'm not broken. Look at me, darlin'."

I raised my head, my eyes locked on hers.

"Every day I'm growing stronger. I don't want you to be a robot. I want you to be you. Honest, kind, incredible you."

My mouth quivered as I swallowed the emotion that threatened to erupt.

"You once told me that words have the power to heal. And you never know the impact you'll have on someone who's going through what you or what I went through. So . . . so speak your truth. Don't worry about your mama. I'm a tough old broad." She gave me a smile brighter than the moon.

"Okay, Mom. I'll do it."

She sniffed and her chest puffed up like a toad. "Good. I'll clean up and you clean yourself up. Let Alston know that you'll be performing tonight."

My shoulders relaxed and the tiny little knots along them disappeared. I didn't realize how much the situation stressed me out until now. Mom and I had never talked like this. For all my important questions, I went to Maya first and then Dad. Never Mom. I'd always assumed she wouldn't have the answers. I grabbed my phone and walked toward the door. Hand on the screen door, I paused before I stepped through. "I underestimated you. I'm sorry. I won't do it again. I won't make you feel bad like Gran and Pop do."

Her mouth parted open and her breath hitched. Her eyes turned bright and liquid and it made my heart skip. It made me feel good to make her feel good.

I rushed into the house before I could say anything. For once, I didn't need the words. Her eyes told me everything.

Friday night, August 7ᵗʰ
152 days

"Glad you could make it," Alston whispered, startling me from my trance. The dancers were on stage now. After their performance, I was up next.

I turned to face him. The gel in his hair attempted to tame his curls, but some of the spirals still pushed through. He was close, so close I smelled cinnamon from his gum.

"You ready?"

"No."

"I'm sorry about what I said to you. It's just that—"

"I know. Besides, it wouldn't work out between us anyway. Not in the long run."

"Why?" he asked, his voice low and impatient.

"The entire summer you taught us to speak our truth. Yet, you can't take your own advice."

The muscles in his jaw clenched. He looked away. I leaned closer, right next to his ear. "I'm going out there. And I'm speaking my truth. Maybe you'll learn something from me today."

When I leaned away, his eyes were now on mine. His chest heaved. He stared at my lips with a look so starved, it gave me hunger pains.

Applause broke the tension. Someone called my name. I looked away, heading toward the stage.

I marched to center stage. Mind clear, heart full, bursting with energy. "Hello, everyone. My name is Ryder Bennett. I'm seventeen years old and I attend Whitfield Academy. Over the summer, my teacher Alston taught us spoken word. I've . . . I've written poems, but I've never performed. So please forgive me if I'm a little nervous." The audience clapped and a few people cheered, "Go, Ryder."

"Let's talk about it." I took a deep breath. "Let's talk about babies . . . armed with rattles, and coos, hugs and kisses. Milk to make their bodies good. Lullabies to make their minds strong." I tapped my temple.

"The world seems brighter, the grass greener, the sky, ocean blue. You send thanks to heavens for the miracle you've created. The wind caresses your face and you know, you just know that you've been touched by God.

"Then . . . a car swerves into your lane. A man with mud-brown eyes and earth-brown skin looks alarmed. And with the same mouth and in the same breath and in the same sentence you scream: GO BACK TO YOUR OWN COUNTRY!" I yelled into the mic; my fist punched the air. "The baby cries from the backseat of the car, scared of Mommy and Daddy. Let's talk about it.

"Let's talk about the young black man you passed by on the street with the Kaepernick jersey. You tighten your purse straps, lock your doors, and roll that beautiful bouncy baby so fast the wheels lose their tracks. ALL LIVES MATTER! But when the black and blue beat men black and blue and when boys who play with toys raise their hands, gunned down by overzealous men before they can become . . . a man . . ." I breathed into the mic, pausing for effect.

"If you squeeze your eyes shut, you can pretend those lifeless brown eyes look nothing like your baby's blues. And those youth size, over-the-head hoodies are worlds apart from your pastel-colored, zip-up hoodies. Let's talk about it.

"Let's talk about pasty, old white dudes, robbing intelligent women of their personal agency, forcing us to a lifetime in prison if we don't bend to their will. Let's talk about hundreds of women dying from pregnancy-related complications. Let's talk about the fact that black women are four times more likely to die in childbirth. Yet, we're the MURDERERS!" I yelled into the mic. "I'm talking to you, *Georgia*. Let's talk about it.

"Let's talk about toppling the age of racism and patriarchy. Let's talk about embracing our differences. No. Let's stop talking. Let's *do* something. Let's teach our kids to be each other's keepers. To care about their fellow man. Let's do that."

I stepped back from the mic. The room was silent. The spotlight suspended above me baked my skin. I couldn't see into the audience, so if someone aimed tomatoes, or—I dunno, what did people throw at bad performers on stage these days? I wouldn't see it coming.

But I could hear just fine. A loud whistle pierced through the silence. Claps started, slow and clunky and unsure, until it aligned to one beat, one booming sound. It was like God himself gave me his seal of approval.

Alston rushed the stage, picked me up and twirled me in the air. He carried me offstage. "My God, woman, you're incredible." He lowered me to the ground, a grin split his face. "That wasn't the poem you practiced."

"No, I . . . I just did it."

"Improv?" He grabbed my shoulder. "And so, the student surpasses the teacher." He dropped his grin. His eyes went serious. "You surpassed me in a lot of ways. You're right, you know. About what you said earlier."

I nodded. "Yeah. I know."

"I'm sorry. Are you still . . . ?" He cut himself off, but his mouth moved as if he were searching for the right words.

"Am I into you?"

"Yes. Because if you are, you're right. We can figure it out. I'd want to meet your mom, of course. Your sister, too—well, formally. I want them to feel comfortable with who I am and understand that—"

I leaned up and kissed him. Adrenaline and energy zipped through my lips. His fingers dug into my hips.

I broke the kiss and took a few steps back. My heart drummed like the Energizer bunny. I tried to gather my thoughts and play it cool.

"So that's a yes?"

"It's a maybe." Though my words were noncommittal, I couldn't control my grin.

"Ryder!" Maya yelled from behind me. I turned around, straight into her arms.

"Girl, I was snapping so hard for you. That's what you do, right? You snap when things are good?"

I shrugged. "I don't know. This is my first time."

A throat cleared from behind Maya. Mom. Tears brimmed her eyes.

"You're so good. Through and through," she whispered to me. "You didn't have to—"

"I spoke my truth. Just like you said." Instead of disparaging Mom, I made it a tribute to Dad. To the life he led, to the things he did. His words were powerful, but his actions, what he taught his daughters through love and lessons, made the world just a little bit better.

"Let's celebrate," Maya cut in. "Waffles and shakes at Lenny's."

"That would be nice," Mom agreed. She leaned in and asked, "Do you want to invite Alston?"

"No." I shook my head. "Tonight, it's Judge's girls."

CHAPTER 18

JEANIE
THE SPACE BETWEEN

Saturday afternoon, September 12th
188 days

It'd been six weeks since my time at Straight Arrow. Ryder returned to school, finishing out her senior year, and the weather had begun changing from uncomfortably hot to a lingering chill in the air. Vic finished doing time, as she put it, in rehab.

She was visiting today, and as I promised, I cooked my famous pot roast. Classical music drifted from the speakers installed in the ceiling. The moving cadence of the piano set the pace of my cooking. Right now, the piano was speedy. I quickly sliced the potato wedges. The carrots were already chopped and chunked. I threw them into the pan, covered it and put it into the oven.

A purr from a car came from the driveway. I quickly washed and dried my hands and then hurried outside to find a black sedan parked in the driveway.

A man in a starched white shirt and black pants hopped out of the car. He had one of those black chauffeur hats on his head. He opened the back door. Vic stepped out, one long leg at a time, and gave him a regal smile.

Her eyes met mine. I fanned myself and mouthed, "Fancy." She winked and blew me a kiss.

The chauffeur pulled out a red and black bag and rolled it to the front door.

I opened my arms and she stepped right in. Vic squeezed me tight. "Damn good to see you, girl."

"Good to see you, too." I grabbed the suitcase from the guy. Vic tipped him.

"Come in, come in."

"Your home is beautiful." She scanned the living room. "Look at the natural light in the kitchen. You can get a lot of painting done in there."

I followed her into my kitchen. "Yes, but I prefer painting outside in the mornings before it gets too hot."

"You've got some work done?"

I nodded. Boy, did I. When I was bored, I painted. When I wanted a drink (which was a lot), I painted. When I was sad and thinking of Joseph, I painted. I could fill up a coliseum with all my pictures.

"Well, then . . . show me."

My hands gripped around the suitcase handle. My paintings were . . . different since she'd seen them. I'd been dabbling in abstract paintings—well, my version of abstract. I played with colors and objects on the canvas. Ryder told me my paintings looked like colorful quilts. I guess that was a compliment, but I wasn't sure. "Let's, uh . . . let's get you settled first, huh? Dinner will be ready in about an hour."

Vic cut me a look and then shrugged. "Okay, then. We'll do it your way."

I tossed her a paper-thin smile and guided her upstairs. She would stay in the spare bedroom, across from Maya.

"Your girl is at school. Ryder, right?"

"Yes. She'll be home at four. She and some friends are meeting up to critique college and scholarship applications."

Maya stepped into the hallway and waved.

"Vic, this is my stepdaughter, Maya. Maya, this is my friend from . . ."

"Rehab." Vic chirped oh-so-helpfully as she offered her hand for a shake.

I gave a nervous giggle. "Yes. Rehab. We're having dinner downstairs in a few minutes, if you want to join us."

They shook hands, Maya smiled. That had to be good, right?

"Thanks, Jeanie, but I'm good. I need to meet up with my business advisor."

"You found someone? That's great." Maya had been debating hiring a consultant to help her drum up more business.

"First meeting, and she's squeezing me in over the weekend. And I better hurry before I'm late."

"Okay, good luck!"

Maya smiled and hurried downstairs while I showed Vic to the guest room.

"That wasn't awkward at all." Vic flopped on the bed.

"Yeah. You were the one that said you were the friend from rehab." I wagged my finger at her.

"Girl, she knows you went to rehab. Hell, didn't she drop you off?"

"Yeah, but . . ."

"But nothing. Rehab is a part of your story now, whether you like it or not."

"It's my past, not my future."

"It's a life-shaping event. You went to rehab, found a new best friend—"

"Soon to be ex if you keep shouting from the rooftops that we met at rehab."

She rolled her eyes and continued. "And you re-discovered your passion for painting. Speaking of which, I want to see your work."

"After dinner."

"Fine. After dinner." Maybe she would be so full she wouldn't want to see them. And besides that, she'd be leaving early tomorrow morning. My goal was to keep her fed and distracted.

"Okay, well, you settle in, and I'll set the table."

"Sounds good." She patted her flat belly. "I'm starving."

While I set the table for us, Vic changed into silk red pajamas and furry bedroom slippers. She sauntered downstairs as if she were lady of the manor.

"Now this is a spread." She settled into her seat, rubbing her hands together.

I started with appetizers. Bacon-wrapped shrimp with a special dipping sauce, smoked salmon over flaky hash browns. She muttered, "Jesus Christ," when I poured her a glass of lemon, lime and orange–infused water. "All this good food and no wine?"

"We don't have alcohol in this household."

"Tell me you put red wine in the pot roast."

"Red grape juice. Reviews online said it's just as good."

Vic looked so horrified I couldn't help but to laugh.

"So, what does sis do when she wants something to drink?" I assumed sis was Maya.

"I'm not sure. I don't ask. We don't . . ."

"You don't talk about it." She sighed. "Trust me, pretending doesn't help."

She quickly switched topics after dishing her sage advice. We talked about her daughters instead.

"How are things with Lesha and Dana?" I asked about her daughters.

"Tense." She sighed. "You know, I broke their trust. I'd been sober for two years and then I slipped up. No." She shook her head. "I crashed and burned. Dana is the oldest. She's patient and kind, like my momma. It's always a clean slate with her, no matter how much I've hurt her. But Lesha is spitting mad."

She put down her fork. "She's engaged. Good guy, though he's a little nerdy and stuck up. But he loves my baby and sometimes he'll laugh at my jokes. Anyway, she's getting married in March. She told me straight up that if I embarrassed her at the wedding, she was done." Tears filled her eyes.

I grabbed her plate and served up my world-famous buttered potatoes and placed them on her plate. If we weren't recovering alcoholics, I'd pour her a glass of wine.

Vic looked from the plate and then to me, her lips twisting with laughter. "Do these potatoes have healing properties?"

"Yes. Butter." We both laughed.

I squeezed her hand. "You won't embarrass her, Vic."

"But what if I do?"

"You won't."

"What if I can't control myself? There's an open bar at the wedding."

"Aren't you still talking to the counselors? Maybe they can help you."

"Yeah, but they won't be there to stop me."

"True." I nodded. "Why don't you ask your plus one to help out? If you feel overwhelmed, then step out and get some fresh air."

She nodded. "Good idea, except I don't have a plus one." She nibbled her lips. "Will you be my date?"

"Huh?" I scrunched my nose.

"I'm allowed a plus one. I was going to take Nick, a friend of the family, but he's been getting on my damn nerves."

I shook my head. "I don't know anyone."

She put up a hand. "You know the mother of the bride. C'mon . . . I could really use a friend. A non-judgmental friend."

"Fine. Yes. I'll help. Just as long as you don't say that we met at rehab."

"Sure, I won't." She grinned as she put a hand over her heart, as if to make the promise real.

I knew all too well she was going to crack a joke. I was beginning to realize it was her way of coping.

A few minutes into dinner, I finally gathered the courage to ask her about drinking. "Have you stopped drinking?"

She nodded. "Thirty-five days and counting."

"Does it get . . . easier?"

She sighed and leaned back into her chair. "I want to tell you yes. I want to tell you that you'll never drink again, and you'll beat this. But . . . yeah, it's hard. Every day is a battle. Doesn't matter if you become a hermit and never go out. The cravings are unavoidable. You've just got to build good habits, have a solid support system and believe in yourself."

"I keep thinking back . . . and I don't understand how it got out of hand. One glass of wine a day became three. Three glasses became three bottles. Then, even that wasn't enough. I went to the hard stuff. The stuff I never liked. The stuff that made Daddy hit me and Momma. I swore I'd never touch it. Just a glass of wine here and there. But look what I've done."

"You know there's some research out there, says alcoholism can be genetic."

"Genetic?"

"As in, your genetic makeup can cause you to be predisposed. Not sure if it's legit or not. But it makes sense to me. I've got a lot of alcoholics in my family. And when I was young, I told myself the same thing, when my grandfather stumbled around town, smelling of a distillery. Maybe its social or familial. I don't know. But it seems like there is something to it."

"Well, that sucks. I don't want to be anything like my racist, a-hole father."

"Racism isn't genetic, so you're covered there."

"But it's social, and it comes from family, too." I sighed. "I just . . . maybe I'm not as freethinking as I think I am."

"It's called racial bias."

I nodded, thinking through some of my past thoughts. "So how do I stop it?"

"I'm really going to have to send you my Cash App." She shook her head. "Just be aware of your thoughts. When you find yourself jumping on the other side of the street when you see someone who doesn't look like you, check yourself." She stood. "Now let's go check out your work."

I groaned. "Now, really? We were just having a great conversation."

She tilted her head and stared at me for a full minute. I broke the stare-off. I was never good at those things.

"Fine, it's in my room." I waved at her to follow me.

I switched on the light in my room. There were stacks of art, mostly finished, while some were still works in progress.

Vic went to the wall, flipping through the stacks, moving some of them to the other side of the room. She leaned over and observed the paintings, muttering things to herself. Frowny lines etched her forehead. She looked so serious. God, was she contemplating how much these sucked? I hopped from one foot to the other. She pulled out a phone and snapped a picture.

"Hey! What are you doing?"

She straightened. "I have a confession to make."

My mouth went bone dry. "What is it?"

"I'm an amateur artist. But my full-time job is an art dealer."

"A-a what?"

"Art dealer. I buy and sell art. I co-own a gallery in Atlanta. Midtown area. It does well and I want to feature your art. This is . . . this is phenomenal work. But I want a theme from you. You're all over the place. I like the abstract, but I love the contemporary more."

"Okay . . . well . . . I . . . this is just a hobby. This isn't a big deal or anything."

"Let me ask you something." She crossed her arms and narrowed her eyes. "How do you feel when you paint?"

"I don't know. Good, I guess?"

"Describe it. Describe the feeling."

I closed my eyes and went back to just this morning. I'd jumped out of bed. I had an idea about how to get the lake in my painting to sparkle. I was painting something from Joseph's point of view, his Sundays on the lake.

"It's like . . . warm apple pie with lots of cinnamon and a side of ice cream, falling in love for the first time and winning the lottery because I feel so damn lucky to be able to do what I do."

She bit her lip. "Even I don't have that feeling. Maybe it's because I don't have as much talent as you—"

"That's not true," I interrupted.

She shook her head. "Girl, I don't need a hype man. It is what it is. But what I lack in talent, I have a great eye for art and you, Jeanie . . . you are good. And the exciting thing is, you've just scratched the surface. Let me take a painting back for my partner, okay? We both have to agree on this. She isn't one to invest in new artists, but I think I can convince her."

The breath in my lungs stalled. They were filling up and ready to burst. "Okay." The air whooshed out of my body. My shoulders sagged from the release.

"Okay. I want the one with the porch and—"

"No. That one won't be for sale."

"But it's your best one . . . so far."

"It's a gift." I looked down at my shoes, clasping my hands behind my back.

"Understood." Vic's voice broke the silence. "I'll get the painting of the shoes by the fireplace with the lit cigar."

My heart thwacked against my chest. The painting repre-
sented some of Joseph's favorite things. I had a dozen paintings of Joseph, but each one was precious. *Let it go*, someone
whispered in my ear. A someone whose voice sounded like
Joseph's distinctively warm and low timbre.

"I . . . okay. Yes."

Sunday, September 13th
189 days

Vic and I talked until the sun rose. We talked about our
childhoods. I'd discovered Vic had an interesting upbringing.
Her mother and father divorced when she was a teenager and
her mother moved in with her best friend and lover, a woman
named Cassie. Vic loved her stepmother and, somehow, her father and mother still got along.

Her stepmother, who is an artist, cultivated Vic's love for the
arts and was Vic's gallery partner.

We had just finished up breakfast—quiche, fresh fruit and
baked cinnamon apples—when a black town car arrived at
noon.

I helped her with her things outside. The young woman who
drove the luxury vehicle opened the car door.

I reached for Vic's hands and wrapped my own around the
rings adorning her fingers. "Thank you."

"Don't thank me yet. You still have a lot of work to do, and
I still have to convince Cassie."

"No." I shook my head. "Not just that. For everything. For
barging into my apartment—"

"*Our* apartment."

I laughed and rolled my eyes. "Yes, our apartment. Thanks
for giving me perspective for free. You made me uncomfortable because you told me the truth. You put a mirror to my

face, and you didn't let me look away. I never would've been able to do that without you."

Vic pulled me into a hug. "You, Jeanie, are stronger than you realize. Don't ever doubt that about yourself." She stepped back. "This is a great place. I see why you love it so much."

"It is." I looked back at my house. The marigold leaves on the trees framed our two-story home. The wraparound porch, with two rocking chairs—chairs that Renee, Maya's mother, had purchased—still stood strong and proud on the porch. I'd added a long bench with sea green pillows and a cushion on the seat. The lake caressed by the breeze was the sweetest lullaby to my broken heart. And yes, it was still broken. But every day it grew stronger. The love of my daughter, the passion for my art and—maybe—the forgiveness of my stepdaughter.

"If you need a place to stay, I have a three-bedroom condo in the city."

My heart stalled at the thought of horns and traffic and smog. I was a country girl, through and through. I'd shrivel up and die in the urban jungle.

"I . . . I'll think about it." I needed a place to stay. Although Maya and I had come a long way, this was still her home.

Vic nodded and slid into the vehicle. I waved at her until the car was swallowed by the distance.

I stood in the driveway, my back to the lake, staring at the majesty of the field of lilies across from me when Maya pulled into the garage.

I hurried into the kitchen to meet her. "How did the meeting go?" I hadn't realized she would be gone overnight.

Maya grabbed a bottled water from the fridge and then settled at the kitchen table. "Exactly how I expected it to go." She rubbed her temples. "Everything my business advisor said made sense, but I guess I'm just not as ready as I thought I would be."

"What did she say?"

"If I want to have a successful practice in civil rights law, I need to be closer to the action."

"The action?"

"The city. Atlanta. All two of my clients so far have been in Atlanta. I don't want to make a two-hour commute every day. It'll kill me."

"Are you sure?" I sat down beside her. "You can always stay in the city during the week and come back home on the weekends. Or only travel up there for client meetings and court."

"No. I'm sure. I loved living up there during undergrad and law school and all my friends are there. But I came back home. I guess I just wanted to be here, with Daddy and Ryder."

I nodded my head. "And your father loved every minute of it."

"I'm glad I did. I spent time with Daddy, and I met—" She stopped herself mid-sentence and took a deep gulp of water. From the way that she pulled the water, I could tell she was wishing she had something a little stronger. I knew that feeling.

"You met your young man," I finished for her.

Her eyes darted to me. She smacked her forehead and groaned. "You knew, too? Hell, the whole town must've known."

I shook my head. "I only knew through your father."

"Daddy knew?" She frowned.

"You introduced them. You remember, at the Mayor's Ball."

She tilted her head, nodding it slowly. "But I only did it because Roland stood beside me and literally flung his hand out for Daddy to shake. Besides that, I introduced him as a friend."

"A *friend* you snuck off with for over an hour. A friend who, once you returned to the party, had stains of your fire engine red lipstick on his lips. A friend who put a lopsided grin on your face." I snorted. "Of course, Joseph noticed. As a matter of fact, your young man came by for a visit."

"What? When?" Her brows snapped toward the middle of her forehead.

"Had to have been a few weeks before Joseph died. He told your father he loved you and asked for your hand in marriage."

"He . . . he what?" Maya jumped out of her chair. "No way. There's no way that happened. I mean, we weren't even thinking about it. We never discussed it. Hell, we were secret—apparently the town's worst kept secret—but still a secret."

"Joseph said that Roland wanted to let him know man-to-man that he respected you and he planned to take the relationship at your speed. He told your father that he had all intentions of marrying you."

Maya stopped pacing the floor. She gripped the top of the chair. "And what did Daddy say? Did he accept?"

I laughed and leaned back, remembering Joseph's laughter over the matter. "He told your young man that when it came to relationships, glaciers were quicker than you."

Maya scowled.

"And he told him, 'If you want something to happen, son, you better *make* it happen.' He said that you needed a man who'd take a stand. He said you needed a partner, not a yes-man."

Maya squeezed her eyes shut. "God, Daddy." She shook her head and opened her eyes. "Here he is, telling Roland to push me, but yet he acted all sweet and gentle with you. Why is that?"

"Me and your dad . . . our relationship was wonderful. But I want to make something clear—he treated me the way I wanted to be treated. I wanted a home, I wanted to take care of him and raise my girl. Maybe my ambitions weren't as impressive as his or yours or Ryder's, but I loved my life. Yes, he treated me like fine china. But not like I was the inferior sex. It wasn't up to him to give me power and strength or to know my worth. It was up to me."

Maya crossed her arms. "That may be true, but sometimes I resent this narrative that I have to be so strong. Maybe sometimes, I want someone to hug me. I want to be the little spoon. I want a safe space to cry. Daddy made me feel like all of that was a weakness, yet he reveled in being your knight in shining armor." Maya rubbed her hands together. She didn't look angry or hurt, she just looked tired.

"I remember when Joseph found a wounded bird by the lake."

"Okay." Maya's voice held caution.

"You were in college. Anyway, the bird's wing was damaged. I couldn't bear to leave it behind, so Joseph and I decided to take care of Tweetie together. Joseph bandaged the wing. I gave him food. Day by day Tweetie got stronger. Joseph and I argued about what to do—he wanted to take off Tweetie's bandage and let him fly away. I wanted to wait. What if he damaged his wings again? What if a predator swooped in and killed him? What if the bird lost its instincts to gather food?" I took a deep breath and stared out at the lake.

"I said all those things to your father, and he looked me straight in the eyes and he said, 'If the bird wants to stay, he can stay, but the wing is healed. It was never broken. You can sit there and be afraid to let the bird fly, stunt its growth and development, or you can believe Tweetie knows by instinct how to survive. We can't force him to be ready and we can't force him to stay. We just have to be ready for when that day comes, and it will come.'"

Maya's brows furrowed. "You think he was talking about me?"

"No." I shook my head. "You've been ready to fly since you were a little girl. I think your father was talking about me. At the time, I didn't know it. Think about it: your dad was never a broad-strokes guy. He adjusted his advice and his approach to the person. I was the broken bird. I caged my dreams, my passions because I didn't believe in myself. Your daddy never stood in my way. He just adjusted to what he thought I needed, right or wrong."

I looked into Maya's eyes. "I think in your situation, the way he raised you, to be strong and resilient, in some instances he overcompensated. I have a few theories. One, he didn't want to see that broken girl distraught over her mother again."

"That makes no sense. I was five years old when I lost my mother. I didn't understand the finality of death."

"Still, he was way out of his depth with you. You had an aversion to him leaving the house. You didn't want to ride in cars. You had nightmares. Right or wrong, he wanted you to get better. He knew how scars from childhood carried over. He didn't want you to end up like me."

Tears blurred my vision. "I'm sorry I never saw you. I'm sorry I never validated your pain, but I *see* you now. You're incredible and you deserve all the best things life has to offer. And that includes your young man. Your daddy would've loved him as a son-in-law. He wanted you to find love. He said it all the time. I know you remember."

Maya crossed her arms. "I love that Daddy wanted love for me, but honest to God, I don't need a man."

"No." I shook my head. "You don't. And your father didn't say you needed a man. He said you needed a partner." I gently reminded her. "I know I'm not your mom. I know I haven't been the best role model for you or Ryder, but . . . will you allow me to give you some advice?"

Maya nodded and returned to her seat. "Sock it to me."

"Do you love him? Does he make you want to be a better person?"

Maya looked away. "What is this, a *Cosmo* quiz?"

"Fine, don't answer—out loud, anyway. I know people toss

around the word *love* so much that it doesn't mean much. Especially when the actions don't match up. But if Roland makes you feel half of what your father made me feel . . . at first there was something dead and heavy and cold inside of me. But God, when he was around, I just lit up, brighter than one of those fancy Christmas trees in New York City. He made me feel smart when everyone else told me that I was only as good as my face. He encouraged me to do and be more—but never in a way that made me feel bad about myself. He kept promises to a broken girl who didn't believe in much. He got joy out of my happiness, and I felt the same way about him. Does Roland make you feel that way?"

Maya bit her lip, blinking her lashes as if she were batting away emotions. "Yes. He does. I don't know why he loves me. I haven't done anything to encourage him."

"Maybe he just loves you for you? Love shouldn't be something that is earned, it simply is. Sometimes love doesn't make sense. Joseph and I on paper didn't make sense. But I fell for him. And even though he's gone, I will never regret my time with him. I will always cherish the little time that we had, though I yearn for more." I sat down in the chair and reached for Maya's hand. "Life is too short and love, *true* love, is rare. But when you get it, grab it by the horns and don't let go."

"Okay." Maya nodded and stood. She did a little jig, like a boxer before getting into the ring.

"You're going right now?"

She stopped moving. Her eyes went wide like one of those fish Joseph used to catch. "Yeah, why not?"

I admired this woman, her tenacity, her willingness to give it her all. No, we were nothing alike, but now, I could appreciate the differences.

"Why not, indeed." I tapped the table. "I'll be here all day. Though I don't suspect that you'll be back."

"Cross your fingers." She sighed and looked toward the

garage. "Okay, I'm going for it before I chicken out. Wish me luck."

She grabbed her keys off the hook and rushed out the door.

From the way Roland had stared at her while she gave her City Hall speech, like she was an angel sent to ascend him to heaven, I'd say she had a pretty darn good chance. "You don't need it. But good luck," I whispered.

CHAPTER 19

MAYA
CATCH OF THE DAY

Sunday evening, September 13th
189 days

The tick-tick-tick from the turn signal taunted me. Down the street, make another right, a sharp left and I would arrive at Roland's home.

I'd circled his neighborhood five times. Now I parked in front of the stop sign, a few hundred feet from his house. An old lady with slouchy pantyhose and foam hair rollers stood with a rolled-up newspaper tucked under her arm. She stopped staring and started walking. My hands gripped around the butter-smooth leather. Nosy Nettie was getting closer. She walked fast, despite her open-toed house slippers. I floored the pedal. The tires screeched like the sounds from a getaway car. Seconds later, I pulled into his driveway. Reddish-orange flowers stood on either side of his house. He'd told me last spring his mother had planted the roses to give his plain brick house some color.

A modest-sized stone porch spanned a little past the columns that flanked his front door.

Sweat slicked my palms. Leaning over, I pulled wet wipes

out of the glove compartment and patted down my hands. The smell of rubbing alcohol wafted throughout the car, biting my nostrils and stinging my lungs. I blinked a few times. The smell was ironically sobering. My mind quickly formulated a plan. Knock on the door. Ask to come in. Say sorry. Explain why I'm emotionally constipated. See if he's open to reconciliation. Boom.

No. No. Too clinical. Too cold. I shook my head and erased my plan like an Etch-a-Sketch drawing.

I twisted the wet wipe around my finger. "So now what?"

I should've talked to Jeanie about what to say, or maybe watched a favorite rom com she loved to watch.

"'You complete me'?" Too syrupy and sarcastic. No, that wouldn't do. He would know.

I banged my forehead against the steering wheel. Well not directly, my hands buffered the blow. "I'm not ready," I whispered. I reached for the ignition.

A rap on the window sent my heart soaring into space.

Roland stood there, shirtless and wearing gray sweatpants. Oh, my God did he look fine.

He stepped back and pointed his finger down, miming for me to roll down the window.

I shook my head.

"Maya."

I pressed the automatic windows. As the barrier lowered, Roland bent over to meet my stare.

"What are you doing here?"

"I . . . ummm . . . was in the neighborhood? I have a client here."

"Really?" He squinted his eyes. "Who? I'm the HOA president. I probably know them."

"Confidential. Super-duper high-profile case." I cleared my throat. *Smooth, Maya. You should leave. Leave right now.*

"Can I come in?" My voice squeaked. *What the hell is wrong with you? Drive, woman. Drive away!*

"Ummm . . . sure." He stroked his beard and stood at full height. His abs were still tight and glistened with sweat.

"Okay." I whispered it more to myself. I turned the car off and scrambled out, almost making contact with the chest I remembered all too well. I hurried up his walk, admiring his ass in the loose sweats, and followed him into his house.

He closed the door and then led me to the living room. "Have a seat."

I sat on the blue suede couch and ran my hands over the material. "Is this new?"

I'd only been in his house once or twice, but the couch wasn't here before.

"Yep." He leaned against the wall, arms crossed and eyes guarded.

Also, it was important to note that his forearms looked corded and strong. Like maybe he squeezed stress balls or maybe tossed a lot of medicine balls.

"What are you doing here, Maya?" His voice snapped me away from his buff forearms and sent me straight to his eyes.

"I came to confess my love."

"Oh?" He lifted an eyebrow coolly. Wholly unaffected by my profession of love. "Do you know what love is?"

I snorted. "Of course, I do."

"I know you love Ryder and you loved your father. I'm talking about romantic love."

"Yes, I know what romantic love is."

"Have you ever loved someone before?"

"Romantically, you mean?" I clarified.

"Yes."

"No. I haven't. But that doesn't mean I don't know what love is and how to love. Like I said, I love you."

"So you said."

"I say what I mean, you know that." I bit my words. This was not going as planned. Wait, I had no plan. That was the problem. I should've said "you complete me" first. *Goddammit.*

"Really. When you love someone do you think it's appropriate to break off contact and tell him to go to hell? Is that your definition of love?" His voice was smooth and steady. The voice he used in the courtroom. I hated it. This wasn't a cross-examination. This was real life.

"No. It's being human. I'm not perfect. And I was wrong to make you feel like you didn't matter to me. I'm sorry."

He nodded. "I accept your apology." He pushed away from the wall, "But—"

"Furthermore, I think love can mean a lot of things," I cut in before he sent me on my merry way. "It can mean cooking someone's favorite meals because they can't cook worth a damn. It can mean spending late nights poring over depositions and strategies because you want them to win. It can mean spending countless hours searching for a rare art collection because the person you love wants it. Or thoughtful messages stuck under coffee mugs and cups."

Roland clasped his hands behind his back. He wasn't looking at me, but his eyes were trained on the floor. He was working on a counterargument as he listened to my rebuttal. His mind was made up. I was running out of time.

"Roland, baby, listen to me." I stood, then walked forward until my face was mere inches from his. "I know what love is. I learned from the best, my father."

"But that's not—"

"The first people you love are your parents. They teach you the meaning of love so just . . ." I raised a halting hand. "Just listen."

He sighed and dipped his chin. "Go on."

"The greatest thing about love is that true love keeps no

tally marks. But still you want to do your best and be your best. It's about acceptance, that no matter how grumpy or bitchy or wrinkly you get, you will love that person no matter what, thick and thin. There are the squishy parts, the soft looks, the hugs and the kisses and the passion. But it's also about being a damn good partner and lover and friend. Lucky us, we've got it all."

He uncrossed his arms. I stepped into them. "Somehow, some way, you embedded yourself in me. And everywhere I go and everything I do, you are right here." I pointed to my heart. "And that's where you'll always be, whether you take a chance on me or not. But you really should, because I'm awesome, you're awesome and we'll be awesome together." I held my breath, searching his eyes.

"Damn, girl. I need to pause for a recess."

"Why?"

"I need to get my mind together."

"Don't. Just feel, just be. No more secrets, no more sneaking around. I can't promise you peace—we argue too much. But we'll make a damn good team."

"How?"

I pulled away from him and rummaged through my pockets. I pulled out a piece of paper. A crumpled piece of paper. One that I never intended to see the light of day because it reeked of presumption, but mostly hope.

"Here." I stuffed the crumpled paper into his hand.

He raised an eyebrow. "This is going to answer my question?"

"Maybe. Anyway, just read it. It's cool if you don't want to."

He unfolded the paper and stared. He didn't say anything, just swallowed; his breath became shallow, like he was losing oxygen.

He showed me the letterhead. It was something I'd done on the computer, playing with letterhead options. After a really late night of watching sappy TV, I played around with the law firm name. Hill & Hill.

"I'm the first Hill." I tried joking, but my shaky voice messed up the delivery.

"You want us to have our own law firm?"

"Yes."

"Seriously?"

"Yes. E-even if it's Donaldson and Hill."

"Hmm."

"But I really, really want Hill and Hill." My face heated like a blow torch to the face. I'd never put myself on the line when it came to love, but I knew I needed to. He needed the reassurance because I'd hurt him. Even if he settled at us being friends, he deserved the truth—that I was ridiculously in love with him.

I pulled back my shoulders and shot him a look I reserved for court when my back was against the ropes and it was do or die. "I want to have your babies. I want good meals and great sex. A good home in an excellent school district for our two-point-five kids. I want us to be the heads of the PTA and irritate the hell out of the administration and other parents. I . . ."

I lowered my head, taking fortifying breaths. He didn't say a word. I squeezed my eyes shut. "I want to be there for you. Rub you down when you've had a hard day. Support your dreams, listen to your fears. I want to protect your soft side. I want you to be my man. I want to share my load with you."

I held my breath. Still, he said nothing. Tears gathered. He didn't want me.

Exit stage left, Maya.

"No."

"No?" I heard the heartache in my response. *It's okay, girl. You did your best.*

Don't cry. Don't cry, I repeated uselessly in my head. The tears came all the same.

"I'm sorry," I said as my tears fell.

"For what?"

"Crying. I'll be fine." I sniffed. "I'm just . . . emotional right now."

"Don't apologize." He stepped closer, crowding my space. His brown eyes pulled me in the undertow.

"It's Hill and Hill." His voice went as deep as the Grand Canyon.

My head snapped up. "Really?"

"Yes. As soon as possible. I'm tired of waiting."

"Where's my ring?" I wiggled my finger, sniffing away the tears that rushed to the surface.

"Where's my contract?" He rubbed his fingers together.

"I'll draft one tonight. For now, it's the honor system." I gave him my hand. "A good ole-fashioned handshake."

"I'm giving you more than a handshake." He softly cupped my cheeks, so gentle, so reverent, I knew that he'd never break me. He kissed my face, tracing the trail of tears.

"My God, Roland, I love you. I love you, I love you, I love you, I—"

His lips, his tongue swallowed the rest, replacing my revelation with delicious, honeyed kisses. Gripping my hips, he pulled me closer. We stripped each other down until we both stood together, nearly naked and open not only in body, but in mind and spirit.

"Bedroom," he growled against my lips. He lifted me up and carried me upstairs. His dark hungry eyes never left mine. Not when he opened the door, not when he tossed me on the bed and crawled closer. Not even when he reached for a condom in his nightstand. He lifted the package—but instead of a foil packet, it was a small leather box.

He swallowed another deep gulp. The intensity in his eyes, God, I couldn't think. Nothing mattered but the present.

"Will you marry me?"

"Yes."

His eyes went soft as he slid the ring down my finger. He still didn't look away. "No turning back. No secrets."

"You can put an ad in the *Hope Springs Gazette* if you want to."

"I do." His fingers skimmed my collarbone, then traveled lower and lower until he found my lace underwear. He pushed my panties down my legs. His fingers scaled back up and slid deep into my folds.

I licked his lips, not satisfied until his tongue dueled with mine. We fought for dominance, but the frenzied thrust of his fingers made me quickly lose control.

His fingers slid out. He pushed down his loose jogging pants and boxer briefs. "Have you been with someone else?"

"No. No sex." I shook my head, then tucked it to my chest. "You?" I asked, looking away from him.

"No." His answer sounded like a vow. "There's been no one since you."

My eyes lifted to his. A gust of breath whooshed out.

Lowering himself, he lifted my legs and placed them over his shoulders, lowering himself inch by inch until there was no resistance. Kisses rained on my cheeks, my neck.

I grabbed and held him close. Not moving, waiting until we were stuck together like glue. But we weren't and thank God. Because that man of mine could move. Time had no meaning, the sun set, and after, we settled back into his bed. His strong arms wrapped around my middle. I'd never slept over before. This was nice. I was so very stupid to not realize this gift of a man. I shot my hand out, admiring my ring, certain a dopey smile had settled on my face.

I licked my lips. "When did you get the ring?"

"A while ago. I even asked your dad for your hand, I don't know, maybe a month before he passed away."

Although Jeanie had told me, it still hit me hard. "Wh-what did he say?" I wheezed the pocket of breath out of my throat.

"He asked about my lure."

"Y-your what?"

"Lure. Bait. He said that you weren't a woman who's gonna snatch up a regular ole dry fly. He said you deserved a greased grasshopper. Someone who'd take the time to go below the surface and wait it out until you were ready. I said, 'Sir, is that a yes or a no?' He just laughed, you know that Santa Claus laugh he was known for, and he said, 'Son. I think you're a good man and you've got my vote. You'll figure it out.' I had no idea what the hell he was talking about."

"It's a fishing trick. If you want a trout, you have to drown the hopper—a grasshopper—and grease it so it sinks below the surface. That's how you get the big fish."

"And you're a big fish." His arms wrapped around me.

I continued staring at the ring. The ring look hard enough to cut through rock. "I'm a catch, yes."

"Glad I didn't have to bait you. You figured it out."

"Oh, really? Katy wasn't a greasy little hopper?"

"Of course not, baby." His arms wrapped tighter around me. "She's not a grasshopper. She's just not the woman for me. She's not you."

Monday morning, September 14th
190 days

Roland and I returned to my place the next morning to announce our news. Jeanie burst into tears. Ryder jumped into Roland's arms and gave a two-minute monologue not-quite-apologizing for Milkshake Gate. Her confession was met with gasps from Jeanie and laughter from me and Roland.

Roland left after Jeanie made breakfast. It was just us three, outside, on the porch. Jeanie chatted away about her art projects. She tried to make light of it, but the joy in her voice gave it away.

I was happy for her. My only regret was that Daddy wasn't here to see this. From the paintings I'd seen around the house, I knew she was super talented. I had no doubt her friend would be able to sell her art.

Jeanie hopped from her seat. "Oh, I've got a gift for you. Think of it as an engagement present." She ran into the house, leaving Ryder and me outside.

"What is it?"

"Beats me." Ryder shrugged. Her phone dinged. She looked down at the screen and blushed.

I knew who it was without asking. Her beloved Alston. "Ah, to be young and in love."

Ryder quickly typed a response. "You're young and in love."

"Mhmm. That I am."

"Smug is a good look on you."

I slapped her shoulder. "Smart-ass."

She giggled then got quiet. "When are you and Roland leaving for Atlanta?"

I shrugged. "A few months. We've got to find a place to stay and we need to find office space. Then there's merging our contacts for business and resolving other business matters."

"What you're saying is you're going to wait until I graduate."

I rolled my eyes. "Maybe not that long, but how about this—you can come up and visit for weekends. I'll show you around the city, so you'll feel good once you start Emory."

"I haven't gotten in yet. It's not official."

"You will. And then you and Alston can graduate from holding hands to dry humping."

"Oh, my Gawd, Maya." This time she punched my shoulder.

Jeanie cleared her throat. I straightened in my seat. She had a painting behind her. "If you don't like it, you don't have to keep it. I just . . . I just thought it would be nice for you to have a little piece of home while you carve out your new life." She flipped the painting around, revealing a picture of three women sitting on the porch.

"It's us," Jeanie pointed out, though it was quite obvious the porch looked exactly like our home, with the long bench and two rocking chairs. She pointed at stiletto red heels. "The heels are you. The tennis shoes are Ryder and the pumps are me. Anyway, I painted this when I got home. It's like an affirmation—I wanted us to have a close relationship where we all can sit on the porch and talk, like we're doing now." She beamed a bright smile that could warm the coldest of hearts.

"I love it but . . . are you sure you want it for me? Don't you have that art gallery gig?"

"I can paint more pictures, but this is my gift to you. I have a lot to thank you for."

"Really?" I scrunched my nose. I hadn't always been kind to Jeanie. We hadn't been kind to each other.

"Of course. You didn't put up with my issues. You forced me to make a better life for myself. If it weren't for you, I'd have let myself float away. Now, I've got two daughters and a blossoming career. And though Joseph is gone, I got to experience true love that'll last me until my homegoing."

I stood and wrapped my arms around her waist. I didn't realize until now that she gave good hugs. Ryder joined in, making it a group hug.

Jeanie stepped back and dabbed her eyes with a cloth handkerchief. "Look at us. Judge's girls are together and stronger than ever."

I shook my head. We had gone through our personal storms and came out on top. We weren't mere girls. "No. Judge's women."

I grabbed their hands, knowing there was another tradition to create before we moved on into our separate ways. "Next Sunday, let's take the boat out on the lake."

Jeanie's eyes filled. "Looks like another one of my paintings came true."

A strong gust of wind grazed my face and lifted our hair. A warm feeling started at the base of my head down to the soles of my feet.

Jeanie looked awestruck. Ryder smiled big and wide.

And me, I didn't need Aunt Clara Bell to tell me Daddy was happy that the women in his life had taken hold of their second chances. Ryder and Jeanie weren't my family of blood but had become the family of my heart.

JUDGE'S GIRLS

Sharina Harris

ABOUT THIS GUIDE

The suggested questions are included
to enhance your group's reading of
Sharina Harris's *Judge's Girls*.

DISCUSSION QUESTIONS

1. Do you think Joseph was right in stipulating in the will that Jeanie can stay in the house although it belongs to Maya?

2. How would you describe the relationship between Maya, Jeanie, and Ryder?

3. Why do you think Ryder isn't as close to Jeanie as she is to her stepfather and stepsister?

4. Do you think Ryder is too judgmental of others, including Dani and her mother?

5. Maya realizes she has unresolved anger with her father based on how he treated Jeanie's emotions versus her own. Do you think he was aware he enabled Jeanie's feelings and stifled Maya's?

6. How has Joseph's stance on making sure Maya is tough and ready for the cruelties of the world impacted her as an adult? Do you think it was more helpful or more harmful?

7. How would you describe Maya's relationship with her aunts?

8. Maya said she didn't want to publicize her relationship with Roland because that would kill her chances of becoming a partner at the law firm. Are her suspicions accurate, or do you think this is a product of her not trusting others?

9. As the novel progresses and knowledge of Jeanie deepens, does your perspective for Jeanie's struggle with alcohol change?

10. When Maya argues with Jeanie about weaponizing her tears, and Jeanie accuses Maya of being mean, which perspective do you agree with and why?

11. Have you met someone who reminds you of Maya, Jeanie, or Ryder and their issues? After reading this book, do you think it's possible to understand and form a better relationship with this person?

12. How do Maya, Jeanie, and Ryder evolve during the novel? How do they make peace with Joseph's death and their identities? What have they learned?

Connect with 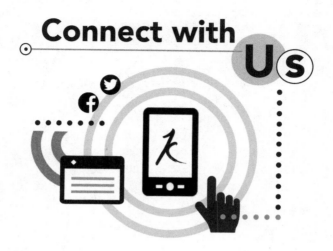 Us

Visit us online at
KensingtonBooks.com
to read more from your favorite authors, see books
by series, view reading group guides, and more.

Join us on social media

for sneak peeks, chances to win books and prize packs,
and to share your thoughts with other readers.

facebook.com/kensingtonpublishing
twitter.com/kensingtonbooks

Tell us what you think!

To share your thoughts, submit a review,
or sign up for our eNewsletters, please visit:
KensingtonBooks.com/TellUs.